WHITE GOLD

AN AFRICAN WILDLIFE THRILLER

DAVID MARK QUIGLEY

Published by Hashbooks Publishing

Paperback - ISBN: 978-1-955388-05-4

First Edition Published 2021

This book is dedicated to Hymna Shalomith, Papa Hy, my grandfather, for giving me the impetus to publish this book. Thank you, I will be forever grateful.

ABOUT THE AUTHOR

A NATIVE NEW Zealander, David Mark Quigley worked variously as a farmer, vineyard owner, clinical hypnotherapist, and serial entrepreneur. Travelling extensively chasing adventure across Europe, Australia, and Africa, he has been obsessed with animals and nature ever since. Inspired by his travels, he decided to tackle his dyslexia by writing a book, *Scars of the Leopard* and unexpectedly discovered his love of writing, and wrote two further action adventures, *White Gold* and *African Lion*. He is a sculptor and produces striking wildlife sculptures cast in silver, alongside running an international environmental consultancy. He is also the innovative architect of Hashbooks, the multi-layered publishing platform where life-changing anecdotes and insights meets adventure. He lives in Naples, Florida, with his wife and numerous furry freeloaders, in a home he built in his spare time.

PROLOGUE

ON THE DAY he was murdered the sun stood high above the African veld. The shining orb of angry, fiery gold was the only thing gracing the far blue of the distant heavens. Although the sun's harsh piercing rays of noon had now abated, its scorching, determined presence still bathed the surrounding land and vegetation with layer upon shimmering layer of unrelenting heat. As each wave of lava-like air bore down on the earth, nothing stirred, nothing moved. Only the sun readily exposed its face in this sweltering corner of Africa.

Although this area of bushveld was lavishly adorned with vegetation, a tall grassy bush-studded plain, interspersed amongst stately forests of greens, yellows and browns, appeared like a wasteland devoid of animal life. The open plain revealed no hint of ever being embellished by game.

An oppressive silence accompanied the scene, compounding a heavy feeling of desolation hanging like a sad and dreary cloud. For mile upon uninhabited mile, the bushveld was bare as if robbed of wild game.

Eventually, the morbid silence was broken. A bleak and lonely zephyr wind tumbled in from the north. With the wind came at last relief from the afternoon's unyielding heat. As it rolled untidily across the open plain, sending the tall stands of golden grass rustling in its wake, it carried with it a hint of moisture from a nearby tree and bush-lined river.

This wide slow-moving river, the nearby forests and the abundance of other vegetation covering the fertile plain should have shown an otherwise perfect face of African wilds. However, although the sun still shone, the river flowed, and the grasses grew, it had been turned into a sad and lonely place.

Eventually, as the wind played with the vegetation in its fickle manner, the previous feeling of desolation seemed to fall away. There was now a distant, unrecognisable sound. It rose and fell with the wind; at first faintly, then ever louder. Finally, the wind was unable to keep the noise at bay. It rang out from the depths of the surrounding woodlands – a noise that betrayed the misconception of this land being a barren, lifeless place.

Crashing, snapping and the boisterous destruction of trees and branches within the forests, like that caused by a marauding army, told there was indeed life, albeit hidden, in this stretch of African wilds.

Undaunted by the sun and the ever-present heat, with trumpets blaring and the echo of marching feet, it was an army of sorts that eventually emerged en masse from the forest to descend upon the open plain. Using well-rehearsed manoeuvres, the army's combined ranks numbered in the thousands.

He had hung back – barely able to tolerate the noise of the advancing hordes – and only now did he emerge from the forest. With an expression of resignation etched across his deeply creased and wrinkled face, he looked out across the open plain. The first thing that hit him was the heat. Previously, it had been like a living thing weighing him down, but now with the cooling breeze, he felt it bearable to advance towards the river.

It wasn't until he walked into the sun that his true bulk became obvious. The profile the huge bull elephant presented to the army of other elephants that had emerged onto the open plain was truly awesome. Every part of him was huge. From the flattened spoor left by the gigantic, padded soles of his feet, his vast flapping ears and colossal head extending from his mountainous frame to the python-like twisting and turning appendage of his trunk. But his most outstanding features were his massive ivory tusks.

Stained a purple-black from vegetable juice, these giant pillars marked him a bull amongst bulls. Extending from his upper lip, the oversized incisors were the circumference of a grown man's thigh. Measuring just under ten feet, each near identical tusk stretched, with little curve or taper, from their enormous base out to their equally impressive, rounded tips.

Having reached his sixty-second year, the bull was now in the twilight of his life. Onto his sixth and last set of molars, yet still in excellent health, he wouldn't usually associate with so many other elephants. Now normally a solitary creature, even the once tantalising scent of a cow in season only triggered memories of an all but forgotten period of his life. The prolonged and unrelenting heat of the driest season he had experienced for many a year was why he found himself close to so many of his kind. The lure was water of the nearby river and the riverine vegetation, presenting a virtual oasis in this otherwise dry and parched land.

The elephant stopped and peered out through sad weepy eyes across the plain. He saw that a multitude of other African game had joined the countless herds of elephants. They too had taken refuge within the cooler depth of the forests against the fiercely hot ever-present sun.

Raising his trunk like a periscope, he used it to test the air. The smell of

Africa, of home, filled his head. In a delicate gesture, before dropping his trunk and continuing on with his wary ambling gait, he used it to wipe away the weeping moisture from around his eyes. He wished he could leave the offensive, boisterous behaviour of the other elephants behind. He longed to live out the rest of his life in peace. But still the smell of water lured him on.

A few paces on, a new scent carried to him on the wind. A well-remembered smell, an enticing smell. His strides lengthened as the gentle, cooling flapping of his ears became more pronounced. Saliva shot from glands at the back of his throat and began to fill his mouth. It was the aroma of near-ripe, protein-rich acacia pods that beckoned. As he thought of this, his last true pleasure of life, the other elephants and wildlife were finally forgotten. He was gripped with delicious anticipation of the feast he knew was soon to come.

He walked up to and gently rested the flat area of his tapered head against the acacia's trunk. With eyes closed and their delicate almost feminine eyelashes resting upon his cheeks, he began to rock his incredible bulk to and fro. To begin with, the tree resisted even his most determined efforts. But slowly, ever so slowly, the tree began to sway until he had its upper branches whiplashing back and forth as if caught in the centre of a violent storm.

Gradually at first, but then in a steadily increasing shower, the acacia pods rained down upon his body. Eventually, he drew his head away from the shaking tree. With saliva now dribbling from his mouth, he surveyed his work. A carpet of bean-like acacia pods, inches deep, littered the ground. Using incredible dexterity, he began to pick up the pods one by one in-between the two finger-like projections at the end of his trunk. Delicately, he placed them into the back of his mouth. With his normal doleful weeping eyes closed in relish, and gently rocking from side to side with something approaching ecstasy, he chewed down upon each bittersweet pod.

As the great bull stood, rumbling contentedly, devouring his feast – standing as a symbol of the sheer majesty and grandeur of the African wilds – a fleck of mud was flicked from a spot on the side of his head. Immediately, a spurt of rich, ruby-red blood leapt from the spot. For a moment his gigantic head contorted out of shape as a smashing void of darkness hammered into his skull.

A split second later a resounding rifle shot cracked out across the open grassy plain. As its thunderous volley echoed violently about the woodlands, it stilled all other noise. The bull's legs collapsed beneath him as his immense weight crashed to the ground, with his trunk untidily thrown beneath him his head slumped forward down upon his massive tusks. His once sad droopy eyes were now open wide in shocked amazement, but their sparkling sheen of life was quickly fading.

A wondrous beast, a creature of authority coupled with sensitive dignity, had just died and with him had died a part of Africa.

CHAPTER I

Present Day – Lausanne, Switzerland

ANTICIPATION HAD GROWN to fever pitch in the main concourse of the convention hall. The atmosphere was so thick the tension could be cut with a knife. All the major news sources were there: *BBC, ITN, CCN* and *The Times* to name but a few. Their people, as well as other camera crews and journalists, jostled one another while hurriedly scurrying back and forth looking for the choicest interviews. They accosted anyone with a name badge, asking for their views on the pending meeting but more particularly their beliefs regarding what the future held for African elephants.

Although he was slightly confused by the raucousness, Peter Nkomo tried to ignore the throng of bustling people as he entered the concourse. He had nearly made it through into the main meeting hall when the fierce arc of a television camera light stopped him dead in his tracks.

Damn! he cursed inwardly at his stupidity. This was the last place he wanted to draw attention to himself. He should have taken off his nametag before entering the hall. A reporter shoved a microphone into his face.

'Sir, Greg Manners from CNN, can you give us a comment on the pending discussions involving African elephants? In your view will the elephants gain Appendix One? Will the meeting ban worldwide trade in elephant products?'

Pointing to the legend beneath his name on his nametag, Peter said in a naturally clear yet resonant voice, 'As you can see, I am just an observer.'

'Well at least, sir, a comment on the EIA's report, *A System of Extinction,*' the reporter countered. The reporter thrust a copy into his hand. 'An African perspective would be appreciated.'

'I'm sorry, this is the first time I've seen it,' he said honestly, looking with interest down at the report.

'Come on, guys. We're wasting our time here,' the reporter said, dropping the microphone to his side. 'We've still got three minutes of footage to shoot before we can get this to the studio.'

'Do you mind if I keep it?' Peter asked, holding up the report.

'Not likely, pal. Get your own,' snapped the reporter. 'The booth's over there.' He indicated with a curt flick of his head to where Peter could acquire a copy, before snatching the report away, turning to follow his departing camera crew and looking around anxiously for a more worthwhile prospect.

Peter, who usually expressed little outward emotion, was aghast at the arrogance of the reporter. 'Bloody Westerners,' he muttered, as he dismissed the incident before making his way to the booth the reporter had indicated.

Peter was a tall, black man in his late thirties. Dressed as he was in a dark three-piece suit, it was clear to see he was cast in the typical Zulu warrior mould of old. He walked with an athletic grace, with his head held high and the sheen of intelligence sparkling within his liquid dark brown eyes. He was handsome, with broad distinguished features and charisma that lured men to his side.

Being a black African and educated in South Africa, he was a man at home in two usually disparate worlds: the traditional and the modern. A factor that, to date, had allowed him to prosper beyond most people's wildest dreams.

He was born in South Africa, but looked upon southern and eastern Africa as his home. He was affiliated with no group nor tribe due to his great grandfather's fate of birth, and because of this he was accepted into most societies throughout the continent. Being a loner, his only real interest lay with the wildlife of Africa, especially its elephants. This interest had been first cultivated courtesy of the South African Parks Board, where he initially trained and worked as a game warden. However, now was a different story. Instead of conservation, he was lured by a much greater and more absorbing compulsion – that of greed. He had moved into a far more lucrative vocation involving African game. This was why he was at the CITES meeting in Lausanne, the cultural and intellectual capital of French-speaking Switzerland.

Peter Nkomo was an observer at the CITES Secretariat's seventh biennial meeting of the conference of contracting member countries. He was attending at his employer's insistence and also for personal reasons. First-hand knowledge of new regulations restricting wildlife trade across the globe could help their interests considerably.

Peter shook his head as he thought of CITES and what it stood for: Convention on International Trade in Endangered Species of Wild Fauna and Flora.

What a mouthful, he thought. Waste of time in my view,' he reflected as he came upon the booth the reporter had indicated.

There was a throng of CITES delegates and representatives from wildlife societies from around the world crowded about the booth, intent on gaining a copy of the report.

Because of his height, Peter had little difficulty reaching over the heads of those in front of him and retrieving a copy. This time he had a chance to study the report more thoroughly. Its full title read: *A System of Extinction: The African Elephant Disaster*. It had been compiled by the Environmental Investigation Agency, the EIA, based in London.

Its front cover showed two dead elephants somewhere in the African bush. Superimposed over the dead animals was an official-looking seal, declaring: **Approved CITES Secretariat.**

Peter quickly read through the forty-six-page report. *Bloody hell!* It contained detailed, explicit evidence of the illegal ivory trade currently rife across the world, it pulled no punches, was well researched and a publication that couldn't possibly be ignored.

After flicking through it a second time, Peter dropped his arms limply to his side and gazed vacantly across the concourse. The report was comprehensive; itemising names, addresses, dates and figures. The only thing he felt he could be thankful for was, somehow, they had missed his poaching network, and though they'd listed a number of his associates and competitors, they hadn't mentioned him by name.

Now feeling conspicuous, he guiltily looked about the hall. A feeling of impending doom engulfed him like a tidal wave. His intuition told him that this meeting wasn't going to go well at all.

If elephants were upgraded to Appendix One, the proportion of the illicit ivory trade he controlled (and the network of poachers he commanded for his employer) would quickly grind to a shuddering halt, but the most appalling aspect of it was his possible loss of income. The meeting that was supposed to – in Peter's view – indirectly ratify the illegal ivory trade looked like destroying it completely.

No, things don't look good at all, he mused unhappily; everything he had built up could soon come crashing down.

With the report's exposé, the spotlight would be firmly focused on a possible ivory ban. *Screw the elephants*, he thought as he tried to rally himself, *I've got too much riding on this.*

Pulling himself together, Peter forced the possibility from his mind. He looked around at the milling crowd and although he was rubbing shoulders with the very people who were trying to stop him and people like him, he was glad to be at the meeting. It would give him vital first-hand knowledge for his own report, the one he would soon have to file with his employer. Still clutching the EIA's report, Peter walked into the main meeting hall.

So the decision is going to come down to the wire, Peter thought, as he waited for the CITES decision on trading elephant ivory to be made.

After several days of subtle probing while at the CITES' meeting, Peter realised the vote to ban ivory trading was going to be close – extremely close.

He was at the back of the main meeting hall watching over, and listening to, the proceedings of the meeting of CITES' Committee One, the committee that dealt with changes to appendices. They were about to vote for the third time on the Appendix One listing for the world's elephants. Two amendments and a full proposal for a total ban had recently been defeated, showing how much feeling there was about the issue.

Peter looked around the hall, assessing the mood. The vote for the third and final proposal was about to be called – the proposal most likely to succeed. It advocated a total ban, yet allowed countries to downgrade from Appendix One in the future, providing they could prove they controlled poaching and that their elephant populations were stable.

Out of the corner of his eye he caught movement; the United States delegate. He swore inwardly. For the listing to be changed, two thirds of the member countries would have to support the vote. With the damaging EIA report, and the likelihood of the US backing the ban, the lobbyists had been able to achieve a ground-swell of support.

It's going to be close, Peter decided, *too damn close.*

He reflected how easy it had been to circumvent CITES' regulations in the past. Using bribes and coercing the right people at the right time, he had been able to operate his racket as if the regulations never even existed.

Damn the environmentalists… and the bloody elephants, he thought, before looking up at the raised podium at the front of the hall, the chairman was calling the meeting to order.

As the vote was being cast Peter's mind was flooded with memories of the most exciting period of his life. He had been initially lured away from the Parks Board by the prospect of money, by way of a percentage of turnover, to set up what was now one of the most highly sophisticated poaching networks in Africa. He remembered the secret meetings in the dead of night, the brutal discipline he had to occasionally exert over his massive ring of poachers and most of all the enormous amounts of money he made. Everything he had worked for, like a carefully weighted pendulum, now hung delicately in the balance.

He was an entirely selfish man with little consideration for the world he lived in or the people and animals he shared it with. To him life was just a game: winner takes all.

The official announcement was about to be presented. Peter Dollinger, the Swiss delegate chairing the meeting, stepped onto the podium. He cleared his throat. 'The results are as follows. There are four abstentions, eleven against, and seventy-six in favour. Therefore, the motion is carried.'

Peter's world collapsed, he was stunned and to make matters worse the sickly feeling he felt in the pit of his stomach seemed to be compounded by the weighty hush that settled over the entire hall. No-one uttered a sound as the full meaning of Dollinger's words hit home.

The ivory trade that had given Peter such a lucrative living, and had slowly pushed the world's elephant population towards extinction, was finally illegal. Never in his worst nightmares had he thought it could ever be possible.

Somewhere in the hall, clapping began. Like a surging wave, it swept forward engulfing the crowd. Peter noticed amongst the now elated crowd there were many handshakes, back-slapping and hugs of congratulation. All those present were more than aware of the ramifications of the meeting's decision. In theory, Africa's elephants had been given breathing space from what was previously certain extinction. 'But for how long?' many delegates would soon be asking.

Environmentalists, Peter thought bitterly, as he turned to leave. They were systematically destroying the Africa – his Africa – that he had grown to know and use.

As he left the hall, the deafening roar of applause taunted his every step. He stepped into the main concourse and towards the phone booths beyond. His American employer would have to know and a trip to Los Angeles would have to be made.

If anyone could make something out of this fiasco, he was the man to do it.

CHAPTER 2

1875 – Southern Africa

'YES, IT IS SO,' the man agreed in the Zulu language. 'We have taken far more ivory than the wagons can carry. And yes, many trips will have to be made back to pick up those tusks we have had to bury. But this …' the man said, slowly shaking his head in wonder, 'well, this spoor belongs to an elephant larger than any I have ever seen before.'

The man who spoke was black, wearing only a simple leather loincloth; nothing more. Yet simply dressed as he was, he still commanded a captivating presence. His shoulders were broad and the muscles of his back and arms bulged beneath the sheen of his glossy black skin. His language of choice was Zulu, for his bloodlines could be traced back to the legionary Zulu kings, Shaka, Senzgakona and beyond. He was squatting on his haunches and tracing with the tip of his *assegai* around a huge dustbin lip shaped imprint on the ground.

'What do you mean, Nkomo, larger than any you have ever seen before?' How on earth can you tell its size? It's only a footprint,' the man beside the Zulu responded dubiously, speaking in the same language. He too was squatting on his haunches but he was a white man and fully clothed.

Jarrod Donovan was in his early thirties, an American of Irish descent. He couldn't be described as a handsome man but was a man with an engaging personality all the same. Well-built and standing just under six-feet tall in his stocking feet, he had a shock of wavy black hair, an unremarkable face and penetrating eyes of walnut brown. Notwithstanding his eyes, his most distinguishing features were the breadth of his shoulders and the bold cocky self-confidence he exuded.

He and his companion were coming to the end of two hard years of hunting elephants in the African bush for their ivory. With his wagons full of ivory once again, it was time to turn and leave the elephants and bushveld behind. He would take his booty south; his wealth once again restored.

Hiding his irritation, the Zulu rose and surveyed the varying shades of brown and yellow that adorned the surrounding mopane woodlands.

Although he was well-muscled and tall, standing well over six-foot, his facial characteristics were his most distinctive features. He had a strong powerful jaw and prominent cheekbones protruding beneath dark fathomless eyes, with a deep intelligent forehead topped by peppercorn curls of jet-black hair.

Ignoring the white man, who by now had also risen and was watching him curiously, he deliberately took a pinch of powder from a small leather pouch at his belt and delicately inhaled a pinch through each of his broad nostrils. When his induced bout of sneezing had subsided, he composed himself, turned and looked evenly at Jarrod.

'*Nkosi*, some of the white man's knowledge and ways I do not understand, nor choose to question. Now myself, well, I have lived all my life tracking and hunting the animals of the wild. There are certain things I too have learned.'

The rebuff may not have been a direct one, but Jarrod felt its lash as surely as if it had come from a *sjambok* whip.

Without taking offence and chuckling lightly, he replied, 'As it'll be you carrying his tusks, tell me anyway, Nkomo. Tell me about this great elephant of yours.' It was clear he still doubted the black man and had no intention of trekking after ivory his wagons couldn't possibly carry.

The two men squatted down beside the huge imprints once again, and with his index finger this time, Nkomo traced around the spoor.

'This spoor came from the front footpad of an elephant. See how it is circular, you will find rear pads are oval. Now this particular spoor, as with the others around it, must belong to those of an elephant bull – because of their size.' Nkomo paused and cocked his head to the side as he made a quick mental calculation. 'Now *Nkosi*, if the distance around this print was laid out lengthways, would it be longer than I am tall?'

Cocking his head to the side as he considered the print, having no idea why he was asked the question, Jarrod made a quick judgment, 'Yes, much longer.'

'Well then, that is why I have never seen a bigger elephant. He will stand twice that height at the shoulder. An elephant's height is twice that of the distance around one of his front foot pads.'

Jarrod's mouth gaped open wide as he rocked back on his heels. 'No!', he eventually managed to breathe in awe. 'Surely not!'

But instinctively he knew what Nkomo was saying was correct. Although he had little interest in it himself, when it came to reading spoor Nkomo had a rare and valuable gift. He had been astounded at times by the accuracy of his ability and predictions.

Nkomo felt somewhat vindicated and was now thoroughly enjoying himself. He gained no greater satisfaction than confounding Jarrod with the extent of his bushcraft and tracking skills. He judged his next comment finely, waiting until the white man had recovered from his shock.

'Now, because of the size of the impression left at the front of this print, it tells me the ivory this elephant carries is substantial.' He indicated the deep indentations with his finger. 'And on this journey, we have seen no other bull carry tusks larger.'

'Surely not,' Jarrod whispered fervently. 'Not as big as the one we saw in the Matopo Hills?'

He still dreamt about that bull. It had been just on first light when he and Nkomo had first glimpsed it on the crest of a hill above their camp. With the brilliant gold of the rising sun as its backdrop, its silhouette had presented a truly imposing sight. To date it had been by far the biggest tusker he had seen in the two years he'd been hunting ivory in the bush.

They chased that bull for three days and nights, curling up exhausted, sleeping like dogs in the dust when it became too dark to work its spoor. Yet each day they had lagged further and further behind; the elephant had easily outdistanced them. Not once did they catch sight of it again.

'Surely not that big?' he repeated hungrily.

'Does a man compare a lion cub with its father?' Nkomo queried with a raised eyebrow. 'There is no comparison. These elephants are also like father and son.'

Jarrod jumped to his feet, the thought of turning south forgotten. Running for his horse, he yelled over his shoulder, 'Take the spoor.'

The fervour of the Matopo Hills had taken hold once more.

CHAPTER 3

DONOVAN HAD BEEN born in 1845 in Dublin, Ireland, yet he never came to know the country of his birth. Just after his fourth birthday he emigrated with his parents to the United States of America. His father, disillusioned with the life of subsistence in Ireland, and lured by the prospect of gold joined the Californian gold rush of 1849.

Jarrod's father became one of the few forty-niners to strike it rich and sensibly, at his wife's insistence, left the rush with his hard-earned money intact. He went on to take advantage of another natural resource, this time the country's indigenous forests. Originally selling back to the mines and miners he had chosen to leave, he carved out an empire in the timber industry.

Jarrod never got on well with his father, and after a series of blazing rows he was offered and accepted a full and final payment of his inheritance at the early age of twenty-four. Like his father he too had been bitten by the mining bug, but one of a very different kind.

He was one of the many thousands of hopeful prospectors who flocked to a place called Kimberley, in a country that would later be called South Africa. Upon arrival he acquired a number of small-claims and worked as a *digger* in the 'Big Hole', as the Kimberley mine became known.

The mining industry wasn't to be as kind to him as it had been to his father. Four years after his arrival, with less than one hundred pounds to his name and harbouring a badly dented morale, he walked off his claims. The disillusioned young man headed north, this time lured by gold – white gold. His family's lust for ivory had begun.

Immediately, Jarrod began to experience his first of many setbacks as an elephant hunter, his lack of skill and even the most basic of equipment being paramount amongst these. Although he hated to admit it, once Kimberley had been left behind he was totally inept out in the African veld.

Three months later and three hundred and fifty miles north of Kimberley, using fair means and foul and learning quickly, he found himself with two salted horses – resistant to the bite of the tsetse fly – a single shot bolt action Mauser and as much ammunition as he could carry. Several hours earlier he'd had to make a rather hurried departure from the Transvaal Boers' capital of

Pretoria.

Upon his arrival at Pretoria the men-folk of this budding frontier settlement immediately became suspicious of the confident brash talking young American, but to the settlement's women he made a welcome change from the conservative, silent male demeanour they were used to. Jarrod's main goal was to equip himself as quickly and cheaply as possible for an extended period of time as an elephant hunter in the African bush. 'And by God if these Boers won't help me, their women-folk will,' he declared.

It took him several days of researching and planning to decide on a strategy to achieve his goal. He targeted a general store dealer named Avril Le Roux who operated from a store on Church Street on the west side of the town's Church Square. The reason he chose Le Roux was because he stocked, or had access to, all the necessary equipment a budding elephant hunter needed. However, the unsuspecting storekeeper also had two other factors in his favour, one; a domineering wife and two; a not so attractive strong-willed daughter of marrying age. This buck-toothed, overweight redhead's name was Mary.

His assault began when he walked into Le Roux's store early one Friday morning, armed with a shopping list in his hand and a winning smile painted upon his face. Appearing to aimlessly wander amongst the vast, confusing array of goods, he eventually solicited help from Mary, and while he spent considerably more time than money on his selection, she was naively convinced he found her attractive. A tentative courtship began and much to the horror of the browbeaten yet traditional thinking Le Roux, a budding romance ensued.

Jarrod was able to move closer to his goal when Mary found out he was in need of work. With help from her mother she strongly suggested that her father gave the young American employment. Although he began working for a pittance, it suited his aims – it was just the stolen moments behind the maize sacks in the shop's storeroom at the rear he found difficult to endure.

Executing each step of his plan as necessary, Jarrod was forced into the next unenviable phase. Even though he worked amongst his sought-after supplies, it didn't mean Le Roux would part with them for less than the full retail price, unless of course there were exceptional circumstances. To her father's alarm, Jarrod announced his engagement to Mary.

As Mr and Mrs Le Roux were of Voortrekker stock – their parents having been involved in the Great Trek north from the Cape – it came as no surprise when Mary demanded a substantial dowry so she and her soon-to-be husband could discover new lands in the north. It just so happened that the dowry exactly resembled the supplies Jarrod sought. Now, even though the engagement and dowry had been agreed upon, Jarrod was thankfully able to delay the date of Pretoria's wedding of the decade.

The plans, however, weren't without their minor problems. On most occasions while they were alone Mary tried to have her wicked way with Jarrod. At these times, forced to grin and bear it, he performed his duty, although perhaps not with the same gusto as his fiancée, by continually reminding himself of his goal. The only other hitch he'd experienced so far was that he could only procure a down payment of the promised dowry before the wedding – the horses, rifle and ammunition. The wagons, their accompanying oxen and mountain of supplies would only come after the marriage.

Jarrod was at a loss to figure out a way to acquire the remainder of his needed supplies but decided to bide his time and wait, that was until he was informed that his future parents-in-law were leaving for an extended holiday visiting cousins in the Orange Republic and the store was to be entrusted to their daughter and future son-in-law. The prospect in itself didn't unduly worry Jarrod; it was the knowing looks Mary settled in his direction and her whispered comments on the days leading up to their departure that had him seriously questioning his method of achieving his goal.

Their first day alone between customers was bad enough, but the prospect of the hours of darkness to come was too much for him to bear. So, slinging a rifle over his shoulder, packing the ammunition and what food he could carry on one horse and up-saddling the other, he bolted for the sanctuary of the wilderness to the north. Yet his hurried departure didn't go unnoticed – Mary had spotted his fleeing form.

Riding like the devil and being hounded part way by a distraught Mary, Jarrod eventually found the road behind him clear. Breathing a huge sigh of relief, knowing he was beyond Mary's reaches and Boer jurisdiction, he stopped at the next European settlement. It turned out to be the home of the renowned Italian adventurer, Joao Albasini. Jarrod's luck had finally changed.

Still totally unskilled in the art of African bush-craft, and lacking basic supplies and equipment, Jarrod turned to Albasini for help and guidance. Taking advantage of the Italian's knowledge of the bush and love of gambling he received far more from him than he would've ever dreamt possible.

Some two weeks and several lucky card games later Jarrod was on his way again now heading northwest, only this time he wasn't alone. Trailing behind him were four ox-drawn wagons, their accompanying Sotho handlers and enough supplies to keep him for two years of solid hunting in the bush. His only other acquisition gained from Albasini, albeit grudgingly, was a tall black man running at his stirrup. The black man turned out to be his greatest asset. His name: Nkomo.

Nkomo had been born of royal Zulu ancestry during the reign of chief Dingane, the half-brother of the legendary Zulu king, Shaka. From the moment of Nkomo's birth, his destiny within the mighty Zulu empire should have been one of privilege and affluence. It was never to be. Nkomo never grew to know Zululand or the finer intricacies of its culture. He grew up to know the life of a virtual nomad, traveling the African veld.

The name 'Nkomo' – meaning 'head of cattle' – should have secured him the birth right of eventually succeeding in his father's once proud footsteps. His father, Mazibe, had been King Shaka's *induna*, directly accountable for royal cattle. As the nation's wealth was measured in cattle, this was no insignificant appointment. Yet it was this appointment that led to the ostracism of Nkomo's family, before his birth, by Shaka and the entire Zulu nation.

During the forging of Shaka's mighty Zulu Empire, Mazibe had first come to the attention of the Zulu king because of his reckless bravery shown in battle. Being in control of a fledgling and fast-growing empire, Shaka was in constant need of strong yet trustworthy *indunas*. He found such a man in Mazibe.

After only a few short years of his succession as chief, Shaka was the ruler of a huge empire experiencing a perplexing problem. With tribe after defeated tribe either incorporated into his swelling empire or driven away as homeless refugees, Shaka had thousands upon thousands of plundered cattle. Still involved in a never-ending series of military campaigns, Shaka solved the dilemma by appointing Mazibe as the new custodian over the ever-expanding royal herds – an appointment he was to hold for but a few short years due to the defiant actions of a fellow *induna*.

One of the first tribes to join Shaka during the infancy of his kingdom was the Khumalo. They came as a consolidated group voluntarily offering their allegiance, rather than as a defeated tribe, under the leadership of their young chief, Mzilikazi.

Impressed by Mzilikazi's qualities of courage and intelligence, Shaka made him a military *induna*, with his regiment largely consisting of members of his own tribe. This arrangement produced a serious weakness within the Zulu State. Mzilikazi could command the loyalty of his followers not only as the commander appointed by the king but also by virtue of his hereditary position.

A serious breach finally occurred after Mzilikazi had been sent to conduct a raid against the Sotho tribe in the northwest of Zululand. He returned victorious with an enormous booty of cattle. But when Mazibe arrived to take charge of the plundered herds, Mzilikazi told him he would be keeping the cattle for himself. The action amounted to a direct denial of Shaka's authority and an open declaration of war.

With the majority of his warriors, his people and the looted cattle still intact, Mzilikazi was eventually able to escape Shaka's wrath, which would not only lead to Mazibe's downfall but also give birth to a new kingdom within southern Africa; the Matabele nation was born.

Seething with anger at Mzilikazi's escape, yet unable to seek retribution against the rebellious general, Shaka chose Mazibe as his scapegoat. Mazibe was stripped of his rank and banished from Zululand along with his family.

Fiercely proud of his heritage, Mazibe was never able to lower his pride and seek a home amongst any of the lesser tribes in and around southern Africa. Thus, Mazibe and his family were damned to a self-imposed exile as wanderers of the African veld.

Mazibe raised Nkomo in the proud Zulu fashion, giving him the name that indicated his rightful station in life. Yet growing up as a nomad Nkomo developed a fierce independence, with neither respect nor allegiance to another man or his tribe – until he met a single-minded white man named Jarrod Donovan.

CHAPTER 4

THE START OF their relationship could never be called amicable. To begin with, Nkomo hadn't even been part of the arrangement Jarrod had struck with Albasini. The tall Zulu just sort of came along. Although the Sotho drivers treated him with contempt, and Jarrod looked upon him as an unnecessary addition, instinct told him not to turn the black man away. So, for the first few days as the wagons lumbered onwards, Nkomo received scant attention.

In Nkomo's case, the feelings of those about him preyed little upon his mind. Although he could never explain why he had chosen to accompany the white man, he reasoned that another's sentiment would never prevent him from continuing his northward journey.

From the start he knew Jarrod had little knowledge about or experience of the African bush, yet his attitude towards him remained neutral – but the Sotho tribesmen were different. It wasn't until the hunting started that his contempt for them really took hold. Tribalism aside, Nkomo found them woefully lacking for the tasks they had been hired to do.

Jarrod was more than aware of his limited knowledge of the bushveld and hunting elephants. However, that wasn't to say he looked upon that as a handicap. He had heard there were elephants by the thousand, waiting to relinquish their ivory. He felt with his entourage of indigenous tribesmen to drive the wagons, keep his camp and point out these thousands of elephants, he would have his wagons full in no time at all. He soon found this wasn't to be so.

Jarrod had learnt within days of arriving at Kimberley how to get the best from the Xhosa speaking tribesmen he had hired to help him work his claims; it was with the use of respect. By gaining true respect, Jarrod was envied as having one of the best and hardest working crews at Kimberley. So, he felt it was fair to assume things would be the same with the Sotho tribesmen. How naive that belief turned out to be.

Jarrod's first problem was one of language, which in itself should never have inhibited him. He had found since arriving in Africa he had an exceptional ear for languages. The problem lay with his reluctant tutors. Not only were his drivers unwilling to teach him their dialect, where they would often forge ignorance, they soon became slovenly in their manner and generally lazy in all facets of camp life. Unlike the hard-working Xhosa of Kimberley, the four Sotho drivers hadn't even given Jarrod the chance to gain their respect. To them he was just employment, a free meal and nothing more. How wrong their assumption turned out to be.

It came to a head late one afternoon when he was hunting alone. He had never known such frustration. He couldn't effectively communicate with his drivers let alone solicit their help or gain their respect, and because of it he was experiencing failure unlike he had ever experienced before. Then, like a thunderbolt from heaven, realisation struck.

The bastard, he softly swore. Albasini had used him to rid himself of his reprobates. As he cursed his stupidity, it became blatantly obvious none of the Sothos possessed the slightest desire, let alone the skill, to perform the duties they had been hired for. His anger burst into flame, and pivoting his horse on the spot, he brutally kicked it into a gallop back to camp.

Nkomo solemnly shook his head. The white man had gone off on his own again to hunt. He noticed his attempts to hunt were mostly unsuccessful. Sometimes he did succeed, but the Zulu was sure only the *amadlozi* would know how on earth that happened.

Nkomo had followed him out of the camp on two separate occasions; both times he had turned back in stunned disbelief. The white man was obviously a natural marksman, but in other regards, like an orphaned child, he was woefully lacking. He almost felt sorry for the man – almost but not quite.

Nkomo could hear the rhythmic thunder of horse's hooves vibrating in the distance. Sitting where he was at his own camp, slightly removed from the main one, he shaded his eyes with a hand and with interest looked out across the bush-studded plain sweeping out before him. The horse was lathered with sweat and blowing heavily, but this wasn't the sight that captured Nkomo's attention, it was the unmasked rage on Jarrod's face. Never before had he seen so much anger.

Savagely hauling the horse to a halt, Jarrod threw the reins over its head and left the heaving animal to stand where it had stopped. As he deliberately stepped from the saddle he was like a raging furnace, seething with fury, boiling inside. With his fists balled like hammerheads at his sides, he quickly scanned the camp. It was set on the edge of a small acacia woodland that made way on all sides to bush-studded grasslands of golden-brown. Although it seemed impossible, his anger intensified; he had located the Sotho.

The four tribesmen were lounging around the remnants of the camp's untended fire. They had made no attempt to start the evening's meal and didn't even acknowledge Jarrod's hurried return. Jarrod felt the last threads of his sanity tear away.

In a few quick strides he reached the fireplace. His first punch was thrown low and hard; it had the full weight of his massive shoulders behind it and connected with the ringleader of the four black men squarely on the side of his head, just above his jaw. He was immediately rendered unconscious and toppled sideways off the log he had been sitting on like a sack of potatoes.

Jarrod swivelled on the spot, dropped his other shoulder and executed a near identical blow to the second tribesman on his opposite side. His bony fist smashed untidily into the side of his jaw, causing him to tumble from his hand-carved stool. He lay stunned, spread-eagle upon the ground, and before the fallen man could recover Jarrod turned, stepped between the man's parted legs and swung a hefty boot into his unprotected groin. As a groan of anguish was driven from the Sotho's lungs, Jarrod knew he would have no more trouble from the man.

Swinging around with his anger still unabated, Jarrod faced the two remaining tribesmen. They were rallying quickly; one had deliberately reached to his side and retrieved a pair of ebony fighting sticks. With the gleam of contempt smouldering like ignited coals within his eyes, Jarrod stepped towards the stick-carrying tribesman. As the man rose, in practiced harmony, he began twirling the sticks about his body. All Jarrod saw was the liquid blur of black, rock-hard ebony.

Blind to the mortal danger of the flying sticks, Jarrod stepped in boldly. Like an inexperienced boxer meeting a seasoned champion, he was met by a flurry of blows he had no hope of defending – one catching him a resounded *crack* to an eyebrow, cutting him to the bone while another brutal *thud* caught him on the point of his left shoulder, crippling the joint and lastly, a telling *whack* that deadened the opposite thigh. With his limbs paralysed and a snake of blood streaming from above his eye, he slumped forward to the ground.

The Sotho stepped in for the final killing blow. Raising a fighting stick like a sword-wielding gladiator, the black man aimed for the vulnerable spot at the base of Jarrod's skull.

When Nkomo saw the Sotho rise, swirling the ebony fighting sticks like the wings of a starling in flight, he knew the white man had fought his last fight. He stood to gather his scant possessions and leave; he wouldn't be staying once the white man had died.

Having only retrieved his *assegai* he heard the first few blows strike about Jarrod's body. He looked over at the fallen white man who now had no hope of rallying against such well-placed, crippling blows. Yet it was at that moment Nkomo developed the first hint of respect and grudging admiration for Jarrod. Seemingly oblivious to the pain and the paralysing blows, he delivered a far more debilitating blow than he had ever received.

Although Jarrod's body had slumped to the savage pounding of the whirling sticks, his mind was blind to all but his rage. Oblivious to the pain and blood now swimming in his eyes, Jarrod drove up a brutal punch, sending it hurling into his attacker's groin.

The impetus of the agonising blow lifted the Sotho off his feet and sent him hurtling backwards to the ground; with fighting sticks forgotten he lay on his back writhing about in pain. Jarrod then started to rise to meet the assault of the fourth and final man.

Nkomo knew Jarrod was doomed – the fourth Sotho was moving towards him with a battle-axe dangling at his side.

As he rose Jarrod was crippled with pain; it was as if white-hot spikes of steel were being driven into his thigh and shoulder and he could feel his rage subside as the pain paralysed his battered limbs. Standing with his vision washed red with running blood, he could do no more than wait for his executioner's axe to fall.

The Sotho's arm was thrown high as he held his aim, and like an ancient priest performing some satanic rite, he seemed to be drawing out the climax of his killing blow.

Through his blurred vision of red, and bitterly accepting his fate, Jarrod caught a glint of shining light flicker before his eyes. Unable to comprehend, he saw a flash of silver thrown across the axeman's throat. There was another taller figure now standing close behind the man.

With the flat surface of his gleaming *assegai* resting on the axeman's throat, and the sharpened edge resting up against his chin, Nkomo had stilled all movement from the man as if he were now cast in stone. After reaching out with his free hand and retrieving the battle-axe, he began to speak in Sotho.

'If the white man is harmed again, you and your leper-spawned hyenas will die a slow and painful death.' Nkomo slowly drew his *assegai* from the Sotho's throat. As he did so, he purposely pressed its razor edge lightly up against his chin. Leaving a thin red line, he continued to speak. 'Make sure your whore-rutting brothers understand.'

On a number of occasions since leaving the Italian Albasini's property, Nkomo had heard Jarrod trying to converse with the Sothos in Xhosa. Because Zulu is closely associated with the language of the southern Xhosa, he had little difficulty understanding what he had been trying to convey. He walked over to Jarrod and switched to Zulu. Having never heard the tall Zulu speak before, Jarrod was surprised he understood him.

'Tonight, I will treat your wounds. And tomorrow, I will teach you how to hunt.'

Now forgetting the Sotho tribesmen and staring dumbfoundedly up at the big Zulu, Jarrod's uninjured arm was draped around the black man's shoulder. He said the first thing that came to mind. 'How are you called?'

'Nkomo,' the Zulu answered. A bond of sorts had been established.

CHAPTER 5

AT DAWN FOR the next few months, as the iridescent rays of Africa's morning sun inched above the horizon, Jarrod rode from camp with Nkomo running at his stirrup. With Nkomo as his tutor, Jarrod began to learn how to harvest ivory. He was a willing pupil and by following Nkomo's lead he found that hunting elephants was as easy as he'd previously believed it would be. Unaccustomed to man, the beasts were easy targets when tracked and hunted correctly, and Jarrod found it easy to displace his first bumbling efforts from his mind.

The attitude of the Sothos towards Jarrod and Nkomo had changed dramatically. There was no more disdain or slovenliness, only respect and order. Although the wagons were constantly on the move, upon returning at night to each new outspan the camp was always spick and span; the oxen were fed and kraaled behind thornbush stockades, while the evening meal was ready to be served. Camp life had finally settled down to a regular routine.

Jarrod's role was hunter, Nkomo's tracker, while the Sotho tribesmen were left to sort out themselves; one was in charge of camp duties and the other three were detailed to recover the ivory.

During these months the small company of men left scores of plundered elephants in their wake. Jarrod and Nkomo left the great beasts where they fell and proceeded on to their next determined killing field. Following their trail of destruction the Sotho axemen brutally hacked the ivory from the elephants' skulls. As each day progressed, Jarrod's hoard of plundered ivory grew steadily larger.

Although Jarrod found the Sothos' attitudes towards him had vastly improved he could never bring himself to cultivate more than a superficial relationship with them, not with men who had shown open defiance and murderous intent. He learnt their language and ensured they were able to do their appointed tasks to the best of their abilities. However, in all other regards he kept his distance. Yet with Nkomo, what developed was something very different.

Other than their time spent hunting together, the only other outward change in Jarrod and Nkomo's relationship was their sleeping arrangements.

Not that there appeared to be a need, but taking the threat of the Sothos seriously, Nkomo moved his sleeping roll under Jarrod's wagon.

Nkomo had reasoned, 'Some baboons may be clumsy but most have long memories.'

With every successful hunt, their compatibility as hunter and tracker improved and as it did, so did their grudging respect for each other. Jarrod couldn't help but be impressed with Nkomo's tracking ability, knowledge of the bush and its game, and his infinite patience. He was amazed at how accurately Nkomo could predict the number and size of game from a series of smudge marks left on the ground, while Nkomo was equally impressed with Jarrod's speed of learning and his marksmanship. He had seen Jarrod turn impossible shots into shots clean and true.

Instead of travelling due north, Nkomo guided Jarrod and his wagons northwest. Jarrod knew of the need to be granted 'the road' by the new Matabele chief, Lobengula, into the heart of the rich hunting grounds in the north. On discussing it with Nkomo, he was first shocked and then intrigued by Nkomo's fervent hatred of the Matabele king and his tribe.

It took several days for him to glean the full story – Nkomo's past. However, it wasn't the Zulu's blatant prejudice against the Matabele that led Jarrod to heed his advice.

He had heard of the Rudd Concession where Cecil Rhodes representatives several years before, were given mineral rights, and hunting privileges by Lobengula for all of Matabeleland. As near as possible Jarrod wanted to hunt on uncharted land. He also had no desire to be caught up for many months discussing with the chief the possibility of being granted 'the road' and a hunting concession within his empire. So he chose to accept Nkomo's advice and skirt his wagons around to the west of Matabeleland.

Having taken several days to manhandle each wagon across the sandy riverbed of the tree-lined Limpopo, they headed slowly northwest following the Shashi River, harvesting ivory.

It was a chilly, early winter morning when Jarrod and Nkomo left camp on this particular day. In the half-light before dawn the air was still and a light frost had tinted the open plains around their camp a ghostly white. The dry brown winter grass crunched frozen underfoot as the two men passed, however, only briefly was the frost able to hold the bushveld in its ice-bound grip. As it rose from the east the sun, painted an ignited yellow, banished it and its icy tentacles from one horizon to the next. The sun's welcomed warmth and golden rays made for a perfect start for that day's intended hunt.

The previous evening, upon returning back to camp, Nkomo had cut the spoor of a small herd of bachelor bulls. Only minutes after leaving camp they intercepted their spoor once again.

'The even size of the prints tells me it is a herd of bulls. They are moving slowly, feeding along the way.' Nkomo stood up and looked along the line of the spoor. 'See the branches they have torn from the trees up ahead,' he pointed with the tip of his *assegai* at the half-eaten leafy foliage on the trail up ahead.

Standing in his stirrups gazing hungrily into the distance, Jarrod demanded, 'Are they worth following? Is there big ivory among them?'

Nkomo didn't answer. He turned and began to run along the spoor towards the sparse woodlands ahead. He knew the white man's lust for the elephant teeth would have him follow the tracks no matter what he said.

Why bother answering? he thought. Yet the thought held little contempt. Jarrod may disregard his advice at times, but for Nkomo it was good to be hunting again, good to be with a man of action.

Nkomo had been running continuously for an hour since first cutting the spoor. A light sheen of sweat had only just broken to cover his glossy black skin, a testament to his body's fitness. As the woodlands began to thicken he slowed and eventually stopped beside a huge spongy heap of yellow dung. The mound, interspersed with undigested twigs and seeds, rose halfway up his shin. Despite the morning's rising heat wafting in from the Kalahari Desert to the west, the dung was steaming. Squatting down beside it, Nkomo thrust his hand deep into its warm spongy centre.

'Well?' asked Jarrod, leaning forward in his saddle. He had seen Nkomo perform the action many times before.

'It holds the heat. They are close. We should hear them soon.' As if in confirmation, a distant toppling shudder of a fallen tree carried to them through the forest. 'They are still feeding.' Nkomo spoke over his shoulder, now standing to face the noise.

'Go,' Jarrod commanded.

It took less than ten minutes before they came upon the herd. There were four mature bulls standing in a small grassy clearing, around a huge green umbrella-shaped acacia tree they had pushed to the ground. With a light breeze carrying the scent of man away from them, the elephants were oblivious to their presence and were absorbed, feasting leisurely on the acacia's rich green leaves.

Jarrod withdrew his horse to a safer distance and dismounted. Leaving the horse he went back on foot to Nkomo.

'The one on the far right – it has the biggest pair.' Nkomo indicated the bull with the largest set of ivory.

Without a word and accepting the advice, Jarrod went down on one knee and raised his rifle. He unconsciously steadied himself and sighted along the barrel, controlling his breathing.

A shot crashed out as the Mauser violently bucked and sent the heavy grained bullet smashing through the side of the elephant's head, up into its brain. Jarrod was reloading as the elephant slumped and fell lifeless to the ground.

Pandemonium struck. There was an ear-piercing squeal of terror mixed with the shot's resounding volley. One bull bolted, careering headlong through the acacia's leafy branches, escaping into the woodlands beyond.

A second shot crashed out and another bull fell, leaving only one confused animal remaining. Deft hands worked the Mauser's action and seconds later a barking cough dispatched the third and final bull. Like the others, it slumped to sprawl unmoving on the ground.

After the final echoing report faded into the distance, all was quiet. In undignified poses of death, all three bulls lay untidily around the acacia tree. In a fascinated, dazed silence at the edge of the clearing, the two men watched, both slowly drifting back to earth after soaring high upon wings of a killing rage. Nkomo spoke first. 'It was a good bull, the one that ran.'

Jarrod shrugged indifferently. *There are plenty more where he came from,* he thought. Flicking his head towards the other elephants, he said, 'Come on, that first one I shot must have the biggest ivory we've taken so far.' He walked out into the clearing.

With Nkomo following, Jarrod was halfway towards the elephants when his heart skipped a beat, adrenaline surged into his veins and he leapt and spun around in fright.

'Bloody hell!' he breathed. An unbalanced, trumpeting scream made him whirl around in his tracks.

The elephant that had previously escaped had come silently in to stalk the two men from their rear. It crashed from the trees with trunk raised, its tusks bearing while screaming in rage as it charged at the men.

Jarrod's world slowed down as his mind began to race. With his rifle empty he knew their only chance of escaping the crazed beast was to make for the partial sanctuary presented by the other bulky lifeless elephants. As he turned to run he saw Nkomo's shoulders slump in resignation; he knew the black man held no hope of escape.

As he'd been pursued by the crashing noise during his first headlong run from the clearing, the elephant's fear had slowly turned to rage. He had seen one companion fall and heard another's ear-piercing squeal of terror. He was a bull into his fifty-eighth year and twice before he had heard that same crashing noise. Once, many years earlier in a land far to the east, a friend from his youth had fallen to a Portuguese musket ball, and more recently, in the highveld further north, two other companions had died, brutally cut down by the heavy lead bullets fired from an Englishman's rifle.

He would never forget the noise, the blood and the pain; both times he had escaped the carnage to circle back around. It was then he had smelt the acid-sweet scent of man. Like the noise, it was a smell he knew he could never forget; an offensive smell, a hated smell he would carry to his grave.

Both those times he had withdrawn, confusion merging with his absorbing fear, but this time it was different. When he circled back into the wind to identify his hunters, something snapped deep within. A burning fury evaporating his fear now consumed his mind. Intent on retribution he threw caution to the wind. Now the hunter, he closed in on his prey.

Silently stalking, using his trunk to test the air, he initially hunted by smell. When he reached the clearing, the sight of man, their loathsome scent and their chirping sounds intensified his calculated fury. He screamed and the two loathsome creatures turned to face him. It was the tall dark one he chose to first seek vengeance on.

Nkomo stood, rooted to the spot. Initially, he was amazed. This was the first time he had ever known of an elephant reversing the roles, from hunted to hunter. By squandering those first few precious seconds in useless thought, he had no hope of escaping its wild charge. He felt his shoulders slump; he knew he didn't want to die, but if he had to die, he'd die like a man.

With arms dangling limply at his side, he lifted his chin and fixed his gaze upon the maddened beast. With its tusks like tapered spears of creamy white, bearing down upon his body, he accepted his fate.

With frantic fingers trying to fumble a cartridge into his rifle, Jarrod risked a look at the charging beast.

Ow Christ! The sight sent chilling fingers of fear whispering down his spine; the beast was impossibly close. He finally managed to ram the cartridge home but the bull was now towering above Nkomo, presenting an impossible shot.

As the shadow of the great bull loomed above him, Nkomo felt no fear. He might not die the death of a Zulu warrior but it would be a respected death all the same. He watched the closest lance of ivory come slicing on; he didn't flinch, he stood his ground. Then with brutal force he was driven violently to the ground. Lying there with his eyes wide in shocked amazement, he gaped upwards to the side.

Jarrod had hooked his free hand around Nkomo's shoulder and thrown him sideways to the ground. With his other hand clutched around the rifle's stock, he thrust its barrel toward the charging beast.

Although it was unaimed and a reflex shot, the rifle barked sending a bullet slicing upward towards the elephant's angered brain. It nicked the brain's frontal lobe, instantly killing the bull, yet its momentum carried its lifeless body on. In a billowing cloud of dust, the great carcass slumped forward, towards Jarrod and the ground.

As the dust cleared Nkomo leaped to his feet – Jarrod was nowhere in sight. Eventually, a groan and a breathless curse carried from beneath the fallen beast but there was still no sign of life. Then he heard, 'Don't just stand there, you big baboon, get me out from under here.'

Nkomo fell to his knees and peered beneath the elephant's trunk. On his back and hidden behind the trunk Jarrod was neatly nestled between the elephant's tusks and tucked up legs.

'Well?' he asked, looking up at Nkomo's disbelieving stare.

Jarrod was badly bruised but miraculously, otherwise uninjured; only the devil's own luck had saved him from a gruesome death. Both tusks had narrowly missed his shoulders and driven into the ground, preventing the elephant's head from flattening his chest, while its folded legs had protected his lower body.

Several minutes later, with Jarrod limping heavily as both men left the clearing, Nkomo stopped and looked evenly at the man who had unselfishly risked his life to save him. Knowing no words for 'thank you' in Zulu, he was at first at a loss to know what to say. Eventually, he found his tongue. *'Nkosi,'* he respectfully praised, 'I am your man. My family will always owe a debt to yours for the thing you did today.'

The tentative bond between the two men was now cemented in place and would last for generations to come.

CHAPTER 6

MONTH AFTER MONTH Jarrod and his wagons slowly trekked northwards, leaving littered in their wake hundreds upon hundreds of slaughtered elephants. Jarrod was so successful during his quest to harvest ivory that many times they had to stop, empty his wagons and bury his plundered ivory along the way. He placed each cache with care, accurately sighting their positions off surrounding landmarks before continuing north again.

As they trekked through Africa's great southern wilderness, they constantly passed through prolific wildlife areas. Often, Jarrod had to ask Nkomo the names of the animals they saw; like the gregarious copper antelope the tessebe, the sabre-horned jet-black sable antelope and their fawn coloured cousins, the roan. They also encountered numerous giraffes, spiral-horned kudu and grey waterbucks with the distinguishing white targets around their rumps. The most abundant game they saw were zebra, wildebeest and impala in herds by the hundreds, and buffalo in herds by the thousands, while this ambling game was relentlessly followed by scores of predators. However, more importantly for Jarrod, there was a multitude of elephants to retrieve his ivory from.

While the game they viewed was fruitfully rich and continually changing, so was the landscape. They passed through a timeless African expanse of outstanding scenery, diverse and yet plentiful to the extreme. At times they edged the great Kalahari Desert, but mostly they found themselves well inland from its fiery, waterless reaches. They passed through bright green riverine vegetation, golden-yellow seas of open grasslands, and even English-type meadows at times. Open plains sometimes gave way to bare undulating country only to level out into heavy forests adorned with brown, gold and auburn trees.

Then there was the wild haunting country of the low veld before they passed through and around the rocky majesty of the Matopo Hills, with its mass of granite hills, weathered to fantastic shapes and with its deep valleys shadowed by wind sculptured boulders. At times it left Jarrod and his men touched by something approaching religious awe. However, the countryside they most often hunted in was of shades of greens, greys and browns that embellished the thick savanna-type woodlands and the thornbush studded plains of the southern bushveld.

For the next two years, this great and varied expanse of primeval land gave Jarrod his plundered treasure. His journey had taken him far to the north before he was ready to turn his wagons around and head back to the south. That was, of course, until he and Nkomo came upon those huge dustbin-shaped elephant imprints on the ground.

They relentlessly followed the spoor for days. Because this was the first time they were being truly selective, it was by far the hardest travelling they had done. Mile after endless mile with the baking torch of the sun overhead, they persistently followed the elephant on. At times they lost its spoor in bad, rocky ground, and only by skirting out far and wide were they able to pick it up again. Many a time Nkomo would have given up when even his tracking prowess was stretched to the limit. It was only Jarrod's dogged perseverance that allowed them to pick it up again and continue. Because of the daily distances it travelled, it was clear the elephant was struck by some kind of wanderlust.

Each evening after the last red flash of day, the two men slumped bone-weary to the ground. They ate their unappetising meal of biltong and stodgy maze cakes and slept where they lay.

'Maybe tomorrow, *Nkosi*,' was the last thing Jarrod heard each night before falling fast asleep, sleeping through the night like a dead man. However, each morning he had Nkomo up as soon as it was light enough to read the spoor.

'Come on, you tired old woman. People die in bed,' he'd say to rally his companion.

'*Hawu!*' Nkomo would exclaim from beneath his blanket, 'But remember this old woman does not have a horse and the way we travel, this is where I choose to die.' Yet before full light, with much mumbling and many mildly obscene oaths, they would be on the trail again.

They were well into their fifth day's hunt and had just found the spoor after losing it for the umpteenth time; the temperature had soared to the extreme. Jarrod had dismounted and was standing beside Nkomo. The heat seemed to compound an oppressive eerie silence that veiled the encompassing scene.

At mid-morning they came upon a huge slow-moving river, its width stretching for over a hundred yards with rich vegetation edging its banks. The growth lining the river and its pale blue water offered a pleasant respite after the dust, heat and dryness of the surrounding land.

'What is this place?' Jarrod asked, retrieving his felt hat from his head while wiping sweat from his brow with the back of his hand.

'The people here, the Makololo, call it the Chobe,' Nkomo answered, pointing with his chin towards the river. 'Before it disintegrated, seasons before, their tribal capital verged swamplands several days march to the west. They say this area is one of the elephants' traditional breeding grounds.'

Mystified, Jarrod looked around at the riparian vegetation. He found it hard to believe that it was so totally devoid of animal life, let alone elephants. In fact, since arriving upon the river they had seen no wild game at all. 'Well, what was that smoke we saw before, rising in the distance?' He looked towards the east. It'd been there since early that morning.

'*Mosi-oa-tunya*,' Nkomo said in awe, looking in the same direction.

'The smoke that thunders,' Jarrod translated, as he frowned in query, still none the wiser.

'It is a Makololo name, but it is no ordinary smoke. They say a river, much larger than this one, drops into a huge ravine, and the smoke is the great columns of mists it sends into the air.'

'Ah … of course David Livingstone's waterfall,' Jarrod muttered in English as realisation dawned. He remembered the Scottish explorer had called it 'Victoria Falls', after the British Queen. 'Tell me more.'

'Well, it is also said that where the water drops it is guarded by *Chipique*, a huge snake-like creature with a grey head and a thick body. It is so large, some Makololo have even seen it eat a boat. They say he appears in the night to protect its kingdom.' Nkomo swallowed superstitiously, still staring down towards the now hidden waterfall.

Unable to prevent himself, Jarrod guffawed in disbelief. 'Snake-like creature,' he scoffed, continuing to laugh. He'd never heard anything so ridiculous. 'African beliefs …' he trailed off.

With a start and caught off balance, Nkomo shot a stricken look at him. Stammering slightly he said, 'Not … not that I believe them of course.'

Still chuckling lightly Jarrod shook his head. 'Of course,' he repeated deliberately, before adding, 'Well, come on then, my fine, fearless warrior, we have a far smaller beast to track.' Pointing to the elephant's tracks he said, 'Take the spoor.'

For the next few hours it was unbelievably hot as they tracked after the elephant. It had been drinking at spots along the water's edge and at one sandy spot had taken the opportunity to have a leisurely swim and a mud-wallow. The thick juicy mud helped cool his body and protect his skin from the sun's burning rays.

Although the area was devoid of life, there were many animal tracks leading down to and away from the river. At times they hampered Nkomo's tracking by obliterating the elephant's spoor, but he was usually able to find it again by casting further ahead. That was until it led away from the river, onto a vast bush-studded plain, towards woodlands beyond. Nkomo lost it when it was erased by the many prints from a large troop of baboons, heading in the same direction.

After another hour, totally frustrated, Nkomo came to stand beside Jarrod. He knew the white man wouldn't be pleased. 'It is hopeless. This time we have lost it.'

Damn! So close yet so far away, and the prints were only hours old. It felt as if a life sort treasure he had finally found had been whipped away to just beyond his grasp.

They were standing on the edge of the open plain that seemed to stretch forever into the west. It was fringed on one side by the riparian vegetation and on the other by the green and brown woodlands that swept to the south.

Up until a few minutes before it had been incredibly hot. Only now with a gentle breeze blowing from the river did the men have some relief from the lava-like heat previously weighing them down.

Jarrod looked out across the open plain. 'Come on where are you?' he whispered in English, willing the elephant to show.

Not understanding the words, yet instinctively realising their meaning, Nkomo pointed to the woodlands.

'Because of the heat, the animals will have gone deep into the forest.' He shrugged. 'He may return this way when they come down to drink.'

Jarrod shook his head. *We've bloody well lost him*, he thought, disgusted. He was about to turn away and head for his horse when he stopped in his tracks. 'What's that noise?' he asked, frowning as he cocked his head to the side.

Nkomo could also hear it; it seemed to rise and fall with the wind. Snapping, ripping and boisterous destruction like a marauding army, destroying everything in its path.

With ears cocked, both men slowly turned towards the woodlands when they identified its direction. Finally, the wind was unable to keep the noise at bay. With eyes fixed on the trees both men were cast as if in stone; transfixed by something approaching superstitious awe. Neither had ever heard a noise quite like it before.

Finally, they were able to identify what had caused the noise.

'*My God!*' Jarrod breathed in wonder.

Eventually, his breathless shock turned to stunned amazement, as a tide of animals, like a living sea, flowed from the trees. It was an astonishing array of wildlife like neither had seen before. But what really caught their attention was the thousands of feeding elephants that poured from the woodlands to finally litter the yellow grassy plain. Jarrod's initial amazement turned to jubilation; he had never seen so many elephants in one place before.

He turned to Nkomo and said in breathless wonder, 'Look at those elephants, we could go on harvesting ivory forever.'

Nkomo nodded. 'Yes, with herds like these, there will always be elephants for the taking.'

Jarrod never registered the words. He froze on the spot and placed a hand on Nkomo's shoulder to quieten him.

The black man could feel the hand tremble; he recognised the tremor as excitement. As he followed Jarrod's gaze, his breath caught in his throat as he understood the white man's excitement. A huge elephant bull had materialised from the forest. He seemed to dwarf the trees around him but it wasn't his bulk that held their gaze, it was his monstrous, vegetable stained tusks of ivory. They looked perfect, protruding with little curve or taper in harmony from his upper lip.

Nkomo broke the spell. 'It is the bull I have seen from the prints, the one we have been tracking.'

As he watched the bull walk along the edge of the woodlands, Jarrod couldn't help but marvel at Nkomo's prediction. The elephant was as he had imagined, it was truly a bull amongst bulls.

Still riveted to the spot, Nkomo and Jarrod saw him walk up to and rest his wrinkled forehead up against an acacia tree. They watched in fascination as he shook its bean-shaped pods to the ground. When the elephant began to feast upon his spoils, This was his chance to take the beast. Like a spaniel shaking off a coat full of water, he shook aside his awe and with Nkomo guiding him began stalking towards what would be his grandest trophy of all.

Minutes later a resounding shot crashed out, the elephant fell, as Africa died another death. The brutal slaughter of Africa's elephants had begun in earnest.

CHAPTER 7

Los Angeles

THE RESOUNDING SMACKS and the echoing shots of rackets being struck against the returning rubber ball led Peter Nkomo to his employer. He had arrived in Los Angeles not two hours before and was now walking below ground level down a gloomy short concrete corridor.

At the end of the corridor he quickly skipped up a spiralling metal staircase and entered a small gallery that overlooked two starkly lit squash courts.

Beneath him, two men were playing within the confines of one of the court's white plastered walls. With court shoes squeaking and rackets flaying, they were nimbly hurling themselves across the wooden floor after an elusive black rubber ball.

Peter shook his head. As yet, he was unable to fathom what Western ritual possessed two grown men to compete in such a way. He put the thought aside as he began to study the man who had completely changed his life. As he did so, that man scored an easy point off his opponent. Although he should have been happy, he didn't appear so.

'Damn you, Hank,' he snapped, thrusting his racket in his opponent's face. 'Play the bloody shot or next time it'll be more than a point you'll lose. I may employ you, but I want a game. I'm not here for a picnic.'

Peter nearly laughed aloud when Donovan lost the next three points in a row. He was fuming by the time he noticed they weren't alone.

The walnut-brown eyes that flicked up and met his appeared to be consumed with pure rage. When the man eventually spoke, Peter noticed an instant change come over him. His eyes may have lost their blazing sheen and the voice he used may have been calm, but his aggressive stance betrayed his forced composure.

'Give me five minutes, Peter, and I'll be finished here.'

This was the manner of a man Peter had come to know so well. Cool and calculating, this was his employer: Judd Donovan.

Donovan was true to his word. In the next five minutes he not only finished with his opponent, he annihilated him.

During those brief minutes Peter recognised why he'd been drawn to the man. It was clear Donovan wasn't as skilled as his opponent but he honed in on his weaknesses and ruthlessly exploited them until he was in full command.

Although Donovan was forty years old, Peter could see that he was superbly fit; his balance and the white T-shirt plastered over his sturdy body testified to that. His face, topped by wavy black hair, and his height may have been unremarkable, but his compelling eyes and the breadth of his shoulders gave him a commanding presence. It was this physical presence and the self-assured bearing he exuded that gave him his power, a persuasive type of power that he used to manipulate and influence other men. Just as now on the court, this dominance and authority set him apart and placed him above other successful men, because of this, Donovan was the one man who had earned Peter's respect.

Once Donovan had finished with his opponent, he and Peter left the squash courts; Donovan to shower and change, Peter to wait for him in his outer office. The squash courts were at an underground level of Donovan's company's office block, on the corner of Hill and Second Streets in the heart of Downtown Los Angeles – at the hub of Donovan's business empire.

Donovan owned one of the largest freight-forwarding companies and importing/exporting houses of its kind. He had companies or affiliated concerns, bonded warehouses and agencies in virtually every country of the world. All these interests came under the umbrella of the parent company: Donovan Enterprises.

The company had been set up before the turn of the century by Donovan's great grandfather, Jarrod Donovan. It was first established to cut out the middlemen and export the ivory he had taken during his years as an elephant hunter. Although originally concentrating on ivory, it didn't take long for the company to branch into all manner of other produce. Today it was practically unrivalled across the globe.

The outer office Peter sat in was on the twentieth floor of the huge multi-storied tower block owned and tenanted out by Donovan Enterprises. The black leather and chrome furnishings were nothing compared to the opulence he knew he would experience once invited into Donovan's main office.

There was a gentle electronic buzz from the secretary's desk in front of him. An attractive brunette retrieved the phone and briefly held it to her ear, then with an engaging smile she replaced the receiver, stood up and announced, 'Mr Donovan will see you now. I'll show you through.'

Realising Donovan must have entered his office by way of a private elevator, Peter smiled his thanks and did as indicated. The secretary led him to a massive set of solid teak doors. Stepping to the side of them, she used her body as a screen and stood in front of an electronic locking keypad. As she punched in the access code Peter heard four dull, but different pitched electronic notes resound, then a slight buzz and several audible clicks as a number of deadbolts withdrew. Moving to the door handles she opened them and stood aside for him to enter.

Peter didn't register the doors closing behind him; he had the same feeling of wonder every time he walked into the office. Forgetting to keep up his guard, he gazed around the room in awe. *This is definitely my type of office*, he thought hungrily.

It was a huge split-level office, carpeted in a shag-pile of deep-rich blue. Lining the walls were panels of the best quality North American black walnut money could buy. There was so much movement in the wood; its grain created a banquet for Peter's eyes to feed upon. Gentle waves of black flowed into and through varying shades of orange, brown and gold; with its deep rich lustre this facet of the office alone heightened his anticipation for the other sights that slowly unfolded around the room.

Immediately upon entering its solid teak doors, Peter stood in the office's informal discussion area. It was spacious to the extreme. On his left, positioned either side of a heavy smoked-glass coffee table, were two roll-backed leather couches clad in the finest of elk hide. Opposite the couches, strategically placed, was an array of highly polished solid walnut furniture; bookshelves, drink cabinets and an oval conference table with accompanying chairs.

As he advanced through the discussion area, several steps of Parian marble stretched ahead of him leading up into the office proper. Above the steps, like a lord surveying his manor, was Donovan. Head bowed, he sat behind a desk that was a work of art.

Like the walls and other furnishings, it was fashioned from solid black walnut; exquisitely ageless and stylishly tasteful. As if the flowing grain weren't enough, the handles and grips were carved from ivory with inlays of gold. Conveniently placed about its top was the most sophisticated of electronic and communication equipment. Behind Donovan was a massive floor to ceiling window that presented a picture view of the Los Angeles' Civic Center complex to the right and the sprawling city beyond.

While the fittings and fixtures of the office presented supreme luxury, they were mere accessories to the visual feast that adorned its walls.

Without raising his head Donovan spoke, 'I'll be with you in a moment, Peter. I know you find my works interesting, so look around.'

Without a word, Peter readily accepted the offer. The black walnut walls contained shelves and recesses which were adorned with hand-carved ivory pieces from Donovan's personal collection. The masterful way each carving contrasted against the wood set the beauty of each piece alive. Peter knew this was only a fraction of the collection even though there were scores of exquisitely carved works of art.

There were Japanese netsukes, renditions of human and animal forms engaged in all manner and variety of poses. Even though he was no expert, Peter knew most dated back as far as the Tokugawa period when the hand-carved toggles were exclusively reserved for Japan's aristocracy. He also saw ancient icons covered with hand-beaten gold and decorated by a blazing inlay of jewels. There were combs and fans retrieved from the European civilisations of old, as well as lace balls, flower buds and statues of various kinds. Peter even noticed sitting in pride of place, next to a richly carved Chinese pavilion, a stylised female form. It was about six inches tall and clearly worked with the eye and heart of a master carver. Fashioned from mammoth ivory and discovered at Moravia in central Czechoslovakia, the piece was reputed to be over thirty-five thousand years old.

Peter was in complete awe of the value of the carvings, let alone the hundreds, if not thousands, of hours each master carver had put into his work. With such loving attention bestowed upon them, each treasure revealed the crispest of detail, which easily turned the ordinary into the remarkable, the mundane into the sublime.

Here and there, he picked up one or two of the sturdier pieces. He examined the exquisite workmanship; the creamy lustre and the naturally beautiful crisscrossing grain. He marvelled at each work's silken feel; to him each was as sensuous to touch as the smoothness of an enticing woman's skin.

Peter wasn't aware of how long he wandered around the walls. It was probably only minutes, it could have been hours. He was finally brought back to the present when he was standing in the middle of the office on the white marble steps beneath two massive tusks; both were as thick as a grown man's thigh and they presented a towering archway between the two sections of the office.

Donovan's voice snapped his mind back to the present. 'Truly beautiful, aren't they?' He had come to stand behind Peter and to his side.

As he turned, Peter fancied he saw a symbol of prosperity, a man epitomising success dressed in a dark green double-breasted Giorgio Armani suit, with complementing crisp white shirt, paisley tie and hand-tooled Italian leather shoes.

Donovan was unaware of the reaction he had caused, or the scrutiny he received. He was oblivious to all else as he gazed around his collection. Ivory to him, like power, had become an obsession.

It had started as a fascination as a youngster in his parents' home. From the moment of his birth he had been surrounded by ivory trinkets left to him, courtesy of his family's past generations. However, unlike other children he never outgrew this childhood passion. From an early age, being an only child and entirely spoilt, he was able to start a collection of his own. Yet as his collection grew, so did his fascination, until what finally evolved was an all-consuming obsession.

Donovan had become fanatical about ivory and its trade. Although he had become an exceedingly wealthy man, his thirst for power, the challenges he faced and his addiction was driving him to create a monopoly in all facets of the ivory trade.

'It was in 1875', Donovan continued, still looking up at the magnificent tusks, 'when our great grandfathers came upon the beast that carried these. What an exceptional animal it must've been.' He briefly paused while shaking his head in wonder. 'Both tusks are just under ten feet long, one weighing two hundred and eleven pounds the other, a pound or so lighter.' With reverence he walked up and lovingly stroked one of the tusks. 'Africa of old, Peter.'

Peter didn't answer, he didn't need to. His feelings were the same.

'Yep, gone forever,' Donovan said as he snapped out of his dream-like mood. 'Best we take advantage of what's left of the species while we can. Before somebody else does.'

Again, Peter was in total accord and again he chose to hold his tongue.

'Right,' Donovan said with a clap while rubbing his hands together. 'Down to work.' He motioned to one of the elk hide couches. 'You've a report to present.'

CHAPTER 8

As PETER SAT in the couch facing the nearest wall, he noticed the only picture in the office. It was a full-sized portrait of who he originally thought was Donovan dressed in early twentieth-century attire. Upon closer inspection he realised it wasn't Donovan at all; the man was similar but subtly different in many ways. The eyes, to start with, were a lot softer and generally the man's facial features were milder compared to Donovan's harder, crueller lines.

A man of compassion, Peter decided. *I wonder who he is?*

Donovan, without looking up from reading the report Peter had given him, spoke as if he had heard the silent question.

'Great Grandfather. He founded the company. Look alike don't we?' Then he added, as if an afterthought, 'Don't think you'd ever catch me in clothes like that, do you?'

He fell silent and continued reading as Peter was reminded of how perceptive he had always been. While Donovan read on, Peter thought back over their families' long association, beginning over a century ago.

Peter's generation was the first of his family's to gain a formal education. So, until this point, as is common amongst the indigenous tribes of the world, his family's history was passed on orally, down through the generations. As a youngster he would sit fascinated, listening in rapt amazement, to the stories being told of his forefathers. He had such a thirst for knowledge during those years that he was soon able to tell the stories as well if not better than the tellers themselves. Often, they would have to stand corrected when Peter challenged them for missing the smallest of details. However, there were some stories that had far more appeal and demanded more accuracy than others, especially those involving his family and white men from across the seas.

Because of a debt pledged by one honourable man to another over a century before, Peter grew up to learn of a unique and valuable bond that had developed between two very different families; one African, the other American. A bond that had helped him attain his current station in life.

From its beginning, Donovan Enterprises had been steeped in tradition. As its origins began in Africa, it had maintained solid connections with that part of the world, connections that went hand in hand with those early ones first established by Peter and Donovan's great grandfathers.

Often over the years members of the Donovan lineage made pilgrimages back to the African wilds, back to where Donovan Enterprises had begun. Always during these safaris, the Donovans insisted on their guides being members of Peter's family – Donovan's father was no exception to the rule. So, on a number of occasions during his adolescent years, Donovan found himself and his family on safari in the African wilds.

Working as a camp-boy, it was during these family safaris that Peter first became acquainted with the young Donovan. Being of a similar age, cast from a similar ilk, and uninhibited by social status out in the wilds, the boys struck up an instant rapport. Peter was immediately struck by the power Donovan was able to exude even in those early days. He was a born leader, but one who abused this God-given privilege. He was easily able to manipulate those around him, and because of the accord the two boys had built Peter was shown glimpses of a well-hidden, darker side to his make-up. He remembered clearly one event that would remain fixed within his mind, an event that showed the sheer ruthlessness of the callous, calculating young man. It happened on their last safari as maturing adolescents.

On this particular trip the safari's cook had brought his daughter along as an assistant. Although she was a couple of years his senior, with scant regard for her welfare Donovan intimidated, used and finally abused her while on the safari. With Peter in tow, he was easily able to lure her away from camp. What started as a stimulating and enjoyable adventure turned into a nightmare for the comely young woman.

Allowed close physical contact with a woman for the first time, inspired Donovan's lust, warped curiosity and blatant disregard for others, and eventually led him to brutally rape the young woman. This heartless act in itself didn't impress Peter; it was what happened as a result of it.

Donovan had terrified her so much she never once divulged who had inflicted the abuse. A young guide was eventually blamed for the outrage, and using a *sjambok* whip, the girl's father beat the young man to within an inch of his life. During the beating, Donovan watched with the sadistic relish of a ruthless young man with little or no morality. From that moment on Peter recognised him as a man who took from life what he chose, with no consideration for who or what he destroyed along the way.

When Peter was first enticed by Donovan to leave his job as a game warden and set up his network of poachers, he readily accepted. Knowing

Donovan as he did, Peter saw him as a vehicle to satisfy his own growing hunger, his mounting greed for money.

Donovan's words brought his mind back to the present. 'Right, I've read your comments and the EIA's report. Now tell me in your own words how you see the new CITES regulations. How are they going to affect us?'

As unemotionally as he could, Peter answered, 'I believe it'll be disastrous. Most markets will dry up, and the prices could halve. We could be looking at a very unprofitable business.'

'Perfect,' Donovan whispered.

This time forgetting etiquette, Peter blurted, '*What?*' He couldn't believe his ears.

Sitting back in his couch, Donovan casually replied, 'I said, perfect. Believe it or not, we've been handed an ideal opportunity on a platter.'

'But –'

Hating being interrupted, Donovan held up an impatient hand. 'I don't want to hear it.' He leant forward and slapped the EIA's report down on the coffee table. Poking a finger at it, he said, 'This report alone is worth at least a month's supply of ivory from our current network. It lists, from source to end-user, some of our stiffest competition. Right?' It was more of a statement than a question.

'Right,' Peter repeated dubiously, not entirely following his boss.

'So we start running our operation like a proper business. And to survive these new regulations we have to either be small, with low overheads or large and efficient. I don't have to ask what you want to be. With the accuracy of this information,' he indicated the report again, 'those competitors are now ripe for a takeover, and that's what we're going to do. Only this time, unlike ordinary business, the advances we make for their market share will ignore protocol. The methods we use may not be subtle, but I can assure you they'll be effective.'

The dread Peter had carried since Lausanne fell away. Again, as he had seen happen many times before, Donovan was turning potential disaster into profit.

'Also,' Donovan continued, 'because the price will plummet, it's going to be far harder for the other networks to make a buck. Those that fold, I want *you*,' he indicated with an outstretched finger, 'to pick up, and those that don't … well, we'll see about them. It appears, as you've already got the poaching sown up in Zambia, Zimbabwe and Botswana, you'll have to spend most of your time in Kenya and Tanzania.'

'But what about the markets?' Peter cut in, 'Ivory'll be banned all around the world.'

'In Taiwan, Korea and the like, as they're non CITES member countries, it won't be. But you leave the marketing to me; you'll have more than enough on your plate. The other thing in our favour is the CITES countries that objected to the ruling. Zimbabwe, South Africa, Botswana and Malawi have already stated they refuse to abide by the decision. And my bet is, if they as suppliers are prepared to still market their ivory, there'll be other member countries who'll just as readily buy it.'

With brown eyes now ablaze with passion, Donovan picked up the phone on the couch's end table. 'Sonya, get Mr Bogatin up here right away. Oh, and send him right on in when he arrives,' he added before replacing the receiver.

For the next fifteen minutes the two men laid the foundation of the battle plan they would initiate to monopolise the world's ivory trade. They were planning to play and hard and ruthlessly, for there were no rules on the battleground where they were venturing.

As Donovan spoke, Peter fed off the power he exuded; carried away with the exhilaration of such overwhelming plans. With Donovan it was different, it was like shooting straight morphine into his veins. At moments like this, his obsession for ivory and thirst for power knew no bounds. As with all other aspirations he harboured, he knew he would succeed, and this one would give him the sweetest and most satisfying victory of all.

'Five years Peter, ninety-four is when I want this monopoly,' Donovan declared, thrusting a determined finger at the big Zulu's chest. 'One thing that is constant is change and you can bet those southern African countries will fight hammer and tong to get elephants – theirs at least – downgraded from Appendix One. When that happens, it'll be the icing on the –'

The heavy teak doors opened and in walked a man whose bearing and description could have only identified him as a suit-wearing thug. He was in his late thirties, had Slavic features and was short and squat. Even dressed as he was, in the finest of clothes from Valentino Boutique of Rodeo Drive in Beverly Hills, it was still abundantly clear he was powerfully ruthless and an uncompromising man.

'You asked for me, Mr Donovan,' the man said in a Russian accent.

'Ah, Nikolai, yes of course. Come on in. You know Peter Nkomo. You and he have important business to attend to.'

For the next few hours, the three men laid down the strategy they would use to monopolise the ivory trade across the globe. The plans and methods they discussed could have easily placed each of them securely behind bars for a very long time. It was dark behind the picture window beyond Donovan's desk when they rose with their plans now complete.

'Right, gentlemen. I'll want regular personal meetings with you both. It'll mean a lot of travel for you, Peter, but I want as few records kept as possible. What records there are will be kept here on computer disk,' Donovan said.

As the three men walked to the big teak doors, Donovan spoke again. 'And this Tony Campbell, you say he may not only specialise in ivory? Could he be a problem?'

'From the information I have, I believe so, yes,' said Peter. 'He has been effective in the past.'

'OK, keep an eye on him, but no silly stuff.' Hooking a thumb at the Russian he said, 'If we have to get rid of him, let Nikolai handle that or organise somebody else. We've all got our roles.' Spreading his hands out, he brought the meeting to an end. 'Right, until next time. But remember, keep me informed.'

CHAPTER 9

Present Day – The Zambezi Valley

TONY CAMPBELL HAD hardly moved for the last ten hours. His buttocks were numb and had long ago lost all feeling of the rock he was perched upon. Yet hunched slightly forward as he was, he could feel the tell-tale jabs of his right calf beginning to cramp again. The two salt tablets and the swig of water from his canteen, taken several hours earlier, hadn't helped at all. He knew he would soon have to rise and exercise his leg. He tried to ignore his calf's insistent ache. With little warning, the diamond-shaped muscle of his lower leg cramped again. Yet this time it was no nagging twinge that gripped the limb, it was the full-blown thing.

Damn! As if a steel clamp had seized his calf, he involuntarily grunted at the pain.

Slowly he managed to straighten his leg. Trying not to make another sound, with a hand stretched forward he pulled back the toes of the troublesome leg. The grabbing pain subsided.

Not trusting his body, he left his leg stretched out. To accommodate his body's new posture he repositioned the polished walnut rifle butt of his Ruger .458, previously resting on the thigh of his leg. Then with his hunter's patience restored, he settled down to wait. He knew his intended prey would eventually come – when really didn't matter. The prize was worth the wait, especially with rhino horn fetching $23,000 a pound.

He, more than most, knew that he was dealing with one of the most stupid, cantankerous, nervous but inquisitive, single-minded game in all of Africa – the black rhinoceros. An animal that charges anything that provokes its wrath; man, beast or inanimate form. Unlike its placid grassland cousin the white rhino, the black rhinoceros is a browser, feeding on the thick bush where it makes its home. This is why Tony found himself in the middle of such dramatically beautiful yet rugged scenery in the unspoiled wilds of the Zambezi Valley. It was in the dead of night and he was perched beside the river the valley's name was taken from – the mighty Zambezi.

Those who knew Tony Campbell would describe him as an

uncompromising man, but since he lived by his own set of values he felt other's opinions were of little consequence. He was a tall well proportioned, muscular man with short sandy hair and an intelligent, lightly chiselled face that was dominated by fathomless, cool blue eyes.

It had taken him only a few short days to unravel this particular rhino's nightly routine. The dramatic increase in poaching from Zambian peasants had made the rhinos of Zimbabwe's Zambezi Valley increasingly difficult to find and shoot. The persistent threat posed by the poachers had triggered their survival instincts making them wary and nervous animals, hiding by day and moving to water at night. It was this habit that had led Tony to his night's vigil.

He was sitting in a game hide he had constructed the previous day. The hide's peephole and firing slot opened onto a small sandy spit, close to the end of the Kariba Gorge on the Zimbabwean side of the Zambezi River.

Once the rhino's spoor had been located, and its nightly routine established, Tony had sighted his hide with care. When he heard the animal come down to drink, he would activate the battery powered jacklight positioned above the hide illuminating his prey. And before long the Zambezi Valley would have one less black rhino living amidst its woodlands. It would be just one of many that had succumbed to Tony's rifle.

The Zambezi Valley had always been one of the last strongholds of these prehistoric beasts. In the past, Zimbabwe's rhino population had been relatively stable, but those days were now definitely gone. Previously, badly administered National Parks and government corruption within the north countries had supplied the insatiable market of North Yemen and the world's largest illicit trading centre, Taiwan, with the rhinos' eagerly sought after horn. But as the rhino's northern populations dwindled and (despite an international hunting ban) became extinct in certain areas, demand for their horn easily outstripped supply. The inevitable happened; greedy eyes finally focused south on Zimbabwe.

The use of rhino horn for the handles of the Yemenese *djambia*, as an aphrodisiac in India and to a far greater degree for traditional medicine in China and Japan had effectively decimated Africa's once abundant rhinos. Once numbering in the millions a few short years ago, now less than a few thousand roamed the African wilds. They were described in the late nineteen hundreds by hunter and naturalist Courtney Frederick Selous as the 'most common big game today.' A hundred years later the hook-lipped rhino was facing extinction. But these weren't thoughts that preyed on Tony's mind, far from it. While there was valuable game to poach in Africa, using his acquired skills, Tony would always have a job.

Although Tony hadn't looked at his watch since beginning his patient vigil, he knew dawn wasn't far away. He lifted his hand and spread the fingers before his face, presenting a faint silhouette; he could just make out their darkened outlines.

Time of the horns, he thought, then he wondered how often had he waited like this and repeated the old Zulu maxim. Literally hundreds of times.

The saying was derived during the days of the great Zulu Empire when chiefs, warriors and herd boys alike recognised the new light of dawn as their first chance to glimpse the horns of their cattle against the morning sky. Yet Tony uttered the maxim for a very different reason; it reminded him he would have good shooting light in ten minutes. The jacklight would be unnecessary. When the rhino came to drink, Tony would find it easy to sight his prey.

As the morning light quickly strengthened, Tony assessed the lie of the surrounding land. In front of him was the untamed Zambezi River, flowing ever onward in its entire majestic splendour towards the sea. The silence that accompanied him during the night had been broken at times by the occasional splash of eddies forming and disappearing as the river commanded a life of its own.

On the opposite bank, lining the water's edge, he could see bare quartzite boulders. They had been eroded by a millennium of floods and now resembled sculptures from an alien world. Above the sculptured rocks a dense green canopy of trees, festooned with woody creepers and twisted vines, rose up the gorge's wall to eventually give way to the changing woodlands beyond.

As the soft golden light of dawn fell upon the river canyon, Tony could hear its animal life slowly coming awake. He heard the sporadic honking of purple louries, the haunting cry of a hunting fish eagle and a lone red-crested cuckoo echo its monotonous call, but there was still neither sight nor sound of the rhino. Half an hour later Tony knew it wouldn't show. It was now fully light, so he decided to leave his hide and return in the early evening for another night-long wait.

Tony had constructed his hide from an old canvas tarpaulin and tufts of long golden-brown grass. It blended well with the bright greenish-yellow bark of the group of fever trees it was nestled amongst.

He had just backed out of the hide and was kneeling on the ground with his rifle and haversack at his side when, as if somebody had walked across his grave, he felt his instincts flare. All noise had ceased. Triggered by some unseen presence, the surrounding scene had taken on a veil of deathly quiet; it was the ensuing silence that had set his alarm bells ringing. The birds had stilled their morning's chorus, and even the river seemed to hush its watery turmoil.

Now with all his senses unerringly focused, the fever trees seemed to crowd in around him. Instinct told him there was danger at his rear, with speed that betrayed his size, Tony swung his body around. He was met by nothing more than oppressive silence. Noiselessly, he rose and assessed his position. Around him was a small copse of fever trees, to his right the trees ran into a thicket of dense riparian woodlands, while above him and to his left was open rocky ground, interspersed by clumps of stalky grass. It ran from the river's edge to the undulating woodlands of the Zambezi Valley beyond.

Tony quietly moved to the edge of the small clump of trees. There he waited. Out in the open ground before him he could see the road-like game path that the rhino regularly used. It descended from the lip of the gorge, gently meandering down the rocky slope, and swinging in front of his hide on its way to a stagnant pool and the river further on. The game path and open ground were empty of animal life, but still the eerie silence persisted.

With the eye of a seasoned hunter, Tony began to scan the top of the gorge. As he did so, a shaft of sunlight pierced the canyon's rim, bathing it in early morning warmth. Finally, above and out to the left, a movement caught his eye.

A young tan-coloured impala doe had materialised to stand stock-still on the edge of the gorge. She had her head thrown back, looking over her shoulder while her eyes bulged wide-open in fright. She hesitated briefly before plunging headlong down the open slope. Moments later, dissolving the misconception that they never hunt, two spotted hyena followed in hot pursuit.

The impala leapt clear of the rocky ground and stopped on the river bank with her flanks heaving while she quaked in fear; her nose quivered nervously as she stared into the water's turbulent depths. An ear flicked back, listening for the hyenas; she then risked a quick glance behind her. Her hunters by now baying for blood had reached the edge of the sandy spit. Galvanised by the sight she suddenly jumped and disappeared beneath the swirling current. After what seemed like an eternity her head finally bobbed clear of the surface and, struggling wildly, she forged her way across and clambered exhausted onto the opposite bank. Panting heavily in obvious relief, she gazed back across the river where she was met by the two hyenas' forlorn stares. Not trusting the river to protect her she turned and, in two swift bounds, was swallowed by the dense green vegetation above the rocky bank.

The hunters and hunted, Tony thought as he watched the hyenas slink dejectedly back up the slope. Forever trying, but mostly unsuccessful.

A lack of success was a fact for most hunters, but one he chose not to accept.

CHAPTER 10

As HE HIKED up the slope to the terrace beyond, with the rifle at his side and haversack humped on his back, Tony could feel his calf resisting his efforts to stretch it out. He chose to ignore it and using his tracking skill, concentrated instead on the trail in front of him. When he had moved into the open woodlands above the gorge, he knew the rhino hadn't followed its normal nightly routine. The spoor he was following was over twenty-four hours old, though not by much.

After an hour of hard walking he had ascended one of the valley's terraces and found himself in front of the vast area of near-impregnable jesse where he had originally cut the rhino's cloverleaf- shaped spoor. He had a choice – either cut through the jesse and possibly save several hours or skirt around it to his Toyota Land Cruiser in the mopane woodlands beyond. He chose the direct approach and stepped into the jesse.

As he intended to return to the hunt later in the day, and had no desire to confront a short-tempered rhino at such close quarters, he headed through the dense bush away from its spoor. Within minutes of entering the jesse he wished he had taken the roundabout route. He could see no more than a yard and a half in front of him, and every step of the way he was hampered by thorns and barbs protruding from what seemed like every bush and tree. What's more, the closeness of the bush had driven the heat skyward. It was unbelievably hot and humid; his khaki shirt and shorts were now plastered to his skin.

He finally found a negotiable game trail and as his old training came flooding back he fell into his practiced mode of travel. While forging silently on, oblivious to the heat and closeness of his surroundings, he unconsciously scanned the ground ahead; he was intent on one thing and one thing only – getting out of this godforsaken place as soon as possible. Then, like hitting an invisible brick wall, a rank, gamey smell pierced the grim determination of his mind. He stopped dead in his tracks and froze. A smell like a cattle-crate, but far stronger, closed in like a heavy fog around him. As he stood stock-still, as if forged in stone, nothing around him moved and not a sound could be heard. After five minutes, with ears pricked and eyes darting from side to side, he realised he was alone.

With his confidence partially restored, he took a couple of hesitant paces forward and stepped into a small, thickly walled clearing. He was unable to prevent himself from turning up his nose and turn his head to the side while waving his hand in front of his face – the smell was overpowering. He had found his rhino's midden, the dung-heap it habitually returned to when it needed to defecate.

Trying to ignore the overwhelming stench, Tony squatted on his haunches. Strewn in front of him were remnants of digested bark and twigs. He could tell by the scattered dung that the midden had only been used about twenty-four hours before. As the rhino is a creature of habit, he warily eyed the interwoven branches around the clearing. Intuition told him to leave as soon as possible.

A couple of hundred yards on after leaving the midden, the bush started to thin, the going became easier and he could see open woodlands further along. With alarm bells still faintly sounding, he was able to quicken his pace. The sooner the jesse was left behind, the better.

No sooner had he lengthened his stride, when a hundred yards in front of him exploded a cloud of startled ox-peckers. As these watchful birds live in mutual accord with the larger African game, feeding on parasites and other blood-sucking insects, they warn their hosts of imminent danger. Yet this time their indignant outcries not only warned their host but also signalled to Tony he had found his rhino – his intended prey

'Oh Christ,' he groaned in anguish. 'Not now.' The roaring snorts and out-raged bellows like a steam engine with a full head of steam told Tony he was indeed correct.

As he brought his rifle's padded butt to his shoulder, he knew in such close cover he would have one, and one chance only at a decent shot. He stood, rifle at the ready, leaning forward, with his sights fixed on the crashing overture of sound rumbling down towards him.

With his mind beginning to race, he began to override his initial distress. He was starting to savour the delicious feeling of fear mixing with the adrenaline now coursing through his veins. Once again, he was living on the edge.

How often have I stacked the odds like this? he briefly wondered. *Far too often.*

When the rhino crashed into sight he had to hit it in the flank or shoulder, otherwise he couldn't guarantee the shot would stop the beast.

He tried to still his mind and concentrated on the thrashing bush up ahead.

The rhino's enormous grey head and shoulders burst through the wall of scrub, not twenty yards from where he stood, but unbelievably its tank-like body never followed. It stood blinking short-sightedly through owlish eyes, uttering great gusts of indignation, willing something, anything to move so it could charge. Tony was presented with an impossible shot.

Knowing of the animal's weak eyesight over fifteen yards he remained motionless – hoping the rhino would move – waiting for a better shot. The rhino, sensing a presence close by, chose to stand its ground with impossibly tattered ears flicking this way and that as it tried to pick up the slightest sound. Yet what really grabbed Tony's attention wasn't its ears or its creased and wrinkled hooked-lip, the mountainous peak of its shoulders or even its narrow down-sloping head, it was its long polished double horns – sharpened to incredibly vicious points. It became a stand-off with Tony not daring to move while the rhino was intent on locating a target that it could wreak havoc on.

The unbelievable happened; Tony had to break their deadlock. He felt his calf cramp again and flinched as the gripping pain took hold. The rhino picked up the faint movement and, like a bull at a gate, careered down towards him.

All logic went with the onset of pain and the rhino's charge. Tony turned and tried to run. He hobbled several yards before he realised his folly and with a rush of panic, he shot a look over his shoulder. If the thunderous charging noise wasn't bad enough, the sight he was presented with decimated even his usual unswaying courage. One and a half tons of armour-plated muscle led by a joust-like horn was steam-rolling down upon him.

With his mind reeling in horror he cursed his stupidity. 'Wake up, man.' With his experience he knew he should never have run. One quick step to the side would have easily avoided the lumbering beast.

With only inches to spare he reacted and darted to the side. He felt the wash of air caused by the vicious whisk of the rhino's horn whisper passed his body. Luckily, the animal's momentum carried it on.

Running as best he could, Tony made for the open woodlands. The crashing and violent upheaval of the bush behind told him the rhino had changed direction and was hot on his heels again. Tony, still hampered by his calf, judged his next move finely. Like a gambler with odds finely balanced, he waited until the last possible moment.

The thicker scrub had thinned and he was out in the open woodlands. Feeling the ground from the rhino's charge shaking under foot he sidestepped and ran to the right. After half a dozen paces he stopped dead in his tracks and in one fluid movement he whirled around and brought his rifle to bear. The rhino crashed out of the bush and blundered into his line of fire.

Crack. The rifle bucked and Tony, gasping for air, briefly saw a silver flash then heard the resounding *smack* of the tranquilising dart hit home.

The source of the rhino's rage and his headlong charge were forgotten as he eventually staggered to a halt. He felt confused as a dull pain struck him deep within his chest. Quickly, the area began to numb as a blackened drug-induced void closed in from behind his eyes. With head slung low and his vision swimming, he eventually gasped out one last final ragged breath, before slumping unconscious to the ground.

Another successful hunt had been executed. One more of the Zambezi Valley's precious rhinos had been saved from poachers' bullets. The outcome left Tony Campbell a well-satisfied man.

CHAPTER II

WITHIN VIEW OF the sleeping rhino and slightly hampered by his tightly knotted calf Tony hobbled to the nearest tree, and slipping his haversack off his back he slumped warily down against its trunk. As he massaged his calf with one hand, he unbuckled and reached into the haversack with the other, producing a small hand-held walkie-talkie. Switching it on he held it up to his face.

'This is Campbell One, do you read me, Ben? Over.' Tony had to repeat the message several times before he eventually got an answer.

'Yes, Tony. I read you loud and clear. Hell, you sound close. Where are you? Over,' came a clear, yet somewhat staticky voice.

'Not far from where you're camped. The other side of the jesse where we cut the spoor. What took you so long in answering?' Tony demanded. 'We've got work to do. Over.'

'I was er, I …' hesitated the staticky voice, then quickly changing the subject, hurried on, 'so you got the rhino? Over.'

'You were still in the bloody sack, weren't you? I'll have gotten more than the rhino by the time I see your shiny black backside. Yes, I got it. Now do something useful and get the vehicles and those other useless bastards up here. Over and out.'

As Tony signed off and dropped the walkie-talkie back into his haversack a light smile creased his mouth. Not that he would ever admit it, but he enjoyed working with Ben. He might not be the most effective of game scouts, but he was a brilliant tracker all the same, and someone who got the most from life.

After many months of negotiations, Tony, with Ben as his assistant, had been commissioned by the WWF to help coordinate anti-poaching programs throughout eastern and southern Africa. Until now both of them in their different capacities had been involved with the Departments of Wildlife and National Parks of both Botswana and Zimbabwe. Tony had been born in Botswana thirty-one years ago but looked on both countries as his home. As for Ben, well, nobody was sure when he was born and nobody – including him – really gave a damn. He was one of the many unique characters that helped make Africa the special place it was.

Tony had been raised by his father, who had been a wildlife officer with Botswana's Department of Wildlife and National Parks after his mother had died in childbirth. He was an only child and grew up knowing little more than the game parks and African bushveld that had made up his childhood home. He learnt to know and love the bush, its animals and the people in it. Because of the remoteness of those first early homes, he was schooled by correspondence and (much to his father's distress) gained no formal qualifications; he had only the skills he learnt from the bush. However, not realising (or not choosing to realise) that his lack of qualifications was a handicap, he followed in his father's footsteps and had already carved out an awesome reputation as a young man truly dedicated to wildlife conservation throughout Africa. His single-mindedness and uncompromising attitudes may not have won him many friends, but he gained respect from those who mattered in the wildlife arena. This was why he had been approached, accepted and was about to start his new sponsored position with the WWF. He was ending the final week in his current job and was looking forward to the new and exciting challenge.

For the last few years Tony had been involved with Operation Stronghold, a rhino protection exercise and relocation program in Zimbabwe. The operation was funded by conservation organisations from all over the world. Tony was just one of a hundred or so men who patrolled the seven and a half thousand square miles of the Zambezi Valley and helped relocate the black rhinos from its undulating woodlands. So far he had been involved with well over three hundred relocations, which had helped create viable breeding populations in protected pockets around Zimbabwe. However, what had started as a conservation exercise had now turned into a bloody bush-war.

Tony was involved in a violent battle that was being waged over the black rhino for its valuable horn. Every day, when he wasn't busy with relocations, he and the other armed game scouts patrolled the valley to fight for and protect the world's last large wild rhino herd. Their common enemies were the heavily armed Zambian based poachers and their orders, by government decree, were 'shoot to kill'. As the rhinos hurtled towards extinction, this desperate situation had required more than just desperate measures, it had thrust Tony and his fellow conservationists into a deadly mission that had turned Zimbabwe into the last stand for the wild rhino.

As he looked over at the unconscious beast he felt somewhat relieved. It was one more of the few hundred that remained in the valley that would soon be safe from not only the poacher's bullets but from their real enemy – greed, corruption and ignorance from all corners of the world.

Walking over and dropping his haversack beside the rhino, he began his preliminary examination of the beast. He retrieved a wooden box from the haversack. It was packed with little bottles of the tranquilising drug, M99, for the darts, as well as its antidote nalorphine, a snakebite kit, antibiotics and all the other items required for an effective first aid kit out in the bush.

Using considerable effort he yanked out the tranquilising dart from the rhino's shoulder. Its needle resembled a three-inch nail being just as long and just as thick. After injecting antibiotics into the bleeding hole, he began a thorough investigation of the unconscious animal; its heartbeat and temperature, its length, girth and height at its shoulder and also the diameter of its feet. As he measured its wickedly sharp and highly polished double horns, Tony had darted a truly magnificent bull that would weigh in close on three thousand pounds. Yet what amazed him most was how it had stayed alive for so long this close to the Zambian border.

Over the last few years over five hundred slaughtered rhinos had been lost from the valley, mostly from areas well inside Zimbabwean territory. Only because of its natural cunning had this one out-lasted what must've been persistent efforts by the poachers to kill it for its horn.

Tony was recording the last of his statistics, the rhino's breathing rate when he heard the distant rumble of the recovery vehicles labouring towards him. Buckling his equipment back in the haversack he placed it beside the nearest tree. Looking down through the open woodlands he saw Ben's gang of labourers clearing a path through the undergrowth for the approaching vehicles. Leading his Land Cruiser was the recovery truck, a four-wheel-drive, flat-deck Mercedes-Benz Unimog.

After another ten minutes, the truck's driver had reversed it up to the rhino, switched the engine off and clambered down from its cab.

'Ben, you skinny old rascal, what took you so long?' Tony demanded in English, tapping a finger on his stainless steel Rolex. 'It's been over an hour since I spoke to you. The camp isn't that far away.'

With head bowed, a short, slightly built black man, dressed in a game scout's khaki uniform walked towards him. His jet-black curly hair was cropped short against his skull and as yet Tony was unable to see his face. The man came to a stop several paces in front of him.

'What have you been up to?' Tony suspiciously challenged as he stepped forward and lifted the man's chin. 'You little bugger, you've been fighting again.'

The face he was presented with was clear and shone with good health. A huge smile, displaying perfect white teeth, was splashed across the face. However, a purple-black shiner was ringed around one of his eyes – it was the only blemish on the otherwise beaming face.

'Yes, but you would've been proud of me. Oh, how I fought,' Ben boasted through his cheesy grin.

'Well it can't have been over a woman, we're too far out in the bush,' Ben had built up a reputation as having a thirst for much larger women. 'so it has to be the other.' Tony took an extra pace forward and loudly sniffed the black man's breath. 'You smelly bugger, you've been drinking again.'

'I had no choice, Tony. One of the labourers brought some alcohol into camp. Since you don't allow it,' he shrugged, 'I was forced to take it off him.'

'I don't believe it,' Tony said as he dragged a disbelieving hand from his forehead down over his face. 'And where is he now, this labourer?'

'He is sick.' Ben solemnly nodded. 'I had to leave him behind. We can pick him up on the way back,' he ended innocently.

'And the alcohol?'

'Again, you would've been proud of me. I allowed no others to touch it. I personally disposed of it myself,' he said with a roguish smile and the wickedest of glints in his eye.

'Oh gawd,' Tony groaned, shaking his head in disbelief. 'It goes from bad to worse.' Yet he recovered quickly. Switching to Sindebele, so the other Matabele labourers could understand, he glared at Ben.

'Because somebody has been drinking while away from base, he will be the one that holds the *ubejane's* – black rhino's – head.'

Taunted by the jeering labourers, Ben quickly lost his grin. He rose up to his full five foot six and stalked off towards the truck. Grabbing the nylon straps and other tie-downs, he snapped indignantly at the labourers. 'Come on you bunch of old washer women. We have work to do.'

A padded wooden sledge was pulled down two metal guides secured from the back of the Unimog, down to the ground. It had been placed beside the unconscious rhino. After its legs had been tied together it was rolled onto the sledge and securely strapped into place. A thick cotton facemask was about to be placed over its horns and around its face. Not once had the bull gained even partial consciousness while Tony, Ben and the labourers worked around him. That was until the facemask was about to be put on his head and strapped beneath his chin.

Tony had noticed Ben looking slightly the worse for wear due to the alcohol he had consumed, and because of that he was going to make the man pay.

'Ben you hold him down if he moves,' Tony gruffly teased as he retrieved the facemask and slipped one last tie-down through a metal lug on the side of the sledge. 'He's only a couple of tons. Poke him in the eye if he tries to get up. It'll distract him.'

As if the beast had heard, an eye popped open and fixed a murderous glare on Ben, daring him to put a finger anywhere near his eye.

Ben, feeling far worse than he looked, jumped back and his actions triggered a chain reaction. Even though the rhino hadn't flinched a muscle, half a dozen labourers jumped back with him. 'Aw for Christ's sake, you nervous little pixie. It hasn't moved yet.'

Accepting Tony's comment as a command, the bull immediately gave a huge heave as its horn whisked within inches of his chest. Retreating with the others, he managed to grab Ben and trying to thrust him towards the heaving beast, he implored, 'Now, Ben. With your finger. Poke him in the eye.'

Ben wrenched free, and was running for the nearest tree when the beast gave a great groaning snort only to fall unconscious once again. Realising his folly, with a whinnying laugh and a sickly smile splashed upon his face, he was taunted back by the labourer's mocking laughs to his designated place at the rhino's head.

Thrusting the face-mask into his hand, Tony asked with heavy sarcasm, 'Why is it, Ben, you will fearlessly chase a gang of poachers, but you will run like a frightened child from a quietly sleeping, tied-up rhino?'

Taunted by hoots of glee and much thigh-slapping laughter, Ben was unable to immediately respond. Although the labourers knew of his bravery and virtually worshipped him as their pint-sized champion, they loved it when Tony questioned the little man's courage. All of them knew both men were leaving soon and they would be sorry to see them go.

When Ben did respond it was said rather sheepishly and in English; only Tony caught the words. 'This morning I am not a well man, the spirits have taken my judgment.'

'African hocus-pocus. The only spirit that's impaired your judgment is the one you drunk last night,' Tony scorned. 'Now take the bloody mask and slip it over its head.'

Another ten minutes saw the sledge and rhino winched into place and fixed firmly onto the back of the Unimog. All was set for the grinding two-hour journey back to the rhino's holding stockade. It was the squawk of the Unimog's VHF radio that put a halt on proceedings.

'Campbell One, this is Stronghold. Over.'

As Tony jumped up into the cab he briefly wondered why the main Stronghold base was calling now; it was hours before their next scheduled radio check. It also puzzled him why Glenn Tatum, chief warden of National Parks and the commander of Operation Stronghold was calling him. Usually it would be one of the other rangers. *Tatum has more than enough to do*, he thought.

'This is Campbell One, read you strength three, Stronghold. Over.'

'Tony, we've got big trouble in your sector. Big gang of poachers hit one of our units of scouts, two down, one badly wounded. They're heading for the border. We need you and Ben. I'm sending the chopper in. Over.'

'*Shit*,' Tony silently swore, '*the bastards.*' the scouts had become like family to him since he had been with Stronghold.

'Did you get that, Tony? Over,' came an urgent request.

'Sorry, yes. I'll put up smoke. Here are my coordinates.' He had retrieved a map from the truck's glove box and quickly read off the references.

'Okay, Tony, we've got it. I'll send somebody with the chopper to relieve you. Sorry to do this to you on your last week, pal, but this looks like the big one. Over.'

'No problem. Over and out,' he signed off, hoping Tatum was correct. He had seen far too many slaughtered rhino in his time spent with Stronghold, he wanted one major strike at the poachers before he left, and had hoped this would be it.

He put the thought aside as he turned to look for Ben. Miraculously, the man's hangover was forgotten; already he was stirring the labourers into action. A fire was being set beside the nearest clearing.

Bloodthirsty little bugger, Tony thought as he went to help.

CHAPTER 12

IT WAS THE slight change in air pressure, caused by its spinning rotors, rather than the insistent whine of the helicopter's turboshaft engine that told Tony it wasn't far away.

'Get that damn grin off your face, this is serious stuff,' Tony rounded on Ben.

'Yes Tony,' came Ben's response, with no change in expression.

They were standing near the fire on the edge of the clearing waiting for the helicopter to arrive; for both men this was the worst part of any pending action. Even though externally Tony looked calm and relaxed, inside, his nerves were taut, coiled up like a spring ready to explode. He always snapped at those around him just before any type of conflict and Ben accepted it as a natural part of their build-up. Yet for Ben it was different – like a well-tuned athlete who knew he was about to eclipse his personal best, he relished times like these. This was when the old fighting spirit of his Matabele blood began to course through his veins. Like his ancient warrior ancestors of old, he was gripped with a fighting passion that wouldn't be quenched until the last shot had been fired.

A beige Bell Long Ranger with *John Rolfe, Rescue Service*, blazed across its fuselage flew in low over the treetops to then hover above the clearing. Tony hoped it was John flying today. If it was a bad firefight they were venturing to, his skill and steady nerve could well be needed.

It was Stronghold's commander, Glenn Tatum, running crouched over buffeted by the wash of rotor blades and partially hidden by the swirling dust, who left the helicopter to greet the waiting men. He was a tall man, in his early forties, with short closely cropped dark hair. When he eventually came to stand beside Tony, it was his strong features, his almost military type bearing and his intense gaze that reminded him of the man's dedication to Stronghold and its aims.

'Everybody's busy, I'm going to have to relieve you myself,' Tatum shouted into his ear. 'Try and get John to drop you and Ben back at the holding stockade after you've cleaned up the poachers. We've already sent a boat downstream to cut them off at the river, and other supporting units have been sent in to try and cut their spoor. But don't hold out too much hope; it looks as though your unit'll be it.' A firm hand was clamped on Tony's shoulder. 'Your webbing and weapons are in with the others, I don't have to tell you what needs to be done. Oh, and good work here. Nobody thought you'd ever get it this close to the border,' Tatum said, indicating the unconscious rhino.

Tony nodded; his mind was already on other things.

'Right, fill me in,' Tony ordered.

Tony had buckled on his webbing belt, checked his ammunition pouches and the FN rifle he had been handed. He was sitting beside a huge bald headed Matabele aptly nicknamed Roger-Roger; he had always been the unit's radio operator.

After Roger-Roger had briefed him on what he knew, Tony scanned the other men in the chopper's cabin. He was the only white man, and like him the others were seasoned veterans of Zimbabwe's war of independence. However, the irony this time was, only he and Ben had fought on the losing side. The other five men were ex-ZAPU guerrillas who had fought for and won the country. Even though they had been enemies during those torrid days, he wouldn't swap them for anyone else. Too many times these men had had to prove their dedication and loyalty towards the valley's rhino, and Tony reasoned today was probably going to be no different.

When he joined the Rhodesian Army back in the seventies he had been a young man with the mistaken belief that he was embarking on an adventure. He'd left the army after Zimbabwe's independence with different views; he may have been in one piece and still a young man in body but he had grown old far beyond his years inside.

'And what's more it wasn't even my country of birth,' he scoffed to himself. At least the knowledge gained during those heady days was now being channelled into a worthwhile course.

His thoughts were brought back to the present when Ben nudged him and pointed out the window.

'Aw, Jesus,' he whispered in horror.

Lying exposed on the brown sandy soil amongst open thorn-bush studded scrub was a dead rhino cow and her calf. Both animals had their faces hacked off and their horns removed. And, as if to rub salt into the wound, the poachers had stripped the skin off the young calf and disembowelled it. They'd gutted it for its offal, seeking the choicest milk-flavoured bits.

'*The bastards!*' one of the other game scouts breathed. For Tony the comment exactly summed up the bitter feeling that had grown amongst his men.

Tearing his eyes off the carnage below, he poked his head through into the cockpit and asked, 'How much longer, John?'

'We should be getting a flare any moment now. The first contact was made after the cow and calf were spotted.'

Sure enough, within a minute a red flare arched in front of the Long Ranger's nose.

'Stay close by, John, after you've dropped off the boys. We may need you.' Tony clamped a hand down on the pilot's shoulder before jumping from the chopper to the ground. It was already airborne, heading northward with its tail high, before he had reached the other waiting men.

After a brief discussion with one of the two remaining scouts caught up with the poacher's initial contact named Isacc, Tony was getting the chopper to deploy four of his unit in front of the fleeing gang. If he'd judged their escape route correctly, he and the other scouts would drive the poachers into the waiting men.

Once the chopper was out of earshot, he called Isacc and the other men over to where their dead comrades lay. The third wounded man had only just died, Isacc had done his best but because of the man's bullet-ridden body and his own limited medical equipment, he had watched the poor soul die a slow and agonising death. Even though it was probably unnecessary, Tony wanted them to see the type of men they were going up against.

'Tell the others what you told me, Isacc,' he gruffly ordered.

Isacc, with his mournful black face only half-visible beneath his floppy khaki hat, pointed his FN first at the man who had just died and then at the tracks around him.

'They came back for Alli, we were ambushed. We'd found the dead rhinos and the poachers' tracks. We thought there were only three, but about ten, maybe fifteen others were waiting. They knew we were in the area and ... well, we walked right into them.' He paused while pointing to the other two lifeless figures. 'They hit us in the open ground. Joseph and Hector here went down as we ran for cover. Alli was Hector's cousin so he stayed behind to help. We were cut off from him when they overran his position, he didn't stand a chance.' He sadly shook his head. 'I don't think they're just after rhino horn this time, I reckon they'd come also for us.'

Enough said. The war had intensified. What may have started as a conservation exercise now passed more for a fully-fledged guerrilla war.

'Right, we'll quickly cover these.' Tony indicated the three dead bodies and then turned to Ben, 'While they do it, scout around. Once they've finished, take the spoor.'

The poachers had made no attempt to cover their tracks or use any other form of anti-tracking; they were running in single file and had left a trail a blind man could follow. Tony had his men run in hot pursuit, in a V formation. It allowed them maximum speed while also protecting them against any possible ambush.

Tony was running close to Ben's left – he was at the centre of the V, the big Matabele with the radio strapped to his back was on the other point. The the two other scouts from the initial conflict were running in the rear. Ben was running with his head down, never taking his eyes off the spoor, and Tony would allow no one else to protect him. Ben was the most vulnerable of his entire unit and Tony knew the man had complete faith in him to act as his eyes and ears away from the spoor.

Running in comparative silence as stealthily as they could, only by using a repertoire of bird and animal calls were Ben and Tony able to keep in contact with and direct the other men. Whenever Ben or the poacher's tracks changed direction Tony had them wheeling and counter-wheeling to keep the V formation intact.

Tracking in this particular way was a technique he and Ben had used many times during the war, and ironically on the very men they ran with. It was a technique these men had once loathed but now readily used with brutal effect.

Mile after endless mile of broken scrub, undulating country and open woodlands rolled before the running men and never once in the last three hours had the poacher's tracks deviated from the general direction of Zambia's distant border.

Intently scanning the lie of the land ahead Tony risked a quick glance at the sun. It was standing high overhead turning the distant horizon into a shimmering mirage of ever-changing colours. Only then did he realise how hot it was and that they'd been running for hours. He estimated at their pace of about seven miles an hour. Depending on how much the poachers were carrying, they were probably hauling them in at a little over two miles an hour. Although he hated to stop he knew his men needed to rest so using the warbling call of a white-tailed shrike, he discreetly called for a halt. They stopped in the middle of a wide shallow bowl, studded with thorny scrub, rocky outcrops and several rock-strewn *kopjes*.

'Five minutes, salt tablets, drink and a rest. Isacc, you take the lookout. Roger-Roger, you call in our position, and Ben,' using a flick of his head, 'over here.' They walked along the line of the poacher's spoor until it was undisturbed, squatting down beside it. 'Well?' he asked.

'It's fresh and we're gaining much faster than the loads they're carrying should really allow,' said Ben.

'You mean they're travelling light?'

'Very, but slowly. I don't think they've taken many horns at all.'

'At least that's something.' Tony grunted. 'And they can't know they're being followed. What about their numbers?'

Shaking his head, Ben tutted. 'I counted fourteen when we began. I can't tell now because they're running in single file, but ... well, the last man isn't the same as when we started. His prints are different.'

'You mean he's moved up? Tony queried, showing only slight interest in the comment.

'Well no ... that's the puzzling thing. Since we started following the spoor there's been only one single trail.' Ben had taken off his floppy hat and was scratching his head, clearly confused. He changed the subject. 'You remember during the war that time we chased those terrs into Zambia and ran into an ambush?' Tony nodded; it had been common practice chasing the terrorists, or 'terrs' as they called them then, onto foreign soil. 'and you remember how we lost them when we headed back to the border? Running in each other's footsteps.' The hair on the nape of Tony's neck began to bristle in warning. 'One by one we dropped off the trail until the terrs were only following you, then we ambushed them from behind.'

'Oh God, surely not?'

'Well I can't be certain and I don't see how, but it's like that, yes.'

'Are you positive?' Tony demanded, his alarm bells were starting to sound, 'Surely you would've seen where they dropped off the trail?'

'That's why I didn't mention it sooner – I haven't. They'd have to be damn good and since we've been with Stronghold, no poachers we've tracked have ever been that good.'

'*Shit* and we're at least a good hour, maybe more from where the others will've set up. Damn! I'll have to radio ahead.'

With his nerves like piano wire stretched taut and ready to snap, Tony left

Ben and walked over to Roger-Roger who was rolling up the radio's antenna. He'd had its flexible cable strung out over a scrubby bush beside a small rocky outcrop.

'String it out again and go get the others, we've got problems.' Before he knew what he was doing, he was screaming, *'DOWN, DOWN, DOWN!'* It was the belly whistle snort of the reedbuck, the most urgent of Ben's calls that made him react as he did.

He flew head-first over a waist-high rock, only to be hurried over its lip by a barrage of striking bullets skipping along the edge. Still screaming, he bellowed at Roger-Roger, *'Radio, bring the God-damn radio!'*

The resounding *thumps* of bullets striking the radio within its canvas pack told him his urgent call was wasted.

With the storm of bullets whistling around his head, he risked a look around the edge of his rock. The radio had been blown to smithereens, and worse still the huge Matabele lay dead, shot through the head beside its shattered remains.

'Damn,' he whispered, resting his back up against the rock. He'd heard no return fire from any of his men; like Roger-Roger they'd probably been taken by surprise.

He assessed his position. He was pinned down, the radio was shot, and with the amount of lead flying through the air, he knew there was a hell of a lot more than fourteen poachers.

Suddenly as if he'd received a smack between the eyes, realisation dawned. *These aren't poachers. These are terrorists. But what the hell are they doing here in the valley?*

The question was left unanswered as a fresh onslaught of ricocheting bullets left him cowering beneath a mass of stone chips and flying dust.

CHAPTER 13

'COME ON, COME on think man!'

Tony was trying to stop his reeling mind. He had been pinned down for what seemed like an eternity, though in reality it could have been no more than ten minutes. He knew he was out-gunned, out-manned and outmanoeuvred, so all he was able to draw from was his experience. 'But shit, I've never had odds like these stacked up against me before.'

He had located a few of the terrorist's positions, but what the hell was he going to do? He couldn't retreat, advance or even stay where he was for that matter; it was a miracle he'd lasted this long at all. His mind still refused to work even though within minutes he knew his position would be overrun. Then, as he heard a familiar screaming voice and finally his mind clicked into action. He reacted instinctively, without thinking.

'Cover, cover, give me cover,' yelled the voice.

Tony was up and firing at the positions he'd pinpointed as he saw a small khaki-clad figure, sidestepping like a startled rabbit, running swiftly towards him.

With the sandy soil erupting underfoot, Ben, still running flat out, stooped before Tony's rock and retrieved Roger-Roger's rifle without a break in his stride. He jumped like vaulting a pummel-horse over the rock and landed safely in a crumpled heap at Tony's feet.

Tony, wincing from the fresh onslaught of ricocheting bullets, slumped down beside his panting friend. 'What the hell do you think you're doing?' He rounded on the little man. 'You should've stayed where you were. They obviously didn't know you were there. God knows I didn't.' He didn't know whether to feel relieved Ben was still alive or angry because he'd risked his life to be at his side.

Ignoring Tony's outburst and with an inclination of his head, Ben declared, 'It's good to see you too, my friend.' He ended the comment with a disarming smile.

Initially stunned, but recovering quickly, Tony briefly shook his head. 'You're such a skinny little bugger that even if they wanted to shoot you they'd still miss.' Not that he'd ever say it, but it was good to have the man back at his side.

'Isacc is also still alive. I've spoken to him, but the others are all dead. He is making his way to the top of the small *kopje* in front of us. Hopefully, he'll be able to distract our friends out there and that's when we'll make a run for it. Once we're safe, he'll go for help.'

'Okay, good work. How many are there?'

'Another five have joined the original fourteen. There was an ambush up ahead, and they *had* been dropping men off since we started tracking them.'

Tony groaned; they'd walked right into it.

'That's not all, 'Ben continued, 'I heard them talking before I joined you. It's you they're after. One asked if the white man pinned down was Campbell.'

Tony was stunned. He knew he was good and had made enemies amongst the Zambian poachers, but only as a team had he and the other game scouts been able to stem the tide of the rhinos' slaughter. The situation was absurd.

'Surely, Ben you must be mistaken. A hit-squad sent in for one man ... the Zambian poachers aren't that well organised.'

'They're not, those men out there are Zimbabwean – they spoke in Shona. They're ex-ZANU guerrillas.'

'But how ... surely not?' Tony queried. 'They can't be ZANU; most of them are now with the army.'

Two main guerrilla factions had fought for the freedom of Zimbabwe, ZAPU from the Matabele tribe and ZANU made up from the Shona speaking tribes. The Shona, because of their superior numbers, now controlled the country and it was their freedom fighters which were mostly incorporated into the Zimbabwe army.

'Surely not,' Tony repeated, it made no sense at all. However, the quandary was thrust from his mind when he realised Isacc was in position and with good effect was peppering the Shona from a new and unexpected quarter.

Taking the brief reprieve Isacc had given them, and following Ben out of cover with FN blazing, Tony bellowed, 'I hope you know where the hell you're going. If I get shot ...'

For both men it seemed an eternity while they were out in the open ground. Ben's FN had fallen silent as he'd already emptied his magazine, while Tony had discarded his and was using the FN Ben had retrieved from Roger-Roger. They had just made it to their new location, a *kopje* strewn with an upheaval of wind-beaten boulders, when the Shona realised the true reason for Isacc's manoeuvre.

They were besieged by a melee of violent ground shuddering welts as bullets kicked up dust around their heels, while they also had to endure a shower of bullets whistling around their ears. It seemed to take forever, but finally they dived into the *kopje's* first narrow ravine. Immediately, upon changing their magazines, they were up and firing again, giving as good as they'd got. Once they'd opened up they saw Isacc disappear over the top of his *kopje* and head for help.

'Run like the wind, boy. If they catch you we'll be doomed,' were Tony's parting words to the fleeing man.

'Hell, these bastards know what they're on about.' Tony was talking to nobody in particular, 'Maybe they are ex-ZANU guerrillas.' He was keeping focused on staying alive as best he knew how. 'Okay Ben, we'll have to fall back again. You first.'

For the last thirty minutes, with only slight reprieves, the two men had fought a raging battle. But every few minutes, with each one of the Shona's determined attacks they had been forced to fall back to a more secure position. Tony had thought he'd wounded one while Ben was sure he'd nicked another. There were too many of them, they were being overwhelmed and would soon have to make a final stand. The one thing both men dreaded above all else was that when their attackers got in range they would be peppered with grenades. Even dying with a bullet through the head would be a preferable option to being mutilated by shrapnel and dying an agonising death.

They were now at what Tony assessed would be their second to last stand before they would be at the *kopje's* summit. Most of the Shona were now sprinkled amongst the rocks on the slope below.

All had gone quiet as they were obviously rallying for another assault.

'Where do you reckon this time?' Ben asked, trying to guess which of the Shona's flanks would close in first.

'Hell, I don't know. You take the left, I'll take the right, but it'll probably be that narrow gut up the middle.'

The only advantage the two men had was that they had already travelled the ground their aggressors were now swarming over. And sure enough. their next assault came up the middle.

'*Shit!*' both men swore in unison. With controlled bursts from their FNs they swung on the advance. They were successful this time as they stifled the assault and saw a Shona flinch in the process.

'Good work, but one of the flanks will move pretty soon. If it was me down there, I'd come from the right.' Again Tony was correct, and again they were successful.

Knowing they had bought themselves some time, they leant warily back against the rocks at their rear.

'How many rounds left? Tony asked, pointing at Ben's sagging ammunition pouches.

'Sweet FA.' After a quick check, 'One full clip and what's left in the FN.'

'Jesus, you're a greedy bugger. Here, take this.' Tony handed over another full clip. 'But use it sparingly; we'll both have to pick our shots.'

'How do you think Isacc got on?' Ben changed the topic. Anything was better than thinking about the prospect of running out of ammo.

'Well, unless he grows wings, he can't help us. They may've already got him; you heard that AK blast soon after he gapped it.'

However, Isacc was quickly forgotten when a small green pineapple-shaped glob landed in Ben's lap, it had come from above and behind.

It was the fastest Tony had ever seen the little man move. No sooner had the grenade landed in his lap than Ben had scooped it up and flung it over the rock wall in front of them. It exploded with a resounding roar just over the lip, showering them with a deluge of flying rocks.

Everything began to happen at once. With the coming of the grenade, Tony immediately realised they had trouble from behind. As he saw Ben toss the grenade, Tony thankfully turned to defend their rear. Then came the grenade's deafening blast and a split-second later Tony felt something crash with brutal force into the side of his face. Momentarily he teetered on the edge of consciousness, but thankfully he was able to haul himself back from the darkness of the beckoning void.

Somewhere beside him, he heard Ben beginning to fire, but the only thing real to him was the insistent numbing ache on the left side of his face. He hesitantly reached up to the spot, and then holding his hand before his eyes, dumbly looked at his dripping, blood-soaked finger. With vision swimming in mild surprise, he realised he was bleeding.

Ben's screaming voice snapped him out of his lethargy. 'For Christ's sake, do something!'

Trying to forget his injury he snatched up his rifle. Even though he was still slightly concussed, he knew danger had crept up upon them from behind. He had only just turned in that direction when he saw, looming before his eyes, the rifle butt of a Kalashnikov AK 47 flying towards his head. Reacting without thought, he ducked and flicked his FN's barrel to the side and the AK's wooden butt was sent crashing into the rock beside his head. No sooner was the butt diverted than a hefty boot was aimed at his groin. He thrust his hip to the side and luckily it landed ineffectively on his thigh.

With bullets ricocheting and rock chips flying, Ben and Tony were caught up in their separate battles for survival and both were unable to give the other any assistance at all; Tony, involved in a hand-to-hand struggle with an opponent who was easily taking advantage of his weakened state, and Ben; desperately trying to hold off the advance of the Shona from the slope below. They both were fighting what had to be a losing battle.

One more concerted thrust and their position would be overrun. While trying to conserve what little ammunition he had left, Ben risked a sideways glance at Tony. The blood splattered figure was making heavy going of his fight with the big opponent that had sneaked up from behind, Ben knew even if he could bring his FN to bare he'd be running the risk of hitting Tony. He turned back to the slope below as the air began to shudder.

Now what? Ben despairingly thought. *Surely things can't get any worse?* Below him and now above the air was filled with tracer left by an ever-increasing barrage of flying lead.

Christ, he's going to have me, Tony thought. Oblivious to all else around him, he seemed unable to rally against the big man's brutal strength.

Even though they were of a similar height and build, the black man had hounded Tony's retreat so he was now bent-over with his back arched up against a waist-high boulder. The two men were chest to chest and the Shona was slowly lowering the stock of his AK 47 down upon Tony's throat.

'Die, whitey,' the black man said through a twisted, leering grin, but his words were sucked from his mouth as the air began to violently shudder while a shadow fell upon the two struggling men.

Tony saw his attacker's eyes flick skywards, towards what had caused the shadow. He took his chance and with all his dwindling strength he thrust upwards with the rifle while also lunging forward with his head, catching the Shona a forceful thud on the bridge of his nose and leaving a bloody mass of bone and gristle smashed across his face. As the man bellowed and staggered backwards, Tony drove upwards with a swiftly driven knee, with a resounding welt the knee was sent hurtling into his groin. The injured man was totally incapacitated and Tony was easily able to yank the AK 47 from his grip, and swinging the rifle by its barrel, he crashed its butt into his bent-over, gasping face. The man fell unconscious to the ground.

Looking up Tony saw John Rolfe's Long Ranger hovering overhead, with its side door open and FNs blaring; his ambush team and Isacc were shafting the now fleeing band of Shona. It was the most pleasing sight he'd ever seen.

Even though his face throbbed like hell, a wave of relief like a warm gentle breeze enveloped his body. Resting his back against the nearest rock, Tony sank thankfully to the ground.

Gingerly fingering the bleeding wound, he managed to retrieve an inch long splinter of rock that had embedded itself in his left cheek. Warily eyeing it, he was content to let the others chase his would-be assassins.

CHAPTER 14

'HELL, YOU LOOK a sight.'

Tony, with blood covering one half of his face and his shirt collar soaked through to a darkened ruby-red, recognised John Rolfe's voice immediately. 'It's only a stone chip,' he replied looking up, 'But it did manage to slice my cheek down to the bone.'

John was middle-aged of average height and build, with short sandy hair. His features were darkly tanned, marking him as a man who had spent most of his life in the African sun. He had just landed his Long Ranger below the *kopje* and was now standing watching Ben working with the first aid kit on Tony's injury.

'Isacc found you, then. What happened to my welcoming party …' Tony began to ask, then quickly forgot the question. 'Ouch! Ya ruthless little bugger,' he flared at Ben. 'Careful what you're doing with that bloody bandage.'

'Oh stop it, ya wimp, it's only iodine,' Ben criticised, 'I haven't even begun to stitch.' Then, as if as an afterthought, he added, 'Oh, and by the way, I notice we've got no anaesthetic.'

Tony let out a miserable groan, as John answered his original question.

'Yeah, Isacc nearly ran into our ambush. As for your welcoming party, they bomb-shelled, all ran separate directions when they saw the chopper. Ben thought he'd nicked one, but the rest, well …' he shrugged 'they're probably across the border by now. But I notice you got one.' He pointed with the toe of his boot at the Shona that Tony had previously knocked unconscious.

'Yeah, at least that's something. He'll give us a few answers.' Tony flicked a sideways glance at the now trussed up Shona. He had regained consciousness and was on his stomach, with his hands behind him securely fastened to his bent up legs. 'Ben,' he continued, 'heard them speaking Shona, he thinks that …' Tony again lost his line of thought. 'Ow, ow, ow,' he cried in quick succession.

John shook his head in amusement and turned to leave. 'I'll leave you and the surgeon to it. You can tell me later.'

As Tony walked down the slope he was followed by Ben's chiding voice,

'Oh for Christ's sake calm down, you're only making things worse. Here, bite on this.'

Showing little regard for his welfare Isacc and Ben hauled the Shona down the *kopje* by his feet and eventually thumped him on the ground beside the Long Ranger's open door. Tony with his face now strained an iodine red and blue nylon sutures hanging like whiskers from his closed up cut was in the cockpit with John, talking on the radio.

'We've buried them, their bodies will have to be picked up later and no, all the terrs bomb-shelled, there was no sign they were carrying any other horn, just from the cow and calf I think. And Ben is pretty sure they were all Shona. Over.'

Glenn Tatum's voice came back to him over the radio's speaker. 'Okay, it looks as though they did come in for more than just rhino horn. It'll be interesting to talk to your prisoner. See what you can get from him on the way back, you know what to do. Till then, over and out.'

Tony hooked the headphones behind the passenger seat and turned to John. 'Okay, you heard him, when we're over the river I'll give you the word. Let's take her up.'

As the helicopter's jet prop slowly wound up, Tony helped his men load their prisoner aboard. They dumped him unceremoniously face down on the cabin floor. When the chopper was airborne he spoke to Ben. 'Okay, take off his gag. We'll question him.'

As Ben began to take off the gag Tony noticed, beneath the man's scruffy T-shirt, a loose-fitting stainless steel chain dangling around his neck. He ignored it as he spoke in English, 'Ben as you're the only one that speaks Shona, you'll have to translate. He knows who I am, so ask him who he is and who sent him in after me.'

Surprisingly the man immediately responded to Ben's demanding questions.

'What did he say?' asked Tony.

'He says he doesn't know you, and that he's just a poacher.'

'He's lying. Ask him why there were so many of them then, and where they learnt to fight like they did.'

'It was a big raid planned over many months and they learnt during the war,' came the translation.

'So they are Shona.' While he watched the prisoner's face, Tony spoke again to Ben in English, 'He's still lying. Open the door; we'll see if a Shona can fly.'

The man's eyes anxiously shifted from side to side. Clearly, he understood every word.

'A very educated poacher I'd say.' Now speaking directly to the man, he demanded, 'Unless you answer me correctly I *will* let them do it. How do you know me?' Silence. *'How?'* Tony yelled the demand as he thumped a veldskoen clad foot down on the side of his neck.

'Okay, Okay,' came a desperate plea. 'A message and a photograph.'

'Better,' Tony said as he took the shoe off his neck. 'Who sent them?'

Again silence.

The pilot stuck his head around from the cockpit, through into the cabin. 'We're over the river.

'Right, to the middle and take us up,' Tony replied as he hoisted a thumb skyward. He was about to use a technique that the Rhodesian army had used with exceptional results while interrogating guerrillas during the war.

'Ben, open the door. Isacc grab his legs.'

The Shona was wailing by the time they thrust his head and shoulders out the door. Below him all the man saw was the deep indigo of the untamed Zambezi River rapidly shrinking in size as they ascended directly upwards.

With a hand clasped around Ben's webbing belt so he could lower him onto the chopper's skid beside the Shona, Tony prepared to continue their interrogation. 'Ask him who sent him.' He turned to Isacc. 'Push him out a little further.'

The man while pleading for mercy, managed to howl a terrified reply to Ben.

'Well?' Tony asked once he'd pulled Ben back to his side.

'I didn't understand, but he repeated it a couple of times. He kept saying, "head of cattle", that was all he knew.'

'Okay, we'll ask him later back at base what it means. This time ask him why he was sent in to kill me.'

As Tony lowered Ben out again he noticed the wind had caught the stainless steel chain around the Shona's neck. While watching it he saw a pair of attached metal tags fall out from the neck of the man's ragged T-shirt.

It must have been the buffeting wind or even the insistent ache of his cheek that had slowed down his perception because it took Tony several seconds to realise what he was seeing. Ben was back at his side before the penny dropped.

'Christ almighty!' he breathed, the metal tags were a set of army dog tags.

Shona tribesmen from Zimbabwe's army involved with poaching and terrorism? Surely not? Knowing he needed a closer look at those tags, he hurriedly turned to Isacc, to get him to pull in the suspended man.

It could have been for any number of reasons, the confusion of Ben giving his reply, the lashing wind, or even the stricken look on Tony's face that made Isacc misinterpret his orders. 'Christ, haul the bastard in!'

As Isacc let the Shona go, Tony watched in horror as the man lurched forward and tumbled out the door.

Dragging Ben back past him into the cabin, Tony hooked a foot around a metal strut holding up one of the passenger's seats and flung himself at the overbalancing man; he only just managed to grab the rope tied to the black man's arms and legs. He cried out in pain as the rope came up taut – it prevented the Shona from falling but also burnt a furrow down into the flesh of his hand.

Ben, also recovering quickly, threw himself onto Tony's outstretched legs and his added weight helped stop both men from tumbling down into the Zambezi River below.

As his suspended prisoner lurched helplessly while hysterically screaming in terror, Tony roared in pain again. He felt the rope cut deeper as the muscles of his arm and shoulder began to painfully tear, yet worse still he could feel the foot hooked around the metal strut slowly lose its hold.

Buffeted by the wind, even with Ben's added weight, Tony was being slowly drawn across the cabin's floor. As a huge gust caught the man, Tony was yanked violently towards the open door. He had no choice but to let the rope and prisoner go.

Transfixed by morbid fascination with his head craned out the door, Tony watched helplessly as the screaming figure tumbled end over end towards a sure and gruesome death.

Everybody was quiet in the Long Ranger's cabin after the Shona's plummeting fall and their subsequent unsuccessful search for his body. Isacc sat hunched dejectedly in one corner and couldn't bring himself to look in Tony's direction. Tony in turn was staring sightlessly out the window. The army dog tags he had spotted and the possibility that members of Zimbabwe's army had been involved with not only his attempted assassination but also poaching really worried him. The ramifications would be horrific, and as yet he hadn't decided if he would pass on the information.

Maybe it'd be better to first make some of my own inquiries, he decided. He didn't really believe the army could be involved.

The body had either already been swept downstream or had been lost to the river's crocodiles. Whatever the cause really didn't matter; the fact remained the only thing Tony had to take back to Stronghold command was the snatched words Ben had been able to retrieve.

At least I know why they came after me, he thought. *But that's all.*

Just before Isacc had let him go and he had hurtled to his death, the Shona had given Ben the answer. It was because of Tony's new position with the World Wildlife Fund; somebody obviously looked upon him as a real threat. It had been then that the magnitude of the task he was about to tackle had really hit home. People were prepared to kill to protect their interests. That was how valuable the poaching trade throughout southern and eastern Africa had already become.

Operation Stronghold's main camp came into view; it was set amongst open grassy woodlands on the Zimbabwean side of the Zambezi River. As dust swirled around the landing machine, thrown up by the wash of its spinning blades, Tony, with Ben at his side, jumped to the ground and walked towards a group of waiting men.

'Oh God, what the hell do I tell him?' He had noticed Glenn Tatum standing among the group, 'Not much, I guess.'

As Tony was trying to phrase his soon to be given report, Ben's words broke his train of thought. 'I've been thinking. You know when I asked the Shona who sent them in, and all he said was "head of cattle"?'

'Yes,' Tony responded eagerly, hoping Ben was going to give him more that he could pass on to Tatum.

'Well, "head of cattle" in Sindebele means "Nkomo". It isn't much but maybe it could help.'

Tony's spirits slumped. 'Nkomo' could have stood for anything, it was a word used in Sindebele and many other Zulu based languages. It was time to face the music; he had stopped in front of Tatum.

'Hell, Tony you look a sight. That cut'll probably leave a scar,' Tatum began, then looking over his shoulder he asked, 'Where's your prisoner?'

'Well, that's something I wanted to talk to you about ...' Tony began.

CHAPTER 15

Los Angeles

As THE SUN permeated through the smog-laden Los Angeles sky, its rays streamed in through the picture window at Donovan's rear. He was sitting in his shirtsleeves at his desk, immersed in the reports and documents that littered its top. A soft electronic hum pierced the concentration of his mind.

'Yes?' he answered absent-mindedly, pushing the intercom button on his phone while still studying the reports. 'I said, no more calls.'

'I know, Mr Donovan, but it's your wife,' his secretary answered in a professional well-cultured voice. 'She's been rather persistent. She wants to know what time you will be home tonight.'

Donovan let out a heavy irritated sigh while staring blankly at the desktop. *Bloody woman*, he thought, *more trouble than she's worth*.

A thought, however, that he knew wasn't entirely true. It was, in fact, their marriage that had allowed him to pull off one of the biggest business coups of his life.

'Okay, Sonya,' he said without a hint of his earlier annoyance, 'Leave it to me. I'll call her.'

'And tonight?' came a quiet, hesitant voice.

'Tonight? You can expect me at seven. Leave my wife to me.' As Donovan broke the connection he heard a faint sigh of relief. *Yes*, he thought, *she definitely still has appeal.*

Donovan knew instinctively that he should never have started the affair, but he'd never experienced a woman like her before. He found her flexibility extraordinary and sex-drive remarkable. Although he didn't like to admit it, he had become captivated. Sex with her was unbelievable and made him feel twenty years younger. *Yeah, what a woman.* Then with regret he put the thought aside. She was a damn good private secretary and he would be sorry to see her go, but she had become too much of a distraction at work. Dismissing the thought, he reached for the phone and dialled his home number. It was answered almost immediately.

'Sitting on the phone were we, Sabina?' It was his wife who had answered.

'As a matter-of-fact, yes,' came an irritated voice, highlighted by the slightest trace of an Italian accent. 'That damn secretary of yours said she would pass on my message hours ago. You know I've still got arrangements to make for tonight – you haven't forgotten about tonight, have you?' she added.

'Well, Sabina, no I haven't, but that doesn't mean I'll be able to make it. I may even have to stay in town tonight.' He was being petty but anything that needled his wife gave him the utmost satisfaction, and this latest attempt would have to beat them all. Standing up his wife on their wedding anniversary. It had to be his most insensitive act so far.

He was met with the heaviest of silences. 'I see,' eventually came down the line. 'What is it this time, Judd? Business, I suppose?' she queried with heavy sarcasm. 'You know I've been planning this evening for months.'

'Yes, business as usual,' he answered.

'Fine, I will let you know how the guests enjoyed *our* anniversary without their host.' The phone went dead.

Donovan sat back in his high-backed chair with a smug expression set upon his face, yet he knew it would only be a hollow victory. Sabina would soon do something just as irritating. He would turn up tonight, but late and not until he'd finished with Sonya – even in Los Angeles there were certain rules that one had to abide by. The thought of his wife, the lavish party she had organised and its multitude of invited guests left his mind as he again concentrated back on the paperwork in front of him.

Donovan's marriage to Sabina had been one of pure convenience, as both of them were aware. However, it had been more than just a marriage; it was in reality the amalgamation of two of the biggest freight forwarding and bonded importing/exporting companies in the world. Their marriage had given Donovan and Donovan Enterprises a controlling monopoly in Europe which was readily added to their stable markets of the rest of the Western world and the swiftly growing trade experienced throughout Asia. Ten years later, Donovan controlled a huge conglomerate of companies unlike any other within its sphere of influence and trade.

Sabina was of Italian stock and over countless previous generations her family had built up a monopoly of importing/exporting houses that had spanned Europe, even including those government-controlled markets behind the iron curtain before it fell. She had been the sole heir to that business empire, but being from a conservative Italian family her aging father had sought to keep the family's hold on their business while also endeavouring to have a male head its operations. Knowing of Donovan and his company's interest in expanding their activities, Sabina's father had approached him with a proposition. At the time Donovan had readily agreed to the marriage, but he would now dearly love to divorce his wife. However, because it could jeopardise the power and monopoly he enjoyed, he continued to endure the relationship.

Once wedding vows had been exchanged it was required that Sabina sit on the parent company's board as well as having the majority holding of her families' company's preferential shares held for her in trust. That Donovan could have lived with since he had negotiated for and won power of attorney over the family trust. However, it turned out that his new wife wasn't just the beautiful Italian girl she had originally appeared to be. Although she had little interest in the day-to-day running of Donovan Enterprises, she was at home sitting on the board. Having been schooled in North America, she had developed a quick and perceptive mind, tempered only by a ruthless well-hidden streak. On more than one occasion she had seen right through some of Donovan's more devious plans of establishing new business and dealing with stiffer competition, and although she had never exposed him publicly, privately she had always collected her pound of flesh.

In public they appeared as husband and wife, but from the first day of their marriage they had lived private lives. She was a thorn in Donovan's side he could gladly do without, and he was a domineering ogre who refused to bend to her every whim and fancy. Donovan knew she loathed him, and although they needled one another incessantly, he felt confident that she was bright and greedy enough not to jeopardise the relationship that served to benefit them both. However, it was an arrangement Sabina was rapidly growing tired of.

She'd had enough; Sabina was shaking with rage when she slammed down the phone. 'He's gone too far,' she muttered, and this time she was convinced she would ask him for a divorce. His constant lack of consideration had become too much for her to bear.

Anger heightened Sabina's astonishing beauty, she was dressed simply in designer jeans and a peach T-shirt, but it was obvious she would've looked at home on any of the fashion boardwalks around the world. At thirty-five years of age Sabina was tall with an exceptional figure and long straight brownish-black hair, today she wore it tied in a plait that fell halfway down her back, and her eyes were a dark, a hazelnut brown, while her Mediterranean features glowed in vibrant health. Normally, she wore a sulky expression that dulled her otherwise staggering beauty, but now as her crimson painted lips were pulled into thin angry lines she had lost that pouting look.

Sabina, like Donovan, was raised as an only child, with a silver spoon stuck firmly in her mouth. Due to the extravagance that had been bestowed upon her since birth, she was often catty and at times vain to the extreme. Although she loathed her husband she also had a healthy respect for him; she had seen far too many of his adversaries fall by the wayside during their years of so-called marriage. But this time, well, it was different, today was their tenth wedding anniversary and though it held little meaning for either of them, she wanted to show Los Angeles it wasn't only the city's celebrities that could set Beverly Hills alight. It had taken months to plan the party – the Wilshire was doing the catering, the scores of invitations had gone out, and their Italiante villa had been redecorated and looked a picture, but now ...

'Oh I loathe that man!' she exclaimed as she stamped her foot in fury. She needed something to break to help vent her rage. She had answered the phone in Donovan's personal study on the ground floor of their enormous three-storied, orange roofed villa.

Ah just the thing, she realised, as she spotted a hand-carved ivory bowl sitting in pride of place on Donovan's mahogany desk, it was one of his favourites from his collection. Her sulky pout returned as she picked up the exquisite piece which fitted neatly into her elegant hand. Holding it up to the light she could see it was so thin it was almost transparent. Although it had no etching of any kind, even she recognised the bowl's simplicity added to its delicate beauty.

Walking from the study through a pair of French doors she entered a red-bricked, pergola-shaded veranda that overlooked a sunken court framed by artistically constructed telescoping walls. She never noticed the court or the sweeping vista of the tree-studded gardens that lay before her, or even the immaculate grass terraces dominated by an extravagantly carved limestone fountain. In this moment she lived rapped in a cloak of absorbing anticipation, as she was about to seek her revenge and destroy something dear to her husband's heart.

She dropped the bowl. As it hit the veranda it shattered into a showering cascade of a thousand creamy-white chips. She didn't watch them settle. Without looking back at the damage she had caused she turned and walked back into the house. *The caterers can take the blame*, she decided.

Feeling somewhat appeased, she decided to call her lawyer before driving downtown to pick up her diamonds from her safe deposit box for the party that night.

'This time he's truly going to pay.'

CHAPTER 16

SABINA WAS DRESSED simply as she walked into the Bank of America on Wilshire Boulevard; high heels, black dress trousers, navy double-breasted blazer with cuffs and a white fitted lacy see-through top underneath. If she noticed the heads that turned to admire her stunning good looks it wasn't apparent, for her eyes were hidden behind tortoise-shell Chanel.

As she walked into the foyer she inwardly cursed. She'd left her card pouch with credit cards, PIN and safe deposit box key back at the villa. *'Blast!'* She hesitated momentarily; she didn't want to have to go all the way back home. She soon made a decision and walked up to the inquiries desk to be served by a polite, pleasant looking redhead. 'Yes, I'd like to see the manager.'

'Certainly, ma'am. What time was your appointment with Mr Troon?'

'I don't actually have one, but I'm sure he'll be available to see me,' Sabina stated confidently. It hadn't occurred to her that he might be busy.

'Oh, well, I'll have to consult his diary. He is normally busy at this time of the afternoon,' the redhead stated politely but protectively.

Sabina frowned; she wasn't used to being treated in such a manner. 'Well, you do that,' she stated indignantly, 'but while you're about it, tell him Sabina Donovan is here to see him. Yes, and tell him it's urgent,' she added as an afterthought.

As the girl disappeared from the counter Sabina, not used to standing in queues, turned and stood well back from the inquiry desk and the bank's row of teller counters. Now feeling conspicuous she snapped at her two burly, suit-wearing bodyguards who had discreetly followed her into the bank and were now hovering at her shoulder. 'For goodness sake, let me breathe.'

Sabina never noticed if they backed away for the redhead had stepped up to her side. She was visibly flustered. Her colour had risen and it was obvious she had just received a reprimand.

'Well how was I supposed to know her husband is the bank's biggest client,' the redhead thought resentfully. The sentiment never showed on her face as she said politely instead, 'Of course Mr Troon will see you. If you'd like to follow me.'

Sabina tersely ordered her bodyguards to wait for her and was eventually shown through to the manager's office. It was large, decorated in pastel shades with patterned print chairs and couch positioned in front of a large modern grey synthetic-coated desk. The man she had requested to see strode from behind the desk to greet her.

Sabina, how lovely to see you.' She recognised the comment as genuine. 'But you must try and make the effort to arrange an appointment next time,' he fondly admonished her before kissing her lightly on both cheeks. 'I do have other clients you know.'

He was middle-aged and cast in the typical banker's mould, average height, average built, and average looks, while wearing the obligatory three-piece suit, crisp white shirt and conservatively coloured paisley tie. Sabina stood back from him and smiled, he was one of the few of her husband's business associates that she liked. Tilting her head mischievously, she said, 'Other clients, Alastair? I didn't realise you had any.'

He shook his head and offered her a seat. 'So tell me, how are the arrangements for the party shaping up?

'So, so. I'll see you and Pamela there tonight?'

'We wouldn't miss it for the world,' he said, taking a seat opposite. 'Ten years eh?' He almost added, *Who would've believed it?* but managed to prevent himself.

As if reading his mind, 'Yes, who would've,' Sabina stated for him, but she said it without malice. She liked Alastair because he was honest and down to earth.

'So how is he, how's Judd? Gosh it must be – hell, all of a week since I've seen him.' Although it was meant in jest – Donovan Enterprises' banking requirements took up a considerable amount of his time – Sabina could easily see the regret in his eyes. Alastair was one of the few people that knew the true state of their marriage and how miserable her husband's actions made her at times. He'd been more than just a banker to her. Over the years he had been a confidante and friend.

'You know him.' But before any dark feelings could take hold, Alastair had changed the topic. 'Now, how is it I can help you?'

Rousing herself, 'Yes, right.' Sabina reclaimed her normal self-confident demeanour. She had plenty to do before the anniversary party that night. There was no time for sentiment. 'I left my PIN number, cards and safe deposit box key at home, and I've got so much to do before tonight. Would you be a darling and organise it so I can get out my jewels?'

'You know it's against procedure.'

'Pleeease?' Sabina exaggerated as she fluttered her eyelashes.

Alastair chuckled lightly, 'How on earth can I say no to that? Come on, I'll have to accompany you.'

Once Alastair had shown Sabina through to the safe deposit box viewing room and seated her at one of the check desks, he got the attending clerk to organise the appropriate forms and lay them out in front of her. Pointing with his finger, he indicated where she was to sign, 'Here, here, and here, and also at the bottom of this one.' As she sighed the last form, a pager beeped on his belt. Unhooking it, he peered at its tiny screen. 'Oops, forgot that one.' he turned to Sabina. 'I'm sorry I'll have to leave you with Jonathan here,' he indicated the young clerk. 'I'm late for a meeting.'

'What, you weren't joking? You do have other clients?' Sabina queried, tongue in cheek.

Alastair smiled and shook his head. 'I'll see you tonight. And Sabina, please don't be too hard on him.' He turned to the clerk, 'The formalities are complete. Draw whichever box Mrs Donovan needs.'

Once Alastair had left with the relevant forms the clerk also left the viewing room and first went to the signature card file to check Sabina's signature, then to the deposit boxes filing-cabinets to find out which safe deposit box to draw. He was new at the job and wasn't used to following anything except the exact procedure. When he eventually walked back into the viewing room Sabina was presented not with her deposit box but an embarrassed young man holding two cards out in front of him. He also wasn't used to dealing with the public, let alone a woman as attractive as Sabina.

'Ah, I'm, I'm sorry Mrs Donovan,' he stammered. 'But, well Mr Troon didn't fill out the number of the box I'm to draw. There are two of them.'

Sabina could see he was embarrassed; he was perhaps just on twenty, short but well built, with slick-backed tawny hair. His embarrassment had turned his face red, which emphasised a number of angry looking pimples.

When he had placed the two cards in front of her, she saw both cards had the surname Donovan blazed across the top and all manner of information beneath relating to their respective deposit boxes. However, in smaller letters beside the surname, she saw different initials; one card was hers, the other obviously her husband's.

With a growing sense of excitement, she stated calmly, 'Oh it probably wasn't explained correctly, I'll be requiring them both.' She held her breath, anticipating some sort of refusal. But when he turned and walked from the room, she let out the breath in relief. She couldn't believe it; she was actually going to get a chance to look through her husband's box. 'God, I never even knew he had one here. This'll be interesting. I wonder what on earth he's hiding?'

Anything she could get hold of that could be used against him, she readily accepted. What little leverage she infrequently gained to resist or confront him with, she had ruthlessly exploited in the past.

By the time the clerk came back into the viewing room, Sabina had risen from the check desk and was pacing restlessly around the room. He walked past her and placed the two rectangular metal boxes he had retrieved from the safe deposit box nests on the desk. Both boxes were polished steel and approximately five inches high, ten wide and eighteen long. He had laid them down side by side. He drew two master keys from his pocket and checked their numbers against their corresponding cards. As he was about to slot the second key into its box he realised his mistake.

'Oh, I think I ah ...' he looked at the card and checked it against the key again. Now feeling a trifle flustered, he carried on, 'I might have made an error. I don't think you're author ...'

By this time Sabina was standing just behind him, she had come that close to seeing what Donovan was hiding and wasn't going to let the chance slip away. She placed a hand on his shoulder in the pretence of looking over it, which had the effect of abruptly stopping his flow of words.

'Authorised? Of course I am.' She leant in and pressed her chest against him as she pointed with her other hand. 'See there, the addresses, they're the same. That card and box belong to my husband. He asked if I could deposit something.'

The clerk flushed red again and slowly turned from the cards to stare uneasily at Sabina's hand. As he swallowed heavily, she saw his Adam's apple bob nervously up and down. She then moved slightly to stand beside him and saw his eyes flick to her lacy top and her generous cleavage beneath.

'I don't think Mr Troon would be too pleased if we were forced to interrupt him from his meeting. Surely the two of us can clear up this misunderstanding?'

'The clerk swallowed again. 'Well,' he croaked before clearing his throat. 'Well, I suppose if he is your husband,' he managed to drag his eyes up to her face, 'and it is only a deposit.'

Sabina lightly squeezed his shoulder. 'Of course, and my, you must work out,' she squeezed his shoulder harder.

The clerk sort of whinnied, 'Yes,' he squeaked, 'A little, there's a gym near home.'

Sabina dropped her hand. 'I've always admired a man who looks after his body.'

He let out another breathless laugh, before finally finding his tongue, 'Yes, well …' but he couldn't think of anything else to say and Sabina didn't offer him another opening. He finally managed to speak. 'Ah, I suppose I had better leave you to it.'

He slotted the second key into the box and turned awkwardly as he made to leave. Sabina made no effort to move and forced him to squeeze past her and the viewing desk's chair. He gave another sickly laugh and turned an even brighter shade of red as he couldn't avoid brushing passed her well-endowed chest – she fancied she could see the back of his ears burning as he hurried away. Sabina knew as she sorted through Donovan's deposit box the clerk's mind would be firmly fixed on other things. She sat down at the desk.

To say Sabina was disappointed as she gave her jewels to her bodyguards was an understatement; there had been nothing of apparent value in her husband's box. Rifling through it she'd found a few insurance certificates, legal documents and a small thin cardboard chit from a company called A Hermann Associates. The chit was the only thing that had slightly aroused any interest, for it had typed on the centre of it numerous numbers and letters. On a whim she scribbled them down on a scrap of paper – *R33, L49, R23, L77* – and slipped it into her wallet. It was a similar type of sequence to the combination she used to open her personal safe back at the villa, but as she shut the deposit box she gave it little more thought; she still had a multitude of things to organise for the party. She had consequently retrieved her diamond necklace, ear rings and brooch from her deposit box and eventually left the viewing room.

As she walked from the bank, the scrap of paper in her wallet was the furthest thing from her mind.

CHAPTER 17

IT WAS THE day after the anniversary party and Sabina, half an hour earlier, had just finished a personal consultation with her lawyer. Inspired by his words she was now about to enter Donovan's office.

'Ah, I'm sorry, Mrs Donovan you can't go in. Your husband won't be back for another twenty minutes.'

The words stopped Sabina in her tracks as she was about to try and push her way through the big heavy teak doors. Dressed in a burgundy Christian Dior suit, she turned to look at the attractive brunette who had risen and now stood defiantly behind the desk in her husband's outer-office.

'Sonya, you may sleep with my husband, but that doesn't give you licence to order me about.' The comment, spoken casually, left the other woman speechless. Sabina turned and tried to open the doors – the handle never gave and the doors were obviously locked. 'Bloody security, this and his own key and keypad operated elevator, his office is done up like Fort Knox. Christ, it's ridiculous,' Sabina uttered bitterly.

Turning back to Sonya and seeing the disconcerted look her comment caused, she demanded, 'Open the bloody doors. I'll not wait for him out here.' Sonya, only hesitated briefly before leaving her desk and stepping up to the keypad to the side of the doors.

As Sonya did as Sabina demanded, her mind was reeling. She'd never suspected for a minute that Sabina knew about her and her husband's affair, and what's more, like static electricity, she could feel the tension bristling from the damn woman now standing at her shoulder.

As Sonya approached and stepped up to the keypad Sabina tried to remain aloof. However, she would've rather reached over and scratched out the bitch's eyes. Disdainfully, she glanced in Sonya's direction and couldn't help but notice the numbered pads she pushed. She saw her push 7, 0, 5, 1, and before Sonya had realised she'd been seen, Sabina was already looking the other way.

Once she'd heard the slight buzz and numerous clicks, Sabina turned and locked a vicious stare on Sonya. The words she spoke may have been uttered sweetly but were definitely laced with venom. 'I do hope you enjoyed your romp with Judd last night.'

Leaving Sonya open-mouthed, she turned and walked through the doors. Sabina knew she would be left alone until her husband arrived.

The beauty of the office that left others in awe left Sabina feeling nothing less than abhorrence. It epitomised her husband and everything she detested about the man; the extravagance, the affluence, even the boldness, that had helped turn him into what he had become today. However, what she didn't realise was that it was their similarities that had kept them from developing even an amiable relationship.

Walking through the towering tusks and up the white marble steps, she passed Donovan's extravagant desk and stood with her hands on her hips staring out across the smog-layered sprawling city of Los Angeles. Even though Donovan had turned up late to the party last night she felt she was finally able to do it, finally able to bring herself to demand a divorce. The party had been a major success. That and her lawyer's comments had buoyed her courage. He was confident that she had an excellent chance of leaving the marriage unscathed and with a massive settlement besides. *That'll throw the cat amongst the pigeons*, she thought with relish.

In irritation she glanced at her watch, remembering that damn woman in the outer-office had said Donovan wouldn't be back for another twenty minutes. *What the hell am I going to do?* she thought. She knew she wasn't going to give that bitch out there the satisfaction of seeing her leave only to return minutes later. She hoped she wouldn't lose her nerve while waiting.

Now feeling a trifle bored, Sabina turned and walked back down into the informal discussion area. Slumping wearily down onto one of the rolled back leather couches she scanned a disinterested eye over the portrait of Donovan's great-grandfather. 'Hello, what do we have here?' she queried as her interest quickened. One edge of the portrait lay slightly proud of the walnut wall. Rising and walking up to it she curled her fingers around the portrait's frame and pulled. 'Good lord!' What Sabina had discovered was a wall safe concealed behind the portrait. 'Just like mine at home, but bigger. Hmm, I wonder?' Sabina uttered, as the slightest glimpse of realisation began to dawn.

Reaching for and rummaging in the large leather shoulder bag she carried, she eventually found her wallet and inside it the scrap of paper she'd used to scribble down the series of letters and numbers she'd discovered in Donovan's safe deposit box.

'Yes, I wonder,' she repeated as she stepped up to the safe and its centrally positioned tumbler.

Holding the scrap of paper in one hand she used the other and deftly twirled the tumbler: Right 33, left 49, right 23, left 77. She tried the handle and pulled – the safe opened. 'Well, I'll be ...' she uttered in amazement, before guiltily glancing over her shoulder at the walnut panels that concealed Donovan's private elevator. Hoping he wouldn't arrive back early, she turned back to the safe and peered inside.

On the bottom shelf were bundles of numerous overseas currencies as well as several gold bars; it was clear to Sabina it amounted to a small fortune. But it was the contents on the top shelf that drew her attention – a container of computer disks. 'Now why would Judd have locked them away?' she queried suspiciously as her intuition flared. After hesitating briefly, glancing again towards the lift, she reached in and carried the disks up to Donovan's desk and computer.

Once she had put down the disks and was comfortably seated in Donovan's high-backed executive type chair she opened the container. The disks were unmarked so she chose the closest one, slotted it into the tower and called up its file menu. Luckily – believing access was protected – Donovan had seen no need to disguise the file names. Most were displayed in English.

After scrolling through the names for several seconds her eyes were immediately drawn to the file name displaying the word *lavare*.

Strange. Why would Judd use an Italian word? He doesn't even know the language. She knew it meant 'launder'. 'Or maybe it's the Latin original?' Ultimately translated it meant 'to wash' if her memory served her correctly. *That'd be more like it.*

Yet she quickly lost interest in which language it came from when she saw the symbol beside it – the $ symbol. With growing interest she called up the file.

'My God!' she eventually breathed in awe, once she had skip read through the file. Nervously licking her lips she looked out into the office. She knew that if Donovan caught her reading this, divorce would be the least of her worries. What she had just read was pure dynamite. Itemised in the file were names, amounts and dates involved in a huge money-laundering racket her husband was apparently running in the revenue-starved countries of Eastern Europe.

Where the funds came from she didn't have a clue. 'Drugs maybe, who knows?' The contraband traded was never specified, but she did notice most of the money seemed to end up in or travelled through Britain. She had to make a decision, take a copy of the file now or come back for it later. This was the type of information she could really use against her husband and was an opportunity she could use to avenge herself and get him off her back once and for all. 'No, I'll have to do it now,' she decided.

Leaving the file on screen, she popped out the disk and slotted it back in the container. After placing the container back in the safe and closing the door, she replaced the portrait back exactly as she'd found it. Sabina had done enough snooping into her husband's affairs to know he had an exceptional eye for detail.

Looking at her watch she saw it had been only minutes since she had first walked into the office. Again pushing aside the worry Donovan might return sooner than expected, she hurried back to the desk and quickly looked for a disk she could use to load the file on. After a minute's fruitless search she knew she would have to print out a copy.

Reaching for the laser-jet printer she flicked it on and set up the computer to print out the text – she hoped there weren't too many pages. She could feel her palms beginning to sweat as page after page spilled from the printer into its tray.

God, it's taking an eternity. She had lost count of how many pages had already been printed; she hoped she could fit them into her shoulder bag. 'There must be well over fifty by now.'

For what seemed like the hundredth time she looked at her watch, it had been ten minutes since she'd first set the printer in motion. *God, he's going to catch me for sure*, she thought for the umpteenth time as she again looked down towards the subtly concealed doors of Donovan's private elevator.

I'll stop it now, surely that'll be enough. But as before her greed prevented her from stopping the machine. The more she got on her husband the better.

After several more agonisingly slow minutes the printer finally dropped the last page into its tray. She scooped up the thick sheath of paper and stuffed them into her bag. Then in horror she heard a gentle whoosh behind her, the walnut panels sliding open that concealed the private lift.

Oh God! she thought, close to panic; she could hear her heart pounding like a locomotive within her chest while her lower abdomen cramped with fear. She flicked off the printer's switch as she quickly jumped in behind Donovan's desk. Breathing a sigh of relief she could hardly believe she had pulled it off.

Donovan walked into the office and with an irritated frown of recognition marking his face, he began striding towards her. It was then Sabina realised her mistake – the computer was still on. The evidence was there. Donovan would know she had opened the safe and accessed his files.

'What the hell are you doing here?' Donovan snapped. He was in a foul mood; wherever he had been it was obvious he'd had a bad meeting.

'Sonya let me in, so I could wait for you,' she managed to respond, but recognised the tremor of fear in her voice. *Christ, now what?* she thought in mounting terror, *He's caught me for sure!* Donovan had reached the marble steps. Trying to appear calm but with her mind reeling in anguish, she found she was unable to maintain contact with his piercing walnut-brown eyes. She couldn't help but drop her gaze.

'What the hell are you up to?' Donovan demanded suspiciously as he briefly stopped on top of the steps. Instinctively, he knew she was up to something. Without dropping his eyes from her face, again, he began to walk towards her.

It was then that relief, like a gentle wave, washed over Sabina's body. She had noticed under the desk, beside her foot, the computer's power-lead plugged into an electrical socket recessed into the floor.

'I am your wife you know,' she responded in a wounded voice without raising her eyes. She slowly moved her foot and touched the plug's switch with the toe of her shoe; thankfully the screen went blank. Trying to conceal her relief she spoke again, 'It's just that,' she lifted her head and looked evenly into his accusing eyes, 'well, I came in to thank you for making the effort of showing up last night, that was all.' She walked from behind the desk and swept past her now flabbergasted husband. 'Not that you'd care,' she ended with a convincing sob as she passed him by.

Her comment and subsequent actions had thrown Donovan completely; it wasn't what he had expected at all, not after the cutting remarks and scowls that she had thrown at him during the previous night. She was out through the teak doors before he could respond or even attempt to stop her.

For an hour after Sabina had left Donovan's office she had shaken like a leaf, feeling fear, exhilaration, and tremendous relief all wrapped into one. She couldn't imagine what Donovan would have done if he had actually caught her, also she couldn't really believe she'd had the nerve to pull it off. Even if she never took any more action it would have to be the sweetest victory she had ever scored against the man who for the past ten years had successfully manipulated her life.

It was now two weeks since she had taken the file and during that time while she'd tried to absorb its contents, with all thought of divorce forgotten, she had avoided Donovan like the plague. It had made him all the more suspicious and Sabina suspected he was having her watched. *No matter,'* she thought. She had already decided on her next course of action.

The screeds of printouts had not only minutely detailed the huge money laundering racket her husband was running, but also a vast multitude of payments to destinations across the globe, with destinations in Britain and Africa mentioned most often. Although, in comparison to his companies' total turnover the amounts were small, it still showed Donovan was laundering tens of millions of dollars. Even though she didn't fully understand the intricate workings of the racket, it appeared vast sums of money were coming in from Asia into the network spread throughout the old Soviet Union.

She decided she wanted to cause maximum damage to her husband while still protecting her interests. Yet she didn't trust the American authorities to take the appropriate action as she was in no doubt Donovan hadn't got where he was today without lining a few pockets along the way. It would be too ironic to have the material that should rid herself of the man she despised used against her. Since a large proportion of the laundered funds were being channelled into Britain, it was the British she decided to pass the information on to.

Sabina decided it would be wise to drive herself today, and being extremely careful that she wasn't followed, she drove her Porsche 944 towards downtown Los Angeles. Parking on Wilshire Boulevard she walked several blocks down to the British Consulate General located at 3701 on the same busy thoroughfare. It didn't take her long to find the consulate situated in suite 312, where she placed her carefully wrapped bundle in a drop-off-box. She was out of the suite in less than a minute. Positive she hadn't been followed either into or out of the building, she was back in her Porsche heading west towards Beverly Hills in next to no time at all.

Even though an investigation could take many months, she began to revel in an overwhelming feeling of triumph. At least the British would have to take some kind of action, and with their intervention the authorities in the States would be forced to act. The United States government couldn't afford to be associated, through their customs department, with international crime of this magnitude.

Sabina felt confident that he would have to be exposed and charged with fraud. Now, because Donovan Enterprises was too big to fall and with her substantial interests, she was positive she was looking at a far greater windfall than any divorce settlement could give her – ultimate control of her family's trust and independence from her domineering husband.

As she turned off Loma Vista Drive and pulled her car onto the red-bricked driveway, sweeping passed the wrought-iron security gates and kiosk which led up to her lemon-shaded villa, she really saw for the first time the beauty of the manicured gardens and artfully situated dwelling. As she stopped her car under the villa's porte-cochère she couldn't help but gloat.

'Eat your heart out, Judd Donovan. You're about to lose this and much, much more.'

CHAPTER 18

London, England

RICHARD BLACK WAS staring absent-mindedly out of his office window, down into the small oak-lined courtyard at the rear of his third-story flat. In theory it was part of a small complex of six other residential flats, yet in reality it was much, much more.

Richard had been born in South Africa just over forty-seven years ago. However, he was a British subject and worked for Her Majesty's Government. He was a handsome man and a bachelor; he had short brown hair, dusted with the lightest flecks of grey at his temples and his face was clean-shaven which emphasised a strong powerful jaw. He had humorous yet probing blue eyes with the lines around them, and those that marked his face, formed from laughter; his temperament was one that naturally allowed him to see the humorous side of life. He was a well-built man, but his body bore witness to the fact that he spent most of his time behind a desk.

Richard ran an information-gathering agency simply called 'Network', which was frankly the best of its kind in the world. Those people seeking to use its services thought they were dealing with an independent company with no association with any government organisation or security service; a front that had been elaborately cultivated to allow Richard and his tight-knit group of agents to work anonymously across the globe, gathering information to protect Britain's sovereign interests.

Network was loosely attached to the British Secret Intelligence Service, yet was affiliated to none of its many branches. Its main policy was that as long as the information it was asked to gather didn't jeopardise Britain's national security, and the price was right, it was readily collected and given. Adopting this approach, Richard and his agents were able to gather a vast volume of information otherwise unavailable to Britain's other security services. Another factor that allowed it to perform so well was that of its financial independence. Having no budgetary constraints its self-sufficiency allowed it to operate as a law unto itself.

Richard's office was at Network's base and main coordination centre, part of a three-storied brick complex situated on Sutton Court Road in the west of London. It was on the corner of Ellesmere Road, an extension of the M4 that led into the heart of London. It was also conveniently close to the London Underground's District Line, with its nearest tube stations being Chiswick Park and Turnham Green.

Although the base was suitably close to the M4 and Heathrow Airport for international travel and the underground system for domestic, the main reason for its location was as a residential dwelling. To date, none of the subversive factions of the world had been able to locate its whereabouts or even realise it was an integral part of Britain's security services. Its autonomy and security had remained intact; even most of Richard's agents were unaware of its true location. If anybody did happen to notice the screed of aerial satellite disks subtly positioned amongst the stately oaks at the building's rear, well, it was well-known amongst Richard's neighbours that he and his 'flatmate' were keen ham radio operators. It was Richard's so-called flatmate who brought his mind back to the present.

'I think you'd better take a look at this. Came in a couple of days ago,' the man said. 'I wanted to follow up on a few leads before I presented it.' He placed a thick report on the desk blotter in front of Richard.

His name was Johnny – it wasn't his real name but a code name and he was Richard's assistant. Where appropriate, he was the man who spoke to and vetoed incoming calls and outgoing information.

He was a nondescript man who seemed to lack any distinctive features; the sort of man people found hard to recognise twice. He was practically bald with only slight wings of wispy grey hair above protruding ears, and of an indeterminable age. Those who knew him would say he was born somewhere in-between thirty and fifty years ago. He had a round fleshy face with a body that testified to his lack of physical exercise. Standing well under six foot with a protruding paunch and rounded shouldered stoop, he carried an inquisitive, searching look upon his face; characteristics that were the mark of his trade.

For what seemed like countless years he had sat hunched over a huge desk cram-packed with all manner of sophisticated recording equipment, computer screens and terminals, elaborate phone systems, and radio receiving and transmitting devices. Johnny was arguably the best information gathering expert in the world. Richard had given up trying to keep track of his many informants; he knew they numbered in the hundreds. If the information was available, the little man had the knowledge to gather it.

Wearily, Richard looked down at the bundle of information Johnny had placed in front of him. Because of the cutbacks in the old KGB and the like, he had been forced to redirect Network's efforts towards industrial espionage, an area that wasn't his cup of tea. Yet it was a field that had proven to be as debilitating as the more blatant forms of coercion, experienced during the bitter years of the cold war.

Johnny watched Richard slowly sit upright in his chair as he quickly scanned through the pages. It took him several minutes to skim through them and read Johnny's accompanying report.

'Bloody hell,' Richard breathed in awe, sitting back in his chair, once he had finished. 'Christ, this is disastrous.'

'Yeah, interesting reading isn't it? I thought you'd be intrigued.'

'Intrigued? Mortified would be more to the point. Who the hell dropped this in our lap? This stuff's dynamite, straight out of someone's files.'

'It was left in the drop-off-box in our consulate in Los Angeles. Our man, the Vice-Consul for information there, actually saw the woman who dropped it off. He followed her, but only managed to get half of the registration number off the car she was driving.'

'You're joking! Why the hell would he follow her? That's not procedure,' Richard queried, it sounded too convenient.

'Well. apparently she's quite a looker, and would probably cause heads to turn wherever she goes. I suppose he was intrigued, suspicious or maybe both. I dunno. Remember all our agents are handpicked.' He shrugged. 'Anyway, once he'd picked up the package he tried to have what he'd got of the car's number-plate traced. He wasn't able to and her identity should have died there.' Johnny fell silent.

'Should have, but it didn't. Come on, get on with it.' Sometimes it was like pulling teeth trying to get information from Johnny. It was his only fault, playing theatrics; he loved trying to build a story to a climax. 'You did name her in your report, remember?'

Now thoroughly enjoying himself, Johnny continued, 'Yes, that I did, but come on, you have to admit this is the best one we've had in for years now that the Russians don't want to play.'

'Get on with it,' Richard cut in, he was more than aware, from his initial glance at Johnny's report, that the information held disastrous implications.

'Okay, that evening our man went and reviewed the footage from the consulate's security cameras, he recognised her from there. Apparently she's one of LA's elite, she often appears in the society mags over there. With a name and the partial registration number he was able to trace the car,' Johnny reached over and tapped a name on the top of his accompanying report, 'Its owned by Donovan Enterprises and she's the owner's wife, Sabina Donovan.'

'Well, I'll be! It looks as though we're dealing with one bitter lady. I wonder what her husband did to annoy her? With this sort of stuff she could break him.'

'Hmm, yeah, I know what you mean. Look, I've still got a bit to follow up on, call me when you've decided how to play it.' Johnny turned and began to walk from the office, but as he got to the door he stopped and turned around. 'Hell, Richard, this Donovan character needs to be stopped, even if it's just for the elephants' sake.'

Richard whistled softly in disbelief. It had been a couple of hours since Johnny had first placed Sabina's printout on his desk; he had finally finished his scrutiny of the file and was flabbergasted, not only by its accuracy, but also its contents.

The printout had been split into three separate parts. One concerning the dates, amounts and the weights of the contraband that was being traded, the next where the money from its proceeds was being laundered, and finally the distribution of the laundered funds.

From Johnny's initial investigation of the first part, as Donovan had seen no need to disguise them, he had managed to put faces to most of the names the file had mentioned. As it turned out, all but a few were actually registered individual or company traders operating legitimate businesses in mostly Asia, and to a lesser extent, other countries around the world.

Although the file didn't state in as many words what merchandise the laundered funds were for, Johnny had successfully been able to deduce it was ivory. The file had clearly stated the amounts of money, and the accompanying dates and weights of whatever was being sold. Meticulously, Donovan had recorded all corresponding data except regarding what was actually being sold.

Taking figures directly from the file and using his black-market contacts in the countries where the majority of the transaction had taken place, Johnny was able to find out the only commodity that sold for around $60-$123 per kilogram – or $27-$56 per pound – was ivory. Richard wasn't fully versed with the international ban on the trade of elephant products, but because of his deep affinity with the continent of his birth he was very aware of it, he knew the ivory had to be illegal. So from an unspecified source it appeared Donovan had passed on huge amounts of poached ivory to willing buyers in Asia and, to a smaller degree, other countries around the world.

The second part of the printout was simple enough – it referred to the actual laundering process. It had turned out to be just one more of the many problems the West was now encountering with the countries of the old communist East since they had been exposed to the open trading and monetary markets across the rest of the world.

Richard knew from colleagues of the former Soviet bloc's booming drug trade that their home-grown gangster elements mainly viewed democracy as a fast track to wealth. But until now he hadn't truly appreciated the ease with which money could be laundered throughout Eastern Europe.

It appeared Donovan was taking advantage of the blind eye the new governments within the recently formed Commonwealth of Independent States were now turning in their desperate quest for tradable currencies. He was having his ivory customers deposit funds directly into numbered bank accounts spread across the CIS. And it seemed from there the money was being converted straight into roubles. Reading between the lines, Richard surmised the roubles were then used to purchase CIS goods such as gold or possibly silver. Though not actually stated, specified under numerous names in the third part of the printout were various amounts itemised alongside the word 'bullion'.

Although they were listed, Johnny as yet hadn't been able to give him the identity of the names to whom the bullion had been exported. Bitterly, Richard realised this was the simplest part of the laundering process. Donovan, using his conglomerate of companies, would have easily and legitimately been able to move the bullion around the world.

Scribbling notes on a legal pad, Richard began itemising the information he needed. In theory, this was outside his jurisdiction, but technically because the majority of the laundered funds seemed to be traveling through or ending up in Britain, he was entitled to make inquiries. However, morally he also felt obliged to take action if only to help stop the needless slaughter of the African elephants. He also had another ace up his sleeve as he was accountable to virtually no one, 'I'll do as I please,' he decided. It was time for him and Johnny to plan their assault.

Rising from his desk, he left his office and walked down a short dark hallway to Johnny's office. Poking his head in the door he saw his assistant in his customary working pose, head bent intently forward, insistently tapping away on a keyboard in front of him.

'Everything you can find out on this character Donovan and his companies, as well as the other individuals or companies that either bought the ivory or received the bullion. Especially the bullion, I want to work backwards on this one.'

Johnny, still intent on what he was doing, waved a half-hearted acknowledgment and mumbled an incoherent response. As Richard walked back to his office he knew the information would be on his desk in next to no time at all.

CHAPTER 19

OVER THE NEXT few months, Johnny was able to collect a sizable dossier on all facets of Judd Donovan, from his personal life to the companies he governed, but most importantly right through into the ivory and money laundering racket he controlled.

'But why the hell would he do it?' Johnny asked Richard. 'He controls a huge business empire, earning him far more than ivory ever could. And legitimately, I might add.'

'Greed, power, who knows?' Richard answered. 'One thing that's obvious from his file is that he's controlling upwards of thirty per cent of the estimated 750 ton of poached ivory coming out of Africa a year, and even presuming he gets the lowest price of US $30 per pound and loses half in laundering, it'll still gross him over thirteen million. His companies may net him far more but, well, I think you get my point. But what really gets me, is the twenty thousand odd elephants he's having slaughtered each year. You've gotta hand it to him. However he's done it, he's approaching a monopoly in the ivory trade.'

'Okay, let's review what we've got so far. From the top,' Richard instructed.

It was the standard approach they took for each of their weekly review meetings regarding Donovan and his ivory racket. Only after the review would they add new information. Richard leant back in his chair and stared vacantly out through the window into London's late afternoon sky as Johnny began to speak.

'Firstly, Donovan himself appears squeaky clean because of his involvement with the US government. He partially owns and controls a huge conglomerate of international importing/exporting companies. He was one of the youngest men to take over the presidency of a top 500 company and is acclaimed throughout the United States for his astute business aptitude and negotiating skills.

'Probably his most profitable business decision was marrying his wife, and we can safely assume because of her actions it's a marriage without love. On the surface he has never invested in any field other than importing, exporting or freight-forwarding, which also includes shipping, warehousing, transportation, etc.'

'Okay, so we have an astute rich boy who married into more money, now heavily involved with governments from all over the globe.' Richard snorted in disgust. 'We're going to have to have a watertight case against him,' he repeated for the umpteenth time since starting their investigations, 'otherwise any allegations will easily be dismissed. Give me his personal,' he asked, dropping his previous concern.

'Still not much, I'm afraid. Marriage we know about, collects ivory, and seems to live for the company.'

'Yeah okay. Tell me about the ivory again.'

'Right, where are we?' Johnny mumbled looking through his screeds of notes before finding what he wanted. 'As we know, his great-grandfather originally started Donovan Enterprises through his dealings with ivory, and following in the family tradition he now has one of the largest collections of its kind in the world, even including Asia. He collects anything remotely involved with the stuff, mammoth, early Japanese, you name it, he has hundreds of pieces on loan to museums around the world. Few people have seen his personal collection, so all I've been able to find out is that most of it's housed in a special room at his home in Los Angeles. Guarded of course.'

'Hmm, guarded, and a special room you say. Interesting,' Richard uttered with no change of expression.

'Yes, apparently,' Johnny responded suspiciously. The fact Richard had commented normally meant something had attracted his attention, but as he made no further comment Johnny shrugged and carried on. 'It's probably a rumour, but they say he cried the day Kenya's President Daniel arap Moi set fire as a gesture of protest against poaching to those two and a half thousand tusks back in eighty-nine. Other than that ...' Johnny shrugged.

'It always gets back to the same; he must be obsessed with the stuff. Right, next, the laundering racket.'

Johnny quickly flicked through a few more computer printout sheets before composing himself to speak, 'Okay, right, most of his customers are Chinese Asians who are paying him as we know in the CIS. From the brief investigations of our people in Asia, it seems the ivory comes in through various, and as yet, undetermined routes. We're probably safe to assume it's smuggled in with legitimate goods shipped via one of Donovan's many companies. The Asians seem to have cleverly disguised their involvement by a maze of silent partners and investment holding companies. Once they've got hold of the ivory, it's cut up, carved and sold as all manner of things –

trinkets, name seals, statues and the like.'

Richard shook his head in disgust. Over a century of wanton slaughter. *You'd think we'd learnt after all the other species now extinct. It's happening all over again,* he thought, then focused back on Johnny as he continued.

'Now, because it's become so lucrative or entrenched in their heritage, about sixty countries, a lot of them Asian, refuse to participate with the CITES ban, and in certain places the ivory is still sold openly to collectors and tourists.'

After Johnny had finished Richard remained silent, staring vacantly at the opposite wall. It took him several seconds to snap out of the morbid mood that had gripped him. 'I can't see how they sleep at night what with the elephants that are being slaughtered. Ivory isn't exactly a necessity.' Leaning forward, he rested an elbow on his desk and cupped his chin in his hand. 'Skip over the actual laundering in the CIS, it's the same as the far East. At the moment there's not exactly a lot we can do. What about the bullion?'

'Okay, we've got the list of names it has been sent to in Britain and Africa, but not much else. The names in the UK appear to be investment related companies, and they seem to briefly hold the bullion on reserve in banks spread around the country before it's shipped overseas again.'

'Hmm, that's interesting,' Richard commented, with his vacant look again.

'Yes,' Johnny replied suspiciously again, he was intently watching his boss, 'but I've been unable to find out where it goes. It's as if it disappears.' As Richard made no further response, just briefly squinted, Johnny reverted back to something he knew. 'In the short time I've had to search the companies' records he uses here, I haven't been able to unravel the interconnecting trusts, dummy companies and nominee shareholders that hide their ownership. In fact, may never; we can only suspect the companies' ownership will eventually lead back to Donovan.'

'That's something I think we can safely assume,' Richard agreed, 'Yet at the moment we can't prove the connection between the bullion and ivory – we'll need a hell of a lot more information for that. What about the names in Africa?'

'Just two individuals. The bullion is transferred into banks in South Africa, Botswana, Zimbabwe or Kenya, and then immediately sold. These two will have to be involved with the actual poaching.'

Richard murmured an agreement. Even though they had such detailed information from Donovan's file, he still felt they were hamstrung. They knew so much which led to some glaringly obvious conclusions but had no facts to actually back them up. He knew elephants were being butchered in their thousands, but as yet couldn't do a damn thing to help them. He hoped new information would soon come to light.

'Okay, the areas we're going to have to concentrate on are the bullion and Donovan himself. Anything new on either?' he asked hopefully.

'Nothing on the investment companies, but I'll keep pushing there. As far as Donovan and the African connection goes, a bit of a breakthrough on both. But I'm afraid you're not going to like it, Richard,' Johnny warned as he flopped first one then another photocopied article on his desk. Richard began reading through the first article; it was a couple of years old:

The Herald, Harare, Zimbabwe.

In a recent turn of events Captain Edwin Bhundani Nleya, investigator with the Zimbabwe National Army, was recently found hanged in Hwange National Park in the northwest of the country. It is believed the Captain was investigating a major elephant and rhino poaching operation running throughout the country. It is thought Captain Nleya was followed by his assassins on a train from the capital Harare to Hwange. Just before he was killed the Captain phoned his wife to warn her he was in imminent danger.

A close friend and fellow officer, Captain Abel Sithole vowed the Zimbabwean Army wouldn't rest until the villains that had perpetrated this crime were brought to justice.

'*Bloody hell!*' Richard swore as soon as he had finished the article. 'This Abel Sithole character, he's one of the ones receiving the bullion. You're telling me I don't like it, the Zimbabwean Army involved with poaching. Christ, what could possibly be worse?'

Johnny respectfully stayed silent. He truly felt for the elephants and their plight, but he couldn't understand how his boss felt, having not been born in Africa. Although he rarely spoke of the continent and its wildlife, on the few occasions he did, it was clear to Johnny Richard treasured them as a significant part of his heritage.

'What about the other one,' Richard eventually began, still saddened by the new information. 'The one that's receiving most of the bullion, what's his name again?'

'Nkomo, Peter Nkomo.'

'Anything on him?'

'Not a bean.'

Richard briefly shook his head, still wrapped up in the increasing enormity of Donovan's poaching and laundering racket. The Zimbabwean army. He couldn't believe it. In a country like that, the army was practically able to operate above the law; they could virtually do as they pleased with little fear of being exposed.

'Leave this one to me,' he finally declared, 'I've got a few people to talk to. I seem to recall reading somewhere the World Wildlife Fund have set up an anti-poaching squad now operating in eastern and southern Africa. Somebody down there needs to be told. I'll talk to a friend I know who works in their US office.'

Picking up the photocopied article and putting it aside, he quickly read through the one beneath it. Although it mentioned Donovan and ivory, he couldn't understand the significance, yet somehow his intuition told him it was an integral part of his ivory and laundering scheme.

The article was from a *American Scientist* journal and briefly stated that a huge quantity of mammoth tusks had been found in a small valley in northern Siberia between the Yana and Kolyma Rivers. Speculation was rife how such a quantity came to accumulate there, mammoth graveyard, ancient hunting pit and no one theory had yet been decided upon. The article also estimated that probably half a million tons of fossil ivory still lay buried in the Siberian permafrost.

However, the thing that most interested Richard about the article was that despite a huge uproar from the Russian Academy of Science, the newly formed government of the Russian Federation had sold the lot to an American citizen, and none other than Judd Donovan, for an undisclosed sum with first right of refusal for any more uncovered. Although puzzled, Richard realised Donovan was again taking advantage of the need the new governments of CIS had for hard currency.

'But why had he purchased it?' he had to ask himself, 'Especially when he could acquire poached ivory for probably a fraction of the price.'

'You're wondering why he bought it?' Johnny asked, apparently reading his mind.

'Just seems absurd, that's all.'

'I know what you mean. But if it's any help, when I found the article I did some checking. Because of the CITES ban, mammoth tusks are now the only ivory able to be traded legally throughout the world.'

The truth hit him like a ton of bricks. 'God it *does* get worse!' Richard voiced in horror. 'Christ, having unspecified but documented amounts of mammoth tusks, Donovan can easily trade his poached elephant tusks as legal mammoth ivory.'

Although in its raw state mammoth tusks were far more curved, Richard had read somewhere when it had been worked only by using highly sophisticated scientific procedure – isotope or something or other analysis – could it be effectively told apart from elephant ivory, and by then it would be far too late.

'That's if he did buy any mammoth ivory. For all we know Donovan may be bribing some Russian official to get the appropriate documentation,' Johnny reasoned.

Richard, rubbing a disbelieving hand over his face, slumped back in his chair as he tried to gather his thoughts. This was definitely no amateur racket they had stumbled across; it was highly professional and well-organised international crime. The laundering racket probably accounted for only a portion of the total ivory poached now that Donovan could appear to legally supply outlets when mammoth documentation was used.

'How much has already been sold as mammoth ivory?' he wondered. 'What a perfect cover.'

What had started as a hunt to stop a laundering racket channelling tens of millions of dollars around the world had now turned into what could be a desperate fight to save the African elephants.

Richard needed a plan and quickly, he made his decision.

'Okay, Johnny. I'll be concentrating on Africa and Donovan himself. You take everything else. First I need to talk to this Donovan woman. Set it up and book me a ticket to LA as soon as possible. His expression hardened, 'she's committed now so I'll make sure I get it. I also want somebody to put pressure on Donovan from the States.' Looking at his watch Richard calculated, 'Eight hours behind, that would make it the middle of the morning in LA.' The man he wanted should be at his desk. 'Get me Mitch Hagan at the FBI's Californian headquarters in LA. I know we haven't used him for a while, but he's good. When you've put me on, come back through.'

It only took Johnny a few minutes to get Richard connected. 'Good to hear you, Mitch,' Richard greeted him sincerely.

'Long time, Rich. Obviously not a social call. What can I do for ya?' came a friendly voice back down the phone.

'Got a naughty boy in your neck of the woods, right up your alley as you Yanks would say. Have you still got the same fax number? It's too detailed to try and explain on the phone. You have? Good. I'll send it over and be back to you in a couple of days. Oh, and Mitch, get rid of the fax once you get it. Who we're investigating won't like it, so be careful.'

Johnny was already sitting in front of Richard's desk waiting for him to finish the call. 'Anything else new since last week?' Richard asked him once he'd replaced the receiver.

'One other thing. It may fit in with both the mammoth ivory and laundering in the CIS. It came in as I was putting through your call. It appears Donovan has a Russian working for him, a real nasty piece of work. He'll probably bear watching.'

CHAPTER 20

Kowloon – Hong Kong

IT WAS A hot humid day when Nikolai Bogatin stepped from the British Airways Boeing 747 onto the tarmac at Hong Kong's Kai Tak Airport on Kowloon peninsula. Carrying only a small handgrip he was sweating profusely by the time he had passed through customs, after indicating he was only there for a stopover of a few short hours.

As Kai Tak is one of the busiest airports in Asia, nobody took any notice of his heavily accented English; to them it was obvious he was Russian. But so what?

When he stepped from the main terminal complex he immediately took the nearest taxi and asked to be taken to Nathan Street in the sprawling mainland city of Kowloon, opposite Hong Kong Island.

'Ah, plenty good bargains there. I have cousin who works on Nathan Street, has best-priced goods in Kowloon.' The taxi driver chirped as he screwed around and hooked an arm over his seat, 'I take you there if you like?'

Bogatin never said a word, just stared at him from beneath drooping eyelids.

What the taxi driver saw was a heavy-set man with Slavic features dressed in an expensive light-weight Pierre Cardin suit. And what he soon recognised was a menacing presence that no amount of external refinery could ever hope to hide. Feeling somewhat ill at ease, he gave an embarrassed laugh and turned to concentrate on his driving, thinking it best if he said no more. He definitely wouldn't be getting a kickback for guiding this one to his so-called cousin's store.

Bogatin had been an employee of Donovan Enterprises for five years now, and he wasn't exactly what could be called the model employee, more like one usually hidden from public view. Nobody, except Donovan, knew exactly what he did; he took orders from him and him alone. That suited the other employees fine because the further away they were from him, the better. He was the type of man who would easily send shivers down anyone's spine. It was fair to say Nikolai Bogatin had developed a unique repertoire of skills, but putting people at ease certainly wasn't amongst them.

Posing as a Soviet-Jewish refugee, Bogatin had entered the United States through New York's JFK airport, telling immigration inspectors that he was thirty-two, born in Saratov, in the Russian Soviet Federated Socialist Republic, and was a jeweller by trade.

In reality, Bogatin was nothing more than an extortionist and cold-blooded killer, just one of the many career criminals that had been hardened by a decade in Soviet jails and dumped on the West by the KGB. The Soviet's plan was to rid itself of violent and troublesome offenders while also helping to discredit legitimate migrant communities. A plan that worked remarkably well.

Upon entering the States, he settled in Brooklyn's teeming Brighton Beach community – home for tens of thousands of Soviet migrants already living in the United States. Within days of setting up residence he had already established links with the Organizatsiya – a unique confederation of tight-lipped gangsters who were pouring in from Russia. In those days he undertook any crime that paid, from counterfeiting to contract murder. Yet after only a few years with the Organizatsiya he decided to move on. The increasing risks he was asked to take seriously jeopardised his newfound freedom.

He first gained employment with Donovan Enterprises as a security guard. In a matter of months he'd moved up the ranks to where he eventually became head of security and Donovan's main hatchet man – positions he still held because of the loyalty he had towards the man who had given him independence and money beyond his wildest dreams.

After paying off his taxi Bogatin stepped onto Nathan Street, a magnet for tourists intent on purchasing all manner of goods; videos, cameras, stereos and a vast array of jewellery. There were storefronts adorned with clothing encroaching upon the footpath, while the street teemed with people. What space was left was packed with hawkers. He was immediately spotted as a new arrival and became besieged with a barrage of young Asian boys, each dancing about and displaying their wares, while the more pushy ones shoved watches in his face and shrieked in English, 'Copy watch mister! Copy watch, cheapest in town!' It only took a few menacing scowls for the boys to scamper to accost a more likely and less threatening suspect.

Looking around and studying the tourist map he carried, it didn't take him long to gain his bearings. After walking several blocks he turned down a narrow side street, Cameron Road, away from the noise and bustle of the main shopping area. It was shaded and quieter on this road, while the shops lining its cobbled surface had their heavy metal shutters hooked back, displaying themselves open for business.

As he walked along the road he soon came to the entrance of a metro station and knew he was near his destination. He stopped beside it and placed his handgrip at his feet. No sooner was it on the ground when he noticed out of the corner of his eye a small Asian boy dressed in scruffy white shorts and a baggy green T-shirt dart from the shadows to scoop it up and drop an identical one in its place. He didn't watch the boy scoot away or try to stop him, the transfer was expected. Instead, he studied the sign above the shop opposite him, which read: *Tat Hing Trading*. It was the heart of one of Donovan's biggest ivory competitors, and Tat Hing's owner, a Mr Poone, had been offered on numerous occasions a modest partnership deal by Donovan. Bogatin had been sent in to finalise the arrangements.

From the research he was required to read before any form of 'negotiation', Bogatin knew Mr Poone was a Hong Kong real-estate speculator, jewellery-store owner, and one of the *kingpins* of the world's illicit ivory trade. He and a handful of other families – mostly Hong Kong based Chinese – had controlled the vast international trade of ivory for the last few decades. Most of them were exorbitantly wealthy and many remained above the law. However, on this particular trip Bogatin wouldn't be abiding by anyone's law. In fact, quite the opposite.

Poone's ivory consumption accounted for something approaching twenty to thirty per cent of the world's ivory trade, a percentage Donovan had decided he wanted a part of. To maintain this percentage, Poone, in recent years, had to constantly move his carving factories when countries suspected his involvement in the illicit trade. Taiwan, South Korean, Hong Kong and the United Arab Emirates had each at some stage housed his factories, factories Donovan was positive would soon help increase his growing monopoly in the trade.

Bogatin picked up his new handgrip, walked across the cobbled alley and entered the entrance of Tat Hing Trading. It was dark and cool inside the store and Bogatin instinctively stepped to the side as he closed the door. As he let his eyes accustom themselves to the dull interior, he scanned his surroundings. It was obvious that none of the millions Poone's operation had taken from poached ivory had been spent on the inside of the store; it was starkly furnished in bare aging wood. The Russian recognised it for what it was, a sham, left as unpretentious as possible to protect the enormity of Poone's worldwide business.

In front of Bogatin was a bare waist-high wooden counter and around the walls, wooden shelves stacked full of brown cardboard boxes. There was an overweight Asian of average height with a round chubby face, wearing a white silk shirt, standing behind the counter. He had looked up from studying an accounting ledger as the Russian stepped through the door: it was Mr Poone himself. Bogatin recognised him from the photos in the research package he had studied.

Once Bogatin's eyes had adjusted, several paces carried him to the counter, the ledger was snapped shut.

'Yes, may I help you,' Poone said in accented but easily understandable English.

Bogatin also spoke in English; it would have to be their common language, 'Mr Poone, my employer, I believe you know him as Mr Franks has sent me to discuss the terms of your new arrangement.'

Poone was trembling with rage even before Bogatin had finished and started jabbering in outraged Cantonese. He eventually switched to English, 'Out, out of my store! Under no circumstances will I even consider such ludicrous terms.' Poone had advanced from behind the counter and was standing in the shop proper, gesturing with an angry shaking finger pointing towards the door. 'I will never consider taking on a partner. Out! And tell your Mr Franks, if that's his real name, not to bother trying again. Now, out I said!'

Bogatin hadn't moved from his spot beside the counter. He had one hand placed on its wooden top, resting beside his now partially opened handgrip. He watched and waited for the Asian to stop his ranting.

Eventually, yet still exasperated, Poone fell silent, his black eyes shone like glistening specks of coal, betraying the darker well-hidden side of his life. This would be a man to watch Bogatin decided. He selected his next words carefully.

'Mr Poone, a number of the other traders have already seen fit to include Mr Franks as a partner, he feels it –'

'Never,' Poone cut in, 'Now out!'

Bogatin sighed heavily, 'That is, I'm afraid, what my employer thought you would say.'

In one swift movement, that betrayed his size, he had scooped out a pistol hidden in the handgrip; a silenced 9mm Beretta, loaded with the safety catch flicked off. Poone staggered backwards as it was pointed at his face.

'I am sorry you do not approve of Mr Frank's terms.'

There was muted *cough,* Poone's head whiplashed back at the pistol's shot. He was violently thrown backwards against the shelves at his rear, covered with a cascade of cardboard boxes, to eventually sit slumped with his back up against the shelves. He had a neat red hole between the eyes and a snake of rich ruby-red blood trickling down his nose; it splashed in cushioned silence onto his brilliant white shirt. Tat Hing Trading had just lost its owner. Mr Poone was very dead.

Showing no emotion and retrieving his handgrip Bogatin walked to the now lifeless man. *One less competitor for Donovan,* he thought.

Kneeling down on one knee beside him, he first placed the silenced Beretta back in the hand-grip, then, in keeping with an ancient Russian custom, used his index finger to gouge out both of Poone's blank lifeless eyes. Dropping them on the wooden floor he stood and crushed them under foot. It was a ritual he performed after each assassination. Since ancient times it had been believed that a murder's image would be recorded in his victim's eyes.

Rubbing his bloodied finger on a silk handkerchief, he stepped out of the store back onto Cameron Road. The handkerchief and the hand-grip would be disposed of later. Walking back to Nathan Street, he congratulated himself on a job well done; it would have been disappointing if Poone had agreed to Donovan's terms.

It was now back to the Kai Tak Airport to catch a flight on to Teipei, in Taiwan. He still had several more 'terms to negotiate'.

That would make Donovan's monopoly complete, he thought. *Yes, it's certainly good to be a part of the free world and out of Russia.*

He hailed a taxi.

CHAPTER 21

Antarctica

BLOW AFTER POUNDING blow smashed into her face and body, and only by using her grim determination was she able to plough through the brutal onslaught. Her face felt numb and swollen, she was chilled to the bone and as she struggled to lift her head she couldn't see a thing. It wasn't blackness that had closed in around her; before her eyes was a solid impregnable wall of white.

She had never experienced violence like it; putting her head down again she trudged forward while the howling, bitterly-cold blizzard continued its savage assault. Never before had she heard anything so terrifying. The howling hurricane-force wind had taken on a life of its own. Just when she thought the violence had reached its peak, unbelievably the katabatic wind seemed to grow in intensity. Its insistent whistling grew louder as its biting cold lanced deeper right through into the core of her bones.

Now she began to panic. Although she knew she had only been outside for less than a minute, it felt like an eternity, despite the short distance she had chosen to travel. Somehow, this vortex of swirling white had made her lose her way. As another brutal blast of horizontal wind-driven snow and ice flung into her face, she decided she would soon have to turn around. 'Five more paces,' she told herself.

Leaning into the raging storm she had only counted off three of them in her mind when thankfully, she crashed headlong into a solid man-made wall. Even though her forehead had hit with a resounding *thud*, she nearly cried out with joy.

Groping her way along the building she soon worked out where she was – outside the Scott Base mess building. Overcome with relief she soon found the nearby entrance and stumbled inside. Once out of the lashing wind she slumped back against the nearest wall and laughed out loud; a throaty, delighted cry of pure joy.

'Hell, what an experience.' She laughed through even white teeth. It was an experience she would be sure not to repeat.

Her name was Anna Hagan, Doctor Anna Hagan, she was a scientist involved with a joint venture project between the WWF and the United States National Science Foundation. She was employed by the WWF and had lived for the last four months at the Foundation's McMurdo Base, in Antarctica's McMurdo Sounds.

Anna had a doctorate in zoology and specialised in mammal adaptations. Using this expertise she was coming to the end of a southern hemisphere's summer, spent in biological study, down on the Antarctic ice.

Only after Anna had taken off her goggles and pulled back her thick felt-lined hood was it obvious she was a woman. The high-tech cocoon of clothes she wore didn't exactly flatter her shapely figure beneath. As she stood like a stuffed dummy, with her padded arms angling outwards at her sides, she nearly laughed out loud again. Her earlier fear had rebounded as elation, and for the first time in her life she had experienced the thrill of meeting and overcoming mortal danger.

She was thirty-one years of age, of average height with long straight raven hair; she had a finely featured face, highlighted by high cheekbones and a clear olive complexion. Anna had dark brown eyes and a series of faint wrinkles from hours of concentration lining her forehead; these helped give her an intelligent type of poise which added to her natural beauty. To the outside world, having being born in southern California, Anna was a typically confident, naturally fit, carefree American girl, which was only tempered at times by a quiet type of self-disciplined independence.

Her olive complexion and agreeable features were due to her father's side of the family. She was part Mohave Indian, a branch of her heritage she was aware of but not drawn to. She had two loves: her father, a special agent with the FBI in Los Angeles who raised her and her work. She was dedicated to a profession she was exceptionally knowledgeable about and found extremely fascinating, and if unnecessarily hindered she showed a feisty disposition, courtesy of her Indian blood.

Although it was her fine beauty that first attracted people to her, it was her temperament that finally won them over. Being relaxed, carefree and exuding a quiet self-confidence she was easily able to put most people at ease. Anna was the type of person that took people as they came. Back in California she had a large circle of friends, due to her likable personality, but her independence never allowed people to get too close. Often in the past she'd had proposals of marriage, but so far had never found anyone she felt truly comfortable with and who was willing to allow her to put her career first.

As her elated buzz slowly drifted away her mind was drawn to her circle of friends. *If only they could see me now*, she thought, looking down at her shapeless form.

Since she had been down on the ice it had taken her an age to get properly dressed each time before venturing out into the Antarctic cold. First, there was her full-length thermal underwear, then her two pairs of trousers, not forgetting to mention her Mukluks – cold weather boots. On her upper body she piled on numerous woollen shirts and sweaters before covering them with a down-filled vest and parka while also wearing heavily padded gloves. To top it off, for days like today, she was ready for whatever the Antarctic could throw at her wrapped up in her heavily lined and hooded outer-jacket. 'Yes, a far cry from the string bikinis on Newport Beach,' she decided, 'but no way is this Californian girl going to get cold.'

'G'day Anna, what are you doing over here?' A voice carried to her from just beyond the entranceway. 'MacTown too busy for ya, after some good old Kiwi hospitality?'

'Stewie, me old mate,' she tried to twang in a New Zealand accent, 'Just wandered over to Scott Base to see what me old Kiwi cobbers were up to, so we could have a yarn.'

As he walked up to stand in front of her he grimaced at her woeful attempt at New Zealand colloquialisms. He was one of Scott Base and New Zealand's resident scientists, but he looked more like your average Kiwi sheep farmer; six foot, well built with a ruddy complexion while wearing a brown home-spun woollen jersey.

'I think, Anna, you should concentrate on what you're good at, being the Californian babe. You didn't come over in that, did you?' He asked full of concern, flicking his head towards the howling blizzard outside. Although the American and New Zealand bases were virtually side-by-side, nobody in their right mind should have ventured out in weather like that; visibility was down to zero and with the wind chill factor, the temperature had plummeted to 56°C below.

'Not likely, buddy,' she switched back to her normal voice, 'I've been here since early this morning before the blizzard struck. I had some stuff to drop off at the museum.'

'Oh, and you only walked in from over there, and I suppose that's all right then, is it?' Stewie asked with heavy sarcasm. 'It's a wonder you didn't lose your way.'

'Oh, stop being such an old prude. For that you can buy me a cup of coffee,' Anna rounded on him as she lightly dismissed his concern, but she was well aware of the risk she had taken. On her way from the museum she had actually walked between two sleeping quarters which were side by side, B Hut and the Swamp, and missed them completely. Any further off course and she'd still be out there, wandering helplessly around in the raging blizzard. It wasn't in her temperament to worry so she dismissed the thought, part of her philosophy of life was if it happens, it happens and if it doesn't, why worry?

After peeling off several layers of clothing she hooked her arm around Stewie's elbow and while cheerfully chatting away, walked with him down the corridor to the mess.

All the faces in the mess lit up when they recognised her. She may have been a Yank but the New Zealanders had adopted her as one of their own. She was everyone's favourite.

'G'day, Anna. Ya dumped that scoundrel John Summers yet? You need a decent man,' somebody called from a corner table as she entered the mess. 'Look, we took a vote on it after your last visit, it was unanimous. You need a good Kiwi bloke.'

'Hello, Bruce, but I'm after a real man, not a Kiwi that scratches around for a living, lives in the dark and when he eventually finds a mate takes her out and only eats, roots, shoots and leaves,' she responded, which immediately brought a howl of laughter.

She enjoyed it amongst the Kiwis; most of them were a lot of fun and pretty well down to earth. It was one of the reasons she spent quite a bit of time at their base. The other reason was that they were far enough away and of a different enough culture for her to keep her distance.

'How are the seals today?' someone asked.

'Tucked up under the ice, if they've got any sense.'

'Not venturing out with your box of tricks today then?' came another voice.

'Ah, not today, no,' she confirmed.

Anna was one of the American scientists involved with a research project that studied the adaptations of a self-contained population of Weddell seals around White Island in McMurdo Sounds. It was the isolation of the White Island Weddells, due to the twenty kilometres of McMurdo Ice Shelf which prevented them from reaching the open sea that really interested Anna. Mammal adaptations and genetic viability were her main fields of interest and expertise.

She was there to find out if the colony could effectively survive with no ill effects without the introduction of new bloodlines. From her research Anna hoped to discover how, if at all, an isolated group of mammals, effectively surviving on a limited gene pool, could prosper. She knew this type of information would be vital for the earth's animal population in the years to come. As the human population grew and the world's wildlife shrunk and were forced into smaller and more isolated pockets, could they adapt and survive, and if they could, what had to be done to help them?

The diminishing population of the world's animals was bad enough, but to have those isolated groups dying because of weakened gene pools; that was too much to bear. Anna hoped her research would help them to not just survive but prosper.

'Anna, so you're here.' Lester Forrester, one of the army signalmen who operated the bases' radio, declared as he walked into the mess. 'I've only just come from the Command Centre. That so-called casual acquaintance of yours you keep telling us about, John Summers over at McMurdo, has been pulling his hair out trying to find you. He wants you back.'

The mess erupted with a barrage of catcalls and some undisguised comments of envy. Her relationship with John, another scientist, may have been a casual one but one, strangely, most single males at McMurdo and Scott Base took an intense interest in.

Anna tried to ignore them as she replied, 'In this weather? I could be stuck here for days. He'll have to wait.' More cat-calls followed as Anna could feel her face flush, wishing she had used a better choice of words.

'Well, it must be urgent,' the man responded, scratching his head while looking down at a hand-written note. 'He said if you were here to put you in one of the all-terrain Hagglunds and bring you straight over. He sounded pretty anxious.'

'I'll bet he did,' Anna tried to say lightly, but the comment held no conviction. She was worried; it didn't sound like John at all. One of the reasons she had been attracted to him was because of his carefree and relaxed attitude to life, the other reason was that the relationship was non-threatening and she knew it wouldn't last.

CHAPTER 22

IT HAD BEEN a rough – and at times terrifying – trip from Scott Base to McMurdo in the fully enclosed Hagglund. Buffeted violently by the raging blizzard Anna was certain at times they weren't going to make it. Yet by the time she got to the American base she was even more worried; the trip wouldn't have been made if it wasn't important.

Anna found John in the base library. He was alone and on a day like today when there was little to do outside, that was most peculiar.

'What is it, John?' she asked anxiously, standing like a stuffed over-sized rag doll in front of him. She had hurried in when she knew where to find him and hadn't bothered to take off any of her many layers of clothes.

John was a tall handsome man with blond Scandinavian features; however, his normally restful bearing was betrayed by a haunted, sorrowful look in his pale-blue eyes. *God, why me?* he thought despondently. He took a deep breath and placed both his hands on her shoulders. 'I'm sorry, Anna. It's your father. He's been shot.'

Tears immediately welled up in Anna's eyes as a hand flew up to her mouth in shock. 'No, not Pop. What happened? Is he –?'

'I'm afraid so, yes. He died in intensive care at Los Angeles County Hospital this morning. I'm sorry, Anna.' He gently took her into his arms.

It took another five days for the blizzard to finally blow itself out. During that time Anna had sat quietly in her own room, accompanied only by her grief. It had been planned she would winter-over on the ice but instead was now on the last summer flight out of McMurdo, on her way back to the States to settle her father's affairs.

It was a brilliantly sunny day overhead and the only clouds adorning the Antarctic's pale-blue sky were painted lavish shades of glowing oranges and peach. The temperature had risen to a warm minus eight degrees and only a low rolling mist, a few feet off the ground, reminded those that cared to notice of the previous days blizzard. After the wind's constant howling, a tuneless silence seemed to now ring insistently within Anna's ears.

Several minutes before she had entered the open cargo hold of a US Army

C-141 Starlifter, she was now slumped dejectedly into one of the blue nylon sling-seats that ran the length of both sides of the hold. She was waiting for the big jet aircraft to take off and begin its five and a half-hour journey to the Operation Deep Freeze base located at Christchurch International Airport, in New Zealand. From there she would catch a commercial flight straight through to Los Angeles' LAX.

'You all right?' came a concerned, distant voice.

'Sorry, what? Oh, yes John,' Anna answered automatically, before adding honestly, 'Well, no. I feel bloody awful.'

She couldn't believe it, her father dead and what's more gunned down in cold blood, Who could do such a thing? She had looked on him as being immortal. He had always been there for her, ever since her parents had separated when she was a little girl. It was his belief and constant encouragement that had allowed her to follow her heart and pursue her dreams. He had been her rock, her source of inspiration that had allowed her to succeed where others had failed; it was his philosophy of life she had adopted as her own. Now that security blanket and well of inspiration had gone. 'No John,' she repeated, 'I'm not.'

He didn't really know what to say; grief wasn't something he handled well. 'I'll still be here next summer,' he declared, trying to reassure her.

'Thanks, I'll look forward to it,' she replied, but with little conviction. She knew the WWF wouldn't be sending her back; the research here was too valuable for her position to remain vacant throughout the winter.

Standing in front of her, John eventually gave her an awkward farewell. As he walked from the plane he was sorry to see her go. Theirs had been an uncomplicated yet rewarding relationship. However, he was pleased all the same she would be taking her sadness away.

As the cargo door of the Starlifter was closed and locked into place, Anna's mind wandered for the first time from her father to the continent she had grown to love. She viewed it as the last true wilderness of the world and the earth's cleanest continent; she had experienced it as one that was uniquely rich in wildlife, harsh in weather, yet extremely fragile all the same.

Where on earth was she going to find another place like this? she wondered. The isolated colony of Weddell seals at White Island had been unique. Maybe in a few years the position would become vacant again? *Fat chance.* However, as the exploitation of the Antarctic's minerals slowly moved closer, setting in motion an irreversible process of untold consequences, she wondered if she actually wanted to return.

As the Starlifter began to roll down McMurdo's ice-runway she realised she would rather remember Antarctica for what it was now; the last true untamed wilderness on earth.

CHAPTER 23

Los Angeles

ANNA COULDN'T PREVENT the tears from streaming down her face; in fact, she made no attempt to stop them. She was standing in front of a black marble headstone in Hollywood Memorial Park Cemetery, the white writing etched upon it read:

MITCHELL J. HAGAN.
Died in the Line of Duty

It was her father's grave. It had been bad enough that he was murdered, but not being able to attend his funeral had been like rubbing salt into the wound. She had been here for the last twenty minutes trying to pay her final respects, but she couldn't stop thinking, 'Why, Pop? Who on earth would do it? You were always such an honest man.'

Richard Black felt terrible, he always did when one of his agents died, 'What was it?' he asked himself. 'A month since I sent the fax on Donovan?' Although he had only spoken to Mitch once since then, to confirm he had received the fax, he was left in no doubt that it was Donovan who'd had him killed. 'He must've gotten too close.'

Richard had his head down and was deep in thought as he walked up the cemetery's crushed gravel pathway, the groundsman had told him where he could find the federal agent's grave.

Over the past month he and Johnny had made little progress with their investigations. He had met with Sabina Donovan and for a first meeting it had gone remarkably well, yet no new information was forthcoming. A lot more work still had to be done on her, but he was sure once he had won her confidence, she would be the link that would finally bring her husband down. He was due to meet her again that evening.

Time to set the wheels in motion,' he decided, *Especially now.* The embittered thought of Mitch Hagan's unnecessary death was still fresh within his mind.

From memory, he again ran the official police report through his mind. It stated Mitch had been shot once between the eyes at close range, in an alley in downtown Los Angeles. It said there was no sign of a struggle, so it was suspected to be a professional hit. *He'd probably only just come from Donovan,* he thought bitterly. But the thing that really stuck in his mind about the murder was the subsequent mutilation; both his eyes had been gouged out and left squashed on the ground beside him. 'God, there's some deranged animals living in the world.'

As his mind flicked back to the present, Richard knew he couldn't be far away from the grave. He raised his head to gain his bearings and recognised Anna immediately. It was a requirement of Richard's to have a complete dossier on all the agents who worked for Network, whether they were full-time or not. She was facing him, looking down at her father's grave and had just finished wiping her eyes when she looked in his direction.

'Bugger,' he swore softly to himself; he had planned to be alone when he paid his last respects, not meeting anyone here, especially not Mitch's daughter. Realising he had been spotted and was too close to turn away, he walked the last few paces towards Anna and the grave. As he did, he realised the photograph of her he had seen hadn't done her justice; she had a natural type of elegance that the camera hadn't captured. Although she was dressed simply in jeans and a burgundy patterned shirt, these only enhanced her beauty.

'I hope I'm not intruding?' Richard asked as he came to stand in front of her. 'You must be Anna.' He stuck out his hand in greeting.

'Well, no. Not at all, I was just leaving. And yes I am,' she answered as she accepted the hand; however, even in her anguish she noticed he hadn't offered her a name. 'And you are?'

He had done it on purpose; he had no desire to tell her who he was. 'The best form of deceit,' he had schooled his agents, 'is to lie by omission.' However, not that he was a religious man, but openly lying in a graveyard? *What's the harm; in her state she'll never remember my name,* he thought. 'Richard. Richard Black. I was a friend of your father's.'

'Don't recall the name and Pop was very particular about his friends.'

'We go a long way back,' he said before trying to throw her off by adding, 'My condolences, I'm terribly sorry.'

'Yes, so am I.' But she wasn't going to let him off the hook that easily. 'Your accent, where are you from?'

'South Africa.' In Richard's book, a half lie in a cemetery was acceptable.

'Hmm, and Richard Black you say. My father seems to have a past I don't know about.' She looked down at her watch, 'I'm sorry Richard, I have an appointment with my father's lawyer. Thank you for the sentiment and the gesture,' she pointed at the flowers he carried in his hand and with a slight inclination of her head she turned and walked away. Yet as she strode down the gravel pathway she was puzzled. Her father and she had always been close, and she had never heard him mention a Richard Black before.

Richard wished he hadn't approached her at all, but felt there was little reason for concern. *Why would our paths cross again?* He dismissed the thought. His direction lay with plans for the exposé of Donovan. *And Mitch's daughter's, who knows?* Yes, he was positive their paths would never cross again.

Richard Black. It was that man's name again. That was twice she had seen it now, once in her father's black personal diary and now on this fax dated 18th January this year.

After leaving the cemetery Anna had spoken with her father's lawyer and instructed him to sell the old Santa Monica family home, lock, stock and barrel, then to wind up the estate and distribute its assets. Her brother could have sorted out the arrangements but as he had grown up with her mother and they'd never been close, she didn't even bother checking to see if he had actually gone to the funeral.

After the lawyer's she visited the house, which had been particularly bad; wandering through the rooms the essence of her father had still been very much alive. He had been such a kind and compassionate man. He certainly didn't suit being a federal agent and it was only his fierce sense of justice that had kept him dedicated to the job. After packing up a number of boxes with his personal effects, she had locked the house, dropped the key at the realtor's and driven home.

When Anna was at home she shared an apartment with an old roommate from her UCLA days, it was on the second floor and in a complex called Bay Court Apartment on Bay Street in Costa Mesa, about forty-five miles south of downtown Los Angeles. She was now sitting in the middle of her living room, in front of an old comfortable couch and coffee table, with all manner of her father's memorabilia spread around her.

'Richard Black,' she repeated comparing his open black diary to the facsimile she held in her hand. She had never known her father to keep a personal diary; normally he used the Bureau's official issue. Although she had looked at it she thought it had been strange when she had found it and the fax tucked behind the breadbox in the kitchen, where he kept his passport and other important papers. 'And who the hell is Donovan?'

The fax, which was the first and only remaining page of five, had asked her father to make initial investigations into a Judd Donovan of Donovan Enterprises. From what Anna could fathom he appeared to be involved with some type of money laundering. *Right up Pop's alley.*

Scrawled across the top of the fax in her father's print was *Richard Black, 18th Jan 93*. Under the corresponding date in the diary was again his name followed by a month's worth of what looked like incoherent entries. They must've been written in some type of code, for no matter how she viewed them, she couldn't make head nor tail of them.

After puzzling over them for several more minutes she came to a decision, 'Right, Richard Black and Judd Donovan, let's see who you really are.'

Since the WWF had given her a couple of weeks off, while trying to organise another position for her, she didn't exactly have a lot to do. 'Pop has taught me enough about criminal fraud. Tomorrow I'll start.'

And so, in walked Anna, right in up over her head.

CHAPTER 24

RICHARD HAD TO concede Sabina Donovan was one of the most attractive women he had ever met, and possibly the most intriguing. Compared to what Richard assumed would have been her normal lavish evening wear, she had dressed down for their meeting, wearing beige drill trousers and a rusty-coloured shirt, beneath a dark green sweater. Eyeing her casual attire, Richard was thankful he didn't look out of place in his dress jeans, khaki button-down, and navy sports jacket. To those who noticed them, together they looked a well-matched couple.

They were sitting at a secluded corner table in Alice's restaurant on the pier at Malibu, on Los Angeles' Pacific Coast Highway. Sabina probably would have preferred eating at Chasen's, the Ivy or even the Citrus, some of the more exclusive southern Californian restaurants and some of her more regular haunts. However, tonight she had no desire to be seen frequenting any of her normal eating places, especially ones her husband and his many cronies habituated. Alice's would do fine.

Until this meeting Richard had questioned why she would jeopardise her luxurious lifestyle, by helping to expose her husband. He had mistakenly believed his ruination would also cause the destruction of the life she had become accustomed to. How wrong he had been.

'So all your family's old company shares are held in trust you say, and in your name,' he stated, clarifying her earlier explanation. 'Interesting. So correct me if I'm wrong, if your husband is exposed and has to forfeit his power of attorney over the trust, you stand to acquire a substantial controlling chunk in Donovan Enterprises?' Sabina nodded demurely. That was confirmation enough. 'I'd say you have rather a lot to gain.'

'More than you possibly realise. Richard, what you must understand is I came from a conservative Italian background where my marriage was arranged. I've lived for the last ten years in a marriage of convenience, a marriage my husband has merely viewed as a useful business arrangement, one that he probably loathes yet jealously guards all the same.' She let out a heavy dejected breath. 'Because of the power and influence he has, and not just in LA, it has become virtually impossible for me to nurture any kind of relationship outside the marriage and I don't think you, or anyone for that matter, can know how frustrating that can be.'

Richard nodded sympathetically as he noticed her eyes had begun to moisten. Here was a woman who probably had it all except the one thing she hungered for – love. No wonder she carried an occasional pout.

Like a chameleon changing its colour, she shifted her desires. Though her face never altered, her eyes took on a determined cast. She lifted her head and declared, 'You see, Richard, by helping you to expose my husband I may gain my freedom, but I also look upon it as a business proposition. A potentially profitable speculation you might say. I will virtually inherit the company.'

Although he felt sorry for her, after that comment Richard had trouble concealing his jubilation. Revengeful and a profiteer. Two of the finest qualities useful when controlling an informant. However, he recognised that although they had struck up an amiable rapport, for some reason she had still been hedging.

Sabina had chosen the pasta, while Richard stuck with the seafood and salad. As they ate and talked he was amazed at how she was able to eat the sauce-filled dish with such grace and poise. And as for her figure? He was having enough trouble concentrating each time he looked at her remarkably attractive face. If it weren't for her occasional pout, she'd be stunning beyond words.

'Tell me, Richard, who are you actually with? You say you're not with any of your government's security services, yet it's obvious you must have huge resources to draw from, especially if you're able to do what you claim you can.'

It had been a risk giving her his name, but as she was such an important contact it was a risk worth taking. The last thing he wanted was for her to be suspicious. But telling her about Network was another matter. 'Put it this way,' he began, 'I'm attached to the British SIS, but not part of it. Wheels within wheels you might say. As you originally chose to keep your identity a secret, I'd rather do the same.'

'Ah, but within a week you'd already found out who I was,' she countered.

'Within the day actually. But surely, doesn't that prove to you the effectiveness of my organisation?'

'Admittedly I was shocked when I realised I'd been found out, but after our first meeting it was one attribute, amongst many I might add, that impressed me about you – and your organisation, of course,' she quickly added. To emphasise her not so subtle come on, she placed her fork beside her plate and laid a hand on his sleeve. She was flirting, but he was a handsome man and the secrecy surrounding him added to his appeal.

Due to her sheltered upbringing it was probably the first time in her life she had experienced true excitement. Sabina felt like an excited schoolgirl playing truant. However, as a fully grown woman with the allure of possible freedom from her husband, and the tantalising mystery of events to come, this man in front of her was doing the strangest of things to her body.

As with the other advances Sabina had dropped throughout the evening, Richard pretended not to notice. He hurriedly thought of something to say. 'The material we've received from you so far has been exceptional.'

'I know, as you have already told me.' She had withdrawn her hand and reached for her wineglass, and was now watching him over its rim.

Oh God! Richard's normally cool mind began to race. *This isn't how it's supposed to work*, he thought. 'Maybe I should've gotten somebody else to deal directly with her.' Yet he dismissed that thought. The operation was far too important and she was too vital a contact to have somebody else in control. *Fraternise but don't flirt*, he reminded himself.

'From the printouts did you realise what your husband was dealing in? It's probably not what you think.' It was the next thing that came to mind and thankfully it had the desired effect; it interested Sabina.

Putting her glass down, she slightly cocked her head to the side in interest. 'I wondered, but I just presumed it was drugs. Isn't it?'

'Couldn't be further from the truth. It's ivory.'

Sabina shook her head as realisation dawned. 'Now that's something I should've guessed. Ivory – Judd and his collection. He has always been obsessed with the stuff. He even has a specially guarded room at the villa he calls the "ivory room" did you know that?' She didn't wait for a response but again shook her head, this time in pity. 'Those poor elephants. If he hasn't already, with the way he operates he'll have organised an operation so polished they'll be dying in their thousands.'

'Hmm, I believe he has, or at least is starting to, with the amounts of money changing hands.' For some reason Richard decided to reveal the true reason for his interest in the case. It may have been her earlier honesty, he couldn't rightfully say. 'I was born in Africa, so you see, Sabina this may be personal to you, but it's personal for me as well. I'll do my duty to stop your husband's laundering, but I'm not prepared to stand by and let him destroy a part of my heritage.'

It was as if Richard had sworn undying love. This was obviously more than

Sabina had hoped for, having him personally involved. She didn't hesitate in offering him the commitment of support he had been trying for. 'Tell me what it is you want me to do.'

Inwardly, he breathed a sigh of relief. Although he'd instructed his agents to do what was necessary to solicit help and gather information, he didn't know if his ego could handle trying, and possibly failing, to cajole a woman like her by using more than mere words.

'What do I want you to do?' he said to mask his relief. 'Much of the same really. I need a lot more information. We know what your husband is doing and how he's laundering the money, but we're unable to prove it. I need you to fill in the middle ground, the gaps. I'll take whatever you can give me.'

'And who will be – I don't know, running me. Is that the right word?' This secret agent stuff sounded so exciting.

'Ah, not quite, Sabina, I'll be your controller if that's what you mean?'

'That's exactly what I wanted to hear.' She leant forward as her eyes lit up. 'How often will we meet?'

Oh God, he inwardly groaned, *Here we go again. As little as possible if I'm going to have to fence like this with you,'* he thought uneasily. He felt like screaming, *What about my poor ego?* but instead he said, 'As often as necessary.'

'Good, I think we're both going to get what we want.' Sabina placed her hand on Richard's sleeve again.

Trying to ignore it, Richard declared, 'So we're agreed then. All that remains is to formalise the arrangements.'

'And the agreement, of course,' Sabina added, squeezing his arm. She knew she was in the driving seat, her whole bearing clearly stated it. 'And it'll be more than a handshake I'm after.'

Richard was stunned, he had been backed into a corner, and this wasn't the way it was meant to be at all. *I'm supposed to be controlling you!* he wanted to scream. He was getting too old for this. Even though he knew exactly what she had implied, he felt his mouth go dry as he queried, 'What exactly do you mean, Sabina?'

'Put it this way Richard, I find you attractive and a man finally beyond the influence of my husband. I have ten years to make up for, so what hotel are you staying at?'

Richard swallowed heavily. 'The Bel Air.' He couldn't help himself, he was staring, fascinated by her lips.

'Ah, truly the most romantic hotel in Los Angeles.' It wasn't a statement or even an invitation, Richard read it as a request.

I'm shocked! This is bribery! he tried to convince himself, but instead his mind teetered on the edge of indecision.

'Well?' Sabina quietly asked. A waiter had materialised and was standing with the bill beside their table.

'Come on Richard, it's lust, sex is all she's after,' his conscience yelled at him, 'What about the elephants?'

'Yeah, what about the elephants?' whispered another voice, 'And too bloody right it's lust.'

'Ah, what the hell,' Richard said, he didn't bother checking the bill; he peeled off three one hundred dollar bills and gave them to the waiter. As he rose from the table he looked at Sabina and commented, 'I noticed you arrived in your own car. A Porsche wasn't it?'

'Yes it was,' she replied with a satisfied grin as they walked out of the restaurant, arm in arm. And as they stepped into the mild evening air Richard's mind was, understandably, on anything but checking for surveillance.

'I must say this secret agent stuff is rather more than just exciting, that was wonderful.' Sabina declared. She was lying naked on top of the huge king-sized bed in Richard's suite; he was lying beside her in a similar state of undress. 'Marvellous,' she purred as she reached her arms over her head and stretched like a cat.

'That is quite an understatement, my dear lady,' Richard declared as his eyes roved over her body.

She was indeed beautiful. Her brownish-black hair was tossed to one side as her head rested leisurely on one of the bed's many pillows, and her eyes were closed as the memory of their sensuous love-making gave her already handsome face a tranquil, contented look. As she lay quietly, the mounds of her well-formed rose-tipped breasts rose and fell with her every satisfied breath. He also noticed how the darkened even shade of her skin contrasted starkly with the bed's white satin sheets, showing off every line and curve of her sculptured body.

He allowed his eyes to wander further down her tantalising form, over her concave stomach, to briefly rest on her silken triangular mound of pubic hair. He sighed contentedly. It had been better than anything he had previously experienced.

As he took in her long shapely legs, and noticed where the wetness from their lovemaking had dampened her inner thighs, he wondered what she saw in him. Compared to hers, his body was overweight, and if he wasn't careful would soon be running to seed, but strangely he had felt no embarrassment. In spite of the circumstances it had seemed like the most natural thing in the world to do; he vowed to get back in shape, that was all. However, he quickly lost the thought as he felt Sabina's hand idly play with his soft, slightly moist member.

'Did I tell you he goes to Africa once a year? He's actually due to leave in a month or so.'

'Who?' Richard asked, having difficulty concentrating. His mind was firmly focused on her hand. He could feel himself beginning to harden.

'My husband, I always wondered why. He must go to view his poaching operation. What do you think?'

'Hmm, could do. I'll try and remember that. I fly down there tomorrow. But for now, concentrate on what you're doing will you?'

Thoughts of Africa, Donovan and the elephants were forgotten as Richard reached over and drew Sabina on top of him.

CHAPTER 25

Zimbabwe

IT WAS GOING to be another scorcher; it was only ten o'clock in the morning and already Africa's blazing summer sun had turned the distant horizon into a shimmering mass of distorted shapes and colours. Tony Campbell was sitting on a large *kopje* just below its summit while in front of him, rolling towards the horizon, was an undulating plain of stalky yellow summer grass, interspersed with dull green trees and grey thorny shrubs. He sat with his back slumped up against a large granite boulder, hidden from view amongst shadows cast by an over-hanging acacia bush with his elbows resting on his knees and a pair of binoculars pressed to his eyes.

Ignoring the sweeping vista the yellow plain presented, he instead relentlessly scanned the immediate foreground. Intent in his search, he never saw or heard the black gnome-like figure sneak up noiselessly to his side. A hand reached out and grabbed his unsuspecting shoulder.

'Hey!' Ben harshly whispered as he shook the shoulder. Tony, taken totally unaware, nearly jumped a foot in the air with fright.

'Oh, you little bastard!' he breathed self-consciously once he recognised Ben, while holding a hand above his pounding heart. 'Don't ever do that to me again. You scared the living daylights out of me.'

'Yes, Tony,' the Matabele replied with a deadpan face. But his sparkling eyes exposed the lie; Tony knew he would be sneaking up on him at the next opportunity.

Although Tony was probably the best European he had ever met at all forms of tracking and hunting, Ben knew he would let down his guard all too often. It became Ben's self-designated job to keep him on his toes, especially now with their current occupation. For the last thirty months, since leaving Operation Stronghold, Tony and Ben had been active with their new anti-poaching position sponsored by the WWF, and needless to say, they'd made numerous enemies along the way.

For the first few months pretty much all they did was gather information and acquaint themselves with the many game parks and their wardens scattered across eastern and southern Africa. They had targeted Kenya and Tanzania in the east, and Botswana and Zimbabwe in the south; the other countries were either out of their jurisdiction or over-poached and beyond their help.

Although it was a massive area to cover, Tony being already well-known amongst these countries' wildlife conservationists had made their job far easier. Yet it became abundantly clear right from the start that they would have to specialise; they were simply unable to cover the whole spectrum of wildlife poaching in these areas. So they decided to target the illegal ivory trade. Once the decision was made they encountered another problem. Because of the sheer enormity of the task, they were unable to become involved with the day to day protection of the elephants and the tracking and apprehending of their many poachers. This they had to leave to the countries' game wardens and in some cases their armies.

However, they did involve themselves in the bigger tracking operations. but only in the context of their determined role; gathering information, identifying and then exposing the larger networks of poachers, middlemen and traffickers that controlled the illicit trade. By concentrating in this particular way they had already been instrumental in uncovering numerous poaching rackets. One of their biggest coups had been executed within the first six months of operation, in Tanzania.

Just as the two men had defined their area of specialisation so they did with their individual roles. It was decided Tony would take the head-on approach while Ben would sift for information in the background. Because most attention was focused on Tony and his forthright demanding style, Ben usually went unnoticed, and it was from him most of their information was learned.

Purely for business reasons, of course, Ben had taken to frequenting the odd bar in the Tanzanian capital of Dar-es-Salaam. 'A terrible job,' he would declare, 'But one that's got to be done.' With a wry smile tugging at his lips he'd then walk into the city's evening air, leaving a disgruntled Tony grumbling away while he updated the operation's books.

On one particular night in the street level patio bar of the New Africa Hotel on Makataba Street in the city centre, after bestowing a number of drinks upon certain likely looking locals, Ben was able to eventually manoeuvre the conversation on to ivory. Now experiencing a particularly lucid period later that evening, he clearly remembered the words 'ambassador', 'Indonesia' and 'container'. The next day, ashen-faced with a head throbbing like hell, he passed the information onto Tony.

As it turned out the Indonesian ambassador, Joesoef Hussein, was about to complete the most lucrative posting of his career. That was until Tony, with a very sick Ben in tow, and the Dar-es-Salaam police seized one hundred and eighty-four tusks hidden in a container of household belongings being shipped to his home in Jakarta. Upon further investigation, much to Tony's disgust, it transpired that the ambassador had installed a fully equipped carving factory in his official residence. But as the ambassador's partner was a high ranking Tanzanian official and above the country's law, Tony was unable to trace the many tons of poached ivory they'd smuggled from the country; every witness he interviewed was too scared to talk. However, the most bitter of pills that Tony had to swallow was when the ambassador was let off scot-free, and by claiming diplomatic immunity was allowed to leave the country unscathed. Although no arrests were made, there was at least the satisfaction that a huge poaching racket had been destroyed.

They had also in their first year of operation, using similar methods, uncovered another far larger and more devastating poaching ring operating this time in Kenya. The network had employed the most ruthless and deadliest of all east African poachers, the southern Somali *shiftas*; heavily armed bush-wise veterans of many brutal cross-border and tribal conflicts. For years, as Tony and Ben discovered to their horror, they had been systematically destroying entire elephant populations supposedly protected within Kenya's national parks, game reserves and wildlife sanctuaries.

Picking midday when the Kenyan heat and silence was most oppressive the *shiftas* would sneak up to within yards of their peacefully drowsing prey and then the carnage would begin. Shattering the African stillness with a deafening rattle of automatic fire they would wipe out the elephants in one cruel, agonising blow; not even the calves were spared. Hardly allowing the silence to re-settle a just as merciless noise would start up to ring out across the wilds. With chainsaws whining the *shiftas* would hack into the elephants' faces so their tusks could be ripped from their skulls. Within minutes of the carnage, the poachers would shoulder the bloodstained tusks and melt back into the bush.

Once the *shiftas* had done their job the ivory was trucked in relays to the coast. When about seventy odd tons – tusks from approximately eight thousand slaughtered elephants – had been stockpiled, a dhow registered in the Kenyan port of Mombasa and owned by a Yemeni sheikh would be sailed and moored just offshore. The tusks would be ferried aboard by small fishing boats to begin their seven thousand mile journey first to Dubai in the United Arab Emirates, to be cut up and carved, before the last leg where it was distributed and sold as fashioned ivory trinkets across central and eastern Asia.

Because of the lawlessness allied to the racket, Tony, Ben and the game scouts they had recruited were forced to use just as brutal methods to break it apart. However, the difference was that Tony and his team were doing it by government decree. Taking care of the sheikh's dhow was easy enough once the caches of ivory had been discovered. As they were being ferried aboard, several RPG-16 rockets were launched. Blasted amidships, saw the dhow and its crew's seafaring days come violently to an end.

With the *shiftas* it was different.

The hardest and most soul-destroying part was that the *shiftas* not only had to be caught in the act but left to their gruesome work. Tony and Ben needed a trail that led back to Somalia and it wasn't until after months of painstaking watching, waiting and listening that they eventually obtained the information they needed.

It was here they employed the same techniques they'd used with the same callous indifference during Zimbabwe's war of independence. Using their hot-pursuit methods they tracked the *shiftas* back into Somalia, then ruthlessly hunted and tracked them down. It was barbaric but brutally effective, and with every poaching gang of *shiftas* they culled the message spread quickly across southern Somalia, *Poach in Kenya and suffer the consequences.* Needless to say, it may not have stopped all the Somali poachers, but it diminished their activities.

Using unconventional methods like these which became their trademark, Tony and Ben had helped give the East African elephants a much-needed reprieve. So with this partial success, it was then time to focus further south. As yet they hadn't been able to crack any major poaching rackets in the south; it was sit, observe and wait, although by working in accord with the likes of Zimbabwe's National Parks and Forestry Commission they had experienced limited success, helping to apprehend a number of small operations and individual poachers.

One advantage they did experience in Zimbabwe over and above the other countries they operated in was the government placing at their disposal a crack unit of army scouts led by a young captain, Abel Sithole. Although Tony hadn't yet had to use the captain and his men, he felt it was reassuring to have hardened soldiers of such calibre in reserve if the need arose. Tony had found Captain Sithole to be most helpful whenever he and Ben were active within the country, not only with his resources but also with the supply of information. In fact, because of the apparent dedication the Captain had shown towards wildlife preservation, it was in him that Tony had eventually confided regarding his suspicions of a possible poaching and assassination squad operating from within the Zimbabwean army. The Captain had appeared both distressed and shocked at Tony's revelations and seemed to have taken the allegations seriously, but as yet neither he nor Tony had gained the slightest lead in the matter. It appeared that the captain was treating his government appointment of helping Tony and Ben with the utmost importance by undertaking several investigations of his own. This was one of the reasons why they had found themselves for the last three days and nights concealed on a rocky bush-studded *kopje* overlooking a small Zimbabwean village.

It was situated just over the northern boundary of the Hwange National Park, in the northwest of the country. Zimbabwe along with Botswana had approaching one fifth of the elephants still left in the African wilds, and because of this Tony had found the poaching in both countries had dramatically increased. Although he had no proof he knew there was a huge, well-concealed racket operating throughout both countries. From a tip-off, also confirmed by Captain Sithole from another source, they had learnt the village's headman allegedly recruited the racket's poachers. The tip-off indicated that during the coming week the headman was meeting with his employer, the racket's main middleman. This was why they had the village under surveillance; it was the break they had been waiting for. Once the middleman was identified and apprehended, the racket would fall apart.

'So, you skinny little bugger, what did you find out?' Tony asked as Ben slumped down beside him. He had been away since before daybreak scouting for in or out-going spoor around the village.

'Nothing, our man didn't turn up. Maybe it'll be today.'

'Yeah, maybe,' Tony said unconvinced. He was beginning to wonder if they had been led on a merry chase. Nobody had left or entered the village in the three days they had been perched above it. 'Here, take these.' He handed Ben the binoculars. 'As you nearly scared the life out of me, you can take the next two shifts. I need to rest and recover.'

Ben, mouthing numerous obscenities, retrieved the binoculars as Tony made a show of sliding down on his back while sighing contentedly. He placed his floppy canvas hat over his head and was soon fast asleep.

Tony didn't know how long he'd been asleep or what had woken him. Without moving a muscle he lay quietly intently listening while his eyes stared up at the dull light on the inside of his hat. He could feel Ben's presence beside him, and then as his friend sucked in an excited breath and restlessly shift position, he knew something had aroused his attention. Pulling the floppy hat off his head he quickly glanced at the sun and realised he had been asleep for less than half an hour. He looked over at Ben who, oblivious to all else, was intently sitting forward peering excitedly through the binoculars. He sucked in another slight breath while craning further forward.

'What is it? Has he come?' Tony demanded. This time it was Ben's turn to jump.

Puzzled, unable to remember the last time he had startled the little man, Tony sat up and reached for the binoculars. He never noticed the disconcerted look on Ben's face as he pressed them up to his eyes. Scanning the village he was initially unable to see what had attracted Ben's attention, there was virtually no movement down in the village at all, that was until he focused in on its vegetable garden.

The headman had obviously only just risen, in more ways than one. He was still naked when he walked from his hut and it was then he spotted one of his wives hoeing the vegetable patch. Having walked up behind her and lifted her dress he was now engaged in a vigorous act that proclaimed his virility to the world.

'You dirty bugger,' Tony declared still with the binoculars pressed to the eyes. The wife was still intent on her hoeing but had picked up the rhythm and was in the process of decimating a row of maize.

'Well, if you're so disgusted, give them back to me,' Ben replied, reaching for the binoculars.

'Piss off, ya pervert,' Tony, with the binoculars still pressed to his eyes, had to twist his head to the side while fending Ben off with his other hand. The headman's erratic movements had reached an unbelievable frenzy, while his wife's hoe was now frantically uprooting a row of millet.

The headman eventually reached his frantic climax to collapse exhausted in the dirt behind his wife, and she in turn, without breaking her stride, was finally able to bring her hoeing back under control, managing to concentrate on a truer line.

'Well I think they'll be buying in food this year,' Tony declared, still looking at the exhausted man surrounded by his uprooted garden.

'What, why what's happening?' Ben managed to grab the binoculars, but alas he saw it was too late.

'Come on, you horny rascal. Grab your stuff. We're leaving. It's been a setup,' Tony was already rising.

'What do you mean?'

'I mean, with that display down there our headman isn't expecting a visit. We've been setup,' he repeated bitterly. 'I want to get back to Main Camp at Hwange. Something's up. I can feel it. I'll drop in at the ranger's HQ then you'd better talk to your friend who gave us the info. My bet is somebody wanted us out of the way.'

'Three bloody days, wasted,' Ben heard Tony mutter as he followed him down the *kopje*.

CHAPTER 26

'WHY ARE WE going to Vic Falls? Shouldn't we be tracking the poachers that hit those elephants early yesterday morning?' Ben asked, mystified. Both men had just jumped in their Toyota Land Cruiser and were heading north out of Hwange National Park.

'Well, I'd like to, but a fax came through two days ago from the US office. We've been told to meet some chap up at the Falls,' Tony replied. It was obvious as he shifted through the gears that he was annoyed.

'Must be important. Who is he?'

'Wouldn't have a clue, and yeah, it better be.'

Tony hated being taken away from his job, especially now when a gang of poachers had wiped out just under a hundred elephants virtually from right beneath his nose.

Several hours earlier Ben had dropped him off at the ranger's headquarters at Hwange Main Camp and gone off on his own to find his informant, who by chance had conveniently disappeared. When he eventually got back to Tony after several hours of fruitless searching he found him in a quiet all-consuming rage. They had indeed been set up. Just over twenty-four hours earlier while they'd been watching the village, a small well-drilled gang of poachers had gone in and massacred several family groups of elephants deep within the heart of the national park, and like the Somali *shiftas* further north, with causal disregard, even the calves too small to carry ivory had been killed and left to rot beside their parents.

The poachers had hacked the adults' faces off with machetes, retrieved the ivory and whisked it off into the bush, but the worst thing was that the poachers had left a trail a blind man could follow; it was as if they knew they wouldn't be followed. Tony and Ben had originally set aside a whole week to watch the village and it was if the poachers knew they had all the time in the world. Yet as they'd cut their vigil short Tony felt sure they could've caught the gang – that was until he was handed a fax from the WWF's United States office in Washington. Giving no explanation it instructed them to drop whatever they were doing and meet a man who would contact them at the Victoria Falls Hotel.

Tony contemplated ignoring the fax, but as he'd had plenty of run-ins with the Swiss, Belgian and US offices in the past they had learnt not to waste his time. He hoped on this occasion they'd sent the fax because it was important.

'Jeez it bloody well better be,' Tony fumed. He forgot the thought, and still half concentrating on the road up ahead, turned to Ben. 'What about this chap who gave you the information? Anything?'

'No, he's gapped it. No one's seen hide nor hair of him since yesterday. And what about Captain Sithole? I noticed his army Land Rover sitting outside the office.'

'Apparently he's just come down from Harare, said he was hoping to question the middleman once we'd caught him,' he let out a bitter snort. 'Fat chance now.'

'What about *his* contact?' Ben asked with disdain, 'Remember, it was him who confirmed from another source the middleman would show.'

Ben hadn't liked nor trusted the captain from the first time they'd met, and had specifically asked Tony not to mention that he understood his language. 'There's something about the man,' Ben had said on several occasions.

However, his reaction hadn't unduly concerned Tony. He'd put it down to tribalism, a too common a problem across the continent; Ben was a Matabele and captain Sithole a Shona. Ever since the Matabele had broken away from Shaka's Zulu nation in the early nineteenth century and settled north of the Limpopo, they had looked on the menfolk of the less war-like Shona tribes as convenient sport and their woman as handy slaves. Tony had assumed that as the Matabele looked upon other tribes with open contempt, this was the reason for his friend's mistrust. It never occurred to question him further.

Tony had his eyes fixed on the road up ahead and it took him several seconds to answer Ben's question about the captain – he was still brooding about the slaughtered elephants. 'Oh, I dunno,' he eventually replied, 'I think he said he'd look into it.'

'Well I don't trust him, that's all. It's not the first time he and his goons have conveniently turned up just after a big poacher's strike.'

'Yes Ben,' Tony breathed out heavily as he flicked his eyebrows skyward. He'd heard it all before.

Both men fell into silence. There wasn't much more either of them could say, they'd been led a merry dance and until they got back from Victoria Falls there wasn't much either of them could do. As their Land Cruiser's heavily lugged tyres droned them monotonously forward, each became lost deep in thought; Tony with his butchered elephants and who they were to meet, while Ben couldn't get the thought of Captain Abel Sithole from his mind.

For the last hour, Tony and Ben had been sitting on the Victoria Falls Hotel's flagstone patio, at a table in a quiet corner to the left under one of the patio's sweeping shade trees. As they sat gazing sightlessly over the Zambezi Gorge to the north just in front of them, neither registered the multi-coloured mist that rose above the falls, or heard the thunderous roar that the giant cataract caused. Tony was fuming. As yet nobody had approached them and more than once he had threatened to leave. Ben was taking it in his stride, with an ice-cold can of Castle Lager saying, 'What more in the world could a man ask for?'

Tony got up, rising again.

'Oh sit down. There's not much we can do about those poachers. They'll be long gone by now.'

If looks could kill, after that comment, Ben should've died a horrid death. Tony sat down, retrieved an object from his pocket and prepared to snap a retort. But before he could, he was interrupted by a man, just under six foot with short brown hair, who had come to stand beside their table.

'Tony Campbell is it?' Richard Black asked as he stuck out his hand in greeting, 'You obviously received the fax.'

'About bloody time,' was the only greeting he received. Tony ignored both the question and the proffered hand. 'I don't know who you are, pal, or what sort of clout you've got with the Wildlife Fund, but if you're interested, poachers just wiped out about a hundred elephants in Hwange National Park, and we would've caught those bastards if it wasn't for you.' He stabbed an accusing finger at Richard's chest. 'So what you've got to say better be bloody good.'

As if he'd been struck a physical blow Richard flinched at the words. 'I'm sorry, I didn't expect for a minute that you should've –'

Tony could see the man meant the words. 'Yeah, all right. Not much that can be done about it now. Here look, take a seat. Now what's this all about?' he asked as his guest took a sat. 'And I didn't catch your name.'

Richard had already had his people run a thorough check on both Tony and Ben, and he had also been watching them discreetly since they had arrived so had formed his own opinions. What he had learnt and seen impressed him; they were the type of men he needed to accommodate the plans that were slowly beginning to form. He knew they were both dedicated to wildlife conservation and had achieved exceptional results since starting with the WWF. *All the better*, he'd reasoned on numerous occasions. If he was to have any hope of stopping Donovan these were the type of men whose help he needed, so had already decided to be forthright right from the start – well, on the surface anyway.

'Richard Black, I'm with British Intelligence.'

'You don't sound British.'

'Born in South Africa ... look I'm not interested whether you believe me or not,' he shrugged indifferently, 'but currently we're both working in the same field, trying to stop ivory poaching. Elephants are dying and I believe I can help stop them.'

'Since when has British Intelligence become interested in ivory poaching?' it was Ben who dubiously asked the question.

'I didn't say they were, I said I was. But don't believe me.' Richard pulled out two thick manila folder reports from a brown leather satchel he was carrying. 'Believe these.' He placed the copies on the table in front of them, then sat back and watched both men tentatively open the reports. As each of them sat forward and became increasingly transfixed by what they read, Richard knew he'd taken the right approach; he sat, watched and waited. 'Good men,' he decided. 'A pity really.' He had to prevent himself from sadly shaking his head.

Both Tony and Ben were stunned, slowly lifting their heads once they had finished the reports to gazed dumbly at one another, it was as if they had forgotten Richard's presence. It was Ben who broke their dumbfounded silence.

'Head of cattle, that Shona who fell from the chopper, kept saying, "head of cattle" when I was questioning him.' He pointed at a name in the report. 'And its translation in Sindebele is "Nkomo", remember Tony?'

'How could I forget.' He brought up his hands to cover the lower half of his face. 'God, this is terrible.'

'I knew we should never have trusted him.'

'Who?' Tony asked, looking at him as he dragged his hands from his face.

'That prick Sithole. It's probably his band of goons doing the poaching.'

'Bloody hell, the army is involved,' Tony breathed, then repeated, 'God, this is terrible.' He slowly turned to face Richard, 'Where the hell did you get this from?' he asked pointing at his copy of the report. 'Nobody's ever been able to expose a racket of this magnitude before. And who the hell's this

Donovan character?'

'I take it you're prepared to listen then?'

'Prepared? That's an understatement. But I think first I could use a drink. Do you mind?' He asked, already looking for a waiter.

Once the lagers had been delivered Tony and Ben sat back and let Richard explain the well-documented report and accompanying figures. Occasionally they interrupted when they needed to clarify a point, but for the most part they listened, transfixed by the enormity of what they were hearing. All the while, while Tony listened he was rubbing and revolving what he'd retrieved earlier from his pocket in the fingers of his hand.

After about an hour Richard finally fell silent.

'Bloody hell, an American eh,' Tony uttered, 'I imagined it would be some Asian monopolising the trade.' He briefly shook his head in stunned amazement. 'And by using documents for mammoth ivory you think he could have more than thirty per cent of the trade?' Richard gave a slight inclination of his head; it was all in the report.

'But he's already rich.' Ben cut in. 'Why the hell would he want to risk being involved in ivory poaching? Christ, why kill elephants, full stop?'

'Who knows? My people believe he's obsessed with the stuff,' Richard answered. 'As you've read, he's got the largest ivory collection in the world.'

'Okay, okay that's been covered.' Tony looked evenly at Richard, 'You've obviously realised we're convinced. Where do we go from here?

Richard had already anticipated the question. If these two were prepared to give him the support he needed, he would do the same – well at least that was what he'd decided to imply.

'Right, this is the way I see it. I'll continue as I am. My people are working at getting the facts we need to expose the money laundering and the ivory sales of Donovan's operation, and I think you two need to find out who this Peter Nkomo character is and close him and this army captain friend of yours down. I'll be feeding you whatever information I can.'

'It's a wonder we haven't heard of him before, this Nkomo fellow. I would've expected to have heard at least a whisper. If he is running the show here in Africa he must run one hell of a tight ship,' said Tony.

'Well, we believe he does. Just from the amounts of bullion he receives, he has to be coordinating the African side of Donovan's operation.'

'Okay, Richard. I'm asking this because we need it clarified – what rules are we running by?'

Richard never hesitated, 'Your own. You'll have no official support, but put it this way; I'm not here in an official capacity either.'

'Point taken.' He and Ben would have to lay some careful plans. Knowing Captain Sithole was now heavily involved they would have to tread carefully, especially as Tony suspected an element within the Zimbabwean army was somehow involved with poaching. 'Right, what else is there you haven't told us?'

Richard was impressed, from the short time he'd spent with the two men he felt confident they would achieve excellent results, especially if events ran according to plan. 'Other than I heard somewhere that Donovan comes to Africa once a year to observe his operations, and is due out soon, you know as much as me.' Richard nearly grimaced as he said it; he hoped he hadn't been too subtle with the comment. Inwardly he breathed a sigh of relief at Tony's next remark.

'Is he now? That could be interesting.'

'Don't worry; I'll keep you informed of the dates. But my bet is he won't be an easy man to target, if that's what you're thinking.' Richard stood up to leave – he had planted the seed which was enough for now. Only time would tell now if his plans for Tony and Ben would mature through to fruition – everything he wanted to cover had been said.

Still standing, Richard pointed down to the object Tony was still playing with in his hand. 'What on earth is that? I noticed you've been toying with it since I arrived.'

Tony held it out, 'A talisman I suppose. The boys from Stronghold, the rhino protection operation Ben and I were with, gave it to me as a parting gift.'

Accepting it Richard immediately saw it was made from ivory, it was a disk about the same diameter as an American silver dollar but thicker. On one side it had a raised, life-like carving of a huge bull elephant in miniature and on the other side an inscription which read; *Tony, All the best. Regards, Stronghold.* 'Magnificent,' Richard couldn't help himself from uttering. Tony misread his word as a show of appreciation for the artistry with which it had been carved.

'Yeah, Glenn Tatum, the commander at Stronghold had it carved by an old African craftsman.'

'Hmm, interesting. Glenn Tatum you say?' He was definitely somebody Richard wanted to talk to. That simple ivory disk had given a whole new dimension to his plans. Handing it back he hurriedly changed the subject.

145

'Oh, and by the way,' he reached into his satchel. 'I have a friend in your Washington office who asked me to give you this.' He handed over a sealed, officially addressed envelope. Tony opened it.

'Aw Christ,' he cursed, 'Now of all times.'

'Anything I can help with?' Richard asked slightly concerned. The last thing he wanted was delays, not now. The sooner Tony's investigation got underway, the better.

'Oh, it's nothing. It's just the WWF are sending somebody out to Kenya to review our operation, some bloody doctor from the States by the look of it. They do it every year. It has to be done to keep the Board of Trustees and International Council happy. As I said, it's nothing, just a trip up north that's all.' Placing aside the thought of his pending trip Tony stuck out his hand, he also ignored the vague sense of disquiet he felt, putting it down to the enormity of Donovan's ivory racket. 'Good to meet you, Richard, and how do we contact you if we need to?'

'There's a phone number on the back page of the report,' Richard said, feeling a twinge of guilt as he shook the proffered hand. 'It's a London number and it'll be answered by a chap called Johnny. He'll pass on any messages.' He then shook hands with Ben, before adding, 'Oh, and for security's sake, burn both reports once you've absorbed their content. I'll be in touch.'

Richard turned, and not expecting to see either man again, left them to plan their assault against the men who were helping to systematically destroy the African elephant.

CHAPTER 27

Zimbabwean Capital, Harare

PETER NKOMO HAD arrived in Harare from South Africa in the early afternoon. He had already worked out at the Athletic Club before having an early evening meal at the Bagatelle, where he found their grilled Kudu steaks exceptional; he regarded the restaurant as his favourite in the town. He had returned to his hotel suite at the Meikles on Jason Mayo Avenue in the centre of the city, and was now in its lounge in front of the picture window, gazing out across a small park into the quickly mellowing early evening air.

He had no expression on his face and only the sparkling expectancy of his eyes told of the growing anticipation he experienced for his impending meeting, as he stood waiting with his hands comfortably clasped at the small of his back. He was wearing a white silk shirt open at the collar, which contrasted against his glowing black skin, and a pair of khaki brush cotton trousers and hand-tooled Italian leather pumps upon his feet. Dressed as he was, and added to the commanding aura he exuded, he looked a picture of affluence. There was a knock at the door to his rear.

'Come,' he ordered with a deep resonant voice. He didn't bother turning around.

The door opened and in walked a man just as compelling as he, yet dressed entirely differently, wearing British army style fatigues with the three stars of a captain on his epaulets. He wasn't as tall as Peter, yet he moved with a similar athletic grace, and his features were completely different. Where Peter's nose and jaw were broad the Captain's were finer and far more defined. They appeared alike in two regards; they were both black men and their eyes were similar – dark, hungry and compelling – but that's where the similarities ended. At a glance it was obvious their origins were from two very different tribes.

As Peter stood waiting for his guest to announce himself, all he was presented with was silence as the seconds slowly ticked away.

'A truly cosmopolitan city, a harmonious blend of old and new, wouldn't you say Peter?

Peter was able to prevent himself from starting in fright only by using an extreme force of will. The army captain had noiselessly crossed the lounge to stand just behind his shoulder. He too was gazing out across the Zimbabwean capital; the difference was he had a smug expression set upon his handsome face; he knew he had startled Peter.

Slowly turning his head, to then fabricate an easy smile of recognition, Peter showed no sign of the alarm he had just experienced. 'Abel, I'm sorry. I thought it was one of the maids,' he easily lied, 'How good it is to see you.' He turned to reach out and shake the man's hand in greeting.

'*As smooth as silk*,' Captain Sithole thought as he applauded Peter's charade. 'No wonder he is able to easily control the number of men he does.'

As the men shook hands they may have been smiling but the warmth never permeated beneath the depth of their healthy black skin, they may respect one another but that didn't mean there were any feelings of friendship. Far from it. In fact, they loathed each other. The abhorrence they experienced went further than normal tribal hatred. Although Peter didn't class himself as one, he was born a Zulu and Captain Sithole was a Shona, it was because both were powerful men and had achieved that power at the expense of others.

These men, while it suited them, may have worked together but they were also potential rivals, and at the slightest sign of weakness neither would hesitate to crush and destroy the other. Money was their source of inspiration and greed their God, and if killing one would give the other the slightest turn in profit, appropriate action would be taken. But for now as neither had shown any previous weakness they were both content to sit, watch and wait. For now, they chose to work as colleagues, directing other men to work as poachers and harvest ivory.

'Come over to the coffee table, we can get the meeting underway.' Peter indicated a soft tan leather chair beside the glass-topped table, and seated himself in an adjacent chair. 'I am due to fly out and meet with Mr Donovan in the next few days; I believe you have a report to present.'

Although it wasn't said in as many words both men knew the comment was an order. For the Captain to continue receiving his monthly cut from Donovan's poaching racket he had to produce the appropriate documentation, weights and numbers that coincided exactly with Peter's figures. If for some reason they didn't match, it was simple – the Captain's bullion wouldn't be sent.

Sithole produced a red foldered report from the black attaché case he had been carrying, and placed it on the coffee table in front of Peter. As Peter picked up the report Sithole's eyes blazed with hunger, his first sign of emotion. In spite of Tony Campbell's time spent in Zimbabwe it had been another record month, two thousand nine hundred and ninety two kilograms the report stated, just under three tons of ivory, US $368,114 worth – tusks from three hundred and forty-eight harvested elephants.

Peter noticed the greedy flame of passion flare within the captain's eyes, and while weighing the report lightly in his hand he looked directly at his so-called colleague. They both knew their figures would exactly coincide, but over the years meetings like this one had turned into a ritual both men chose to perform. 'I'd like to first hear it verbally, so I can gain an insight into your activities. Mr Donovan will want to know.' Peter placed the report on the arm of the chair as he sat back to listen.

Because the Zulu and Shona speaking tribes weren't historical enemies and as Peter had openly denounced the tribe that had ostracised his family generations before, he was usually viewed by the people he met as a loner with no tribal bonds. Thus, he was able to solicit help throughout the African continent where previously none would have been forthcoming. So any tribal animosity that existed between the two men mainly came from Captain Sithole's quarter.

Peter had first come in contact with the captain when he was involved in the initial tentative phases of setting up a ring of poachers for Donovan in Zimbabwe, Botswana and Zambia. As he already commanded what approached a monopoly in the poaching trade in all three countries, Captain Sithole quickly heard of the new and potentially powerful rival. After some rather unaccustomed restraint on the Captain's behalf and some delicate negotiating from Peter, he was able to convince the Captain he should supply Donovan's rapidly growing network instead of his previous, and at times unreliable, buyers. However, it wasn't Peter's well-phrased words or his articulate manner that impressed Sithole the most – as always it came down to money. The vast increase in revenue he could see he would achieve, and the safer methods of disposing of the ivory convinced him to swallow his pride and tribal animosity and accept the lucrative offer.

In turn, the arrangement was a major coup for Peter. Gaining the supply of an already well-established poaching ring immediately turned Donovan into a major player within the world's illicit trade of ivory. Regularity of supply allowed Donovan to command premium prices and so pass on a far larger bonus to Peter. Peter had handed Donovan a major poaching network on a platter while also allowing him to vastly increase his income, an income he had continued to receive over the years with little effort.

Peter's role in the racket was a multifaceted but simple one. Firstly, he was the intermediary and thus the safety net between Donovan and the actual poaching. Secondly, he ensured the ivory met the demand of the racket's insatiable Asian customers, and finally, he organised the smuggling and safe export of the plundered ivory, made incredibly easy because of Donovan's exporting companies.

The main method used to smuggle out the ivory was a simple one. A truck driver who had delivered raw materials from South Africa to Malawi would backload his now empty container with tobacco, tea and sugar destined for customers back in the South African Republic. After being inspected by Malawi customs the container would be officially sealed and the appropriate documents issued, so during its southward journey there was no need for other custom services to open or search it along the way. Once it had reached its destination it was then a formality for the Republic's customs service to break the seals, inspect, and consequently clear the load. However, just as documents can be altered so can custom seals be broken and exchanged.

Once a month a truck carrying a Donovan Enterprise container only partially filled with tobacco, tea and sugar, would leave Malawi on the Lilongwe to Lusaka road. Almost immediately upon clearing Zambian customs, just across the border at the township of Chipata, it would make its first unscheduled stop. Entering a small warehouse on Kapata Avenue just near the town's bus station, the container's seals were broken for the first time and tusks poached from Zambia's South Luangwa National Park were loaded. After being re-sealed, with identically numbered seals, the container would continue southward once again.

After entering Zimbabwe, ninety miles south of the border post at Victoria Falls, another much longer unscheduled stop would be made. At a warehouse near the township of Hwange, just after Thomson's Junction and behind the Baobab Hotel, was stockpiled in neatly sorted rows all the tusks poached from Botswana's and Zimbabwe's national parks. After the tusks were loaded and the container resealed, it wasn't tampered with again until it reached its final destination; Donovan Enterprises' massive bonded warehouse in South Africa, on Maydon Wharf in the port of Durban.

On the first night, within hours of it being unloaded from the truck, the container's seals were broken yet again. It was here, under bribed supervision, that Peter personally inspected and weighed each tusk. Once the weighing was complete the container was re-sealed for the final time. The ivory was immediately reloaded into another container recently cleared through customs, this time destined for a port in Asia. Once this container's new seals were attached Peter's job was done. When the Asian customer had taken receipt of the container his share of the profits was guaranteed.

Another factor that worked in Peter's favour operating in joint accord with Captain Sithole was the fact that just as he was Donovan's safety net the Captain worked as his. To date, this was the main reason he had been able to operate as successfully as he did with little fear of being discovered.

Compared to Peter the Captain had, in relation to his earnings, far more work to do. He coordinated and disciplined the poachers, directed their movements, and organised the stockpiling of the ivory for transportation and export.

His government appointment to help Tony Campbell crack down on poaching had given him inside knowledge of the areas throughout Zimbabwe and Botswana which were being targeted for anti-poaching. Being privy to such information allowed him to ensure his poachers were operating elsewhere at the appropriate times. He did send in the odd sacrificial lamb, but in most cases he was able to ensure his gangs operated unmolested.

In Zimbabwe he had his own soldiers and poaching gangs operating in Chimanimani National Park in the east, Mana Pools National Park in the north, and in the west the country's largest national park, Hwange. Employing the technique of using cross-border sorties, he had also found Botswana relatively simple to poach. He only operated his gangs in the country's Chobe National Park because it virtually bordered Hwange. However, because he was unable to keep track of the anti-poaching operations running in both countries he still had to operate with a certain amount of caution, but not so in Zambia.

Zambia had virtually become a lost cause as far as wildlife conservation was concerned. With official corruption and the cost of conservation it had become too prohibitive for the country's near-bankrupt economy to effectively sustain. Sithole was ruthlessly able to operate his gangs at will, even to the extent of hiring from the Zambian army weapons for his poachers to use.

It was enough to say both Peter and Sithole had covered every possible contingency in their quest to poach and harvest southern Africa's ivory, all except Tony Campbell that was.

Sithole had fallen silent after giving his report and Peter studied him carefully. *He's damn effective, I'll give him that*, he thought reluctantly. 'It's been another reasonable month then,' he commented instead, before quickly changing the subject. 'And what of Tony Campbell?' He didn't want to give the man too much praise.

'Tony Campbell? Nothing I can't handle. He is active in Hwange at present.'

'Can we expect trouble?'

'On the contrary, we took out just under a hundred elephants three days ago, right from under his nose,' the Captain responded, triumphantly. 'It'll be in my next month's report.'

Time to bring him down a peg or two, Peter decided. He was aware of what had happened three days earlier. Ever since Tony had started with the WWF he'd had him under surveillance – the man worried Peter.

'That's not what I heard. It was only by chance you and your men weren't caught. If he hadn't been called away you'd be exposed by now.' Peter spoke quietly but it was as if he had struck the man a resounding slap across the face. For the most fleeting of seconds, Sithole's head propped slightly forward as his mouth nearly dropped open in shock. Although the Captain quickly masked the movement Peter couldn't help but silently declare, *Got ya, ya bastard.*

Sithole immediately realised he had let down his guard. He had started to become too confident with Peter, and would have to watch his step. He was also more than aware of the risk he had taken; he didn't need to be reminded.

He and his men, using army equipment and arms, had actually driven to within several miles of the elephants that had been killed. They had walked in, butchered the lot and carried the ivory back to the waiting trucks. If Tony hadn't been called away he would've eventually found the tyre prints, and then by using simple detective work would've easily pieced the rest together.

Yes, it had been a risk. But as he'd seen to it that the tyre tracks were now gone, it was a risk worth taking. *But how the hell did you know about it, that's what I want to know?* He silently asked, while looking at Peter. *One of my men probably, I'll have to look into that*, he decided.

'Have you run a check on this person he met at Victoria Falls?' Peter definitely wasn't going to let him off the hook.

Sithole contemplated feigning ignorance but decided against it. He'd put it down to a cheap lesson, one he'd luckily gotten away with. 'Just a British tourist. I've checked with immigration. He must've been a friend, that's all.'

'Hell've an important friend wouldn't you say to leave a fresh trail left by poachers? I'll need a description of him. We can't take any chances. Get one of your men to drop it off.'

Sithole never answered. Though his face showed no expression his eyes cried out for blood. Because of the humiliation he felt settling just beneath his temples, somebody was going to pay.

'Is he going to be a problem?' Peter asked. It would be a risk killing him but this Campbell bastard was starting to get on his nerves.

'As I said before,' came a terse reply. 'Tony Campbell is nothing I can't handle.' However, Peter wasn't so sure.

When Donovan had originally heard a whisper that the WWF was setting up an anti-poaching team he'd ordered Peter to investigate and it hadn't taken long for him to find out the potential dire consequences if Tony was allowed to start his new project. Tony's reputation was formidable, hence why Donovan had ordered his execution. Yet somehow he had got away when Captain Sithole had sent in his hit squad. It had caused a huge uproar when it was exposed to the international press and worst of all, as far as Donovan and Peter were concerned, it had boosted the anti-poaching cause and cemented the WWF's project in place. Because of the worldwide media backlash, Donovan had ordered Peter to leave Tony alone and still hadn't rescinded the decision.

'I'm going to have to talk to Donovan about him; he's becoming more trouble than he's worth.' He looked evenly at Sithole. It was time to twist and thrust the knife deeper, 'You believe you can handle him, but I'm not so sure you can. I'll be talking to Mr Donovan about it, so be prepared to have your hit squad ready when I return. For now just keep an eye on him.'

Enough of the heavy hand. Time to sugar him up a bit, Peter decided. 'Unless you've got anything else, I can organise your bullion to be transferred.'

What a note to end on, and for what'll be coming through I can probably put up with Campbell and even you for a little longer, Sithole thought as he rose from the leather chair to leave.

'Not at the moment, Peter. I'll look forward to hearing from you after your return from Los Angeles,' he said aloud.

CHAPTER 28

Los Angeles

ALTHOUGH HE WORKED at keeping it hidden, Donovan had a growing sense of unease. The only trouble was he couldn't pinpoint why. Donovan Enterprises was booming and he was already several years ahead of his scheduled plans to monopolise the ivory trade across the globe. There were little things, unrelated things that were irritating him, similar to several small festering cuts that refused to heal. Sabina for one. Ever since he'd found her in his office she'd become civil beyond belief and that really worried him. Although he had discovered she was having some kind of an affair, if he could call it that – one meal wasn't exactly an affair – there was something more. 'It's her bloody smugness,' he decided, 'I'll have to keep Bogatin watching her.'

However, it wasn't only Sabina, it was the ongoing business stemming from the bloody FBI agent that Bogatin should have sorted out. That would have to be tied up. But also it was that bastard Campbell.

He was becoming a real thorn in Donovan's side, ever since the day he'd heard the whispers about the WWF's anti-poaching scheme. He certainly didn't want him kept around, not after the damage he had caused in Kenya, but he definitely didn't want the bad press that his murder would cause either. Christ, that last fiasco was bad enough. Donovan's thoughts were distracted as he began to focus on what Peter was saying.

'So he met some Englishman up at Victoria Falls, so what?'

He and Peter were in his office down in its informal discussion area, sitting opposite one another on the roll-backed leather couches. Lying in front of Donovan on the smoked-glass coffee table were Captain Sithole's and Peter's latest reports.

'It seemed an incredible coincidence that he would drop everything and rush off to meet him, especially when ..'

'Yeah, yeah, okay, especially when Sithole nearly screwed up.' He knew Peter didn't like the Captain. 'But remember he didn't, and on more than one occasion I've learnt that that can be the difference between success and failure. What do you know about this Englishman, if that's what he is?'

'Not much; his description, carried a British passport, where he flew in from, his destination and dates, etc. Other than that, nothing,' Peter spread out his hands. 'It's all in the back of my report.'

Donovan picked up the report: destination Heathrow, and he'd flown into Harare using a roundabout route from LA, Peoples Express to New York, then a direct Air Zambia flight to Lusaka and onto Harare; description meant nothing. 'But hang on a minute, the description *and* the dates – surely not?' He frowned heavily, then looked up at Peter. 'Did Sithole get a photo of him?'

'No, not that I know of. Is it important?'

Donovan was quiet for a couple of seconds; the description was similar to the photograph Bogatin had taken of the man Sabina had dined with at Malibu, and the dates. 'This guy left LA the day after she'd had that meal.' He shook his head. The thought was absurd. It'd have to be a coincidence. He flicked the report down on the coffee table. 'No, Peter. It's nothing. Tell me your thoughts on this Campbell character again.' However, his disquiet had risen to the surface again.

'Well, he hasn't closed down our *shifta* poachers working out of Somalia, but we're receiving only a trickle of ivory at present, compared to their normal quantities. To sustain levels I've had to push the Masai and Baron tribesmen to up their kill rates in both Kenya and Tanzania. We've been getting good numbers out of the Tsavo, Mount Kenya, Amboseli and Masai Mara parks in Kenya and the Selous game reserve in Tanzania. But without Campbell, well, we could sustain those levels plus get the quantities from the *shiftas* back up again. It'd vastly increase our profits.'

'Okay, so you want him out of the way?'

'It would help,' Peter responded tentatively. He didn't want to upset Donovan, not with the mood he appeared to be in.

'You realise it could bring some unfavourable press, and the last thing I want happening is any of our outlets closed down because some African official is starting to feel the heat. You know what happened last time; markets got jumpy and the tonnage dropped because of the international pressure caused by the bloody media.'

'I am aware of the ramifications,' Peter tried tactfully, 'I just feel it would be wise to… I suppose, dispose of him now before he becomes too much of a menace.'

'But he is indirectly helping Sithole, is he not?'

'Yes, but only until Sithole slips up again.' He couldn't prevent himself from adding the not so blatant slight against the Captain, 'And in both Kenya and Tanzania we have no such control over him.'

Donovan shook his head, still clearly irritated. He hoped his judgment wasn't impaired, but with all these incidental problems he was experiencing, things didn't feel right for some reason. However, he knew some course of action was needed to tidy them up and made a quick decision. 'Okay, get rid of him, but make sure it looks like an accident. And I don't need to tell you why,' he said with a threatening finger. 'Are there any loose ends that need tying up with him?'

'Only a Matabele. He's Campbell's assistant. He's nothing important.'

'See to it then. Anything else?' Peter shook his head. 'Right, I'm due for my trip down to Africa to view the operations in the next few months so start organising it. I want it to be a comprehensive one this time. And since there's nothing else, I've another pressing matter.' He rose indicating the meeting was over. 'We'll cancel your next month's visit; it can be incorporated with my trip. Until then,' he shook Peter's hand, 'get Sithole to sort out Tony Campbell, but remember, I want no screw-ups.'

Just as Peter reached the heavy teak doors, Donovan spoke again. 'Oh and see if you can get a photograph from Sithole of this Englishman Campbell met. As Peter walked from the office Donovan had already settled himself back onto the couch, he had another meeting to prepare for.

'Good work in Honk Kong and Taiwan, Nikolai; we've either acquired several Asian business partners or picked up some more rather profitable carving factories and outlets. Well done.'

'Thank you, Mr Donovan, I only did as was instructed,' the Russian replied modestly in heavily accented English.

'Yes, I am more than happy with the way things are proceeding.'

Unlike Peter Nkomo, Nikolai Bogatin was privy to all facets and the true extent of Donovan's worldwide poaching racket and money laundering activities. Bogatin had no outlandish dreams of grandeur or desires for exorbitant wealth, he was content to work for his vastly inflated salary and service the man he respected above all others. Also, Donovan found his connections into the old communist East and his animal-type cunning gave him entirely different perspectives into his illicit activities. For those reasons he found the Russian an excellent and a completely impartial sounding board.

'With the help of the mammoth documents you've organised from Siberia, we're now involved with or controlling upwards of seventy per cent of the worldwide market.' It was over 500 tons annually, over sixty-five million US dollars in the raw trade and that didn't even include finished products. Donovan gloated. 'Yes, in that quarter things are going well, but in other areas not as I'd like. Tell me, is there anything new on my wife?'

Although his expression never showed it, this assignment definitely wasn't the Russian's cup of tea. 'Nothing since she had the meal in Malibu.'

'And afterwards? Were you been able to find out where they went?'

'Ah, no, Mr Donovan,' the toad like-man said despondently.

'After they left the restaurant, I have still been unable to trace their movements.'

He had lost Sabina and Richard on the Pacific Coast Highway as they headed west back towards Beverly Hills. Sabina had floored her Porsche and left him reeling in its wake. At the time her disappearance had seemed unimportant, he had reasoned he was no goddamn babysitter, but when he realised how important it was to Donovan to know his wife's exact movements he had taken it personally. It felt as though he'd failed his biggest assignment.

'I am still looking,' he stated lamely. Looking to Bogatin meant scouring every inch of LA and talking to every contact he had acquired in the city.

'Yes, find out, but don't let it concern you,' Donovan said absent-mindedly. He'd been looking at the picture Bogatin had taken of his wife and her dinner guest while leaving Alice's Restaurant at Malibu. Feeling uneasy, and not knowing why, he placed the photo aside. He was convinced they had a more pressing problem to attend to.

He picked up another photograph; it was an eight by ten-inch colour print of a rather attractive young woman. She had raven shoulder length hair and several faint lines of concentration lining her forehead. Her eyes were dark and it was obvious she didn't know she was being photographed; the shot was taken from a hidden security camera in reception. From her dark complexion and finely proportioned facial features, she had either Mexican or Indian blood running through her veins.

He looked up at the Russian. 'I thought you said this Hagan business had been sorted out?'

'I believed it was,' Bogatin looked pensively at his employer; he'd always prided himself on leaving no loose ends. 'I took care of the FBI agent over a week and a half ago.'

'His daughter,' Donovan placed the colour print of Anna in front of him. 'Anna Hagan. She's been snooping around.' This he could certainly do without.

About two weeks ago an FBI agent had approached him and made some vague allegations. Somehow he had gained partial evidence that indicated he possibly controlled a huge money laundering scheme operating in the CIS, which of course he did. Although it appeared the federal agent hadn't got all his facts right, it was enough to have some rather searching questions asked of him if his investigations went much further.

Donovan made a few inquiries and found out it wasn't an official investigation, and though he had no idea where the information originally came from, he immediately involved Bogatin. He directed him to find out what the agent knew and then to silence him. Thankfully, or so he'd thought at the time, Bogatin was able to tidy up the whole potentially untidy affair before it got out of hand. He met with the agent, under the guise that he had further information that could incriminate his employer, and subsequently killed him. As the agent had disclosed no incriminating evidence and had none on him or at his home, the matter should have died there with him, but somehow he'd obviously managed to pass some on to his daughter.

Bogatin had picked up the photo. 'What do you want me to do?'

'Find out everything, and I mean everything she knows. Destroy whatever you find and get rid of her. Trace whatever leads you have to, but make sure you sort this one out once and for all.'

This is more like it, the Russian thought callously. *I think I'm going to enjoy this.* Already he could feel a slight twinge at his groin as he looked at the attractive face. 'I'll get on with it right away,' he promised.

As Bogatin walked from his office, Donovan felt the pensive cloud that had surrounded him lift, he felt things were finally back on an even keel. 'I think work can wait for now.'

He reached for the phone on the coffee table. 'Sonya, could you please come on through? No, no. Divert the phone to reception downstairs, and leave your notepad behind. It'll be more than notes I'll be wanting from you.'

CHAPTER 29

Costa Mesa

ANNA HAD A light sheen of sweat covering her forehead as she walked in through the front door of her apartment. She was dressed in a blue and white Adidas T-shirt and similar coloured shorts, while wearing the same brand of running shoes on her feet. Although her breathing and outward appearance didn't show it, she had been out for a run, and by most people's standards, a rather long run.

'Been out marathoning again?' she heard a voice call to her from the apartment's kitchen. It was her flatmate, Sarah.

'Ah, no. Marathons are out, it's now multi-disciplines. Triathlons are in.' This was one thing she enjoyed about being back in California, McMurdo Base had been so restrictive – she'd always been physically active. However, Anna soon forgot about her physical activities. 'My God, Sarah. What've you done to your hair?' She was shocked.

'Do you like it? Isn't it divine?'

'But … but it's …' Anna stammered into silence. She was standing in the middle of the living room and out of the kitchen had walked her roommate, a blonde, blue-eyed, Californian bombshell. Well, that's what she'd been last time Anna had seen her. She knew Sarah had always been so impulsive, but this, this was too much.

'Well don't stand there gaping, say something – and close your mouth,' Sarah said as she did a pirouette in front of her friend.

Regaining some of her old composure Anna shook her head in bewilderment. 'I did. What've you done to your hair? Where are your beautiful blonde locks?'

'I know. Isn't it great?' Sarah simpered as she briefly hunched her shoulders in delight.

'But we'll look like sisters.'

'Oh phooey. Anyway, I've always wanted my hair black,' Sarah declared with a flick of her head as she ran her fingers through her hair. 'I like it.'

'No, come on. Come and have a look.' Anna grabbed Sarah by the hand

and dragged her into her bedroom. Standing in front of her oval dressing-table mirror, she implored, 'See?'

The two girls standing side by side could have been easily mistaken for sisters, their complexions were similar, Anna's courtesy of her birth, while Sarah's was gained from diligent hours spent under the Californian sun. They were about the same height and build, Anna was broader across the shoulders, but now that Sarah had dyed her straight blonde locks black it had changed her appearance completely. Yes, people would take them for sisters.

'Hmm, I see what you mean.' Sarah preened, admiring the transformation. 'You always did pull more guys. I think I'm going to like this.'

'Oh Sarah, I did not,' Anna playfully slapped her friend's shoulder. 'Anyway, your face is fuller, mine's more defined,' she stated with a haughty flick of her head.

'What do you reckon?' Sarah had opened her mouth and was squeezing her cheeks together with her fingers. 'Plastic surgery?'

'Ah, no,' Anna said with a shake of her head, and then added more seriously, 'You do realise they will eventually find out it's not your true colour?'

'Oh yeah!' Sarah reached for the waistband of her Levis 501s and popped the buttons of the fly. Yanking the jeans halfway down her shapely thighs she displayed a pair of white, virtually see-through knickers, revealing she had made the complete transformation.

'You didn't!' Anna managed to exclaim, staring at her friend's newly darkened pubic V before they both broke into fits of hysterical laughter.

Anna had to eventually leave Sarah while she struggled to re-button her jeans. Holding her ribs with one hand and squeezing tears of mirth from the corners of her eyes with the other, she staggered back into the living room. As she walked through into the kitchen she realised this was the first time she had really laughed since she'd heard about her father's death – thankfully, the healing had finally begun. The thought of her father slightly tempered her elated mood but only until she heard Sarah coming through from the living room to meet her.

As Sarah walked into the kitchen she fastened the last button into place. 'Did you get the message?' she said while wiping alternate eyes with the palms of her hand. 'Some guy rang from Washington,'

'Well I can say, I'm certainly going to miss you. Yeah, I got the message. They're sending me away again.'

'But you just got back,' Sarah said disappointedly. Even though she knew Anna had been unhappy and she had only come home because of her father's death, she had enjoyed having her company. They'd always been close. 'I'll miss you too.' All humour had gone as the two women hugged each other. 'But I do know how important your work is to you.'

After they eventually broke their embrace Sarah turned to the refrigerator, 'Where to this time, Doctor Hagan?'

'From one extreme to the other, from the Antarctic to Africa. They want me to research the genetic viability of animals trapped in an isolated crater in Tanzania; the Ngorongoro Crater.'

'Really?' Sarah had to fake interest. Anna was probably her closest friend, but she couldn't understand how she, or anyone for that matter, could find that sort of work interesting.

'Yeah, it'll be fascinating,' Anna rushed on oblivious to her friend's lack of interest. 'Similar to what I was doing down on the ice with the Weddell Seals. They also want me to review some other project that's operating in Africa. I'm not sure what yet. I'll find out when I get there, but they'll help me to set up at the crater.'

'Fascinating.' Sarah was frantically searching for something to say that would prevent the outpour of words she knew was soon to come; she'd been trapped more than once in the past by Anna's enthusiasm for her work. 'When do you leave?'

'What? Oh,' Anna's shoulders slumped. 'Tomorrow morning.'

'So soon. I'd hoped at least we'd have a couple more weeks together. Hey, tell ya what,' she ran on excitedly, 'you'll have to pack, but as it's Saturday what about the Pierre Street Annex in Newport later this afternoon?'

'But -'

'Great, I'll arrange it, everybody can view the new me. Better still, when we're not together you can also say you're me so I'll have twice as many guys chasing me while you're away.'

'But like you said, I –'

'Brilliant. I'll go and organise everyone. Be back later.'

'- have to pack …' Anna trailed off as she watched Sarah disappear from the kitchen. When she heard the front door slam, she knew she'd have to go out. 'I suppose it will be fun, but knowing Sarah I won't be home till late. Better start packing,' she told herself.

'Hell of a difference from Antarctica,' Anna stated aloud. She'd showered and changed and was now wearing a red T-shirt and jeans, standing with her hands on her hips beside her bed looking at the vastly different array of clothes she would be taking with her to Africa. She was comparing them to those she'd had with her down on the ice. A few pairs of jeans, one pair of good trousers, a few shirts and sweaters, and a down-filled parka, the rest were mostly T-shirts and shorts. 'Shouldn't I be taking more?' she wondered. The assortment looked pathetically small compared to the Antarctic ware heaped on the floor at the foot of her bed. 'Maybe I could stuff in a few more knickers and socks, and another pair of shoes.' After rummaging through numerous drawers and cupboards she added to her meagre hoard, but even then it still looked pathetically small. 'Oh that'll do,' she conceded, 'Traveling light for a change.' *A new experience.*

It had been arranged Anna would arrive in Africa at Nairobi's Jomo Kenyatta Airport in Kenya. Her instructions, research data, scientific equipment and supplies and so on would be waiting for her at the airport, the WWF's office in Nairobi, or at her new base at the Ngorongoro Crater. After being fully briefed and collecting what awaited her at Nairobi, she would then be taken south across the border into Tanzania to the Ngorongoro Crater Lodge, one of their detached cabins would act as her permanent base. The lodge she was told, was perched on top of the two thousand foot high crater rim and apparently overlooked the crater itself; her designated research area.

She realised looking at her clothes that she'd hardly had a chance to think about her new assignment, everything was happening so quickly. It had been a rushed decision, the WWF needed the position filled, and Anna had been told it may be slightly different from what she was used to, but with her qualifications and knowledge, she would soon feel at home. They informed her she would be picking up somebody's work who had recently left the crater's research project and that everything she needed would either be at Ngorongoro or waiting for her at Nairobi. If it wasn't, she only had to ask.

Her tickets and itinerary were waiting to be picked up at LAX upon departure, so her passport, personal effects and basic research material was all she needed to bring. That and the brief outline of her new assignment was about all she'd been told so far.

But Christ, I've never even been to Africa. The first doubts started to betray her earlier enthusiasm. *And I've never run a full research project by myself before.* But she thrust the thought aside. She'd been told a qualified assistant familiar with the area would be made available, and of course she knew she could do it, it was no different from the Antarctic.

Except for the man-eating animals, the malaria, yellow fever, cholera and the heat. *Yeah, no different, Anna,* her logic stated.

But at least I'll have an assistant and be getting help to set up. What was that guy's name who's going to meet me? She reached onto the top of her chest of drawers beside her bed and started flicking through the book and papers she'd be taking. *Ah, here it is, Tony Campbell.* The name sounded familiar. But she quickly lost the thought and her earlier apprehension as she'd noticed her father's diary sitting beside her papers. She picked it up and sat dejectedly on the edge of her bed.

She'd never felt so frustrated. Her investigations into her father's death had been fruitless, and she felt that was being kind. She had first gone to the FBI's headquarters on Wilshire Boulevard and spoken with her father's old colleagues; they had been sympathetic but not helpful. By all accounts, it appeared whatever he had been investigating wasn't official. There were no records, orders or any information on any of his last few weeks' activities. What's more, though they were polite, nobody seemed to give a damn. She was told in not so few words, 'We have more than enough to do. After all, your father was a loner.' So it was left up to Anna to find out about Donovan and Richard Black herself.

The Los Angeles Public Library had given her an abundance of background information on the high-profile Judd Donovan and his company Donovan Enterprises, but not the slightest lead into how they could possibly be involved with her father's murder. She was left with no other course of action but to confront Judd Donovan himself.

Therein lay her next problem. The receptionist and then his private secretary guarded him as the Buckingham Palace guards would guard the Queen. She had threatened and pleaded, bullied and coddled, but not once was she able to get anywhere near the blasted man. It was always the same, 'I'm sorry Mr Donovan is busy,' or, 'Mr Donovan is out of the city. Perhaps if you'd like to leave your name.' She'd been fobbed off and she knew it. Like with trying to find out about Richard Black it was hopeless, she'd discovered nothing.

She only recently decided to give up when she had seen Sarah's note and spoken to the WWF in Washington. 'Maybe he's got nothing to do with Pop's death after all.' But as she thought about her investigation, she still wished she had never left her name on her last call to Donovan's office.

Oh well, I'm leaving soon. Nothing much holding me here now anyway, she told herself as her crestfallen gaze was directed back to her father's diary. With an effort, she put the thought and the diary aside. She got up to pack.

No sooner had she placed the last item of clothing into her pack, than Sarah breezed through the door. 'Are you ready? They're waiting on the patio down at Pierre Street; we can make our grand entrance together.'

Anna shook her head fondly at Sarah. Maybe there was something she was leaving behind, after all. *But at least you'll be here when I eventually get back*, she thought and felt comforted. As she was dragged from the apartment, she realised Sarah was the last person in the world she really cared for.

'You should see the hunk that arrived with Ryan. Remember, Anna. When we're not together you will say you're me, won't you? I may not be home till late tonight.'

Anna rolled her eyes and chuckled lightly, thinking, *With Sarah here, I may be about to spend a few years in Africa, but California will always be home.* She stopped Sarah at the foot of the concrete stairs leading down from the front door of their apartment. 'But you will make sure I get to LAX on time, won't you? I don't want to miss my flight.'

Sarah gave her a wicked grin. 'I'll make sure you get there. But come on, Africa won't go away, we'll be late for something far more important if we stand here jabbering all day. The hunk awaits me.' Anna had no choice but to follow her excited friend as she was dragged by the arm to the waiting car. 'Let's rock 'n roll.'

CHAPTER 30

BOGATIN HAD PARKED his car on Harbor Boulevard and walked the hundred odd yards to the corner of Bay Street, in Costa Mesa near the Orange County Fairground. Merging with the shadows he waited back off the sidewalk, getting a feel for his surroundings. For the time of night, four on a Sunday morning, the boulevard was busy enough. Party-goers venturing home he assumed. However, nobody took any notice of his squat figure standing in the gloom; he blended in well with his darkened surroundings, dressed in navy jeans and a black bomber jacket with dark basketball boots upon his feet. The clothes themselves were innocent enough but questions would've had to have been asked if anyone had seen his hands which were tucked into the jacket's pockets. People would wonder why on such a mild night he was wearing a pair of black leather gloves.

After about ten minutes, when Bogatin felt comfortable, he walked down Bay Street towards Newport Boulevard at the opposite end. He liked to think it was a sixth sense he possessed. During his years of crime, if at any time the feeling wasn't quite right he would abort the assignment no matter how important it was.

He had walked probably halfway along Bay Street when he came upon his destination, Bay Court Apartments. He already knew where the Hagan woman lived; he'd followed her back from the Hollywood Memorial Park Cemetery after she'd visited her father's grave – he knew she'd eventually visit from past experience – they always did. She lived at number seven; he'd seen her skip up the stairs yesterday morning when she returned. *Yes, I'm going to enjoy this one*, he thought. She was dark and slim, just the way he liked them.

He walked into the courtyard of the apartment block and for several minutes waited in the shadows thrown by the overhanging trees that fringed the road. To his left was the laundry block and garages, in front of him was the central apartment block, and on the right the main complex and Anna's apartment. There wasn't a sound out of place as he stood, intently listening, patiently waiting. Eventually, he decided it was time to move.

He passed the first darkened set of concrete stairs leading up to the first two second-story apartments, twenty more paces and he was at the foot of the stairs. He took them two at a time and made no sound at all; eight paces carried him to the pitch-black recess at the top. Working by touch he selected the door to the left, number seven. Using deft hands and a hardened steel skeleton key, with two quick twists he had the door ajar. Again he waited.

Several minutes ticked slowly by before he slipped into the apartment. It was obviously the living room he'd just stepped into; couch, coffee table, TV and stereo. Standing in the middle of the room he assessed his surroundings, kitchen to the right, small hallway in front of him leading to the bathroom at the end and two bedrooms either side.

He quietly pushed one bedroom door open. The room was empty and an utter shambles, bed unmade and clothes strewn across the floor. That would have to be her roommate's. The door opposite was closed. When he tested the handle, the door eventually gave way. As he pushed it slowly open the noise it made, scraping upon the carpet floor, sounded unreasonably loud. He ignored it as he slipped into the room and quietly closed the door.

The room was surprisingly well lit; it was awash with the moon's pale-grey light tumbling in through the curtain covered windows. If he'd bothered to look out at the early morning sky, Bogatin would have noticed the moon was just past full. He quickly scanned the room. It contained a queen-sized bed and a narrow four-drawer dresser beside it, while at the foot of the bed was heaped a bundle of cold-weather gear.

This had to be the Hagan woman's room. He had found out she had only recently returned from Antarctica when he questioned the apartment block's caretaker.

In the wall opposite the bed was a built-in closet. One of the sliding doors was slightly open, and between the closet and bed was a dressing-table with an oval mirror attached. Looking over at the bed, he could clearly see someone lying quietly in its centre.

Perfect. He noticed there was only a light duvet resting over the peacefully sleeping figure. As he stood staring at the figure for several minutes to ensure it wasn't faking sleep, he could see tossed on a pillow around its head were flowing locks of raven hair, and from where he stood he could see the girl's chest slowly rise and fall with each restful breath. *Perfect,* he repeated to himself as he felt his groin beginning to flare; he knew she was asleep.

It was like the old days back in Russia again, when he had first started his life of crime. Working as a cat burglar, often he would find a woman in bed alone, and often he would satisfy his lust. *And tonight,* he decided, *is going to be no different.* Although he had now moved onto a far grander scale of crime and hadn't used those techniques for many years, he knew like an old well-remembered habit they would quickly return. He reached for a roll of two-inch wide duct-tape in the pocket of his jacket.

As he walked towards the sleeping figure he never took his eyes from the bed as he began unsticking the end-tab of the duct-tape. He stood over her. 'Anna,' he called softly. No response. 'Anna,' he tried again, touching her shoulder. The figure began to stir. 'Time to wake, Mr Donovan wants some questions answered.'

At the word 'Donovan' her eyes slowly flickered open, yet she was still groggy with sleep. 'What... who's that?' She mumbled, then, 'Oh my God,' she came instantly awake, 'The plane, the airport. I've slept in!' She sat bolt upright as the duvet fell to her waist revealing a white, virtually see-through negligee that showed off her pert well-formed breasts sticking out beneath. In an upheaval of sleep and half-muddled thoughts, she realised a stranger was standing beside her bed.

'I'm sorry Anna, you'll have to miss the airport. Mr Donovan wants some questions answered.' She opened her mouth to scream as soon as Bogatin had said the words but the scream never left her lips. He struck a cracking punch to the point of her jaw. Unconscious, she fell sideways as her head hit the pillow with a cushioned thud. Out cold with her raven hair thrown across her face, the plane and airport were now forgotten.

Stripping off the duvet Bogatin indulged himself for the briefest of seconds as he ran a pair of lecherous eyes over her slender body. They lingered momentarily when he made out the silken V of jet-black hair showing through the skimpy negligee at her loins.

Enough time for that later, he thought sadistically. With practiced ease he went about his business and rolled her limp body over onto her stomach. Pulling her arms down behind her back and straightening out her legs, he first taped her wrists together and then her ankles. When he was satisfied both arms and legs were securely held he rolled her over onto her back again. Stretching out a six-inch length of tape and ripping it off with his teeth, he flicked her hair to the side and stuck it firmly over her mouth. *Time to search the apartment.* He grunted in satisfaction as he admired his work; bound as she was, she wouldn't be going far. He decided to search the living room and kitchen first, then the bathroom and roommate's bedroom next, while Anna's room would be last. He started ransacking the apartment.

The rest of the apartment had revealed nothing; he now stood in the middle of Anna's room deciding where to start the final part of his search. Ignoring the now conscious eyes he could feel glued to his every move, he had noticed her slowly coming to as he walked into the room. He chose the dressing table first and emptied its contents onto the middle of the floor. Like the rest of the apartment it revealed nothing. He also bundled the Antarctic wear into the middle of the room. Again nothing, a quick look under the bed, the same. Next the built-in closet.

Bloody hell, he cursed silently, still nothing. *There has to be something, anything.*

Lastly the dresser beside the bed, the first three drawers were empty. He could feel his temper rising then as his hands rummaged through the bottom drawer they struck something hard.

So what do we have here? He pulled out a black personal diary. Resting it on top of the dresser he began rifling through it. He found a fax folded in the front cover and what looked like a month's worth of unintelligible entries at the start of the book. Holding it up to the moon's dull light and looking closely, he could just make out the word 'Donovan'. Jackpot. He had found what he was looking for.

Time to ask a few questions, he decided. He put the diary down and reached for the wide-eye, terrified figure.

Dragging her to the edge of the bed he could see she was visibly shaking; her fear intensified his animal lust. He left one foot on the ground and rested his other knee on her solar plexus, gripping a vice-like hand around her throat. Grabbing a corner of the tape covering her mouth with his other hand he gave it an unceremonious yank. A muffled cry left her mouth as the tape was ripped from her lips.

'Now Anna, what do you know about Mr Donovan?'

As soon as he'd asked the question, only by using a concerted effort was Bogatin able to stop her wildly bucking body and the scream that threatened to escape her throat. Perhaps it was her terror but she was far stronger than she looked. As her head and raven locks shook wildly from side to side and her mouth opened to scream, he had to savagely clamp down upon her throat and brutally thrust his knee deep into her solar plexus. Her head stopped its frantic shaking while her body stopped its wild pounding; her only movement left was the gaping of her mouth as she gasped desperately for air.

'No, no, I'll want you to struggle later, but now, tell me about Donovan!' Bogatin brutally shook her neck and struck her across the face, he noticed her nose had begun to bleed.

'Nothing, I know nothing,' he heard her croak.

'Nothing, you say. Then why the interest after I killed your father?'

'I'm not ..' then when his words sunk home, 'Oh God, what are you going to do?' She breathed hard before trying to cry out again.

'Nothing,' he lied as he viciously clamped down with his hand again. 'I just want everything you know. Now, tell me.' He spat out the words through a twisted leer as he brutally shook her head again, while he shook and squeezed he noticed her eyes flick a despairing sideways glance to where he had placed the diary.

He let go the pressure of her throat as he asked, 'Is this it?' He had retrieved the diary with his other hand.

'That's all I … all I know, but I …'

'Shut up! Answer only what I ask, nothing else.' He was met with a fear-filled nod. 'Now I am going to lift my knee and let you go. You are to roll onto your side, then I will take the tape off your ankles,' He said it deliberately, making sure she understood. 'If you scream, Anna, or move in any other direction, I will be forced to hurt you again.' The threat was clear; he was answered by another nod. 'Good, I'm letting you go now.' As he did his gaze never left her dilated, frightened eyes, they would give the first signal if she was going to disobey. He could feel her body rolling beneath him as he lifted his knee. 'Perfect,' he couldn't help but say.

'Now before I let your ankles go, there is nothing else? Only this?' He held up the diary with one hand while the other hovered at his side. 'You wouldn't want me to visit you again, would you?' he said in a conversational tone.

'No that's all. Leave me alone,' croaked a defiant yet terrified voice.

Bogatin tutted as he shook his head. 'Haven't you Americans learnt anything? You should know by now, never trust a Russian.' With lightning speed Bogatin punched her in the solar plexus.

All air was violently driven from her lungs as his fist sunk home. Immediately, her knees were brought protectively up to her chest. She was winded and now lay gasping for air. It was the position Bogatin was looking for. He smiled a deranged smile. She was as he wanted; entirely helpless. He ran his eyes down her body with her knees tucked up her negligee had raked up over her thighs and hips, leaving her vulnerable and exposed.

Unable to take his eyes off her nakedness, Bogatin spoke again, 'You see, Anna, Mr Donovan can't afford to have you alive and it seems such a pity to waste a body like yours.' He licked his lips as his eyes eventually returned to her face.

Seeing the wild, terror-stricken gaze as she painfully fought for breath, he knew there was nothing she could do. The horror in her eyes intensified his barbaric lust as he rolled her onto her back. Unzipping his jeans and peeling off his gloves he could see she was utterly defenceless and able to be used as he saw fit. As she painfully gasped with her arms pinned beneath her back, as with the other women he had raped Bogatin knew she was about to experience a new type of pain, a degrading pain, but this time one that would be carried with her to the grave.

That night the United States of America lost one of its most dedicated and talented scientists.

As Bogatin casually walked down Bay Street towards Harbor Boulevard, beneath his leather gloves he could feel both index fingers sticky with blood. He'd have to burn the gloves and thoroughly scrub his hands; one of her eyes had burst as he'd gouged it from its socket.

But at least Donovan would be happy. Clutching the black diary in one hand, Bogatin was a well-satisfied man. *Just like the old days and at least this Hagan business is sorted, once and for all.*

CHAPTER 31

Zimbabwe

'I SAY WE cull him, take the bastard out. Just like that, pop, between the eyes.' Ben made a motion with his hand and cocked forefinger. 'It would be a service to humanity.'

Tony rounded on Ben. 'Jeez, you're a bloodthirsty bugger.'

'Well, it's not as if we haven't done it before,' the little man reasoned indignantly.

'But that was during the war,' Tony declared. During Zimbabwe's bush-war he and Ben on several occasions had been sent into foreign territory to assassinate terrorist leaders. 'Come on, it's different now. And remember Sithole is a captain in the Zimbabwean Army.'

'Well, he's a prick.'

'And a Shona, let's not forget that,' Tony cut in.

Ben continued as if he hadn't heard. 'And it'd get him out of our hair once and for all. After all, we did find those tyre tracks and you know damn well they were from one of the Army's Unimogs.' He jabbed a finger at his friend.

It was first light, and Tony and Ben were in their short-wheel based Land Cruiser, heading south on the Victoria Falls-Bulawayo Road, about sixty miles south of Hwange National Park. They were again having a heated discussion about what they should do about Captain Sithole since Richard's report had disclosed the full extent of his involvement in Donovan's poaching racket.

It had been a week since they'd met with Richard Black at Victoria Falls. After spending several more hours at the Victoria Falls Hotel after Richard had left, they'd eventually returned to Hwange, back to their base at the park's main camp several miles inside the entrance. One of the cabins at the ranger's headquarters was set aside for them whenever they were working out of the Park. Neither man had got much sleep that night as they tried to formulate a plan of action against Sithole, Donovan and whoever Peter Nkomo was. It wasn't until the early hours of the morning when they decided to turn in, still none the wiser, without a shadow of a plan yet formed.

After only a few hours' sleep and well before dawn, they left their cabin and drove deep into the park to the shallow pan where the hundred odd elephants had been slaughtered. As an early morning's blood-red sun rose above the horizon it was the pungent, sickly-sweet smell of rotting flesh that first guided them to the elephants killed the day before. Lying with their faces hacked off, already the burning African sun of the previous day had begun to do its work. Most of the elephants were bloated, round and fat with gas, their midriffs blown up while their legs stuck straight out in undignified poses of death.

Also, the scavengers had gathered. Neither man begrudged these animals their dirty work for they knew within days most carcasses would be picked clean, leaving only white shiny bones. They were an essential part of cleansing the bushveld and ridding it of disease.

Those carcasses that weren't bloated had been torn into with hooked peaks, rapier-like talons, and sharp canine teeth. As Tony and Ben looked about the carnage they saw a pack of spotted hyenas, a small family of bat-eared foxes and black-backed jackals, all with disproportionately large stomachs, still hacking into and feeding on the ripped open carcasses. There was also a pack of round-eared spotted hunting dogs doing the same, while sitting about and on top of their rotting feasts were the vultures, Egyptian, white-headed, and white-backed, most having gorged themselves so full with carrion they were now unable to fly. They left the scavengers to their gruesome work as they began to scout around the pan for spoor.

Such was Ben's tracking prowess it only took him about twenty minutes to find the first smudged tyre tracks that Captain Sithole's men had missed. Ten more minutes saw him uncover several more. One particular track nestled close beside a small outcrop of rocks clearly showed they were tracks from the heavily lugged tyres of a four-wheel-drive army Unimog. Ben's statement from Victoria Falls had proven correct; they now knew it was Sithole and his men who had slaughtered the elephants.

All that day they scoured the area for further conclusive evidence that would point the finger at Sithole. But alas, they found nothing and returned to their cabin well after dark, dejected and bone weary, knowing they had identified their main enemy in Zimbabwe, yet without a shred of hard evidence to use against him.

For the next week they cautiously questioned countless tourists, rangers and park personnel but to no avail, Sithole had covered his tracks well. Sure, he'd been seen in the park, but so what? It was known with his government appointment he had an avid interest in wildlife.

'Yeah, more than avid,' Tony had bitterly thought. Realising at the time that they were probably sailing too close to the wind, openly investigating the captain and making no inroads at all, they decided they would have to take a different approach. The only trouble was neither man had figured out what to do, Ben's option had been the only decisive suggestion.

'Well?' Ben had folded his arms and swivelled around in his seat as he questioned Tony. 'You come up with a better idea. I still say we should hit the bastard.'

Tony was staring straight ahead, oblivious to the rugged thorn-veld either side of the black tar-sealed road, the tension he felt made obvious only by the whites of his knuckles as his hands were clenched hard around the staring wheel. He would truly love to do as Ben suggested. Ben opened his mouth again to press home his point.

'Shut it,' Tony cut in, 'It's not practical.'

'But —' was all Ben got out.

'Did you know that children and especially little black men should be seen and not heard? So shut it, you've made your point.' Ben huffed indignantly as he folded his arms across his chest, Tony continued, 'It's better the devil we know than the devil we don't. It would cause all sorts of problems if he was found dead, his men would immediately suspect us for a start, and even if they couldn't prove it they'd get us in the end.' Tony was quiet for several seconds as he began to thoughtfully tap the steering wheel with an index finger. 'Somehow we need to publicly expose him.' A plan had begun to form. 'Look, you agree he's been using us?' Ben nodded. 'Okay, it's time to turn the tables. We know he's a link to Donovan and this Nkomo character, right? So we'll somehow get him to expose himself as well as them.'

'Yeah, but how?' Ben was unconvinced; he still had his arms folded.

'Well, he probably works to some type of quota system, at least we agree on that. Now if we work under the pretext of involving him more closely, one; we can keep an eye on him and his men while feeding him information, and two; he'll have to start taking risks to keep his quota up.'

'Could work,' Ben replied reluctantly, but it was clear he'd still rather put a bullet through the Captain's head. 'What sort of information?'

'Herd numbers, sizes and where, in theory, where we'll be working.'

'Which will be incorrect?'

'Exactly.' Tony could see the man was beginning to warm to the idea.

'Okay, yeah, it could work.' Ben unfolded his arms. 'And it'd help if we could get some inside information from his men.' He looked at pains as he composed his next sentence, he cleared his throat. 'Although he's a Shona, there is one man I could talk to, I ...'

'What!' Tony declared in mock distress, 'Surely not. You, I mean *you*, actually talking to a Shona. Maybe there is hope for us yet.'

'He is part Sotho, so it doesn't really count,' the little man hurried on. 'If he'll listen, we may have a chance. However, money will have to change hands.' Ben ended with a shrug.

'Okay, but the money will have to be taken from the stash of US dollars under the seat or organised when I get back. Until then it'll also give us a chance to plan exactly how we trap and expose our friend the Captain.'

'Ah, by the way, where exactly are we going? Shouldn't we stay at Hwange? Sithole and his thugs are due back in the next day or so, aren't they?'

'Yes they are, but I've got to fly up to Kenya to meet someone in Nairobi.' He lightly shook his head in mild disgust. 'Now of all times.'

'I thought the review was off, that the doctor wasn't coming?'

'So did I, but they still want me up at the Nairobi office for some reason. A fax came through last night.' He pulled it out of the breast pocket of his khaki shirt and handed it to Ben. 'Actually, it's probably for the best, it'll give me a chance to check everything's still in place up there. Once we start with Sithole I don't want to stop until we've nailed him.'

'So, you're taking the Cessna,' Ben commented after reading the fax and handing it back. 'It's due for a certificate of airworthiness, isn't it?'

'Yeah, but I'll have to fly it down to Jo'burg to get it done when I get back. So I'll probably be gone a couple of weeks. While I'm away, talk to this man of Sithole's and get him teed up, then try and find out how they export the ivory. It may be our only lead into this Peter Nkomo. Other than that, I still wouldn't have a clue where to start looking for him.'

'I know what you mean.' Ben changed the subject. 'They must stockpile the ivory first, maybe –' Ben would have continued, but something attracted his attention on the side of the road up ahead. Tony had also spotted it. There had been an accident.

Tony pulled the Land Cruiser up behind the mass of twisted metal. It was a dual-axled, long-nosed Ford truck, and was lying on its side with a rusty coloured cargo container still attached to its deck. One of the container's top corners had been split open when the truck overturned.

Before the Land Cruiser rolled to a stop, Ben jumped to the ground and ran around to the truck's cab. Tony found him there with his head poked in through the shattered windscreen; he was feeling for a pulse on the neck of the truck's driver who was slumped down beside the door.

'Well?'

'No, he's cold. Must've happened sometime last night.' He pulled his head from the cab and viewed the wreck. 'Looks as though he fell asleep and lost it on the verge.'

Tony was already walking around to the back. He had noticed blazed across the container's doors the words 'Donovan Enterprises'. Since first hearing about Donovan and his company from Richard, he'd noticed numerous similar containers on the Victoria Falls-Bulawayo road. Ben found him looking up at the big rent in the top corner of the container.

'Reckon if I gave you a boost up there you could see what they were carting. It won't be long before someone else finds it and if it's valuable whatever's in there will be cleaned out.'

Stepping into Tony's hands, interlaced at the fingers, Ben was hoisted up so he could grab the edge of the container. Hauling himself up and walking to the open rent, he shaded his eyes with his hands from the glare of the rising sun and peered into the depths of the container. Until his eyes accustomed themselves to the gloom all he saw was blackness.

'Anything valuable?' Tony was becoming impatient.

Ben didn't respond straight away. 'No, only tobacco and other stuff,' he paused, peering further down into the gloom. 'Hang on a minute. Shit!' He could see something creamy-white shining back at him. 'Bloody hell,' he breathed as he jumped down beside Tony.

'What is it?' Tony asked full of concern.

Ben ignored him. He ran to the back of the Land Cruiser, opened the back door and retrieved a pair of bolt cutters from the toolbox the vehicle carried. He ran back to the container's doors and reaching up, placed the jaws of the bolt cutters around one of the custom's seals that sealed the doors. Chomp, he cut it through.

'Christ, what the hell do you think you're doing. They're official, you can't do that,' Tony said in horror.

'Watch me,' was the only response he got. Chomp, Ben cut through the remaining seal.

'Bloody hell,' he heard Tony swear as he jumped up and flicked open the locking mechanism of first one set then the other of the doors. He had to jump back out of the way as one of the big heavy doors crashed open to the ground. No sooner was it open than Ben rushed inside.

Anxiously peering around the corner of the door Tony was sure his friend had gone stark raving mad, that was until he saw what Ben was dragging out from underneath the tobacco. 'Christ all-bloody-mighty!' He couldn't believe his eyes.

CHAPTER 32

BEN HAD JUST discovered how Donovan smuggled the ivory. Tony watched in horror as Ben retrieved tusk after tusk from beneath the bundles of tobacco strewn around the interior of the container.

'Leave it for now.' Tony reluctantly called a halt to Ben's work. 'We'll have to think this one through. There could be a couple of tons under that lot.'

Ben, wiping his hands on the back of his shorts, came to stand beside Tony who was staring vaguely at the small pile of ivory he'd uncovered.

In theory, this should have been a major breakthrough in their fight against poaching. *But could it somehow jeopardise the half-conceived plans they were about to put into place against Sithole?* Tony asked himself. He made a decision. Sithole, one way or another, would find out about the load being discovered and if he found out that Tony hadn't reported it, that would immediately look suspicious.

'Right, search the cab and grab all the documents you can find.' As Ben did as he was instructed, Tony yanked one of the custom seals from the container's door, he noted the number and placed it in the glove box in the Land Cruiser's dashboard – it might be of use later. He was still sitting in the passenger's seat when Ben presented him with a large black vinyl document pouch. He began to rifle through it; bills of lading, export certificates and numerous other official-looking documents. He pulled out the original custom declaration stamped at the start of the truck's journey; it was stamped by Malawi customs. Scanning down the declaration he found the seal number the load was registered under. Sure enough, it was the same number stamped into the seal.

'Well either the ivory was smuggled up to Malawi to be loaded before the container was sealed, which is bloody unlikely, or someone's got a seal punch that can duplicate the numbers. Did you find anything that resembled a punch of any sort?' Ben shook his head. 'Okay, what's the closest town?'

'Probably Kenmaur, about another thirty miles further south.'

Tony thrust a notebook and the document pouch into Ben's hands. 'Copy everything that's important out of there then put it back where you found it, I don't want Sithole to know we suspect more than we do. I'll drive to

Kenmaur and report it.'

'What if Sithole tries to cover it up?'

'Already thought of that. I'll talk to that journalist we use, working for the *Chronicle* in Bulawayo, the publicity should stop him.' After closing the passenger's door he scooted over to the driver's side, he started the Toyota's big petrol engine. As it rumbled impatiently waiting to be given its lead, Tony looked back over at Ben. 'When you've finished copying that lot, count the tusks and estimate their weights.'

Ben rolled his eyes theatrically before diffidently bobbing his head and declaring sarcastically, 'Yes *Nkosinkulu*, your wish is my command.'

Tony shook his head briefly in a gesture of resignation, he didn't look at Ben as he shifted into first gear and drove off.

'How many?' Tony asked as he walked up to Ben, he'd alighted from the Land Cruiser and had a khaki-clad policeman in tow. He had been away for just over three hours and as Ben looked up from the rows of tusks behind the container, he could see Tony was nearing the end of his tether.

'Five hundred and twenty,' he responded shaking his head in awe. 'Can you believe it?'

'Good God!' Tony was stunned, 'As many as that. Jesus that's,' trying to calculate, 'that's ...'

'Just over two tons,' Ben finished for him, 'From two hundred and sixty elephants.'

Tony's mouth hinged open as he stood in aghast amazement, his earlier frustration experienced while reporting the crash now forgotten. 'The poor bastards,' was all he could think of saying. 'Five hundred and twenty.' He slowly came around when Ben started talking again.

Ben had noticed the police officer hungrily viewing the rows of tusks. He lowered his voice, 'It's worth a king's ransom, over one and a half million Zim dollars.' He looked again at the khaki-clad constable and flicked his head in the man's direction, and asked, 'Did you get hold of the journalist? I wouldn't exactly like to leave them alone with him.'

'I thought he'd be here by now, I made sure I phoned him before I reported it at the police station. Look, we're going to have to leave as soon as he gets here, I should've been in the air hours ago. We'll have to hope once the tusks have been photographed and you've given the journalist the figures, that'll be enough to prevent any from going missing.'

As if the thought had just occurred to him, Ben declared, 'Hell, we're going to be walking a pretty fine line, poachers are one thing, but this, this is real international crime. People get killed for a hell of a lot less.'

Tony looked over at the policeman. 'You'd better go over and talk to him.'

Tony watched Ben approach the constable, he heard him speak in Sindebele, *'Salibonani mngane. Ibizo lakho ngubani?'* (Hello, friend. What is your name?)

Tony turned to the south; the road was empty. He wished the journalist would hurry up and show. He wanted to get up to Kenya before dark if possible, and he still had to do his pre-flight check and lodge his flight plans. He looked at his Rolex. *No, there's not enough time. I'll have to get Ben to do the check while I lodge the plans.* He'd be pushed, but decided if he cut a few corners he could just about make it.

Bulawayo's airport is to the north of the city and the WWF's Cessna 210R, that was on permanent loan to Tony, was in one of the old private hangers nestled amongst the larger commercial ones near the centre of the airport. There was nobody around as the army Land Rover stopped at the back of the old hanger and one of Captain Sithole's men stepped from the vehicle and stood beside the rear door of the hanger. He carefully looked around before he pushed his way through the back door into the gloom of the building.

The man was short and squat with a scowl permanently etched across his chubby black face. On the upper sleeve of his camouflaged British Army style fatigues he had the three stripes that designated he was a sergeant. As he walked into the hanger he carried a small green duffel bag in one hand. The plane he wanted was easy enough to identify, it was white with broad twin red stripes running the length of the fuselage and had **WWF ANTI-POACHING SCHEME** emblazoned across both doors.

The sergeant went straight to the Cessna's engine cover, placed the duffel bag at his feet and lifted it up. He was undisturbed for the ten minutes it took him to attach and set a small manually timed explosive device; while he worked he whistled a tuneless whistle. He knew unless somebody gave the plane a thorough going over, they would miss the device now taped securely to the fuel line running beside the Cessna's six cylinder, turbocharged engine.

He was out of the hanger and back in the Land Rover before Tony and Ben had even left the over turned container, still whistling his tuneless whistle.

'Did you do the pre-flight check?' Tony asked over his shoulder as he threw his rucksack, webbing belt and semiautomatic FN onto the seat behind the pilot's.

'Yeah, well, sort of,' Ben replied scratching his head. He'd actually forgotten the full procedure since the last time Tony had shown him.

When Tony had run off to the tower to lodge his flight plans Ben had just stood there in front of the plane, hoping it would do the blasted pre-flight check itself, and that's more or less what happened. He kicked a tire, wiggled a flap and did a visual check of the fuel in the wing-tanks as well as the reserves in the outer wings. Other than that, that was about it. He'd never felt comfortable with things that left the ground.

'Either you did, or you didn't.'

'Well, the tanks were full.'

Tony shook his head despondently; he was way behind schedule.

'And all the tyres have got air in them.'

Tony's resolve broke, 'Well then, that'll do me,' he said with a chuckle. It was hard to stay annoyed with Ben for long.

Both men pushed the plane out onto the tarmac, and Tony started talking again once Ben had closed the hanger's door, 'Right, while I'm away, talk to this man in Sithole's unit and follow up everything you can on the container, stockpiles, the works. Even go up to Malawi if you have to, but only if you have to; you've got the name of the customs officer who cleared the container. I'll try and find out what I can about Peter Nkomo while I'm up north. Surely I can pick up some type of lead. I'll be back after the C of A down in Jo'burg, as soon as possible. You know where you can reach me if we need to talk.'

He jumped into the plane before Ben could respond.

Ben waited until the Cessna had turned out of the circuit after take-off and was just a speck in the rich-blue sky, then he walked over to the Land Cruiser. Starting the vehicle up he realised he didn't begrudge Tony his lonely trip up the centre of the continent. On a flight like that, company was appreciated.

As he drove from the airport Ben knew he had more than enough to do to keep himself occupied while Tony was away and gave his friend little more thought, accompanied on his journey only by a small ticking device taped to the Cessna's fuel line.

CHAPTER 33

Nairobi, Kenya

PETER NKOMO OWNED two houses; one in Diepkloof extension in Soweto, a lavish Spanish style villa carefully situated behind a huge security fence and nestled amongst the other homes of Soweto's elite, and the other in Kenya. As he had been spending far greater periods of time in Kenya and Tanzania since the CITES' meeting in Lausanne, he had eventually chosen a second dwelling in Nairobi.

For his first year in east Africa he had lived out of a suite in the historically elegant Norfolk Hotel, on Harry Thuku Road just under a mile from the centre of Nairobi before deciding to take a permanent dwelling in the city. He made his choice with care and eventually bought an extraordinary copy of an English Tudor mansion in the prestigious suburb of Muthaiga on the city's limits. His closest neighbour on one side, living in a sprawling bungalow type thatched-roofed dwelling, was Kenya's Minister of Energy. On his other side, he had the Belgian Ambassador living in a replica of the Grand Trianon at Versailles in France.

Peter was sitting in his study on the ground floor of the three-storied mansion; the room was spacious and furnished solely with solid wood antiques, mostly Chippendale, the Gothic motifs and massive carved furniture suiting the expansiveness of the room. He was sitting behind a solid intricately carved oak wood desk, and beyond the lead-lights at his rear a magnificently manicured lawn swept down to an artificial lake at the bottom of the mansion's beautifully tended five acres of grounds. The sheer opulence around him preyed little upon his mind; it came with the territory. *Africa has a wealth of wildlife, it's only proper some of us become wealthy because of it*, he had reasoned on numerous occasions.

The furniture in his study and the desk he sat behind may have been antiques but not so the electronic equipment strategically positioned around him on the desktop. This was state of the art, the best money could buy; computerised communication equipment, a terminal and screen with the tower tucked away out of sight, and a high-speed fax within easy reach on the edge of the desk.

Peter was perusing the last month's ivory take that had come out of Kenya and Tanzania. He was about to enter the information into his computer and was checking the poachers' weights against what he knew had been unloaded from the containers at Kilindini Harbour in Mombasa. He used a similar method to the one operating down south. Having the ivory stockpiled in caches strategically placed around both countries he would then bring in sealed containers from neighbouring Burundi or Uganda to pick up and smuggle the tusks to Mombasa. However, he was trying to centralise the process; in east Africa he had to do far more work than down south. He had no one central figure like Captain Sithole to work with, and having Tony Campbell virtually destroy his Somali network hadn't helped at all.

He became annoyed just thinking about the cursed man and that wasn't in his nature. *Mind you*, he thought as the annoyance faded, letting out a contented sigh, *It looks as though Tony Campbell is, or soon will be, out of the way for good.*

He reached for a fax just beside his desk blotter that had arrived from Bulawayo several hours earlier and leant back in his swivel-backed chair as he read through it once again. It was from Captain Sithole and was short and sweet. 'Package assigned. Consignment airborne.'

Peter should have felt happy but didn't – his annoyance returned. Tony Campbell had caused too many problems while he was around. His death needed to look like an accident. *Light aircraft are always going down across the continent*, he reasoned. But he was only now beginning to get the Somali *shiftas* back on track again.

Peter had always prided himself on running a tight ship and had become renowned amongst his network of poachers for the type and severity of the discipline he never hesitated to dish out. It usually got results and guaranteed success. But with Tony Campbell and the *shiftas* it had been different; Tony had chosen to play a far more ruthless game. Whereas Peter would perhaps kill a poacher because of a too severe beating, Tony had mercilessly wiped out whole gangs, and only now were the *shiftas* starting to listen to him again.

So Peter had been horrified when he had heard from Sithole that Campbell was flying up, but he was also relieved that Donovan had sanctioned his request to have him removed. His presence in Kenya could've easily tipped the scales, and in the wrong way for Peter.

But now, he thought as he confidently rubbed his hands together, *we'll be having no more trouble from him.*

His thoughts of Tony vanished as the fax machine answered an incoming call and began to print. The distraction didn't last long. Tony Campbell was once again firmly embedded within his mind. Peter was shaking with rage by the time he'd read the fax, his eyes ablaze with shining black fury, while his lips were pulled into thin, tight angry lines, as the rims of his nostrils turned white with anger.

'The bastard!' he exploded as he stood bolt upright, the swivel-backed chair crashed against the vanished sill beneath the lead-lights. 'Jesus bloody Christ, the bastard!' he repeated. His hands shook as he reread the fax from Captain Sithole. 'All five hundred and twenty of them,' he cried in dismay. 'He had no right!'

Peter had been informed Tony had stumbled upon that month's shipment of ivory; the fax stated it had been confiscated and an official investigation in Zimbabwe was ensuing. Still staring at the fax held in one hand, he reached back and groped for his chair with the other. After retrieving the chair he slumped down upon it, placed the fax on the desk blotter and firmly planted his elbows either side of it. With a deep breath he despondently placed his head in his hands.

God this is disastrous. He made a quick mental calculation. *Shit, that's about a quarter of a million dollars US down the bloody drain.* He groaned as he sat back and dragged a despairing hand over his face. *What the bloody hell am I going to tell Donovan?* Even though he knew it wasn't the Captain's fault, he reasoned, *Jesus, Sithole's going to pay for this.* He stared back down at the fax again for many minutes.

It was the first big consignment he had ever lost, even though he'd heard of other less organised rackets losing upwards of twenty percent of their poached ivory to officials. He shook his head and snorted in black humour. *What a parting gift, eh. Virtually from his grave. But at least, Campbell, it'll be the last one you ever give.* The thought should have made him feel better, but it didn't. *All that money gone,* he despaired.

CHAPTER 34

Zimbabwe – Zambia – Malawi – Tanzania

FOURTEEN HUNDRED AND fifty miles. Tony steeled himself. Although he'd learnt to fly years before in the skies above the open expanse of the Kalahari Desert, he still hated flying by himself. *Six, well close enough to six and a half hours and I should be in Nairobi.* He looked at his watch. *Bugger!* Even if he had a tailwind it would be dark by the time he reached the Kenyan capital. He'd have to radio through his amended arrival time.

Tony had only just taken off from Bulawayo airport; he climbed to twenty thousand feet and throttled back to the plane's cruising speed of two hundred and twenty-five miles an hour. After consulting the compass in its glass oil-bath above his head he set the plane on a north-easterly heading and engaged the automatic pilot. He knew with the fuel tanks and their reserves full the Cessna would make the trip with about a hundred and thirty miles to spare, again depending on the winds he met. He settled back for a long tiresome trip, expecting nothing especially exciting to happen. For ninety minutes Tony had flown over the plateau-type landscape of Zimbabwe's high and middle velds, distinguished by the varying green shades of bushveld that were dotted with rocky *kopjes* and bald knob-like domes of sliprock. He'd also seen dusty roads snaking across the vast expanse of primeval country to join the miniature toy-like farms and settlements far below. When he saw the sun reflecting off the shimmering waters of the huge man-made lake of Kariba out to his left, and when the plateau country dramatically dropped away into the broad Zambezi Valley, he knew the Zambian border wasn't far away. Then with a flash of deep indigo, the Cessna crossed over the majestic splendour of the Zambezi River and only then for the first time did he disengage the autopilot and alter course. Using the huge Cabora Bassa Dam to his right as a reference, he began to skirt around the furthest western corner of Mozambique. Tony had no desire to be mistaken for a hostile aircraft and attract a stray rebel Remano or government-backed Frelimo rocket.

Upon crossing into Zambia Tony quickly picked up the mighty Luangwa River and got back on his true north-easterly heading. He let out a tired heavy breath; beneath him the landscape was unspectacular, a gently undulating tableland studded with a few ox-bow lakes and covered with a mixture of deciduous forests, savanna and marshlands. It wasn't until he reached the South Luangwa National Park a hundred and fifty miles across the border, stretching out to the left of the river, that his interest quickened.

Keeping one eye on the horizon he craned his neck to the left. *Luangwa, eh?* he muttered in awe. Tony knew it once or probably still did have the potential to be the most spectacular wildlife sanctuary in southern Africa. Probably all of Africa for that matter.

It had all the 'big five', elephant, black rhino, lion, buffalo and leopard in abundance. If it weren't for the economic plight the country was in, and the inflated cost for the average person to visit it, the wildlife park could have been turned into a spectacular jewel within Africa's treasure trove of game reserves, open to visitors from all around the globe.

Now that would definitely help wildlife conservation and the country's economy.

With his mind firmly fixed on wildlife he decided to make a slight detour. He wanted to view one of the biggest wildlife parks under the Wildlife Fund's anti-poaching scheme, the Selous Game Reserve in southern Tanzania. Grabbing the large-scale map from the seat opposite he made a few quick calculations.

It'll add about fifty miles. Piece of cake, I've still got heaps of leeway, he reasoned after consulting the map. *Should reach Nairobi with plenty to spare.*

He made his decision and changed course towards Malawi and a more easterly heading. Tony was certain he'd reach Nairobi with plenty of fuel to spare.

The small device on the fuel line clicked and began its last cycle as it continued to tick slowly down.

The view beneath Tony was vastly different to those he'd seen in the rest of his trip. He was heading directly over the spectacular mountain scenery and the near tree-less grassy plateaus of Malawi's Nyika Plateau National Park, as well as the small colonial town of Livingstonia, perched many hundreds of yards above the country's huge inland lake; Lake Malawi. Even from his elevated height Tony could see the town would command a dramatic view, probably one of the most stunning in southern Africa, nestled high above the continent.

As soon as the rugged grandeur of Malawi and its lake was left behind Tony was over the green rolling highlands of southern Tanzania. Flying directly parallel and about a hundred miles southeast of the Zambian Highway and Tanzam Railway he soon left the southern highlands behind and found himself above the Selous Game Reserve. Once he picked up the huge coffee-coloured Rufiji River his solitude was forgotten. As he flew directly above it, all he could see for miles around were the varying shapes of brown, grey and greens embellishing the savanna, scattered bushveld and Miombo woodlands of the sprawling game reserve. The sight was awe-inspiring.

'The size of Ireland,' Tony breathed in wonder. It was the largest, oldest and most remote sanctuary in Africa.

Throwing caution to the wind and realising he'd be using up his precious fuel, he declined the Cessna's nose and pointed it towards the river. Once the altimeter told him he was a couple of hundred feet above the water he levelled the plane out once again. Tony knew with its massive tributaries the Rufiji made up the largest river basin in east Africa, sustaining one of the greatest concentrations of big game left on the continent; elephant and buffalo in their thousands, with the greatest number of wild dogs and crocodiles in Africa.

'God, look at them all,' he breathed in wonder as he banked the Cessna to the left. He had come upon a wide open, tree-studded, grassy plain beside the river. There were impala, waterbuck, wildebeest and giraffe by the score, dotted amongst a herd of elephants that must have numbered in the hundreds. 'Bloody hell, a relic of Africa I thought was gone,' he said aloud, as the animals scattered beneath the roaring plane.

Climbing as he banked the plane back to the river, he realised man may have left his mark on the earth's crust elsewhere across the globe, but not here. He was seeing an expanse of wilderness totally untamed and felt humbled by the overwhelming grandeur of the truly unspoiled wilds. Tony felt lost and insignificant, completely in awe. That was until the illusion, like a pane of painted glass, shattered. Beneath him like a shining beacon, a mass of white, sun-bleached bones glared back at him as he climbed. Feeling his blood boil he didn't have to fly back over them to know they were elephant bones, and by their number he knew there were far too many to be caused by natural death.

'Bloody poachers,' he swore venomously under his breath. Even in the virtually uninhabited reaches of Selous the greedy hands of man had grasped and destroyed forever a part of the continent's dwindling wildlife.

They'd use the river to get in and get the ivory out, Tony decided. The rest of the reserve was just a trackless stretch of wilderness that should've been a haven for the animals. *But not now.* He bitterly shook his head.

Tony knew from the work he'd done in Tanzania in the past the Selous Game Reserve was virtually unpopulated, the tsetse fly (causing sleeping sickness amongst man and beast alike) and the poor soil had seen to that. The reserve fell into two parts, either side of the Rufiji River, with the only camps being in the north in comparative easy reach of the country's capital, Dar-es-Salaam.

'Bastards!' he cursed as he silently vowed, *Once this Donovan bullshit is sorted out, this is where Ben and I'll be heading next.* It was too much for him to bear to have a wilderness like this one stripped of wildlife.

Maybe Donovan's lackeys did that. He looked to his side once again. No longer did he see a wildlife paradise below; the Rufiji and its surrounding landscape now looked desolate and forlorn, a gloomy stretch of water.

Feeling totally helpless he tore his eyes away and looked down at the altimeter. He'd only climbed to about a thousand feet. Setting his eyes on the distant horizon he couldn't get Donovan and his poaching racket from his mind, so he began to formulate a plan he'd use to track down Peter Nkomo in Kenya. He was sure with a name, even without a description, he'd be able to get some type of lead and hopefully nail the bastard. But of course Peter had already made other plans.

Tony had flown about a thousand miles and had been in the air for just on four and a half hours when the small device taped to the fuel line made a final click. Tony heard a dull explosive thud as the engine compartment immediately burst into flames. Fanned by the wind rushing by and fuelled by the avgas gushing from the ruptured line, the paint on the engine cover immediately began to blister as smoke billowed from the plane's wounded engine.

'Shit!' Tony swore in horror as he flicked off the fuel pumps and master switches, but still the fire increased in intensity. He tried the radio, it was dead. *Bloody hell, I'll have to land the bitch. But where?* he thought hopelessly. For miles around all he could see was Miombo woodlands. *It'll have to be the river.* He drew his hand away from the toggle switch that would have lowered the landing gear.

Tony steeled himself as he began preparing for a forced landing, but could hardly see a thing; smoke was now billowing in great dirty clouds over the windscreen. Fire: the pilots' horror. Tony recognised the situation as hopeless, with no power and not being able to see a thing he'd either drop like a stone or burn before he'd reached the river. He was thankful he wasn't at twenty thousand feet; he was doomed as it was but being burnt alive as he dropped from high altitude would have been far worse.

The silence, the eerie quiet after the roar of the Cessna's turbocharged engine was appalling as he pushed forward the control wheel and dropped the nose. For the briefest of seconds with the change in elevation the windscreen cleared and he could see in the distance where the coffee-coloured Rufiji was joined by another river.

'The Great Ruaha,' he grunted, 'Stiegler's Gorge up ahead.' The largest of the permanent camps in the reserve was situated above the gorge. *Too bloody far*, he immediately realised as he pointed the Cessna along the line of the river.

'Come on, baby,' he coaxed, delicately playing with the controls as he was again enveloped by smoke, he opened the perplex side window and stuck out his head. Having his hair buffeted by the wind and flicking in his eyes it wasn't much better, but he was going in too fast. Bringing his head back into the cockpit he looked down at the airspeed indicator. *Far too fast.* everything was happening at once. He pulled up the nose and pulled on full flaps to bleed off speed. *Shit!* He could feel his feet beginning to roast and flicked a quick look at the altimeter, down to five hundred feet. He stuck his head out the window once again.

All Tony could see was a smoke shroud haze and distorted shaped that could have been land up ahead. If it weren't for the instruments he'd be flying completely blind and by the seat of his pants, but as it was his intuition told him to look back at his instrument panel. He yanked his head in again. Altimeter: down to three fifty. Airspeed: Hell, too bloody fast again. He pulled back on the control wheel.

Then like the quickly rising African sun, realisation dawned. *Bloody hell!* he screamed silently. In the panic and hidden by smoke he had forgotten the river below was probably already three hundred feet above sea-level; he shoved his head out the window and looked down. The smoke cleared and sure enough, rushing up at him fifty feet below was the murky waters of the Rufiji.

Christ, here's a go. He'd never crashed before, but he knew if he could skim the plane in and land along the water he might have a chance. He brought his head back inside, snapped the side window shut and concentrated on bringing her down, trying desperately to hold up the nose so he could belly her in the river. 'Come on baby.' But it was bloody hopeless, he knew.

Tony pulled up the nose and the Cessna nearly stalled as its nose almost immediately dropped again. Gently playing with the control wheel, he felt his optimism rise; he might be able to make it. With one hand still on the wheel, he tightened his seat belt and shoulder straps; he'd be hitting any second now and hitting hard. He fixed his eyes on the swirling smoke covering the windscreen as he waited for the impact. This was the worst part, not actually knowing when the plane's smooth white belly would touch.

Just as he thought he was about to hit, the smoke cleared. In horror, he saw the river meander off to the right and he was flying directly towards its tree-lined bank.

Oh gawd. He felt like crossing himself, or at least that's what he thought a Catholic would do for some divine intervention.

Looming before him, edging the river, were lifeless looking skeletons of great phallus-like doum palms. He yanked back on the control wheel but nothing happened; the airspeed was far too low as the Cessna continued to catapult towards the trees.

The left wing hit first, whiplashing Tony and the plane to the right. His head hit the door-post beside him with an almighty crack, and he was unconscious when the right wing struck another leafless doum as the wings were plucked from the crippled plane. With his head lolling helplessly, Tony was thrown violently up against his shoulder straps as he and the wounded, wingless Cessna hurtled through the remaining doum palms to a small ox-bow lake just beyond. Nose first, the Cessna crashed into its murky depths sending a cascading deluge of water over the dismembered plane; a great plume of steam immediately quenched the fire. The plane began to sink.

Unconscious and trapped by his seatbelt and shoulder straps Tony wasn't about to be burnt to death nor had he been torn apart as the plane crashed; drowning was more likely. If Peter Nkomo had seen the plane with its sole occupant cocooned inside slowly sinking, he would've known he'd be having no more trouble from Tony Campbell. He would finally have been a happy man.

CHAPTER 35

Los Angeles

HALF A WORLD away, Sabina Donovan had just walked into her husband's outer office. Her hair was severely pulled back and piled high upon her head, while a touch of rouge artfully brushed upon her cheeks highlighted her Mediterranean features. Wearing a tawny suit with a hugging knee-length skirt, she looked a living work of art. She had slung from one shoulder to the opposite hip a tan leather clutch bag. That and her similar coloured stilettos made for the finishing touches of the elegant clothes she wore. Yet her demeanour spoke the loudest message; Sabina was dressed for business.

Walking past the chrome and black leather furniture she stood in front of Donovan's secretary and spoke in a voice as sweet as nectar, yet with undertones laced with venom, 'Sonya, is my husband in his office?' She knew he wasn't; she'd already broken into his briefcase several nights before and viewed his diary. An hour before he'd flown to San Francisco for a morning's worth of meetings.

'No, I'm sorry, Mrs Donovan. Your husband is away. Out of the city for the day,' Sonya said as sweetly but with the same subtle trace of malice. 'However, I may see him tonight,' she couldn't resist adding.

You absolute bitch, Sabina thought, full of loathing. However, she held her smile firmly fixed in place. 'I'd like to use a phone.'

Sonya indicated the one on her desk.

'In private, thank you,' Sabina declared as she turned on her heels.

When she got to the big teak doors guarding Donovan's office she stood contemptuously to the side and waited for Sonya to step up to the keypad and unlock the doors. This time she never saw her push the numbered pads, but immediately recognised the accompanying electronic notes that sounded as being the same.

Once the doors were unlocked Sabina turned to face Sonya again. Time to leave a broadside the little bitch wouldn't forget. 'Don't worry about tonight. You needn't bother passing on I was asking for him.' She then dropped her smile and met Sonya's eyes. 'I'll make sure I'm at the airport to meet him.'

That'd upset their plans.

She pushed through the heavy doors into the office with a bitter feeling of triumph, but her loathing wasn't directed solely at Sonya. She was even more determined now to bring about her husband's downfall as she closed and rested her back up against the doors.

The bastard! she thought resentfully. She pushed herself from the door and walked up to the portrait of Jarrod Donovan. She had no intention of meeting her husband at the airport. That night she had another meeting, a far more important meeting with Richard Black. Within a minute she had swung back the portrait, opened the wall safe and had the container of computer disks tucked under her arm.

Sabina, wholly intent on her real reason for visiting Donovan's office, stepped up the Parian marble steps, passed the towering ivory columns and eventually walked in behind his desk. She never even bothered looking at the panoramic view the picture window beyond the desk afforded of the sprawling city of Los Angeles. She instead placed the container on the desk and reached into the small clutch bag at her hip – it was suspended around her chest and back by a tightly plated leather strap. She withdrew a double sided, double density micro-disk. This time Sabina had come prepared.

Placing it on the desk blotter she first retrieved the phone and dialled LA's pre-recorded weather forecast. Confident that a light would now be showing on Sonya's phone in the outer-office – indicating an outside line was being used – she reached for and flicked on both the computer tower and screen. Impatiently, she waited for the machine to warm up; within seconds the computer was ready for use. She opened the container and slotted into one of its drives the same disk she'd viewed several months before.

Sabina, having being schooled by Richard on what to look for and do, got into the computer's utilities and called up 'copy text' from the disk. Once the function was in place and activated she began scrolling through the disk's file menu.

She first chose *Lavare $* for an update, then a file entitled *Mammoth*, another entitled *East Africa* and one called *Southern Africa*, also choosing one named *Trip '93* – she knew Richard would be interested in her husband's trip to Africa to view his poaching operation.

Sabina was confident she could've copied the vast majority of the files if she'd brought with her enough disks but she had chosen to string Richard along for as long as possible. Destroying her husband was one thing but, well, Richard Black had proved himself quite another – in more ways than one.

She briefly shuddered in delight as her whole body tingled with pleasure.

I'll copy two more, she decided. She thrust the thought of Richard from her mind, but indecision like a murky fog had crept in to cloud her mind. She couldn't decide which ones and spent a few minutes scrolling through the file names.

The cursor eventually settled at the N's. Okay, that one. It seemed unimportant; it was entitled with an obscure name; *Nkomo*. She scrolled back through the menu again and was back to the first page without having chosen another. *Oh, that one'll do.*' It was one the cursor was positioned over, the file simply read: *Campbell.*

She pushed return and began copying each file, one after the other, from the disk to the computer and its screen. Once the copying was complete she popped out the disk, placed it back in the container and slotted in the new disk she had retrieved from her clutch bag. Before returning the container back to the safe, locking it and replacing the portrait, she brought up the command 'save to disk' and pushed return.

When she eventually got back into Donovan's high-backed chair she leant back happily, reasoning she would only have a few minutes to wait.

In the outer office, Sonya was intently staring at the white light blazing on her phone, indicating an outside line was being used. *How long was she going to be in there?* She knew she was being petty, but it didn't seem right, *her* being in Judd's office. Even if she was his wife.

She looked at her watch again; it had been about ten minutes since Sabina had entered the office. She was tempted to pick the phone up and listen in and for the second time her hand hovered over the receiver. *This time I'll do it*, she decided as she placed her hand on the phone. But before she could lift it, out of the corner of her eye a movement attracted her attention. Guiltily she snatched her hand away and looked up.

Oh God! Sonya shivered with dread. Nikolai Bogatin had entered the outer office and was walking towards the big teak doors; he was intent on walking through them.

Sonya steeled herself and swallowed heavily as she rose from behind the desk. 'I'm sorry, Mr Bogatin. You can't go in there.'

Bogatin had already punched in the access code and unlocked the doors. With his hand on one of the door's handles, he partially opened it as he turned to face her. From beneath hooded eyes he swept a lecherous gaze over her shapely body. 'And why not?' he asked in heavily accented English.

'Would you like to try and stop me?'

Sonya swallowed heavily again, the man frightened and disgusted her all at once. 'Mrs Donovan is in there, using the phone, a personal call,' she ended lamely.

Bogatin snorted as he sneered at her and he pushed his way through the door into the office.

The saving seemed to be taking forever. Sabina had actually picked up the phone and listened to the weather forecast – hot, dry and sunny – that's how bored she'd become. *Surely it'll be finished soon.* But still fixed in the middle of the screen in a box read 'SAVE: Now saving'.

She placed the phone back on the desk blotter and looked at her diamond-studded Rolex; she must have been in the office for about ten minutes now. Willing the infernal machine to hurry up, she casually looked down into the office's informal discussion area and towards the heavy teak doors. In horror, she heard the audible clicks as the deadbolts drew back and she saw one of the doors open. It moved slightly and then stopped. *Oh, God!* she thought in anguish, she'd been sure she wouldn't be disturbed. Shooting a distressed look at the computer screen, she noticed the legend on it had disappeared; the save was complete.

First flicking off the switches on the tower and screen, she made sure she saw the latter go blank. Then she hit the button over the disk drive and the disk popped out. Her hand was shaking with anxiety when she reached down to pull it out. *God, I'm not up to this,* she thought despairingly. *Last time was bad enough.*

As she withdrew the disk from the slot, it dropped as she fumbled with it and bounced under the desk. Cursing, half with fear of discovery and half in agitation, she pushed back the chair and followed it under the desk. Groping in the half-light she eventually retrieved it and backed out to kneel beside the desk's pedestal of drawers. Twisting around the tan clutch bag into her lap, still suspended from her shoulder, she frantically fumbled with the flap and managed to finally, thankfully, slip the disk inside. It was then she gasped in fright and nearly died a thousand deaths – a pair of hand-tooled Italian brogues had walked into her line of sight.

Throwing a hand over her chest in fright she slowly raised her eyes. Firstly, she saw a pair of lightweight silvery-grey suit trousers; next, the matching jacket and crisp white shirt with pastel tie; then finally, the bull-neck and face of Slavic features.

'Nikolai, you scared the life out of me. What the hell do you think you are doing?' she blazed trying to hide her guilt. She rose to her feet, reached for the phone and placed it back in its cradle. Her mind was racing. Had he seen the disk? Then she immediately realised Donovan had had the Russian follow her. The thought steeled her. 'Well?' she asked with forced bravery as she placed her hands on her hips.

'I should ask you the same thing?'

'And what the hell's that supposed to mean?' she demanded. She had never liked the man and had already suspected correctly what his true purpose was within Donovan Enterprises. She swallowed her fear and took a challenging step forward. Fleeting hesitation flicked across his hooded eyes. However, he soon braced his resolve.

Orders are orders, even if she is the boss's wife, he reasoned to himself, Donovan's instructions had been explicit. *Do what you have to. Find out exactly what she's up to*. He stood his ground. 'What did you put in your bag?' There was a new firmness to his voice as he reached out for her clutch bag.

He knows. Sabina quailed inside. *And Judd has ordered him to follow me. God, what now?* She could feel her stomach muscles knot as the fear welled up from deep inside.

'What the hell do you think you are doing?' she challenged as she pulled the bag away. 'I dropped and retrieved my notebook.' But she could see he didn't believe her; he was reaching for her bag again.

His hand had just about closed around it as Sabina twisted away, and he took a step forward as he grabbed for an arm instead. This time as she swung her arm out of the way Sabina found herself off balance. Her weight was thrown to the side but her ankle twisted as she toppled off her stilettos.

In horror, Bogatin saw her falling. Roughing up someone else was one thing *but the boss's wife?* He grabbed for her but only succeeded in clutching hold of her suit jacket and changing the direction of her fall. With a meaty whack her head caught the edge of the desk as the jacket ripped.

Sabina ended up on the ground on her knees facing away from the Russian. Slightly dazed she first looked at the tear on her jacket lapel and then felt something warm trickling down the side of her face. With a hesitant hand she reached up to her eyebrow. Bringing bloodied fingers back in front of her face she realised it had been cut to the bone. As is common even with the smallest of head wounds, blood was pouring from the cut.

'Mrs Donovan, are you all right?'

A concerned heavily accented voice lanced the numbness of her mind, she screamed as she jumped to her feet, 'Get away from me you animal!' She brought a hand up to her eyebrow again and rubbed it down her face. Sabina knew exactly what she was doing; she made sure there was plenty of blood over her face and on her white blouse beneath her suit. 'Sonya!' she screamed, she wanted a witness as she positioned the desk between herself and Bogatin.

'But, Mrs Donovan I didn't mean –'

'Sonya!' Sabina screamed again, never letting her eyes wander from the Russian.

'Oh my God!' she heard a woman's voice gasp from somewhere and she looked down onto the marble step. Sonya was standing with her hand thrown up to her mouth in horror, transfixed by the blood-splattered figure she was presented with.

'Call security, the bastard attacked me! Well go on!' Sabina eventually had to raise her voice.

As Sonya ran from the office, Sabina hissed at Bogatin, 'You'll pay for this. If I'm scarred …' she let the statement hang, but she couldn't keep the relief from her eyes.

It had been close, but the accident had been a godsend. She could hardly believe it; she'd gotten away with it.

Even that animal of his couldn't stop me.

CHAPTER 36

'SO MUCH FOR professionalism,' Richard stated as he again checked the bottle of Bollinger champagne in the ice bucket on the sideboard beside the door. He was in the sitting room of the same hotel suite he had stayed at on his last visit to Los Angeles, in the Bel Air on Stone Canyon Road. He was waiting for Sabina Donovan and despite the increasing gravity of the current investigation and the circumstances surrounding it, he was looking forward to the meeting. *And why not?* he thought with a wicked glint in his eye. He was dressed in khaki suit trousers and a plain white shirt; he had only just removed his jacket and tie.

Using an index finger to curl back the shirt's crisp white cuff he looked at his watch, it was just before eight in the evening. When Sabina had rung through two days previously to say she'd have more information they had organised the meeting – if you could really call it that – for eight.

In the past he'd always be adamant, never mix business with pleasure. However, since the last time they'd met, his conscience had eventually given up. He was breaking the secret agents' cardinal rule and strangely it didn't bother him at all.

He walked over to the stereo and selected a disk from the Baroque period. As the soothing strains of Antonio Vivaldi filled the room he walked over to the couch to wait. Crossing his legs and settling himself onto the blue leather three-seater he looked around the room.

It was a spacious sitting room, decorated in subtle shades of gold and blue, with prints of the early Californian days adorning the walls. The rest of the furniture positioned around the room was crafted from solid Tasmanian blackwood, imported from Australia. In front of the three-seater and two accompanying chairs in the centre of the room, was a rectangular coffee table, while behind the suite to the left of French doors that opened onto a small private balcony was a round dining table with room for a comfortable setting of four. Opposite the table was a small hallway that led to the suite's bathroom and bedroom beyond. He nearly rubbed his hands together at the thought of the bedroom but managed to arrest the movement. Then there was a gentle knock at the door.

Well, I'll be ... On the dot of eight. He was impressed as he glanced at his Seiko, getting up to answer the door.

A smile of genuine pleasure spread across his face when Sabina walked into the room; he'd forgotten how stunning she was and how alluring she'd become. His eyes scanned her body. She was simply dressed in red leather ankle-high boots, designer jeans and a floral patterned long-sleeved shirt. His smile quickly faded when he saw her face.

'My God, what happened?' he asked with genuine concern. He closed the door and placed his hands upon her shoulders as he looked at her blackened eye and row of neat stitches in the eyebrow above it.

Sabina recognised the concern as being sincere and totally unforced; it was the most genuine and possibly the nicest gesture anyone had ever shown her, and for that alone she would've gladly endured the ordeal all over again. A prospect that would have gladdened Richard's heart.

When the security guards had arrived soon after Sonya's frantic summons they'd been appalled at the sight. With the copious amounts of blood, Sabina's injury looked far worse than it was. However, the guards may have been appalled, but that didn't mean they would take on the Russian. When Bogatin realised nobody would listen to reason, he left without opposition, but trailing after him were the words, 'My husband will certainly hear about this.'

Sabina was whisked downstairs to the tower block's resident doctor, and after she'd signed numerous release forms he injected the wound with anaesthetic and using five neat sutures had stitched up the cut.

Never once after the ordeal and for the rest of the day had she become emotional; the cold loathing she carried for Donovan was enough to keep her emotions in check. That was until now. Richard's concern had lanced right through into her soul, and as if a dam wall had been breached, tears began to flow.

'Oh Richard,' she sobbed as he gently took her in his arms.

It took Sabina about ten minutes to control her tears and raking sobs; she'd had finally realised how much of a close-run thing the ordeal had been. If Bogatin had found the disk and given it to Donovan ... she shuddered to think what would've happened.

After the tears it had taken another ten minutes for her to tell her story. Although risk was an everyday part of his profession, Richard was horrified. An agent was one thing, a civilian another, but Sabina, now she was swiftly becoming something different yet again.

'He must suspect, otherwise why have you followed?'

'Yes, I know.' Sabina answered, delicately dabbing her red inflamed eyes with a tissue. Both she and Richard were now sitting on the leather couch facing one another.

'We'll have to move with caution, especially up until he leaves on his trip to Africa,' Richard stated, full of concern. 'It may even be better not to try for any more information until he's gone.'

'No!' Sabina let out a gasp. 'I mean, it's too important. Isn't it?' She didn't want to break contact with Richard, not after their last meeting and now especially, after his genuine show of concern; she'd never felt so special in another person's arms.

Richard immediately recognised the true reason for her distress; her sentiment pleased him and worried him all at once. *I should be stepping back, before it really complicates matters.* His conscience immediately piped up in an I-told-you-so-voice, *Forget it, pal. Bit late now wouldn't you say?* Richard tried to ignore the little voice and wait and see what happened. Whatever way he viewed her, Sabina was definitely an important part of his plans.

'Okay, let's have a look at the disk.'

Sabina took it out of her bag and placed it on the couch between them, while Richard reached beside him for a black leather briefcase and placed it on the coffee table. Opening it, he lifted out an IBM notebook, placed it beside the briefcase and switched it on. He grabbed the disk and slotted it into the computer. 'Let's see if the scar you'll carry was worth it.'

'Oh, Richard!' Sabina half wailed, it was obviously the wrong thing for him to say.

'Yes, well …' he tried to cover his faux pas as he made a show of recalling the files from the disk.

The small menu of file names lit up the LCD screen; *Campbell, East Africa, Lavare $, Mammoth, Nkomo, Southern Africa* and *Trip '93*. 'Hell's bells, well done,' his blunder was forgotten, while even Sabina forgot about the possible disfiguration and Richard's ill-chosen words. 'You've got far more than I could ever have hoped for. Well done,' he congratulated her again. His gaze was immediately drawn to two of the file names, *Campbell* at the top and *Nkomo* half way down. He called up *Nkomo*.

'This is brilliant,' he declared reading the file, he now knew exactly who Peter Nkomo was and his relationship to Donovan's poaching racket; dates, residential addresses, the works. Richard reached over and drew Sabina towards him. 'You're brilliant,' he said as he kissed her.

As Sabina melted into his arms he had to use an extreme force of will to prevent himself from sweeping her off to the bedroom there and then. However, there was time enough for that later – instinct told him to call up the *Campbell* file. Sabina sighed a contented sigh as he pulled away and turned back to the computer.

'Oh no!' he breathed in equal horror and regret after scanning quickly through the well-documented file. It gave an explicit resume of Tony Campbell's history since starting with wildlife conservation, his anti-poaching successes and other relevant information, virtually right up to the present day. The file ended with a date and the words; 'Termination of file ordered'.

For many seconds Richard stared in dread at the final words. 'Christ!' He hadn't expected that, not yet at least. He hadn't even begun to initiate his plans for Tony. Sabina snapped him out of his morbid mood.

'One of yours, this Tony Campbell?'

'What? Oh, yes... no, well, sort of. We're working together,' he half explained. 'Damn!' Richard swore as he punched a fist into his open hand that made Sabina jump.

He turned to Sabina. 'Sorry, it's just that I've already lost one man to your husband so far.' This time she gasped as a horrified hand reached to her mouth. 'And looking at that date on the file, which is now several days old, I could've very well lost another. Damn!' he cursed again not just for the loss of another human life, but because his plans for the demise of Donovan had hinged on Tony Campbell remaining alive, for now at least.

He reached into the briefcase again and drew out a small black box with a number of wires attached. He rose and strode over to the sideboard and the phone beside the door. Plugging the wires from the black box into the phone, he dialled reception and asked for an international line. Intrigued, Sabina had come to stand beside him, her earlier disgust for her husband's barbaric action put aside for now. As Richard was given an international line and dialled a number from memory, she asked, 'What is it?' as she pointed at the black box.

'A scrambler unit. The person I'm calling has a similar one at the other end; they'll both scramble and unscramble our conversation at either end so nobody can listen in.' The call was answered, 'Johnny, Richard.' He reached down to the unit and switched it on; he knew Johnny would have already done the same. 'I need you to locate and speak to Tony Campbell or his assistant as soon as possible. Tony needs to be warned, Donovan has ordered his murder.' He paused as Johnny took down the details and clarified the message. 'When? It was ordered several days ago, so it has to be top priority, you know how important it is. No, I'm with her now, and yes she came through. No, nothing else. I'll be in touch.'

He broke the connection, bundled up the scrambler unit and pointed to the bottle of champagne; he knew how bad Sabina must be feeling at her husband's actions.

'Would you like a glass?' Plus there wasn't much he could do at this end; it was up to Johnny to locate Tony now – if it wasn't already too late.

'I think you might have to order another bottle. The way I feel it'll be more than one glass I'll be wanting – amongst other things of course.' Sabina had managed to drop her earlier disquiet as she grinned wickedly and settled a knowing look on Richard.

Trying to keep a grin of anticipation off his face Richard handed her a champagne flute. 'Let's review what else you've got on the disk.'

'Let's not.' With her free hand, Sabina grabbed the champagne bottle by the neck and proceeded to herd Richard across the sitting room, towards the hallway and the bedroom beyond. 'I want you to show me how pleased you are with me.'

Richard managed to evade her shepherding for long enough to retrieve the disk from the computer. After it was tucked into the breast pocket of his shirt, he allowed himself to be guided towards the bedroom. Yet again his professional ethics went out the window, and with Sabina, Richard decided at the moment that's where they could stay.

'You've lost weight,' Sabina accused. She was lying on top of the white satin sheets; Richard was standing beside the king-sized bed. They were both naked.

'Like it? I've been exercising,' Richard stated proudly as he sucked in his stomach and puffed out his chest. Sabina forged a yawn. 'I don't know why I bother.' He dropped his shoulders and let it all hang out.

'Yeah,' Sabina declared, 'now that's my kind of man.' She rolled over and propped herself up on one elbow. With her spine now bowed, it emphasised her smooth shapely hips.

As if in a trance Richard came to sit on the bed beside her. He cupped one of her proud pointed breasts in one hand and stroked her silken hair with the other. Lowering his head he tenderly kissed her blackened eye and sutured cut.

'Oh, if only heaven was like this,' Sabina murmured as she allowed herself to roll onto her back. She was about to speak again but Richard cut off the words as he found her mouth.

He tasted her warm and moist as she opened her mouth and allowed their tongues to meet. With yearning, they enjoyed each other's essence. Richard came up to kneel beside her on the bed. With his mouth still covering hers and one hand resting at the nape of her neck he began to gently glide the other over her sculptured body; smooth, glowing and supple he felt her as her body began to respond.

First, with a feather-light touch he glided his hand over her rose-tipped breasts and down across her concave stomach and her back hollowed in response. Out to her hips, he eased his hand and over down onto her thigh; there his fingers rested.

Sabina couldn't believe how quickly she'd become aroused. *Is it the man or the moment?* She asked herself. *It definitely has to be the man*, she decided as she rolled out her leg, willing Richard to move his hand up to her groin.

Almost desperately she probed deeper with her tongue as she felt his fingers move. With a lover's touch, they glided up the inside of her thigh towards her moistened sex; anticipation filled her mind, yearning consumed her body. She waited, longed for the probe of his fingers but in despair she felt them whisper over her pubis with the lightest feather-like touch. It was too much for her to bear. She pulled away from Richard's mouth, 'Oh please, now, Richard, now.'

He felt like a lion as he came over her, strong, proud and invincible. Then he felt himself shudder at the heat as he entered to cry out with Sabina in the joy of their union. Moist, smooth and gentle he felt they were now coupled as one, each tender stroke, every precious minute of their love-making drove him to a high he'd never before experienced. There he hovered on lover's wings to meet Sabina, only to come tumbling back down with her again. Sensual, heavenly and strong; he'd experienced it all.

Numb, but feeling it all, her body was totally consumed with passion, soaring high and floating free she'd found a lover that gave her it all. Sabina met him on a crest of a wave to first drift, and then tumble down with him to eventually lie exhausted in his arms. Their worlds were one; their love had set them free. In that moment they experienced peace. Peace that have should, but didn't, extend across the world.

CHAPTER 37

Bogatin was wearing Levi jeans and a chambray button-down shirt with brown leather loafers on his feet. He had just let himself into Donovan's massive villa through the kitchen door at the rear of the dwelling. Although it was well past midnight, Donovan had only just phoned and demanded his presence.

He lived in the property's gatehouse, subtly positioned off the driveway at the entrance to the villa; Donovan had always liked having him close at hand. As he had walked up the red-bricked driveway he knew exactly why he'd been summoned.

It'll be that bitch of a wife, he reasoned as he walked through the darkened kitchen, after checking the guards patrolling outside and resetting the internal security alarms.

Walking through the dining room – or more correctly the banquet hall – he passed its disproportionately large mahogany dining table and entered the villa's vestibule. Taking no notice of the Cipolin marble floor and matching staircase that swept up to the second floor beyond, he strode towards the hallway that led into the dwelling's right wing. He passed the lavishly furnished formal sitting- room, the blinking security panel beside the securely locked and electronically guarded ivory room that housed Donovan's treasure, and the villa's library; he was walking towards a light that beckoned from beneath a door further along. He stopped outside the door and respectfully knocked.

'Come,' carried to him through the heavy redwood door.

As he began to push his way into the room he was met with the incessant tapping of keys on a keyboard. He walked into Donovan's study. It was completely different to his office in the company's tower block in downtown Los Angeles. The study had a rustic theme, being furnished with solid wood furniture and with plain redwood panelling lining the walls and bare stained beams crisscrossing the ceiling above.

Carrying a manila folder, he walked up to the solid, highly polished mahogany desk that dominated the room and stopped in front of it. Donovan hadn't yet acknowledged his presence; with his head down he appeared the picture of concentration as he was entering files stacked to the right of his keyboard into the computer. He was dressed in baggy black track pants and a white Nike T-shirt, Bogatin had also seen the Adidas trainers he wore upon his feet, between the drawer pedestals as he approached the desk.

Although the files were upside-down Bogatin could see the top one had scrawled down the margin *Ivory: Kenya & Tanzania, 01/93.* He knew Donovan allowed no one, except himself, to enter any of the facts relating to his laundering or ivory rackets.

He'll be copying this onto disk for storage, Bogatin thought as he watched his boss's hands fly in practiced harmony over the keyboard's keys.

After another couple of minutes, Donovan's fingers finally stopped. He saved the newly created file, copied it to disk, and then deleted the file from the computer's memory. After slipping the disk into a briefcase at his feet he looked up for the first time at the Russian who was met with blazing walnut-brown eyes that clearly proclaimed his previously veiled wrath.

'What the bloody hell have you been up to?' The words may have been spoken quietly but like the eyes they seemed to bore right into Bogatin's soul. He had to prevent himself from stepping backwards.

The Russian spread out his hands, he knew exactly what Donovan was referring to, but had no words.

'Jesus, I go away for one bloody day and find all hell had broken loose on my return. Sabina wants you sued. Let alone demanding I sack you.' Donovan got up and walked to stand facing the closed French doors that opened out onto the pergola-shaded veranda.

'Shit, have you seen her face?' was more a statement than a question. Bogatin was about to answer when he realised none was expected. Donovan continued as he turned around, 'Christ, if it scars ...' he let the comment hang, but the Russian had noticed his eyes had lost their murderous sheen. Donovan indicated a high-backed wooden chair sitting in front of the desk and sat behind it, 'Tell me what happened?' he asked in a resigned, dejected voice. 'You know this one'll cost me, and she'll be after more than just a pound of flesh.'

Bogatin was sitting upright in the chair; he couldn't believe he'd got away so lightly – Donovan had men maimed for less. But the Russian had forgotten it was he that usually did the maiming.

He grimaced lightly as he began to talk. 'Well, I followed her as you directed. An hour after you left she went into your office, using the pretext to use the phone I think. I gave her about ten minutes before following her in. At first I thought she'd left using the private elevator, but I found her kneeling on the ground behind your desk. She said she dropped something, but ...' he hesitated, and then fell silent.

'But?' Donovan prompted.

'Well, I can't be sure, but I think I saw her put a computer disk into her bag.'

'Damn!' Donovan cursed, 'But you can't be sure?' Bogatin shook his head. 'Then what?'

'I reached for the bag; she twisted away and fell, hitting her head on the desk. Honestly, Mr Donovan ...' the Russian began to implore before Donovan held up a hand to stop him.

'The silly bitch probably deserved it. I've seen the security report and heard from both Sonya and my wife, and I prefer your version.' Bogatin tried to thank him, but Donovan held up his hand again. 'I'm more interested in what she was doing in my office. A computer disk you say? Surely she can't have opened the safe? She can't possibly know the combination?' Bogatin never answered, he knew it wasn't expected.

Donovan leant back in his chair and thoughtfully rubbed his chin with his fingers, looking at the darkly stained wooden beams running across the high-stud ceiling. He was unsure what to do. If Sabina hadn't been hurt it would have been a different matter altogether. Unless he played it very carefully she could easily press charges, and the further the police were away from Bogatin, the better.

'You could change the combination on the safe,' Bogatin remarked.

'No, it would – I've got it,' Donovan declared with a flick of his fingers. 'I'll get the security company – what's their name?' he asked, but before Bogatin could answer it had already come to mind. 'Ace Security, that's right. We've got enough security protecting the office, so I'll get them to put a simple trip switch on the portrait itself. It can be linked up to your office and security as a backup. If somehow she gets past the other security measures and has learned the combination I want her caught in the act.'

'But what was she doing?'

Donovan shrugged, 'Who knows? However, I don't believe all that much. She has to somehow break the combination and open the safe?' he grunted, before adding, 'She's not that bright.'

'After she got stitched up, what happened?'

'Waited for your return and ... well ...'

'Come on get on with it man,' Donovan hurriedly prompted him, 'I know she's not at home at the moment.'

'Put it this way, I know where she went after the meal at Malibu. The Bel Air Hotel, she's with the same man again.' Bogatin noticed Donovan deliberately lay his hands either side of his desk blotter as he bunched his massive shoulders, then without moving a muscle he sat dispassionately watching him. The Russian hurried on. 'Her Porsche is parked in the overnight parking; I believe she's planning on staying the night.'

As Bogatin fell silent Donovan continued to stare at him, yet it was as if he was staring right through him. He'd always believed he had never in all his years of marriage felt any emotion towards his wife, and he still did, but what he didn't realise was he was experiencing the most malevolent of all, jealousy.

He had always looked upon Sabina as a possession, one that was perhaps more irritating than he would have wished for but a possession all the same. She had given him power through their marriage, power that under no circumstances was he prepared to jeopardise. In his eyes this current relationship had to be stopped. He allowed his eyes to focus on the Russian's impassive face.

'You know what to do. Find out who he is, everything you can about him, then we'll decide what to do.' *One down, one to go*, he was thinking. 'Okay next, what about this Hagan business, the FBI agent's daughter?'

It was the first sign of pleasure Donovan thought he'd ever seen the Russian show. For the most fleeting of seconds his lips tugged up at the corners. They fell back down again as he began to speak. 'It is finished, the girl is dead.'

'Did you find anything?' Donovan asked, the loss of another person's life not concerning him at all.

'Yes, a diary and part of a fax.'

Donovan cocked his head forward as he frowned in concern, 'A fax? Where is it?'

Bogatin looked slightly taken back, 'Like you ordered, I destroyed them. But I ...'

'What?' Donovan exploded, 'Destroyed them, it could have told us. Shit!' But he knew Bogatin followed his orders explicitly.

Bogatin waited until his boss had fallen silent, and then respectfully spoke. 'I was about to say, but I did copy them. I thought you would want to see them.' He held up the manila folder that he'd had in his lap.

Donovan's face broke into a radiant smile. 'Well my fine Russian friend, yet again you've confirmed why I've got so much faith in you.' It was as if he'd blown a kiss to the man; under his ruddy complexion Donovan was sure Bogatin blushed. He dismissed the thought as absurd and reached for the folder.

As he handed it over Bogatin was overcome with gratitude. Donovan's comment was the highest compliment anyone had ever paid to him. Although he'd made a mess of following his wife Donovan had yet again risen in his esteem, as he'd done many times before he swore a silent allegiance to the man who'd given him freedom and money, but most importantly respect unlike he'd experienced before. He was prepared to die for the man.

'What the hell are these figures?' Donovan flipped over a few more of the photocopied pages as he noticed his, his company's and another name; Richard Black. He looked up questioningly at Bogatin. 'Anything?'

'So far, not a thing. The figures are in some sort of personal code. And the name – nothing on him, either.'

'Damn!' Donovan flipped over to the last page, it was the copy of the fax, now that concerned him. First page of five, with no return number or company name at the top of the page. It asked for an initial investigation to be conducted into him and his company, possible money laundering it stated. And there was the name Richard Black again, scrawled across the top in handwritten script.

'Somebody knows more than they should.' Mitch Hagan and his daughter had only been the tip of the iceberg; somebody could be onto him. He knew Hagan's investigation hadn't been official. But who? Probably this Richard Black, whoever, he is. Choosing to treat it as a business problem – a potential setback – Donovan found he wasn't wanting, his mind unerringly clicked into focus.

'Right, use your contacts and then find out who this Richard Black is.' He stood, indicating the meeting was over. 'And also, I know it now may seem trivial, but also find out about this guy who's knocking off my wife. You haven't got much time. Remember I'm supposed to leave for Africa soon.'

Bogatin had only just closed the redwood door when the fax machine answered a call and began to print out an incoming message. *Ah, Peter.* Donovan said to himself. He looked at his watch. *Eleven hours ahead in Kenya. It'll be early afternoon.* He'd been expecting the call. *Good news I hope, I could do with it.*

He picked up the cover note; it told him it was a short fax, only several pages. *Probably routine.*

Once it had finished printing the first page he took it from the basket and sat back to read it. *This is more like it.* It was a transcript from a Kenya

Broadcasting Corporation report, short and to the point:

"It is believed a World Wildlife Fund light aircraft has gone down over central Tanzania. Its sole occupant a Mr Tony Campbell of the WWF has been lost with the plane. He failed to arrive at Wilson Airport in Nairobi at his scheduled time of arrival and no contact has been made with him since his departure from Zimbabwe. Little hope, if any, is held for the pilot or his plane."

'At least everything is back in order down there.' Donovan reached for the next page. 'What!' he exploded. Peter had obviously chosen to leave the bad news till last; it was about the container Tony and Ben had stumbled upon. *The bastard, he deserved to die.* But at a cost. He'd lose a bundle on that one, and what's more they'd probably have to start smuggling the ivory out through a different route. *More additional costs,* he lamented.

Donovan was in a dilemma. Because of the fax he now wanted to get to Africa as soon as possible, to make sure first-hand that the fiasco was sorted out properly, but the Hagan business could be far bigger than he had first suspected, it could cause all sorts of problems. So should he postpone his trip to Africa and stay and identify the unseen enemy?

No there's nothing I can do, he decided, Bogatin had always come through in the past. *He can tighten up security and change procedures and temporarily halt transactions while I'm in Africa.* It was just a hiccup, Nothing he hadn't tackled before. He looked down at the fax again. Yes, the sooner he got to Africa the better.

I can leave Bogatin behind. Like a dog worrying a bone, he began to tackle the problem. However, no sooner had a series of plans begun to form than he briefly shook his head in annoyance, Sabina had entered his mind. With an effort he dismissed her as unimportant.

No worse than usual, she's the least of my worries. It was the Hagan business and Campbell where his problems lay, but with Campbell now out of the way, he felt confident the other would as easily resolve itself. He'd triumphed in the past and now, he decided, was going to be no different.

CHAPTER 38

Selous Game Reserve, Tanzania

FORLORN, LONELY AND desolate, only the occasional splash of eddies forming, disappearing and reforming from the nearby river seemed to break the eerie silence that accompanied the scene. From high above the swirling coffee-coloured Rufiji a lone fish eagle called out its haunting cry, like a thick dreary cloud, it emphasised the desolation that hung over the river and surrounding land. In this place the river commanded and gave life along its banks, but also dictated death.

On this particular stretch of water the Miombo woodlands, dominated by plain lifeless looking stands of doum palms and thick head-high foliage beneath, fringed right up to the water's edge. One particular stand of palms, edging a large ox-bow lake cut off from the river, stood like the others but with a difference. The palms had huge gouges and fresh weeping scars ripped from their pale trunks, while littered amongst the undergrowth beneath them were scraps of twisted metal, lying along a flattened pathway that led to the edge of the lake. Half submerged, just beyond the lake's edge, was the wingless fuselage of a white and red striped plane. Even though only half of it showed, it was clear the aircraft had taken a terrible beating, there were tears and dents riddling its thin metal skin.

There was a faint splash of water above its cooked and blackened engine cover and in front of the plane's windscreen, two faces peered inside.

'He's dead, that's for sure.'

'How do you know? He could be sleeping.'

'Sleeping? Don't be ridiculous. Why would he sit in water up to his chest, with his face only inches above it? Anyway, look at his face.'

The face they saw was hanging limply to one side and drained of colour to a deadly white. There was a gash on the right side of it caked with dry blackened blood. It was the face of a dead man.

'Okay then, how the hell are we going to get in at him? I've already swum around a couple of times. I can't get in.'

'Hmm, yes a bit of a problem.' He too had swum around the plane with little success of entering.

Both of them stared through the windscreen at the corpse, not really knowing what to do.

'Hey I know, we could ... no, forget it.' It was a hair-brained scheme and he knew it.

His companion turned to him and leered. His face was incredibly ugly, leathery and covered with an infinite number of wrinkles. He had dirty green malevolent eyes while his face was dominated by glistening rows of white chiselled teeth. This was a character most people would gladly avoid. He would've snapped a cutting bite but instead jumped in fright which caused both him and his side-kick to explode into a frenzy, sending a great wash of water boiling over the front of the plane. The dead pilot had popped open an eye and cried out in fright.

'I told you he was sleeping,' came out of the thrashing water.

From miles away Tony drifted in a void of soothing blackness; now and then he'd seen a light way off in the distance. At times he'd started moving towards it, but the increased throbbing of his head made him drift away again.

On this particular occasion he had managed to get close to it with little discomfort, and while he hovered just beneath the darkened surface he remembered hearing the haunting cry of a lone fish eagle. Since the throbbing was bearable he tried opening an eye – eventually, it popped open.

'Ahh!' he cried out in fright.

Leering through the windscreen at him, several feet from his face, were two of the ugliest creatures he'd ever seen. *Christ, this must be hell!*

He began to thrash around in his seat as the two crocodiles exploded into a frenzy of action sending a cascade of water over the plane. Tony had gained consciousness, after drifting for just over fifty minutes in his darkened void.

In desperation he tried to get away from the hideous reptiles but only succeeded in creating his own series of waves; he was held firmly by his shoulders straps and seat belt. Then the pain hit him as his logic took hold. Like a sledgehammer it incessantly thumped at him from the inside of his head. As it pounded while he pushed the heels of his palms into his temples, his current circumstances came crashing back to mind.

'Oh gawd, the crash,' he groaned.

Vaguely surprised he was still alive, he began slowly rocking in his seat. As he willed the pain to subside he realised he was up to his chest in water and cocooned inside the plane, and so for now was safe from the crocodiles.

Finally, it was bearable for him to open his eyes; he looked out the windscreen. He was again met by two pairs of green evil eyes, still staring longingly at him. Lunging forward he gnashed his teeth trying to scare them. However, the lunge had been too hasty and it wasn't the crocodile's violent crash against the windscreen trying to repay the compliment that had made him wince. 'Ow,' he groaned in agony, clutching his head again. It was several minutes before he dropped his hands.

Gingerly, he released his shoulder straps and seat belt, and swivelling around he found his rucksack floating in the water behind his seat. With his eyes closed he concentrated on carefully lifting it over to the front. The small first-aid kit was where he'd packed it, on top of his now sodden clothes.

He was shaking like a drug addict, yearning for the soon to be given relief, when he retrieved the box of tinfoil rapped codeine tablets. Ripping it open he pushed out four of the tablets into his hand. Staring at them he only hesitated briefly before he pushed out another one.

Should do the trick. Either kill or cure. He popped them into his mouth and scooped up a couple of handfuls of water to wash them down. He closed his eyes as he waited for the tablets to take effect.

Fifteen minutes later he opened his eyes again, and still the beady eyes of the crocodiles were locked on him. 'Sorry, fellas. Not today.' He looked at his Rolex, mildly surprised it was still working. 'You'll have to find dinner elsewhere.'

Then like a thunderclap from heaven realisation struck. He looked at his watch again. *Bloody hell, it's just on five thirty in the afternoon, and I must've crashed at about four. Christ, I've been out for about an hour.*

For the first time he looked at his hands; they were wrinkled like the skin of a shrivelled-up prune. *Thank God the water's lukewarm.* It would've been too much, to survive a plane crash in the heart of Africa to then die of hypothermia. Tony thrust the thought aside; he had far more pressing problems. Like getting out of this godforsaken plane and passed a couple of hungry reptiles for one.

It took Tony several dives in the compartment behind the front seats before he was able to retrieve his FN and webbing belt, somehow during the crash they had managed to wedge themselves under his seat.

'I hope you work, old girl,' he said to the rifle. 'I can't swim as well as them out there.' The water surrounding the plane was definitely a crocodile's domain.

He took a full magazine out of one of the ammunition pouches on the belt and slotted it into place under the weapon. Clicking the safety off and cocking it, he opened the Perspex side window, and one-handed he reached up and held the rifle out. He pointed to one side of the crocodiles and pulled the trigger. Three shots barked off sending up small plumes of water before there was an audible click – not surprisingly the fourth bullet had misfired. As Tony watched his two uninvited dinner guests flick their crested tails and swim hurriedly away, he was surprised the first three bullets hadn't been water-damaged and had fired at all.

Bringing the rifle back inside, he ejected the misfire, pointed the weapon at the windscreen, closed his eyes and pulled the trigger again. Three more bullets ripped into and through the laminated glass before it clicked and fell silent again.

The three shots were enough; the windscreen was weakened and Tony was easily able to raise a veldskoen and kick it out. Then like a drowned rat, dripping with water with his rifle and rucksack in tow, he wearily clambered onto the half-submerged engine cover and up onto the roof.

Once on the roof Tony realised how lucky he'd been. *Bloody hell!* He gaped in dismay down the flatten pathway the Cessna had blazed through the doum palms and undergrowth below. Shaking his head he muttered, 'And how am I going to explain this one to the boys at head office? "Hi guys, Tony here. Ah, I totalled the Cessna".'

The plane's half-severed tail was only a couple of yards off the shore, so shimmying from the roof, along what was left of the tail and with one quick step at the water's edge, he found himself on dry land.

'Sorry, old girl,' he said looking over his shoulder at the plane, 'but I'm going to have to leave you here.' It was then for the first time he questioned what had actually caused the fire. He'd probably never know. No way was he risking going back in there again to find out.

He could feel his spirits beginning to rise, with the sun warming his body and colour beginning to flood back into his face; he was starting to feel a lot better. *Right, let's see how I fared.*

First, he patted the breast pockets of his shirt. Satisfied he could feel his ivory disk, he then focused on his body. He knew he had a gash on the side of his head; however, he hoped the other aches and pains he could feel were only caused by bruising. As he had only just started concentrating on himself since gaining consciousness, for the first time he became vaguely aware of a heavy stinging sensation around his genitals.

Oh no! He stated in aghast disbelief; he had his shorts down around his ankles and stared at his genitals in wide-eyed horror. *I know I like a bit of head, but this is ridiculous.* Hanging like elongated grapes from his groin were clusters of fat black leaches. 'How ya hanging, John Thomas?' Tony chuckled. 'Bit too much company down there for you?'

Tony grabbed the first-aid kit again and retrieved another soggy cardboard box with tinfoil wrapped tablets inside. However, this time instead of painkillers they were salt tablets. Crushing half a dozen in his hand he sat down on his bare buttocks and proceeded to delicately sprinkle a pinch of salt on each of the blood-sucking parasites. One by one they retracted their heads from beneath his skin and withered to the ground. He could have plucked them off but knew he would've left their severed heads to fester within his skin. He'd seen it done during the war and only with heavy doses of antibiotics had the wounds eventually healed up.

With the leeches still wriggling on the ground between his legs, he stood, pulled up his khaki shorts and looked around him. Behind him was the Ox-bow Lake, in front of him the path the Cessna had made, but other than that all around him was a head-high tangle of thorny undergrowth beneath the surrounding Miombo woodlands. He was miles away from civilisation and his only hope lay with the river. After liberally smearing his gash with iodine paste he clipped on his webbing belt, humped his rucksack on his back and firmly clasping his rifle at his side he took to the Cessna's improvised landing strip.

'Go on, bugger off.' Tony was perched up a small thorny acacia tree, beside the river, trying to hide behind its sparse leafy foliage. A short time ago he had been amongst the thick riverine scrub. It was late afternoon the day after he had crashed, and after a fitful night's sleep he'd been battling through the scrub since daybreak – and 'battling' was the appropriate word.

As if confused, the river had meandered this way and then that seemingly uncertain of its course. In most places the woodlands and undergrowth had grown right up to the water's edge. He had skirted around, crawled under, waded through and clambered over virtually every conceivable sort of vegetation, from the gnarled roots of great terminalia trees, to the hooked thorns of the leafy wait-a-bit bushes, and the numerous wet bog-like marshes he encountered. What's more, his headache had returned.

He nearly wept for joy when he saw a wide open plain that cut about a mile off the river's twisting course as it did another of its aimless meanders. Relieved, with a new spring to his step and his optimism restored, he set out across the plain. However, his relief was short-lived. Having only walked about twenty paces he found in his elation he had blundered between a pride of lions resting in the nearby bush and its riverside kill.

He looked down longingly at his rifle lying on the ground at the base of the acacia tree, then at the bush lion lying with his paw resting on the barrel beside it. It was a huge beast, much darker than its northern cousins, weighing close to five hundred pounds and probably measuring nine foot from its nose to the black tip of its tail.

Tony had run the twenty paces in world record time, chased by the huge black-maned lion. In his haste to scale the nearest tree he'd dropped his rifle. The old tom had thankfully lost interest in him when it saw the rifle, for the tree he had clambered up was only about fifteen foot tall and threatening to collapse under his weight.

Perched like an over-grown monkey Tony had watched on in horror as the old bugger first played with the weapon like a kitten would with a toy, flicking it around the tree with a bended paw, and then, adding insult to injury, he slumped down with a tired grunt and fell fast asleep.

'Why don't you piss off,' Tony said, but not loudly enough to disturb the cat.

He took another cartridge from his webbing belt and dropped it on the sleeping lion. Again all the cat did, as if irritated by a troublesome fly, was twitch his flank where the cartridge had hit. The cartridge fell with the others littered on the ground about him. Tony tried another, this time with more force, as he aimed for the lion's head. Bull's eye, right behind the ear.

'Oh come on, play fair.' The lion flicked his ear and brought up a paw to cover it.

Tony would have tried again but the lion lifted his weary head and stared out through droopy eyes at his pride; they were just walking back into the bush after finishing off the last of the kill. The old tom decided to join them. Rising, with head slung low, he sauntered after them.

'Hoo-bloody-ray,' a quiet voice followed him as he left.

Another ten minutes saw Tony on the ground again and well away from his precarious perch. He was again walking along the water's edge. *Oh, stuff this*, he had struggled his way through onto a small sandy beach. *Maybe I could try floating down?*

He'd noticed a log about twenty yards out in the water. It'd have to be easier. He stepped into the river. No sooner had he done so when he noticed on the other bank a huge green and brown speckled crocodile slide into the water. *Ah ... no, I don't think so*, Tony wisely decided as he withdrew his foot. He should've known; the Rufiji was infested with crocodiles. Then, as if that weren't bad enough, the log he was going to catch a ride on surfaced. It had been a bull hippopotamus slumbering in the water. Its piggy eyes and great knobby head were now clearly visible.

'Wake up, Campbell,' he muttered to himself. The hippos' reputation for killing more humans than any of the other big game in Africa should have made him more alert, but he was getting tired and hungry and his head still hurt like hell.

He looked around the beach. He found he was standing beside a log washed up by the river, so he unslung his rucksack and slipped off his webbing belt. He placed his FN behind the log and slumped dejectedly down on it. He looked wearily downstream.

Probably another fifty-mile to Stiegler's Gorge. May as well be a thousand and fifty at the rate I'm going, he thought despondently. *It'll be next Christmas before I reach it.*

He looked into the west up at the sun, or what was left of it. It'd be dark in another hour or so. He decided to get up and put a few more miles behind him. Well, his mind had decided but his body refused to respond, stubbornly staying put.

Okay another couple of minutes, he reasoned as he began to look around, and for the first time that day he began taking in his surroundings.

On the opposite bank a small herd of zebra was treading warily towards the river to drink – they were near where the crocodile had slipped into the water. He heard – and saw this time – a black and white fish eagle perched high above the river, like a patient sentinel as it echoed its lonely haunting call. Now he was seeing instead of just looking, he recognised far more than just the dirty brown of the river or the differing shades of green fringing it. He saw flashes of colours, chestnut from a goliath heron, crimson and red from a yellow-billed stork and ultramarine and a deeper blue presented by a malachite kingfisher, all busy in their late afternoon work.

Yep, Tony thought with passion, *If only I could stop the poaching here, the wildlife would truly be free.* With no human inhabitants, and none likely, the Selous Game Reserve would allow not hundreds or even thousands, but tens of thousands of individual species to freely roam its enormous, far-reaching wilds.

Come on boy, enough reminiscing. If you don't get back you'll never be able to help them. He was about to rise when a faint sound carried above the watery turbulence of the river. Tony froze as if rooted to the spot; he looked upstream. 'Well, I'll be ... And what is a rough bunch of scoundrels like you doing this far up the Rufiji?'

CHAPTER 39

AN EIGHTEEN-FOOT ALUMINIUM hulled dinghy, driven by a small ten horsepower Johnson outboard, was plying through the Rufiji's murky water. It was cutting in close to the far bank as it straightened up a lazy meandering corner upstream from Tony. Sitting in the boat were four African tribesmen with only about a foot of freeboard between them and the river's surface – the boat was dangerously close to swamping. In fact, one of them was bailing out with a plastic bucket when Tony spotted them; it was obvious they were carrying a very heavy load.

The men saw Tony before he rose from his log, and ogled eyed they stared in amazed disbelief with mouths hanging open. He thought they were going to carry on past him without stopping.

'Hey!' He'd risen and waved an arm. The man controlling the outboard finally maneuvered it towards the beach.

Yeah, just as I thought. Tony could now see what they were carrying. The engine was throttled back as the boat came to a rest offshore. *Bloody poachers!*

The craft was stacked full with ivory, newly poached ivory, some of it was still dripping wet with blood. Tony's wrath should have boiled through to the surface but instead he nearly laughed out loud. Rescued by the enemy – he couldn't believe it, it was too ironic. He soon lost his mirth when he saw a Kalashnikov AK 47 pointing at his belly.

Shit, here we go. Now what?

But as if he were wading through treacle his mind refused to respond. Transfixed he stood rooted to the spot. His head still hurt like hell and he could feel himself bone-weary; the crash, his injuries and subsequent trek had finally taken their toll. However, one tap on the AK's trigger and he'd be dead.

He slowly began to form some sort of plan; his FN was on the ground behind the log and he knew they hadn't seen it. *Trouble is, how do I distract them?* Then he remembered he still hadn't ejected the misfired cartridge since shooting up the windscreen of the Cessna. It would take vital seconds to cock and load again. *No, too bloody long,* he thought bitterly, *Even then it may still jam.* He'd have to find another way, so he did the only thing left to him. He smiled.

The African with the semiautomatic was immediately taken aback; he was a short fat man with a round fleshy face, wearing an assortment of cast-off Western clothes. Disconcertedly he looked over at his companions. What with the swollen gash on the side of his head which was tinted a crimson-red after being plastered with iodine, and his khaki shirt and shorts virtually hanging in tatters after his river-side trek, Tony didn't exactly look a friendly sight.

The other three were tall men, bare-chested and athletic looking. *Masai tribesmen*, Tony decided; tall, lithe yet powerful, with well-defined features. They appeared as taken aback as their fat friend; one of them began speaking in Swahili.

'What's a stupid *wazungu* doing here?'

The others soon joined in the discussion, speaking in the same language and oblivious to the fact that Tony understood every word. As if viewing a piece of cattle, they discussed his physique and circumstances candidly.

'He is big, even bigger than you, William,' the fat one said, turning to the biggest man in the boat.

The man snorted. Clearly, he was unimpressed. 'He can only be trouble.' He was obviously the leader.

'But how did he get here?' asked another.

'Who knows, who cares? We should leave him.'

'But he is many miles away from anywhere, and look at his cut. And the clothes he wears, they are like rags. We could leave some food.'

'So he can report us?' William had raised a condescending eyebrow.

'Okay then, let me shoot him,' Fatty implored eagerly, emphasising his suggestion with a thrust of the rifle.

Tony had lost his smile, he was horrified, this wasn't panning out well. But his spirits lifted as the other three began to laugh, it seemed like the best joke they'd heard in years.

'You?' howled one of his companions in mirth. 'Why do you think we leave you in camp to do the cooking?' They were all laughing as Tony saw his opening, probably the only one he'd be given.

'I could do it,' Fatty stated indignantly, but soon propped forward in disbelief as he lowered the weapon. The others also lurched forward with similar expressions on their faces as Tony spoke in Swahili.

'Only after I have taken the *banduki* from you, stuck it up your backside and wriggled it while I pull the trigger.'

216

There was complete silence from the four men; they realised he spoke the language like one of them, as if born to it.

Could easily tip the scales, Tony thought.

A stifled guffaw erupted from the leader, immediately followed by a full explosion of laughter from all three men at the expense of poor old Fatty. Thankfully, Tony had judged the men correctly. Despite himself he watched on fondly at their thigh-slapping laughter. Even though they were poachers, like him they were African and had the spirit of the continent running through their veins. They were free and unencumbered, large as Africa itself. After several minutes the laughter slowly began to trail away.

'Stick it up your backside and wriggle,' one of the men managed to struggle out in high pitched tones before breaking into hysterics once again which triggered the others. Even Fatty joined them this time in their mirth.

While they were preoccupied Tony reached behind him, slung his webbing belt and rucksack over one shoulder and cradled his FN in the crotch of his elbow. One by one the Masai slowly fell silent. William was the last to stop laughing, realising their roles had been reversed. He was wiping glistening tears of glee from the corners of his eyes when he realised something was amiss – with a hand shading one eye he spotted Tony's FN.

'William,' Tony spoke casually, 'I would like a ride to Stiegler's Gorge.' It was then that Fatty showed that his bravery matched his prowess with a gun – Tony heard his AK 47 clatter into the bottom of the boat. His bluff had worked, he wouldn't need to cock and load the FN.

Tony didn't smile as he levelled his gaze at William whose eyes briefly flicked to his feet. Tony could see he and the other two had AKs lying on the bottom of the boat in front of them. 'Unwise, might get messy.' He smiled then. 'Wouldn't really worry if I was you, we're all in the same business. *Well, sort of,'* he added under his breath.

The comment had the desired effect as the tension began to dissipate, so without waiting to be invited Tony waded out to the boat. He was initially going to take the helm but decided against it. *These chaps could be a wealth of information if I handle them right.*

Nearly capsizing the craft he stepped on board and the boat sunk even further. He settled himself at the front of the boat so everybody was in view, slumped down and relaxed.

'Good haul,' he pointed with his chin at the ivory, there must've been twenty or thirty good-sized tusks lying before him. He noticed the men relax some more. 'Plenty of them to be found beside the river?'

There was a slight hesitation before William guardedly replied, 'Not as many as there once was.'

And so Tony began to quiz them about theirs and the other poaching rackets operating out of Selous. He had stumbled onto a virtual gold mine, a wealth of information that would help him and his cause.

The boat and outboard were practically new and Tony wondered where on earth they had got them, but what he'd been told made him realise they were part of a well-polished operation.

It was just on dusk and the sun's iridescent rays were fading from pink through to a crimson-red, but the vibrant sunset and his surroundings preyed little upon his mind, Tony was staggered at how much information he had been able to gather; he wished he could've written some of it down.

Tony had mixed with the Masai and men like them since the day he'd been born, and if he chose to admit it he was probably more comfortable amongst African tribesmen than any white man. It had become second nature for him to get the best from the Africans he worked with or from those who had worked for him; show respect and all was possible. With these men, it was no different.

As he had such an intimate knowledge about poaching and its methods it was easy for him to pose as – and be accepted by the Masai – as one. Using a few well-selected words tempered with the right amount of humour, before long all four of them were talking over one another, extolling their virtues and telling him about their work. He mostly directed his questions at William, but when the leader stumbled or even became suspicious he would direct his attention at one of the others, and before long their leader had taken the floor again.

Tony had found out virtually every facet of their operation, from how much they were paid, where they hunted, to where the ivory went, so now he felt it was time to find out about the middlemen who actually controlled them.

'This is a fine boat,' he slapped a hand on its gunwale. 'You must be paid well.'

'*Hauw!*' William exclaimed, 'Not that well. Everything, our guns, this boat, everything is supplied for us by our employer. A very powerful man in Nairobi.' He had puffed out his chest importantly.

This is more like it. Tony could feel his excitement mounting but managed to keep his expression passive and nodded knowingly. 'Hmm, Peter, Peter Nkomo.' His nerves were strung taut as he said the name. For all he knew they might have been run by somebody entirely different. If they were, the name would mean nothing and nothing would be lost, but what if they were part of his and Donovan's racket. *Who knows? This could be the break I've been looking for.* It was a huge gamble, for other than Peter's name that was all he knew about him.

William's jaw hinged open in bewilderment. 'You know him?'

Bingo! 'Yes, well,' he stated confidently. 'well, sort of,' he added, mumbling under his breath.

'You have been to his house in Muthaiga in Nairobi?'

Tony's mind was racing, *Bloody hell, an address.* It was getting better all the time. *Shit now what?* It could be a trap, tread carefully he decided. 'Ah no. I've been invited, but ..' he hurried on. 'we like to keep our relationship on a business level.' Sort of the truth Tony reasoned, but he had to make sure it was the right suburb. 'And Muthaiga you say?' He half queried as if trying to recall whether Muthaiga was where he lived.

'Yes, a magnificent house. One of my wife's cousins works as a gardener there,' William replied, oblivious to Tony's uncertainty.

Just one more question. Tony wanted to find out where Peter Nkomo originally came from. Nkomo wasn't an east African name and knowing his origins would probably help considerably. It would be a risk, but one worth taking. 'Tell me, William. I've always wanted to know, how did a Matabele come to be accepted so readily in Kenya?'

William frowned suspiciously 'He is not a Matabele, he was born a Zulu.' His frown deepened as everyone else fell silent in the boat.

Tony had made a huge blunder. Because he thought Nkomo was a Sindebele word he'd assumed Peter was Matabele. Now what? Things could get very ugly, especially now in the post-twilight gloom. He couldn't see everyone's face, only William's clearly and the dark eyes that locked on his had squinted suspiciously. His face had taken on a hardened resolve as if he'd suddenly realised he had been deceived. The situation was delicately poised.

Only meeting William's eyes for a split second longer Tony lightly shrugged and looked casually out across the water. 'All those baboons down south, Zulu, Matabele, Shangane, all originally fell out of the same tree.'

William tutted lightly and nodded sagely. 'Baboons,' he agreed seriously. Being from a proud Masai heritage he recognised all other tribes across Africa as inferior. He liked the way Tony had put it. 'Baboons,' he repeated again, rolling the word through his lips while frowning deeply.

Tony let out a slow wary breath. That was too close, that's enough,' he decided. He didn't want to push his luck too far. But he still would've loved to have known how even a Zulu was accepted so readily in Kenya and Tanzania.

'We'll have to drop you here.' It was Fatty who'd spoken; the boat had been guided to settle with a gentle bump onto a small sandy spit. 'There is a game trail leading to a track that will take you up to Stiegler's Gorge lodge.'

Tony looked around. He'd been so engrossed with gathering information he hadn't noticed the river edge changing; the river had started to drop on its way to the gorge further down as the bush-lined banks had risen up on either side. He could also clearly hear the muffled rumble of the gorge in the distance.

Jumping out onto the spit with his gear, he asked Fatty, 'Where do you land and unload?' He knew it couldn't be far away.

'Oh, a place just before ...'

William cut in; he'd become suspicious again. 'Just *after* the gorge,' he said. He was wondering why Tony wanted to go up to the Stiegler's Gorge Safari Camp and Lodge. If he was a poacher like them it should be the last place he'd want to go. 'You never told us, how are you called?' he demanded suspiciously.

'Oh, didn't I tell you?' Tony was backing up to the bush and the gloomy entrance of the game trail. 'You probably even know me.' He saw the men beginning to stir. 'When I said we were in the same business I lied a little. It's Tony, Tony Campbell.'

They knew him all right. Just as he worked under the premise 'shoot poachers on sight', they had a similar code which applied doubly to him and Ben.

Tony heard the poachers frantically scrambling for their weapons as he disappeared into the bush and dived to the side. A rattling volley raked the foliage where he should've been. He didn't return fire; it would pinpoint where he was. Instead, he lay quietly listening ready to open fire if they came after him.

Although he heard a whispered discussion he couldn't make out the words. However, before long he heard the gentle whine of the outboard being pushed to gain maximum speed. The Masai had chosen not to follow him.

'Don't bother telling Peter Nkomo I know where to find him,' Tony spoke to the departing boat, 'I'd like to introduce myself personally.'

As Tony walked up the game path he was sure the poachers wouldn't breathe a word of their illuminating discussions, and that was the way he wanted it.

'At last,' Tony breathed in relief as he walked onto the manicured lawns, up ahead a blaze of lights lit up the Stiegler's Gorge Lodge. He could see people sitting on the lodge's veranda.

It had taken him several hours of bumbling around in the dark and struggling through the bush to get to the lodge. As he walked into the light thrown from the veranda, one of the lodge's female guests let out a shrill scream of terror. It was then Tony realised he probably didn't look a pretty sight. He felt and no doubt looked filthy, with his clothes hanging in tatters, the gash on his head and semiautomatic in his hand. *Yeah, I must look a proper sight.*

The woman screamed again. Wild animals were one thing but this had to be a terrorist. God, how many times had she told her husband she didn't want to come? 'Africa is far too dangerous a place,' she'd said. And now she knew.

Tony had reached the top step and gazed around him. There were probably half a dozen guests who had been enjoying the post-dinner G and Ts. Some were cowering in their chairs; others had half risen, while the screaming lady was running for the door and the sanctuary of the lodge beyond. She was met at the door by a bull of a man coming from the opposite direction. He was practically bald with a huge barrel chest and mountainous potbelly hanging over the waistband of his trousers; he had a Mauser 66 Safari in one hand as he barged onto the veranda.

It'd be those bloody scavenging hyenas again. 'Always scaring the guests,' he muttered in German. He stopped dead in his tracks when he saw Tony. 'More than bloody hyenas,' he breathed in awe, slightly shifting his grip on the rifle.

His name was Theodor Rainer. He was an expatriate German and the owner of the camp. He switched to heavily accented English, 'Good God, Tony. You're supposed to be dead.'

'Don't worry, Theo. If it's any consolation, I feel it. I could use a bath, a change of clothes and a ride into Dar-es-Salaam as soon as possible.'

'Come.' Theo waved a great paw of a hand at him. 'Good to see you, my friend.'

The guests stood back aghast, as the terrorist was welcomed into their midst.

CHAPTER 40

Nairobi, Kenya

THE UNITED STATES of America may have lost one of its most dedicated and talented scientists, but Africa had gained one. A very tired, disgruntled and jet-lagged one.

Anna had hardly noticed the nearby far-reaching Athi Plains, or the tree-studded towering skyline of the Kenyan capital as her Pan Am Boeing 747 flew into land; she had never felt so drained.

'Christ, what a trip. I feel absolutely beat,' she lamented, 'And no wonder, girl.' Anna had experienced delay after delay on her way from Los Angeles to Nairobi. It had started even before she left her apartment in Costa Mesa. Sarah was definitely in no shape to drive her to LAX, let alone have her wicked way with the 'hunk'. Sarah's room had been an absolute shambles after Anna had half carried, half dragged her stoned roommate into their apartment, so Anna had bundled Sarah into her own bed.

After carefully explaining to Sarah to look after her father's diary and that she would also write to explain as soon as possible, she kissed her on the forehead and got another friend to take her to the airport.

Continental Airline's flight to New York's J F K airport had been straightforward enough, but her ticketing for the Pan Am connecting flight to Frankfurt had been completely bungled; twenty-four hours she'd had to wait. Then came Frankfurt itself and the same had happened, the Wildlife Fund's Washington office had screwed up again and what's more she'd had her wallet, credit cards, money – the works – stolen. Forty-nine hours she'd had to stay in the airport, snatching what little sleep she could in-between contacting her bank and harassing the Pan Am ticketing office until the error was sorted out.

And now this. If Anna had enough energy she would have stamped her foot. A Kenyan customs official had taken offence to her dishevelled state and was methodically inspecting every item, every garment of clothing she carried, and the more she tried to explain, the slower he went. *I'm going to be last out.*

After another thirty minutes Anna was allowed to re-pack her clothes and pass through customs. With shoulders slumped and her feet aching like hell, she wearily trudged after her trolley through into the arrival lounge.

God, I am the last, she thought dejectedly, there was practically nobody about. *And where the hell's my ride?* She spotted the airport's banks. 'Money first, then I'll worry about where on earth to go to from here.' She walked towards the Kenya Commercial Bank, hoping the transfer had come through this time.

Tony Campbell was fuming. Two bloody hours he'd been waiting and still the damn doctor hadn't passed through customs. He was standing outside the Kenya Commercial Bank in the arrival lounge of Nairobi's Jomo Kenyatta Airport, and was imagining what he could do. *Tear his bloody head off and spit down his throat,* he decided. It was the most gruesome thing his imagination could come up with. *Bit radical, but would get the point across.* He nearly laughed at the absurdity of the thought, but his ire returned before he could.

It was late afternoon and Tony had only arrived in Nairobi just after lunch. That morning Theo Rainer had rustled him up some clothes, which were far too big, and driven him into Dar-es-Salaam's airport from Stiegler's Gorge himself. It was good to catch up with the German, so they had arranged to use his lodge when he and Ben were able to tackle the poaching rackets plundering the Selous Game reserve.

Once he'd flown into Nairobi's international airport he had caught a taxi to Wilson Airport, the city's smaller domestic airport a good fifteen minutes closer to the city centre. He got the driver to drop him off at its long-stay parking bays. As with down in Zimbabwe and Botswana, a short-wheel-base Toyota Land Cruiser had been put at his disposal when he was working in the east of Africa. As expected, the big petrol engine started first turn, so he immediately drove to the WWF's Kenyan office on Harambee Avenue in the city's centre.

Craig Maitland, the office manager, a wiry, sandy-haired little man and an expatriate Australian, had been none too polite with his greeting. He and Theo must have worked on a similar wavelength.

'Christ almighty, you're supposed to be dead,' he said and then added, 'Mind you, didn't believe it myself, though.' Some of Tony's past exploits still left him in awe.

'Good to see you too Craig,' Tony responded sarcastically.

'Well, yeah, I meant that too.' He noticed the gash on the side of Tony's head. 'I don't want to sound rude, but where's the plane? I heard the radio report.' He grimaced slightly as he waited for the reply; part of Tony's funding came out of his budget.

'Oh, that's great. The Cessna's more important is it?'

'It depends.' Craig creased his brow suspiciously. 'It's at the hanger at Wilson Airport ... isn't it?' he asked hesitantly, 'Tell me it is,' he pleaded. He may get results, but Craig always suspected the worst with Tony.

'Well put it this way, you know how the Fund insists on insuring all its vehicles ...'

Craig groaned as if he'd been gut-shot. He threw both hands up to his face and sat, slumped back in his chair for nearly a minute.

'Craig,' Tony tried, with a worried look on his face. 'I –'

'No, I'm all right now.' Craig had slid his hands off his face and firmly planted them on the desktop as he sat up straight. 'You can tell me later. You have that doctor to pick up, the flight from Frankfurt's due in soon.'

'What?' Tony exploded. The Cessna and Craig's anxiety were forgotten. 'I thought ...'

Craig wasn't listening. He'd dealt with Tony before and had no desire to receive one of his tongue-lashings. Tony hadn't achieved what he had to date without making it clear what he wanted, or if he happened to disagree. 'Here are the details.' He thrust out a typed A4 sheet of paper. 'I thought I was going to have to do it myself.'

'So I do have to nursemaid some bloody professor?'

'I wouldn't go so far as to say that. She's ...'

However, this time Tony wasn't listening. 'We'll see about that...' He'd glanced at the arrival time and name on the sheet of paper. 'Doctor bloody Hagan.'

He turned on his heels and slammed the frosted-glass door behind him as he stormed from the office. He never heard Craig's words trailing after him.

'Make sure you bring her back here. Oh and Tony, somebody from London's been ..., and a telegram ... Oh, forget it then,' Craig ended lamely.

'Oh stuff this,' Tony cursed as he decided to have the good doctor paged. It took him a couple of minutes to organise and he had just got back under the bank's sign when the airport's loudspeaker system chimed. As his message was broadcast he noticed a bedraggled, jet-lagged female tourist step out of the bank.

'Would Doctor Hagan please make his way to the entrance of the Kenya

Commercial Bank where he can expect to be greeted,' relayed the plum, well-educated voice that every airport seems to have.

Greeted, yeah, I like that one, Tony thought as he planned what he'd say. *Bloody academics.* He was going to tear a strip off him, he decided. *No way am I going to drag some snivelling bookworm around Nairobi and through the bushveld, especially now.* Tony was still trying to decide how he would track down Peter Nkomo. Even if they weren't formulated, he hated having his plans interrupted.

After a couple more minutes, still nobody arrived, only the tourist who had slumped warily on top of her pack. So Tony sneaked a look at her.

He noticed she had raven hair fashioned into some sort of bird's nest. *Probably some weird overseas fashion,* he decided. She was also wearing a badly creased check-patterned shirt and crumpled jeans. However, if she'd taken more care with her appearance, she probably could have looked attractive. She turned to face him so he turned away.

Anna began her scrutiny. From where she sat she could make out his cool blue eyes, eyes she decided were determined and used to gazing far into the distance. She saw his deeply tanned, roped and muscled forearms crossed determinedly over his chest and the chiselled lines that marked his rough but interesting face.

Man on a mission, she decided, *and, hell, he's tall, but that gash makes him look a bit of a mess ... and as for those clothes ...* Even though she could see he was a big man, his shirt was far too baggy and the shorts he wore weren't much better. *Are those short longs or long shorts?* Anna wondered and then the penny dropped.

'You're Tony Campbell aren't you?' His startled expression was answer enough. Anna struggled to her feet and held out her hand in greeting. 'Anna Hagan.' Tony stared dumbly at the hand then at her face for several seconds. *Boy, a real dipstick, here,* she thought.

'*Doctor* Anna Hagan,' Tony had eventually found his tongue while goosing his head forward in disbelief, he still hadn't accepted her hand. His harsh words were forgotten; even his anger had dissolved, as he looked down into her tired but amazingly dark, compelling eyes.

'Yes, that's right.'

'But you're a woman.' It was the first thing that came to mind, said innocently but still entirely the wrong thing to say.

Anna dropped her hand. Those were fighting words and her tiredness was forgotten to be replaced with something far more consuming – anger.

She now had something – in this case somebody – to vent her last four days of pent-up frustration upon. She'd heard that the men in Africa were male chauvinistic pigs.

'You arrogant, conceited, small-minded bastard.' Anna had thrust her hand out again, but this time led with an accusing finger. She was jabbing towards Tony's chest as she walked towards him.

Although he probably towered six inches over her, Tony retreated at her advance. 'I didn't mean ... I merely ...'

Anna wasn't listening, her barrage of words kept flying. 'You contemptuous, lording, high and bloody mighty male.'

Despite the situation, Tony was captivated by her face. Her eyes had seemed to change colour to an absorbing angry black, while her forehead was deeply furrowed, emphasising her rage. He noticed beneath the clear olive complexion her skin was flushed to a maddened red, right down into the V of her shirt. He saw her flashing white even teeth, high sculptured cheekbones, and her lips pulled back and twisting as she spoke, into lean angry lines. The state she was in gave her a strong, even compelling type of beauty, but still he backed away under her ever flowing torrid of abuse.

'Egotistical, narcissistic ...' Tony was backed up against a water fountain, she had him trapped. 'Yes, I'm a *woman* and a doctor, and a damn good one too. So if you don't like it you can lump it.' Anna had jabbed her finger into his chest and thrust her head forward with her chin jutting out, angrily looking up at him.

Tony tried to cut in, 'I was merely surprised when –'

Anna wasn't listening; she hoisted a thumb back to her gear. 'Since you're so bloody proud of being a man, you can pick them up and take me to a hotel.'

'Well, you're not actually booked ...'

'As from now I am. I've had one hell of a trip, buster, due to the cock-ups of your organisation, and tonight I'm sleeping in a bed.' Anna had taken another pace forward and thrust harder with her finger into his muscular chest. She now had him bent backwards over the fountain.

'Sure, fine, no problem.' Tony managed to squeeze out from in front of her. *My organisation*, he was thinking, That's a laugh. He'd met some strong-willed people in his day but this Yank beat the lot.

He picked up her pack and carryall. 'Follow me.' But Anna proceeded to storm past him towards the car park outside. No way was she going to follow some damn arrogant male.

Tony directed her when Anna faltered once she was outside, unsure which way to go. With a haughty flick of her head she stalked off in the direction he indicated. She'd seen the letters 'WWF' emblazoned on the door of the Toyota he pointed at.

Her shoulders were square while her back was ramrod straight, and though Tony tried not to, he couldn't help himself from staring at her neat little bottom revolving ever so primly within her jeans. *Hell of a nice bod, shame about the temper,* he thought, then he remembered. *Oh gawd, and I'm supposed to help her set up. No way. Craig'll hear about this.* They were halfway towards the Toyota.

Anna was caught in a similar turmoil and what's more her tiredness was starting to rapidly catch up with her again. *I have to put up with him and give a fair assessment of his project whatever it is. Like bloody hell, I'll mark on personality.*

She had reached the Land Cruiser. Walking around to the right she pulled up the door latch and thankfully slumped into the seat. Tony came to stand beside her before she could close the door. This time he was going to stand his ground.

'Ah no, I think I'll drive.'

'I'm not stopping you,' Anna snapped. She wanted to get to a hotel and leave this arrogant prick behind.

'Sitting in that seat you are.' Tony pointed at the steering wheel in front of her. 'It's a right-hand drive,' he indicated, as he couldn't prevent himself from smiling. *That'll bring her down a peg or two.*

Anna let out a weary breath, she'd made a fool of herself and she knew it. This anger business had never suited her. She didn't know whether to scream, stamp her foot, laugh out loud or cry. So she turned to Tony.

Thrusting an accusing finger at his chest, she threatened, 'Not a bloody word, mister. Not one.' But it was his disarming smile that made matters worse.

She clambered over the gear levers to the passenger's seat opposite, firmly crossed her arms over her chest and turned to face the window; she didn't want him to see her face as she bit down on her lower lip. She was threatening to break out into a smile or burst into tears, being so tied she had lost control of her emotions.

'Just take me to a hotel,' she eventually sighed. Hopefully, tomorrow would be better.

As Tony placed Anna's gear in the back he was thinking similar thoughts. *Christ, maybe tomorrow will be better. Hell, no way am I going to go through a week of this.*

CHAPTER 41

'NARCISSISTIC' – *I wonder what it means? I'll have to find a dictionary and look it up.* All the other words Anna had showered him with Tony had heard many times before – 'arrogant' probably being the one used most often.

She's got to be the most unlikely scientist I've ever met, he decided. He'd never got on well with academics of any kind – too analytical he'd found. *And it looks as this one's going to be no different, but at least she's got spirit, some guts. Arrogant, eh?* He snorted lightly. *Hell, gotta be. I wouldn't have got this far otherwise.*

Tony was driving back into the centre of Nairobi after returning from the high-priced suburb of Muthaiga. It was after dusk and several hours earlier he'd driven to the Hilton International on Watatii Street and booked two separate rooms. He would have taken Anna to one of the less expensive hotels, but by the time he had driven the eleven miles into the city centre from the airport she looked absolutely terrible.

Maybe she did have a rough trip, after all, he'd thought at the time. He also booked himself into the hotel. After all he'd been through, he deserved it. Craig would jump up and down. But what the hell.

Having organised to meet Anna the next morning to take her to the WWF's office, he'd then gone around there himself and had a less than satisfactory meeting with Craig before beginning to track down Peter Nkomo.

Tony pulled into the Hilton's car park and snorted lightly again. Speaking of arrogance... It had been incredibly easy to track down Peter Nkomo. His name had been in the last place most people would have ever thought of looking; the Nairobi telephone directory.

The address and house had been easy enough to find, and like William had said, it was magnificent. The only trouble was that as Tony sat on the road outside, the realisation of knowing where he'd acquired the money to buy it detracted from the dwelling's beauty. Although he didn't know what he looked like, Tony had waited, hoping to catch sight of Peter. However, nobody had entered or left the property during his vigil, so after a couple of hours he decided to return to the Hilton and phone through his discovery to Richard Black in London.

With his resources, he reasoned, we may be able to find out a lot more about the man.

Although he'd ordered the cheapest rooms possible, Tony's double wasn't exactly small. It had a double bed, mini-bar, en suite and still enough room to comfortably fit in a four-seater dining-table beside a picture window that looked over Moi Avenue, facing the massive ramparts of Nairobi's downtown Kenya Commercial Bank. Tony had retrieved the phone, sat down at the table, and while he gazed out into the darkened Kenyan sky he waited to be given an international line.

Once the line was available he looked at his Rolex. Only three hours behind – early evening up there. He dialled the number from memory and it was answered almost immediately. *It must be Johnny*, Tony thought – if he'd remembered the name correctly.

'Yes, is Richard Black available?' He was met with a stony silence, and then realised people probably didn't come straight out and use Richard's name. He tried a different approach. 'My name is Tony Campbell; I was given this number at Victoria Falls when I met him.'

'Good God,' came down the line, 'you're supposed to be –'

Tony cut in, 'Yeah, yeah, I know. Dead.' He then added quickly, 'Christ, you guys are on the ball.'

'I think you'd better talk to Richard.' He was put on hold and after nearly half a minute recognised a more familiar voice.

'Tony, Richard. Before we start, this is an open line so be careful, if you follow my drift. Enough of the preliminaries, good to hear your voice.'

Tony was taken back by the genuine relief that clearly resounded through Richard's words. He was puzzled as to why. Especially from a man in his profession. I'm not that important. However, before he could consider it further, Richard was already continuing in the same light tone.

'I thought for sure our American friend had got you. We've been trying to reach you for days. You got the messages and telegram then?' Now even more puzzled, Tony couldn't reply. 'Are you there?'

'I'm not with you Richard,' he eventually responded, confused, 'I got your messages but only later this afternoon. And who got what?'

'Our American friend in LA – the plane crash – it was his doing. He'd ordered a hit on you.'

'God, bugger me,' Tony sent the oath down the phone, Richard's relief was forgotten. Like being struck from above by a lead balloon, he realised the fire and subsequent crash hadn't been an accident.

'Sorry, are you all right?'

'I didn't realise, I thought it was an accident. Anyway, how the hell did you find out?'

'We've accessed his files. He's got a sizable dossier on you, right up to the date when the hit was ordered. And it appears it's not the first time he's tried.' There was a slight rustle of paper, 'What was it, when you were at Stronghold, is that right?'

'Bloody hell!' Tony was thunderstruck, he should have been impressed that Richard had penetrated Donovan's files, but was more appalled that Donovan had ordered and damn-near succeeded in assassinating him, twice. 'All that time, Christ, it's like he's been playing with me,' his voice then hardened, 'Okay, I'll have to watch my back.' It was an added problem he could do without, but one he'd have to live with. He changed the subject. 'I've got some information of my own – an address for Peter Nkomo.'

Richard was impressed, not just at Tony's success but also the resolve he'd recognised in his voice. He applauded his choice in Tony once again. With him his plans had a better than even chance of success. He'd known plenty of men in the past who had been faced with danger, most had shied away, yet with Tony he could tell there would be no backing down.

'Well done. However, I presume it's the house in Muthaiga? There was also a file on him.'

'Well done, yourself,' Tony said. 'We must nearly have enough to nail the bastards.'

'Not quite, not enough hard facts, but we're getting there. Look, we've probably said more than we should already. I'll put a report and everything you need to know that can help you in a diplomatic bag and have it sent down to Nairobi tonight. It should be ready for you to pick up at the British High Commission in Bruce House first thing in the morning. I'll make sure they're expecting you. Other than that Tony ...' he paused and perhaps emphasised his next point a bit too emphatically, 'be careful. For if we can't stop these bastards, I believe nobody can.'

Cradling the receiver once the connection had been broken, he felt it was a fitting note to end on. So, with a newfound resolve and not just for his own preservation, *we'll just have to succeed*, he reasoned.

As he rose from the table, he knew he'd have to walk with a far more wary tread. The trouble was that Tony never considered which direction he'd be forced to take. He walked from the room; it was time to eat.

CHAPTER 42

PETER NKOMO WAS a satisfied man. Things couldn't be better. The only dull spot lurking in the background was the container that had been discovered in Zimbabwe. Yet tonight even that couldn't dull his contented feeling of well-being.

He was at the Carnivore restaurant on Nairobi's Langata Road, about ten minutes from the city centre, sitting by himself at a corner table out on the terrace. Although the terrace was airy and cool, he was dressed only in shirt sleeves, a plain blue silk shirt open at the collar. The refreshing air after the previous afternoon's heat added to the comfortable feeling he exuded from within.

The Carnivore was renowned for its servings of spit-roasted wild and domestic meats, and, of course, its all-you-can-eat menu. Peter could have eaten at any of the more luxurious restaurants around the city, like at the Muthaiga Club or the Hotel Inter-Continental's main restaurant Le Chateau, but because of his expansive mood he had chosen the gastronomical treats offered by the Carnivore, roasted on its open hearth.

Peter had chosen as an appetiser fried trout fresh from the restaurant's trout farm on the slopes of Mount Kenya. Next had come the entrée of homemade soup, and as he smelt the wafting odours from the sizzling haunches of meat inside, he was pleased he had chosen the milky-white crocodile-tail steak that should be arriving at any minute.

The thought of the tender soon to be eaten steak, especially the generous aromas that drifted on the air, had made his *saliva* jet from under his tongue. As he licked his lips and swallowed yet again, he decided, *I'll finish with the Irish coffee. It has to be the best I've tasted outside of San Francisco.* His line of thought was distracted as a movement caught his eye; somebody had walked out onto the terrace. *Ah, the mains. At last.*

Looking up in anticipation, his feeling of satisfied well-being as well as his appetite, dropped to lay discarded around his ankles.

'Good God, you're supposed to be dead,' he breathed in trepidation. Although he'd never seen the man in person, from the photos he'd studied he knew exactly who it was. He was horrified.

Quickly masking the naked anxiety that must've shown on his face, he realised something had gone terribly wrong with what should have been a simple set of plans.

Tony had considered having a meal at the Amboseli Grill in the Hilton, but decided it was much too tourist oriented for the mood he felt. He wanted something ... *something, I don't know, something African ... expansive,* he decided. He wanted to put the constraints and frustration he felt with his job behind him for now. And the Carnivore's all-you-can-eat menu will certainly do that.

Dressed in a loose-fitting denim shirt, tan cotton trousers and veldskoens with no socks on his feet – having had all his clothes now laundered – it was the smell that first hit him as he walked into the restaurant. He filled his lungs with the tantalising concoction of spit-roasted meat. *Ah, good choice, Tony,* he congratulated himself.

The restaurant had a rustic feel to it, enhanced by the ebony-black rough-sawn beams crisscrossing the white plastered ceiling, the substantial pillars of the same colour wood supporting the roof and the square red-brick tiles around the huge circular open hearth. He stopped to chat with a couple of chefs at the hearth for a few minutes as they cooked the haunches of meat. He was known at the restaurant and, as Tony finally began to unwind, he realised it felt good to be back in Kenya.

When the maitre d' appeared to have him seated, he was in the midst of returning a sally to one of the chefs; he carried the humour with him out to his table on the terrace. The first thing he noticed as he walked outside was the cool evening air compared to the heat thrown by the hearth – he'd soon adjust; he was used to extremes. The next thing he noticed was the expression of what looked like unconcealed anxiety from the black man sitting in the corner on his own.

Probably can't pay the bill. He dismissed all thought of the man, taking the seat he was offered on the opposite side of the terrace. He was looking forward to his meal.

As he consulted the menu he could hear the incessant beat of live music drifting to him from the adjacent Shima Saloon, 'Them Mushrooms' was playing. He found he was shaking his head in smiling memory; last year's lavish New Year's bash had been something else. Ben had outdone himself and latched onto a buxom German tourist. He'd looked like a contented puppy enveloped at her bosom on the dance floor, and his soppy smile had remained for many days after.

But mind you, so had mine, although the German's friend hadn't been buxom, 'athletic' would be the best way to describe her.

Tony eventually chose the salad, baked potato and grilled eland, but as he drank the White Cap lager while waiting for the meal, the anticipation he should've felt was seriously impeded by the piercing gaze he could feel locked on him from the man he'd first noticed when he was shown to his table. After his second lager, and when he'd finished his entrée, a spicy wildebeest pate, the man's insistent stare had got too much to bear. He'd bloody well lost his appetite.

Placing his napkin on the table he went over to the man, and standing over him he asked, 'Excuse me do I know you?'

'No I believe not,' came a well-cultured resonant voice.

'Well, what's your problem then, pal? Can't you find a better view?'

The man chuckled lightly as he mocked, 'I believe you have exaggerated your importance. Why anybody would be interested in you is beyond me.' He took a sip of his Irish coffee as he watched for Tony's reaction over the glass.

Tony bridled at that one, he could feel the hairs on the nape of his neck bristling and his fists beginning to ball. Before he could respond the man was talking again.

'I don't believe I've had the pleasure?' said as smooth as silk, yet dripping with sarcasm.

'No, the pleasure is all mine.' Tony stuck out his hand, and as it was accepted, he continued, 'Tony Campbell.' Then he began to squeeze, the man had made a mistake and knew it. As the muscles bunched to stand out like cords of rope along his forearm, he heard the first creak of bone and saw the first flicker of pain in the man's charcoal-black eyes; he was strong but not as strong as Tony. 'And you are?' Tony asked. It gave him intense pleasure to see the conceited prick begin to squirm.

Putting down his Irish coffee and reaching out with his other hand, the black man clasped it around Tony's wrist and pressed in with his fingers. It was expertly done, he'd found a reflex point. Tony's hand immediately opened as he replied. 'None of your business. Now if you would kindly leave.' He threw Tony's hand back at him and deliberately placed his either side of his coffee glass.

Tony witnessed the most malevolent stare he had ever seen. He recognised this as an evil man and one who was unaccustomed to being challenged. He rested his hands on the tabletop and leant forward, about to respond with a cutting retort. However, as he did his ivory disk toppled from his shirt pocket and fell to the table.

As quick as a flash before it had settled, the black man had scooped it up and briefly studied it. Tony thought he saw recognition flare in his eyes as the man began to speak. 'Oh how quaint, but I suppose some of us need a lucky charm.'

Tony snatched it out of his hand. 'Up yours, pal!' he snapped, before continuing. 'I think I may heed your earlier advice and leave. I'm finding the company a trifle tedious.' He hooked the barbed remark and yanked it deeper. 'But I suppose thinking in hindsight I can see why your gaze would've been drawn to me. The strong always attract attention.'

Tony turned without witnessing the murderous sheen that glazed the recipient's eyes, and then with a flick of his hips he bumped the table and sent the steaming Irish coffee into the man's lap. He heard the crash of an over-turned chair and a sworn curse but didn't look back as he walked over and settled back at his table. His appetite may not have returned but he felt a damn sight better.

Tony caught movement to his side; he was expecting it so warily turned his head. The man had finished dabbing the wet circular patch at his crotch and was about to leave the terrace. He walked up to the side of Tony's table, but the aggressive stance he took couldn't be taken seriously – surely, no one can be with a wet patch at their groin.

'Some people attract attention, but the truly strong will always win. Happy flying, Campbell.' He had walked inside before Tony could respond.

It was a threat. But what the hell did 'happy flying' mean?' As the maitre d' walked on to the terrace, he called him over. 'Who was that man that just left?'

Dipping his head to look through the circular hearth to see who Tony meant, he replied, 'Oh that's, ah, Mr Nkomo I believe, sir.'

'Peter Nkomo?' Tony almost jumped out of his chair.

'I believe so, yes.'

Tony now knew exactly what 'happy flying' meant. Several quick strides carried him into the restaurant. Standing, glaring at the figure about to walk out the door, he knew he would never forget his face. Peter turned and the two men stared at each other across the crowded restaurant.

Slowly, in fascination, table by table the restaurant fell silent as all heads swivelled to watch the men. Although they were standing at opposite ends of the room, by their stance and the intensity of the gaze they may as well have been locked in mortal combat. Only the sizzling meat on the spits could be heard. Then like a sentencing judge Tony raised an accusing finger.

'You're finished, Nkomo. You and Donovan both.' As soon as he'd said it he realised his mistake – a startled frown had skipped across Nkomo's face. *Damn.* He'd let his emotions rule his logic; instead of exposing Sithole, Nkomo and Donovan he'd exposed himself. *Bugger!* What plans had been made would have to be changed, yet again.

Peter quickly masked his expression, his jaw firm as he returned a challenging stare, but still his mind raced like a herd of startled game. He knew Tony knew far more than he should.

Nothing was to be gained by remaining, so with an effort he broke Tony's steely gaze, turned and stepped from the restaurant. Thank God Donovan will soon be here. Things are going from bad to worse.

There was an audible release of tension among the diners when Peter walked from the room but Tony never registered it. Instead, his eyes were still fixed on the vacant spot where Peter had been. He had finally met the enemy but, *Damn,* he cursed again – he'd tipped his hand. He was now more vulnerable than ever before, and what's more he'd been forced into taking on a passenger. *That, right now, is something I could definitely do without.*

CHAPTER 43

Earlier

AFTER DROPPING ANNA off at the Hilton before Tony went in search of Peter Nkomo's house, and had his meal at the Carnivore, he had dropped back in at the WWF's office. He had to let somebody have it after his treatment from Anna, and Craig Maitland seemed like the right person.

'No way, Craig, am I going to cart her around the bush with me, assessment or no assessment. I'm onto the biggest and probably the most dangerous investigation since I started with this anti-poaching scheme and I can't afford to watch my back as well as nursemaid her if it cuts up rough.'

'Okay then. What proof have you got?' Craig cut in. He sat smugly back in his chair, he knew from past experience the only proof Tony presented was usually after his investigations were complete.

'Proof, damn it, Craig. You know that's not the way I operate. What's more ...'

Craig sat impassively behind his desk waiting for Tony to wind down. He'd received specific orders from the Wildlife Fund's International Council that Tony's scheme had to be properly assessed this year; too many times he'd ridden rough-shod over his previous assessors. The council was going to have a proper assessment done, and it was Craig's job to ensure they got it. They had even threatened to pull Tony's funding if he refused to cooperate, which Craig decided to keep in reserve, if the need arose. He eventually got his next opportunity to speak. Tony was floundering for something constructive to say, 'But, but, Christ, Craig she's a woman –'

'I could have told you she was a woman if you'd have listened, instead of going off half-cocked –'

'Half-cocked!' Tony roared, before beginning another verbal onslaught.

Craig had to again sit back and wait until Tony paused; he decided the need had definitely arisen. His next comment stopped Tony in his tracks. 'The council is threatening to stop your funding unless you accommodate them this time.' He noticed that had struck home, so hurried on while he still had the chance. 'Plus dinging the Cessna isn't exactly going to help matters

– accident or not. You're going to have to go through with the assessment whether you like it or not.'

Tony had finally started to listen to reason. *Stop funding; now that would pose problems.* But still he couldn't let it go, he tried a different tact. 'Even if I wanted to, I doubt whether I could even get along with her. She's not exactly the friendliest of people.'

'I doubt whether you would be either, if you'd been through what she has.' Craig noticed that at least Tony was listening. 'She had to recently leave a plum job down on the Antarctic because her father was murdered, plus it took her four days to get here from the States, while being ripped off in the process. And what's more if she got the greeting from you I suspect, it's no bloody wonder, mate.'

'Yes well,' Tony lightly rubbed his chest, he was sure she had bruised it. 'I didn't realise,' he ended lamely.

'Tony, face it. This time you've got to go through with it, and help her set up,' he decided to butter him up, 'You and I both know it's results that count, but the council wants an independent assessment.' He could see that sunk home. 'Look, give the Shelia a week,' he reasoned. 'Anyway, I'm not going to be able to get you another plane until then.'

'But …' Tony tried, he wanted Ben up here as back up, however, he was hamstrung without a plane. *Bugger!* He'll have to catch a commercial flight up, *I'll phone him.* However, as far as Anna Hagan was concerned, he'd been forced into a corner and knew it. *Damn!*

Although he was due to embark on his biggest investigation ever, he knew he'd need the full support of the WWF if push came to shove, if and when he was ready to expose Donovan. He'd have to change his plans again. *God, what plans?* he thought despondently.

'Okay, one bloody week and that's all.' He changed the topic. 'Any messages from Ben?' he asked disgruntledly.

'No only these from London, some chap wants you to ring him urgently.'

Retrieving them, Tony walked from the office. He had decided to ring Richard after he'd located Peter Nkomo's house.

It was the day after Tony's encounter with Peter Nkomo at the Carnivore. He was back in his hotel room after picking up and reading through the information Richard had sent to the British High Commission. Although it still gave no hard evidence he could act on, he now knew exactly who the true enemy was, which made his current feeling all the more bitter. He was resigned to the fact that he'd have to delay his investigation and put up with Anna for a week.

But maybe it'll give me time to re-analyse everything I've learnt so far and wait for Ben. Although he hated to admit it, when Ben wasn't around, he did have a habit of acting impulsively. *And now more than ever I'll have to get it right, especially because of that cockup at the Carnivore last night,'* he berated himself.

The material he had received on Peter also indicated there was more information to follow on Donovan's planned trip to Africa. Tony couldn't wait for it so would have to pick it up after he'd helped Anna set up. By then he'd probably have a clear idea of how he was going to take on Peter, Sithole and the racket's kingpin – Donovan. The way things were currently panning out there may be only one option left to him, fighting fire with fire.

After reading through the information for a second time he tucked it into the bottom of his rucksack and tried to contact Ben. No one had seen hide nor hair of the little man in days, so he left a message stating, 'Big developments, I need you up here ASAP.'

I wonder what the bugger's up to? Probably shirking off somewhere no doubt. He placed all thoughts of Ben aside as he picked up his rucksack and squared his shoulders. Time to do battle. He was ready for Anna and to begin her wretched assessment.

Craig Maitland's words from the previous day still stung deeply, as well as those from earlier that morning, and Tony still flat out refused to apologise to the blasted woman. *It's not my fault it took her four days to reach Nairobi and ... oh Christ, no way am I going to apologise first.*

Tony and Anna were in his Land Cruiser on the Nairobi/Mombasa Highway heading south just out of the Kenyan capital. They had climbed out of a shallow bush-clad river valley, around a wide bend and past the game-rich ranching country of the Athi Plains. They were on their way to Kenya's Tsavo National Park, and by their fixed expressions it appeared to be the last place in the world they'd both rather be.

Tony had his eyes locked firmly on the road up ahead while Anna had her arms folded stiffly across her chest, staring sightlessly out the passenger window. In their current state, neither of them saw the great rocky buff of Lukenia thrust up at them on their left as they passed it by.

It wasn't my fault he crashed his God-damn plane in the middle of nowhere and split open his head. It didn't knock any sense into him that's for sure. He could've been more polite that's all. I'm not going to say sorry for my outburst, it was justified, Anna tried to convince herself, still staring determinedly out the window.

After several more miles, as the panoramic large-scale cattle and game ranches of the Kaputei Plains spread out either side of the highway, both Anna and Tony found they had wrestled with their consciences for long enough. They finally turned to each other and blurted out simultaneously, 'Sorry, about ...'

They then both stumbled into silence, thankful the ice had been broken, while still hoping the other would back down first. It was Tony who swallowed his pride and took the initiative. 'Craig told me about the problems you had before and on your way to Kenya. I should've realised by the state you were in. I'm sorry. I wasn't exactly the ideal welcoming party.'

He was finding it hard to believe the transformation in her, after a good night's sleep and compared to her dishevelled state at the airport, Anna looked a completely different woman. Her hair was brushed and tied back in a ponytail and glistening in good health, her face shone and she had a sparkle in her eyes.

'Thank you Tony and I also apologise, I was a little short ... well, perhaps a lot short at the airport. Craig also tells me you had your share of problems on your way up to Kenya to meet me.'

'Yes, a little.' Tony also looked and felt a lot better. Wearing his own clothes and with his cut a lot less inflamed, he looked far more presentable.

Tony had picked up Anna and taken her to meet Craig after he had read through Richard's report. He left them in private as Craig proceeded to give her an in-depth explanation of what her project across the Tanzanian border at Ngorongoro Crater entailed, and what was expected with her assessment of Tony's anti-poaching scheme. While they talked Tony was busy enough, loading up what research equipment was at the office and the initial supplies that had to be taken to the crater. It was at this time Anna learnt of Tony's project and the man that ran it.

Anna's next comment took Tony completely by surprise; she chuckled lightly, 'I should've realised earlier, but you're "the" Tony Campbell. Craig told me.'

'Ah, I suppose so ...' *whatever that was supposed to mean.* 'What exactly did he tell you?' Tony asked suspiciously.

'Oh, no, no, I mean it wasn't Craig, he told me what you did. Most of us working for the Wildlife Fund around the world know you. Well, of you, put it that way.'

Now Tony was really confused. 'Sorry, Anna. I'm not actually with you?' he said, bewildered.

'You're kidding?' she asked, but by the bemused expression on his face she knew he didn't have a clue what she was talking about. 'It's just that you, single-handedly, probably did more in recent years for the WWF than all our fundraisers put together. Money poured in from all over the world.'

'Fund raising money from all over the world? Now you've really got me.'

'Come on, Tony, you were about to start with the Wildlife Fund when somebody tried to have you killed. You were finishing up with that rhino project in Zimbabwe. You caused so much publicity and awareness for wildlife preservation, funds poured in from all over the globe; the WWF has never looked back. Hell, you even overshadowed the re-unification of East and West Germany for a time.'

'Oh I see.' Tony reached up and touched the faint scar on his cheek in memory, he suddenly realised why he'd been given so much equipment and support, and got his demands met so quickly. 'You know, I never thought. I hardly read the papers. I've always been wrapped up in my work.'

Anna chuckled knowingly. 'Plus, you may've been kept in the dark. Well, this will be interesting. So why are they so keen on this assessment? Craig emphasised it was important.'

Again realisation struck; the kudos he had obviously acquired at the start of his project was running out. 'Just standard procedure, that's all,' he answered instead. He wasn't going to ask Anna for support; he could be judged on his past successes and current actions. But he knew no matter what she reported there'd probably be cutbacks forced upon him. And the bloody Cessna wouldn't have helped that.

Notwithstanding the slaughter of the elephants, he'd be soon getting pressure from within. So now more than ever it was imperative for him to crack open Donovan's racket. The continuation of his anti-poaching work could depend on it.

As the assessment was required, and as he wanted to check up on potential trouble spots while in Kenya, he had decided to take a roundabout route to Tanzania's Ngorongoro Crater. He could hopefully kill two birds with one stone, one; having the assessment completed, while two; checking up on Kenyan's largest national park and the extent of any increased poaching in the area.

'Okay, Anna. We've a long drive ahead of us, it's a few more hours before we reach Tsavo. You may as well start asking your questions. I'll answer them as best I can.'

Tony found her first was rather direct. 'You don't really want me here do you?'

Well, she's honest. I'll give her that, he silently applauded, *Maybe we can get along after all.* He was quiet for a few moments, deciding how much he should tell her about his current investigation. She certainly seemed sympathetic, but as she wasn't in danger, he didn't want to involve her needlessly.

Anna intently watched him while he deliberated; it appeared to her as if Tony was torn between two answers. She was disappointed with the one he eventually gave.

'Put it this way, I have a lot going on at present.'

Anna misread Tony's reserve and caution as disdain for her presence. *Two can play at that game, mister. Okay, Tony Campbell. I'll be entirely clinical. Let's see if you're as good as your reputation,* she silently decided. 'So what are your formal qualifications?'

And so the inroads that had been made into a more amiable relationship were torn apart. Anna could feel the tension rise while Tony felt the hairs on the nape of his neck bristle. Those few words were fighting words to Tony.

CHAPTER 44

Tsavo National Park

'Magnificent, unbelievable.'

Anna slowly shook her head in wonder; she had never witnessed anything so breath taking.

Tony and Anna had arrived at Kenya's oldest and largest National Park: Tsavo, a park more than two hundred and fifty square miles, larger even than the British principality of Wales. Tony had ended their not so amicable three and a half-hour journey from Nairobi at the park's traditional centre, the luxurious Kilaguni Lodge.

Anna was sitting by herself on the Lodge's lofty ground-level veranda; she was slouched on one of the veranda's many comfortable chairs. With her feet resting on the foot-high stone and cement parapet, she was gazing in wonder at the scene that was unfolding before her. Entranced, she now ignored the gaggle of beaky hornbills, starlings and other small birds, as well as the myriad of semi-tame hyrax, dwarf mongoose and squirrels that had entertained her since she'd arrived, hopping and scampering about her looking, and sometimes begging for food. Instead, her eyes were now drawn as if by a magnet to the two waterholes in front of the lodge on the dry-brown plains that swept before it.

She drew in her breath in awe; her eyes were fixed on one of the water holes. Cast in a salmon-pink shade and reflected off its mirror-topped surface was Tanzania's Mt Kilimanjaro, standing serene and tranquil not fifty miles away. Like a gigantic icing-topped cake it seemed to float free, suspended above the still, glass-like surface. However, no sooner had the mountain allowed itself to be seen in such splendour, its reflection was plucked away. A herd of zebra had come down to the water's edge to drink, and as their velvet muzzles touched the water the mountain rippled away. But still Anna gaped in wonder. This was the long dreamed of Africa that she had never expected to see.

The gentle chink of two bottles struck together dragged her out of the magical scene and back to her seat on the veranda; the manmade sound made her realise she wasn't alone.

Tony had been watching her for the last few minutes, standing behind her, leaning up against the entrance to the veranda. He cursed himself as the two ice-cold Tusker lagers he was holding lightly touched together. He hadn't intended to interrupt her.

He pushed himself off the door jamb and came to sit beside her. 'She never fails to amaze me,' he said as he shook his head in amazement, 'I've lived amongst the African wilds all my life and I thought I'd seen it all, but at times like this I know I never will.'

Even though they'd had a blazing row on their way down from Nairobi after Anna had asked about his qualifications, she didn't begrudge him being with her to share this beauty. It was strange but during his outburst and her subsequent retaliation she had realised how much feeling and dedication he had for his project and the animals he was protecting.

Tony reached over and offered her a lager. 'I found it too torrid today,' he said, and it wasn't the temperature he was referring to.

Anna knew the lager was a peace offering and accepted it without hesitation. 'Yes, probably a bit hot.' She changed the subject; enough said, 'So this is Africa? I never expected such beauty.'

'Part of it, but I hope while you're with me you'll see a hell of a lot more. A side of Africa most never get to see.'

Tony wanted Anna to get a feel for the wilds and not just its animals, but all facets of what he protected; if an assessment was to be done, he wanted it done properly.

They both fell silent as the sunset quickly faded through pink to eventually envelop the countryside in a blanket of indigo; it was then Africa showed off another of her many hidden treasures. In the breathless still air, like the brilliance of twinkling diamonds reflected against a jeweller's black velvet cloth, popped one, then a hundred, then millions of stars in the domed sky above.

For Anna, it was the most intimate moment she had ever shared with another human being, and though Tony had seen the heaven's sparkling jewels many times before, he marvelled at the riches even the black African night was able to bring.

As the darkness was eventually overtaken by the luminous light thrown by the quickly rising tropical moon, from out of the receding gloom he saw the shadowy bulk of a herd of elephants amble up to the water holes.

'There you go, Anna, those are what I protect. And by the time you get to the Ngorongoro Crater I hope you'll be able to see why.'

'Hmm, I'll look forward to it.'

For the next four days Tony took Anna on a trip of fascination and intrigue, a trip that induced euphoria, sparked by a land untouched by man, still existing in its pristine beauty. As Tsavo National Park is split in two by the Nairobi/Mombasa road and railway, and as Kilaguni is in Tsavo West, this is where they spent these four days.

Crisscrossing past a blur of termite mounds and hammering over the park's network of red dirt roads Tony showed Anna a spectacle of landscape, a land that was mostly semi-arid, rough and incredibly wild, yet amazingly beautiful in all its awesome splendour.

Using his knowledge, from first light to dust, Tony was able to guide Anna through the park while she asked him questions, compiling her assessment, with little or no contact from tourists, game wardens and the like. He showed her the park's main tourist spots, but also areas rarely seen by visitors to the park.

The first contrast to Tsavo's thick hot bushland was the park's centrepiece south of Kilaguni. It was a clump of acacias and doum palms that encircled the Mzmia Springs; a fount of self-sustaining cool clear water, fed by the volcanic porous earth of the nearby Chyulu Hills and the snowmelt from Tanzania's Mount Kilimanjaro. Anna experienced the spring as a virtual timeless oasis, a green outpost amid Tsavo's dry expanse.

From the springs Tony then took her north, through plains with swaying fields of grass so high they would have easily reached up to an elephant's eye, to the Chyulus Hills; the youngest range of hills in the world. By zigzagging up a dirt road, through thorn scrub and a stunted forest of acacias, she was presented with a high-folded range of vivid, velvety green grass-covered knolls, and as if the view of these open grassy ridges weren't enough, stretching to the south was the shimmering, far-reaching plains of the park which sprawled away to Mt Kilimanjaro.

For several days as they explored these plains, Tony allowed Anna to study the park's wildlife until he felt it was time to venture above the heat and bushland once again. Beyond Kilaguni and Mzamia rose another spectacle, the avian paradise of the Ngulia Hills. As much of Tsavo West's northern section is hilly, it was impossible for them to leave the park without first exploring the magnificent escarpments that rose above the plains and the ribbon of the Tsavo River that the hills left far below.

Driving around hairpin bends and up through thick green forest, they eventually came to the Ngulia Lodge; it was posed on the edge of the escarpment and cut out of the mountainous rock. From its numerous vantage points Anna saw birdlife unlike any she had seen before; as they materialised out of the mountain mist she snatched glimpses of thousands of migratory birds.

Using the luxurious Kilaguni Lodge as a base, they returned in the evenings to its veranda or perhaps its manicured gardens outside, where Anna would shower Tony with a deluge of questions. Most of them he would answer, some he would leave to be explained during the adventures of the following day.

Despite their less than friendly start they slowly began to warm to each other, and it was during these frank discussions that Anna soon came to recognise Tony's conviction and understand the man behind the WWF's anti-poaching scheme.

'But surely the CITES ban will eventually stop the poaching,' she had begun one evening.

'I agree. In theory it sounds plausible, but in practice it's entirely different,' he responded before explaining. 'On one hand you have most of the southern African countries refusing to recognise the ban, and on the other the likes of Korea and Taiwan, who aren't signatories to CITES, more than happy to buy their ivory.'

Anna was horrified, 'But why don't those countries honour the ban? Surely it's in their interest?'

'Well, they obviously don't think so. What you must realise is that they feel because of the size of their herds and protection they can offer, they're being unjustly penalised.'

'Unjustly penalised?' Anna queried incredulously. 'How on earth can they be?'

'Because they look upon elephants as a sustainable resource,' Tony simply stated.

'You mean they're actually killing elephants?'

'They would prefer you to call it culling. Believe it or not, over-population is a problem in certain areas.'

'But they shoot them and then sell their ivory?' Anna still couldn't believe it.

'Yes, and by channelling the funds received back into wildlife preservation and awareness they feel they are able to sustain and continue to profit from elephants as a resource.'

'And you agree with this, even in your current capacity?' Anna asked dubiously.

'I never said that,' Tony reasoned, 'each country works to a conservation regime they believes works, and because I'm a guest in these countries it's not my place to question.'

'But ...' Anna began.

Tony wasn't listening, 'Look, Anna, my job is to stop illegal poaching. That's what I do and I'm certainly not here to question a country's protocol. Anyway, whether a country culls or doesn't cull isn't the real issue.'

Tony's rebuff had raised Anna's ire. 'Oh yeah, so what is?' She would have added 'buster' but chose to hold her tongue.

In contrast, Tony was composed; it was a question he'd often had to wrestle with in the past. 'The usual, greed and ignorance. Greed for the profit that can be made, and ignorance for what is lost. The way I see it is I'm fighting Africans and foreigners alike. Foreigners because they don't know, don't want to know, or can't understand the ramification their greed is causing, and Africans because one poaching raid can give them the equivalent of a year's income.'

'So what's the solution?'

Tony snorted lightly, 'Stop the demand, but of course that's easier said than done. It's always the same; it gets back to greed and ignorance. And with them present, there'll always be poaching and I suppose, if the money's there to fight it, men like me trying to stop it.'

Finally, it was time to leave Tsavo West and head across the Nairobi/Mombasa highway to Tsavo East. Leaving by the Maktau gate in the south and traveling across the broad Tsavo plains towards Tsavo East's southern gate at Voi, Tony couldn't prevent himself from taking a brief excursion into the Taita Hills. Although they weren't actually a part of the park he knew they would give a fantastic view of the plains and another facet of Africa Anna hadn't yet seen. Looking craggy and forbidding from a distance, like a bulking mass of blue-grey rocky up-thrusts, they soon took on a gentler aspect the closer they got. Like verdant islands, they seemed to rise out of the surrounding savanna sea.

The contrast of the semi-desert to the Taita Hills Tony knew was one of the most pronounced in Africa. As they climbed the bush fringed dirt roads which were punctuated with crashing creeks and waterfalls, it captured a sense of surprise; the sudden change of both climate and scenery left Anna initially speechless, marvelling at the contrast. Each verdant level they ascended took on a new perspective for within minutes Africa was remote and distant as if left far behind. Tony presented to Anna a series of Shangri-La like valleys and terraced small-holdings that stepped down the hill's steep slopes, looking as if they had been freshly plucked from the southern Italian Alps.

As Tony drove from the hills to the next part of their journey he knew in the last four days Anna had seen a hidden diversity of landscape and wilderness that could've only been discovered in Africa.

CHAPTER 45

TONY HAD DECIDED once they got into Tsavo East they would spend the first half day relaxing, instead of rising before dawn to venture out into the park like they had in the west. It was late morning and both he and Anna were sitting beside the pool at the Voi Safari Lodge. Tony was staring out over the park towards the north. Compared to the previous days today was hot, so he had recently removed his shirt and veldskoens, and forgotten that Anna was somewhere behind him nearby; he had become comfortable with her presence. Taking time off from his current investigation for the assessment wasn't turning out anywhere near as bad as he'd first imagined it would be.

Tony had decided to stay at the Voi Safari Lodge not just because it was perhaps the most beautifully designed of all of Kenyan's wildlife lodges. About six miles inside the Voi Gate the lodge was cut into a large craggy cliff which reflected neither Western nor indigenous themes; it was constructed solely to be in harmony with its setting. It may have offered luxury but the main reason Tony had chosen to stay at the lodge was because of the incredible vista it offered its guests. From beside its blue-tiled pool or even more so from the hill behind it, the panorama that was afforded was truly magnificent.

Whereas Tsavo West was hilly, green and with an abundance of vegetation, the east side of the park looked like a flat burnt-out arid landscape, an uninterrupted plain of empty bushland that seemed to stretch forever to table mountains in the distance. Although the vista appeared to present a monotonous sameness and was touched in the east by the scorched waterless wilderness of the Taru Desert, it still had a majesty of its own. Even by African standards, this part of the park was vast, being not just part of, but now recognised as *the* legendary Kenyan wilderness.

Decades before, much of Tsavo was covered with woodlands, but because of over-population by elephants and years of continual drought, their numbers decimated most of the vegetation in the park. Helped to a certain degree by poachers, they eventually died in their thousands, leaving a desolate wilderness the Kenyan Wildlife Conservation and Management Department were forced to try to save. Today two-thirds of Tsavo East is still off limits to tourists, in part to give the country a chance to recover but mainly it remains a prohibited area because of the continuing war experienced with the Samoli poachers. If it wasn't for the marauding *shiftas* this area of the park had all the ingredients ideal for an undisturbed animal kingdom.

Without looking around at Anna, Tony snorted lightly and shook his head as he gazed down at the two waterholes below the lodge, unconsciously played with his ivory disk.

'Ironic really, but Tsavo to the Kamba people of the area means, "slaughter".' He received no reply, so continued. 'It's been said there were once about seventy to eighty thousand elephants in the park before the poaching and drought of the seventies, and only now are their numbers slowly increasing. The wardens estimate both sides of the park have between six to eight thousand.' Still he received no reply, so slightly concerned, he queried, 'Anna?' But as he turned and glanced over his shoulder he found his breath had caught in his throat.

'Hmm, sorry what,' she murmured, only vaguely aware of his comment and her surroundings.

When Tony had stripped off his shirt and gazed out across the park's dry savanna Anna had done the same, but instead of taking an interest in the landscape she had stretched out on her back, and clad only in the skimpiest of bikinis, she had soon fallen asleep.

Tony again saw a side of the most unlikely scientist he had ever met. Her skin was the colour of wild bush honey, which was contrasted against the white string bikini she wore. With her shining raven hair tossed around her head she looked the picture of tranquillity, lying with her eyes peacefully closed. Although he tried to, he couldn't drag his eyes from her body. Her shoulders were broad, her breasts not overly large, while her waist and hips were narrow and slim. It was then that Tony finally realised he had spent the last few days with a woman, a rather appealing and attractive one.

Notwithstanding her dishevelled state when he'd first laid eyes on her at the airport, the few days she had spent under the African sun had allowed her to bloom like a desert rose after its first taste of rain. He would have gaped for longer but Anna spoke.

'What are you looking at?'

Tony snapped his head back to look across the plains. 'Nothing,' he croaked, having trouble finding his voice. He was sure her eyes had been closed.

'What'd ya mean, nothing?'

'Well … it's just that … well, it should be illegal.'

'What should?' Anna asked as she sat bolt upright and looked over his shoulder. 'Why, what's down there?' Her frown deepened when she saw a small herd of five elephants walking towards one of the water holes. 'Tony, what on earth are you going on about?'

Her eyes had been closed and she hadn't seen him looking at her at all. They had been talking at cross-purposes. He began to laugh. 'Well, you actually. The natives aren't exactly used to seeing people dressed like you, and this native more than most.'

'Oh, I see,' Anna reasoned, as she then thought to herself, *So you aren't made of steel, this'll be interesting.* She'd found a clink in his armour; under his facade he wasn't as cool as he made out to be. She changed the topic, 'What are we doing today? I've had enough of lying around.' Tony laughed again which Anna found strangely appealing. *Twice in one day, things are looking up.* 'Why the mirth?' she asked, intrigued.

Still chuckling, Tony rose, slipped his ivory disk back into his pocket and reached a hand down to help her up. 'Wanderlust. Africa, she's already got into your bones.' He retrieved his shirt and turned to walk back to the lodge.

'And what's that supposed to mean?' Anna half demanded as she scooped up her clothes and walked at his side.

'African fever, it gets into your blood,' he began to explain, 'It's like an addictive need to keep moving on, as if each distant horizon beckons you forward, ever onward.'

'Oh my God,' Anna forged mock distress, but he was correct. She'd been almost disappointed last night when he'd said they wouldn't be going out at dawn. 'What can I do?' she feigned anxiety as she grabbed at his upper arm.

'Nothing I'm afraid, it's incurable.' He tried to play along with a playful flick of his head, but the gesture was the slightest bit forced. 'However, it's been said frequent stops in cities are the only known relief.'

She released his arm with a satisfied smile. For all his rough exterior he wasn't that tough inside. 'Okay then, Doctor Campbell. Where to for my next needed fix?'

'You'll see.' He hooked a thumb over his back at the arid plains behind them, more to relieve the tension that had gripped his arm when she'd grabbed it, than to indicate where they were going. 'But we're venturing out there. You've seen what the wilds can be like with dedicated conservation, now I want to show you the opposite.'

As they walked into the lodge Anna wasn't sure if she liked the sound of what Tony had said.

It had been easy for Tony to get permission from the park headquarters at Voi so they could travel into off-limits area of the park. After leaving the pool Tony and Anna had picked up a packed lunch from the lodge kitchen and headed out into Tsavo East. They had travelled about twenty miles from the lodge and crossed the Galana River, and stopped near one of Kenya's rare displays of white water; the Lugard Falls. They were sitting beside the falls having lunch.

The Galana River ran through what was left of the gallery forest that must have once lined its banks, while the trees weren't necessary full with game there were plenty of birds, the river and shade of the trees giving them some relief from the heat. Like the river the falls themselves weren't grand, but as the main flow squeezed through a narrow crack cleaved through a solid granite rock, the cascading flow beyond, over a ballroom-sized set of irregular steps, made up for their size.

'How did you do it?' Anna asked. 'They told me back at the lodge tourists weren't allowed out here, on this side of the river.'

'Well, we're not exactly tourists.' That was something Anna had immediately realised with the preferential treatment they had received everywhere they'd so far gone in the park. 'The wardens gladly accepted my help with policing.'

'But it's not dangerous here is it?' Anna's eyes flicked to the FN lying beside them on the groundsheet they were sitting on. It was the first time she'd seen it. Until now she hadn't even realise Tony had a gun.

Tony noticed the direction of her glance. 'Africa's a dangerous place, and they're not exactly boy scouts that are killing elephants.' He could see that hit home.

'You mean ... you use that.'

'Anna, all anti-poaching patrols in Africa are armed. Poachers are destroying not just the wildlife but a major revenue earner for all the countries with decent numbers of game. They don't listen to reason, there's too much money at stake. That's why it's a government decree, "shoot poachers on sight".'

Anna was horrified. 'You mean kill them.'

'Yes Anna, dead. Why do you think somebody tried to have me killed down in Zimbabwe before I started with the Fund?'

'But why, why are they prepared to risk their lives? Surely it's the middlemen that make all the money?'

'It is, by our standards. But also look at it this way, the average African tribesman has always lived with wild animals and if they wanted meat they hunted.' He shrugged lightly. 'Would you stop if a foreigner or a spokesman from another tribe said you had to? It's tradition. Plus as I've told you before, one poaching raid can net them a year's income, and many are prepared to take that sort of a risk.'

'And you shoot them, I mean how could you? Can't you catch them or warn them off or something? I mean, surely there's a better way.'

He'd argued this point many times before, he let out a wary breath; he'd hoped Anna would be different. 'Desperate measures for desperate situations.' He held up his hand, as Anna was about to interrupt. 'Before you say anything I'd like to show you something. Come on, let's pack up. There's a reason I brought you out here away from the normal tourist haunts.'

It was the smell that guided Tony to the two dead elephants, he had found out the day before from one of the park wardens that they had been shot by poachers several days before.

He had to take Anna by the arm and drag her up so they could stand beside them. She stood with her other hand thrown up to cover her nose and mouth as she stared in horror through eyes as big as saucers.

'That's what I try and prevent from happening. No mammal, man or elephant deserves to die like that.' He continued to drag her around the stinking, lifeless carcasses. Never once did her eyes leave the dead animals.

Covered in white streaks where the vultures that had fed on them had defecated; their skin now hung in great sagging wrinkles. And with their faces hacked off, Anna was shown the reality of when Tony's work failed.

As he led her away she couldn't prevent herself craning her head back over her shoulder. Although she'd seen plenty of dead animals in her profession, those two elephants had moved her deeply. It was a macabre sight, and with their faces hacked into where the tusks had been, it seemed to speak of the agony the two animals must have suffered. She finally brought her eyes round to meet Tony's when he spoke again. His voice was gentle but filled with sorrow.

'Nobody should have to see a sight like that. I'm sorry, but if you're to do an accurate assessment it was probably something you needed to see. No, Anna,' he reaffirmed, 'I'll do everything in my power to prevent scenes like that.'

Even with what she'd seen Anna couldn't prevent her next statement, 'But surely, is it necessary, shooting poachers on sight?' she queried, 'It's barbaric. There must be another way.'

This time Tony was unable to hold his temper in check, 'Okay, lady, you're the one with the qualifications. You find a better solution.' He didn't want to fight with Anna but before he knew it the comment popped out.

'Qualifications,' she snapped back at him, 'At least I'm more qualified than to lug around a gun.'

Tony would have rounded on her again; probably something about protecting the shrinking African wilds, but Anna had yanked her arm out of his grip and stormed back to the Land Cruiser.

Christ, that bloody woman, he fumed; he'd never met anyone who could trigger so much emotion. *The sooner I'm away from her the better*, he decided as he followed her back to the Toyota.

CHAPTER 46

'THEY'RE SO NAUGHTY, look at them.' Anna laughed. In the last few minutes both she and Tony had quickly forgotten about their latest outburst of twenty minutes previous.

Our arguments may be heated, Tony had thought, *but at least now they're short-lived.*

Oblivious to the afternoon heat they had sneaked up to within twenty yards of a noisily feeding herd of elephants. They were crouched behind the fallen trunk of a long-dead acacia tree, while at their back was the mound of a spire-like termite hill, and fringing them on either side were two over-hanging Nyrika thornbushes. Because of the noise made by the herd they were able to talk in quiet conversational tones.

Anna was enthralled by the antics of two elephant calves. 'Gosh, they're just like children.'

There were ten in the herd, the two calves, an immature bull and an old matriarch, while the rest was made up of breeding cows. All the herd was shaded a dusty red having picked the colour from the park's brick-red earth after covering themselves with dust, using it as protection against the fierce African sun. What had made Anna laugh was one of the calves who had picked a dry branch with its trunk and was chasing the other around and through the herd with it. They were both squealing with delight at the fun of their game.

'They're so noisy; I could hear the calves before you even stopped the Toyota.'

'Yes, one of the things against their defence. A poacher can also hear them from miles away.'

As well as indicating the two dead elephants, the game wardens had told Tony where the nearest herd of elephants were in the park. Although there still weren't many in the area since it was worst hit by drought and more especially poaching in recent times, there were still a few good herds to be found if one knew where to look. He had parked the Land Cruiser when they'd first heard the elephants and instructed Anna to stay close by as they had gone in on foot.

At ground level the arid plain appeared a lot more vegetated than it had done from the elevated vantage-point beside the lodge's pool. The ground was flat but the view was interrupted by stunted acacia trees and the scattering of shrubs and thorny bush. However, it still hadn't taken Tony long to locate the herd once on foot. As the crow flies it was several hours walk from the Galana River and the elephants were congregated in a clearing around a huge Baobab tree.

With her huge ears flapping to dispel the heat, the old matriarch had just dug one of her tusks into the tree and was trying to prise out a chunk of the nutrient-rich, white spongy wood. Nearby, one of the other cows was having a lot more success with the bark of a giraffe acacia tree. Using a similar technique it had wrenched out a strip of bark, grabbed it with its trunk and stripped it off the tree. As Anna and Tony watched, it was in the process of stuffing the strip into its mouth with relish.

'What's it doing?' Anna was horrified, her amusement forgotten, 'it's going to ring-bark the poor tree. It'll die.'

'That's right. In the few minutes you've been here, you've seen how human-like they are. Their calves play like human children, constantly craving attention from their parents and siblings, and you've witnessed the only other species on earth apart from man known to destroy the habitat which it depends on for survival.'

'They must need hundreds of miles in which to live,' Anna reasoned.

'Yeah, another problem they encounter. Although they're common in most game parks they're under increasing pressure. Depending on numbers and suitability of food they need vast areas in which to live, sometimes upwards of thousands of square miles. With boundaries, border posts and human settlements increasingly diminishing their range, that's what they are forced to do.' He pointed at the ring-barked tree. 'However, it does, or once did, have its benefits. They're able to open up normally impregnable thickets and bush for new grazing for the other game. But now ... well, like they did here, they can easily turn it into a near wasteland.'

'So what can be done?' Anna had turned to gaze full into Tony's eyes. At times like this she found he was so easy to read. Normally, it was his facial expressions that gave his thoughts away, but now it was as if his eyes were stripped naked and spoke of the undisclosed feeling and commitment he had for his job. In that minute she suddenly knew she'd found somebody as dedicated to their profession as she was to hers. No wonder we fight, we both believe so much in what we are doing.

'What can be done? As you know some countries cull to try and manage their herd numbers, while others feel the elephants on their own will reach a desirable equilibrium.' He shrugged into silence as he broke eye contact and looked back out at the herd.

'Come on, Tony. I know I've asked you before, but what do you think? Would you shoot, I mean cull, the elephants you're trying to protect? Could you go that far?'

'I suppose it's something I can't answer, but if it benefits the elephant and the proceeds are put back into conservation ... who knows? All I know is, I find it an incredibly arrogant view that the world was made for human beings, so I'm dedicated to a cause I believe in and that's where I'm currently channelling my efforts ... and I feel at the moment that's enough.'

Anna reached out and laid a hand on his sleeve. 'More than enough.' With those few words she knew he was truly dedicated and probably more so than she'd previously envisaged, and the way he acted was due to that dedication.

It was as if her touch had triggered something inside. Tony slowly revolved his head to stare at her, but his eyes had glazed over and gone cold and remote, and then with the speed of a pouncing leopard he had thrown himself on top of her.

Anna couldn't believe it. *God, he's taken the touch as an invitation.*

She began to struggle as she opened her mouth to scream, yet before the first torrent of outrage had left her lips Tony's hand had clamped firmly down over her mouth. It was then she realised how truly powerful he was.

Oh my God, she wailed inside, *and we're miles away from anywhere. He could do anything.*

'Stop struggling and shut up,' she heard him hiss, and with even more strength Anna felt him bore further down on top of her.

Anna was desperate now, so she opened her mouth and sunk her teeth into Tony's hand. Like a dog on a ferret, she began to worry into his flesh.

'Shit ... Ow you bloody little bitch ...' she heard him hiss again.

As Anna touched his arm Tony was sure he'd heard a noise not in keeping with the feeding elephants, he turned his head to the side and stared sightlessly into Anna's eyes. There it was again. He reacted instantly and threw himself forward at Anna, he was sure it sounded like a metallic click. He covered her body and clamped a hand firmly over her mouth to still all noise, as he hissed, 'Stop struggling and shut up.'

Although Anna still struggled, he held her easily as he twisted his head to the side, peering over the log, trying to locate what had made the noise. As he saw a dull metallic glint from amongst the bush to his left, he instantly recognised what he'd seen.

'Shit ...' he began to curse, he knew exactly what he was seeing, then swore again as Anna's teeth gnashed into his hand, 'Ow you little bitch ... for Christ's sake, there are poachers out there. Let it go.'

In relief he felt her teeth unfasten; luckily, she hadn't opened the skin. He placed the thought and pain aside. Right now he had far more pressing problems.

Still on top of her, Tony poked a threatening finger into her face as he reached with his other hand for his FN. 'Not a sound and don't you dare move,' he implored. 'You couldn't have asked to get closer to see how ruthless poaching can be.'

As he rolled off her with his rifle held to his chest, Anna nearly gasped out loud. No longer were Tony's eyes cool and remote. Like glacial ice they were cold, yet calculating, entirely professional while wrought with murderous intent. As he began to move away, he stopped and briefly turned back.

'Yes Anna, I've got no formal qualifications, but the ones I have got are probably about to save your life.' Tony was gone before the words sunk home.

CHAPTER 47

FROM ONE HORIZON to the next the sun's rays beat down like a furnace, sending a wafting heat haze shimmering into the pale blue sky. The air was still, and if it weren't for the clatter of tusks against bark and the trumpeting, squealing uproar the feeding herd made, the scene could've been oppressive. The conditions had turned this into a domain suitable only for animals used to or adapted to the heat. Because of the soaring temperatures, most predators had called a truce and allowed those animals that still chose to feed to do it at their leisure. Most predators that was – except man.

There were five of them, all dressed in an assortment of cast-off western clothes and army uniforms. They were small and wiry tribesmen from the north, reprobates from long-forgotten army days, merchants of death, killers by trade. These were the worst of all poachers; Somali *shiftas*.

Silently moving, cradling their AK 47s at their chests, each man was incessantly scanning the red earth underfoot as they followed the spoor of the leisurely feeding herd. When the contorted limbs of the baobab were visible above the surrounding thorn-scrub, and when the direction of the herd's noise was unmistakable, the leading *shifta* gave an underhand flick with his fingers. The other four men immediately split into different directions. As there was no wind to give them away, it would be easy for them to surround the herd, raise their AK 47s and riddle the elephants – cows and calves alike – with automatic fire until none remained alive. It would be then a simple job to remove the ivory and be gone within the hour to leave the herd to rot where it lay.

The leading *shifta* forged ahead on his own. Scurrying crab-like he avoided the low thorn-bushes to eventually position himself to the right of a tall red termite mound on the periphery of the clearing and the herd. Clearly visible through the scrub he could see the giant, red-tinted beasts; he counted as many as he had fingers on both his hands. He clicked off the safety and put his AK on automatic.

Watching the herd he decided, *today will be a good day* as he clicked the safety on then off again.

In another few minutes he would level the semiautomatic and pull the trigger. By then his companions would be in position ready to follow his lead.

As if he were wading through molten lead, the minutes slowly ticked by. Finally, it was time. He chose the old matriarch, the one with the biggest tusks. He raised the barrel and sighted his rifle. *Yes, today was certainly going to be a good day.*

Running crouched over, Tony left Anna hidden beside the fallen tree; he hoped she'd do as she was told.

If she stays put, she'll be fine, he decided, he then placed the thought of her from his mind.

To stop the ensuing slaughter and the poachers he needed to clear his mind of outside thought; it was imperative he began to think like one of them. But first he had to position them. He chose the one he had identified from where he'd seen the flash of metal.

He changed direction and ran directly away from the still happily feeding herd. As he did so his eyes flicked from the ground in front of him to the bush up ahead; he had no desire to blunder into any of the poacher's line of fire. He knew he should have stayed at Anna's side and waited until the poachers opened up. Once they were firing he could pinpoint them, but he also knew in the confusion most of the herd would be lost. As he circled back behind the man, he realised that with no wind the other poachers were probably circling the herd, and with each pace he took he expected to hear their brutal rattle of automatic fire.

Throwing caution to the winds he reasoned he must now be directly behind the man, then just as he thought he'd have to run in blind, he caught sight of the man's spoor.

Only one of the bastards, according to the single set of tracks, but he knew there'd be more. With the silent footfalls of a predatory cat, he stealthily stalked his prey.

As he moved down the line of the spoor he felt a silent rage well up from within, threatening to burst forth as he noticed a flicker of movement through the scrub up ahead. Using the savage bittersweet taste of anger like fuel, he lightly skipped around the bush up ahead and levelled his gun.

'Bloody *shiftas*.' The briefest glimpse of a man told Tony exactly who the poachers were – the deadliest, most ruthless of them all. His loathing rose within him, threatening to erupt with the explosive blast of his gun, but no sound exploded as Tony saw the man lift his rifle and sight it at his prey.

With the man still oblivious to his presence, Tony managed to check his fury and prevent himself from pulling the trigger. If he did it would send a barrage of bullets into the elephants from the other poachers. He sidestepped just behind the man and smashed the wooden butt of his FN into the base of the *shifta's* skull. The man was unconscious before his forehead slumped to the ground.

Tony wasted no time; he didn't even bother checking the man to see if he was alive. He scooped up the fallen AK 47 and headed back to Anna.

Oh, this is ridiculous. Anna was now kneeling behind the tree peering over the top, *He must be having me on, I can't see anyone.* The elephants appeared to be still happily feeding and she reasoned, *Surely they'd sense something.* She half rose, deciding to find Tony and get him to call off this charade. *He's doing it on purpose, trying to scare me. This sort of thing doesn't happen in real life,* she tried to tell herself.

As she pushed herself off the ground, a hand clamped around her mouth and she was violently thrown sideways to the ground. Screaming noiselessly into the hand, fearfully she screwed her eyes to the side.

'I said stay put,' Tony hissed, 'and I meant it. For Christ's sake, you silly bitch, this is no game.'

From the intensity of his voice and the malevolent mask he wore she knew he was serious. Tony released his grip and rolled to the side, he retrieved a rifle from where he'd dropped it at their feet.

'Where the hell do you think I got this from?' he demanded, not expecting to be answered.

Tony had two guns, one she'd seen him carrying since lunchtime, and now a second one she'd never seen before. It had a dark brown grainy wooden stock and a long curved magazine protruding beneath it. Yanking her into a sitting position, he flicked its safety off and shoved it into her hands. 'Have you ever used a rifle?'

She nodded dumbly, then added quickly, 'Pop showed me once when I was a little girl, but I …'

Tony held up a hand, 'I don't want to hear it. You may have to use it. Look, I don't know how many are out there, and as yet they don't know we're here, but by God, if they do find out …' he never finished as he noticed Anna staring dumbly down at the semiautomatic in her hands.

'Tony I couldn't, I …'

It was then he slapped her across the face. 'Damn you, woman. Those are cold-blooded killers out there. You can't reason with them. Out here its law of the gun – kill or be killed – you're not in some damn classroom now.' He saw her cheeks flush and anger blaze within her eyes. 'Good, at least now you're listening.' He gestured to the AK 47 again, 'Point it at anything that moves and pulled the trigger.'

'You bastard, you hit –'

Before she could continue Tony was gone again, and as quickly as her anger had flared it was snuffed out again, this time to be replaced with fear, gut-wrenching, bowel clutching fear.

Oh God! Anna cringed back up against the tree trunk. *This isn't what it's supposed to be like,* she wailed inside, *I'm a scientist, not some, some ... oh God where's he gone?*

Frantically swivelling her eyes from side to side she scanned the bush. *Come on stay calm, stay calm, he knows what he's doing.*

But the words didn't help. She could feel her heart pounding within her chest and a solid ball of fear in her guts weighing her down. She now ignored the elephants, oblivious to their peril, as she was sure behind every bush and tree there was a dark figure lurking, and her eyes flicked to the right.

Oh my God! She nearly gasped out loud; a small black man had crawled to the periphery of the bush and was pointing a gun at the elephants in the clearing. Anna ducked below the level of the tree, then ever so slowly peered over it once again. He was still there and thankfully hadn't seen her. She brought up the rifle, instinctively doing what she'd been told.

No, I can't ... she realised once she had him in her sights, *not another human being.*

It was then he swivelled his head and with eyes bulging in shock as he saw her, he rolled and flicked himself to the side, trying to throw off her aim. In that split-second Anna knew everything Tony had said was true – it was kill or be killed, but even though her sights followed the man, she couldn't bring herself to pull the trigger.

She saw his sights coming to bear but still she froze. She couldn't duck, she couldn't move, and even before he pulled the trigger she'd already died a hundred deaths.

As Tony ran he quartered off the clearing in his mind. *If they are circling the elephants they'll have sectioned it off.* And sure enough, he came upon the next set of prints where he had expected. *I'd say there are four or possibly five.*

As he followed them his anxiety grew, they were angling in towards Anna. *This'll be interesting.*

He'd followed the tracks nearly to the edge of the clearing when a blur of movement rolled from beneath a bush to the side and in front of him, he reacted instinctively, lunged and drove with his full weight down onto his knees. As his knees thumped into the small of the poacher's back he followed through with his rifle butt, again it smashed into a poacher's skull and again a poacher slumped unconscious to the ground.

Christ, that was close. That time he'd been lucky and knew that it probably couldn't last.

As he rolled to the side he turned his head towards Anna. He saw her huge fearful eyes and her expression of patent relief. With a quick shake of his head he cautioned against any sound. Although she hadn't fired, as he merged back into the scrub, he applauded her the same. At least she'd sighted on the bastard. It was far more than he'd expected. However, his mind was elsewhere as he looked for his next line of spoor. Two down and God knows how many to go. However, Tony's luck finally ran out.

He knew he was running desperately short of time and that one of the poachers he had knocked unconscious must have been the leader. The other were probably at this moment waiting to be given their cue.

They won't wait forever.

He abandoned the possibility of trying to sneak up on the others. He'd have to try to identify their positions.

As he crept back to the edge of the clearing he was spotted. Unbeknown to him his position was marked, but not by one of the poachers. Oblivious to the scrutiny he was receiving, Tony began scanning around the edge of the clearing.

Peering through the legs of the still rowdy elephants he had spotted one poacher, then two. However, it wasn't until he scanned the final quarter of the clearing that he saw to his horror the danger he was in.

In shock he looked back to the elephants. 'Oh, Christ,' he groaned in dismay, 'Not now!'

Tony lay stock-still not daring to move a muscle, at another time he would have probably laughed out loud, but not now. He watched in horror as the youngest of the two elephant calves charged. With its ears spread out, doubling the side of his head and with his arm-sized trunk curled on top of his forehead it let out the most fearsome noise he could muster, but what erupted was a high pitch squeal only a piglet could have been proud of.

As the calf hauled himself to a stop at the end of its mock charge, Tony sadly shook his head, 'Sorry to do this to you, young fella, but you give me no choice.'

Tony raised his FN and tapped the trigger, the calf first stumbled then staggered backwards before screaming with fear to find sanctuary beneath his mother's legs.

Tony's shot caused the herd to bolt from the clearing. But before the dust had settled from around the first poacher he'd fired on, Tony had switched his aim and shafted the next. He didn't have a clue if any of his bullets had hit and he didn't wait to find out. Before they could pinpoint his position, he rolled over twice to the side, rose to his knees and withdrew. The poachers now knew they weren't alone. 'This'll be fun,' he said to himself.

The rattling bark of automatic fire and trumpeting squeals of fright from the panicking elephants made Anna die another hundred deaths, with her heart in her mouth she watched with mounting terror as all hell broke loose around and in the middle of the clearing.

Anna saw the old matriarch break first once the calf was safely in the middle of the herd, and then, in total harmony, all the other elephants wheeled off after her. Although she was quaking in fear she was amazed at how the whole herd instinctively followed her lead, for within seconds the clearing was empty. She then flicked her gaze to where she thought the gunfire had come from; she saw nothing, only dust beginning to settle in two separate spots further around the clearing. One bewildered man had risen, she saw him turn and run, while at the other spot another was rolling in the dust writhing in pain as he clutched at his shoulder.

Now what? she thought on the verge of panic, cradling the rifle to her chest, she sunk back down behind the log. *Come on Tony, where are you?* This would have to be the most frightened she'd ever been.

Okay, keep calm. Stay put. She tried to quieten her reeling mind but her resolve was threatening to break. *Christ, those were real bullets.* She flicked her gaze to the right, to the unconscious figure that had pointed his gun at her. And he was going to shoot me. She would have loved to have run. But to where? She knew she had to do as Tony had said. 'Please God, I'll give him a good assessment, just get him back here.'

Hearing a noise behind her, she felt an intense wave of relief wash over her body. 'Thank God,' she whirled around, 'Where have you ..' the words stilled on her lips as the question went unasked. In numbed disbelief, she saw it wasn't Tony who had walked from behind the termite mound but a slightly built black man, dressed in an assortment of filthy rags with a menacing scowl on his face. Riveted to the spot she watched in mounting horror as the man smiled a hideous smile and pointed his gun at her face.

Anna couldn't move. She'd lost all sense of reality and had even forgotten about the rifle lying idly in her lap. The man deliberately extended his rifle as his finger curled around the trigger.

Time slowed down as the cruel truth of Tony's words stomped their way across her mind, *Damn you woman, those are cold-blooded killers out there, you can't reason with them. Out here it's law of the gun.*

She didn't want to die. Not here. Not like... But the shuddering roar of the red-hot lead and a faint faraway scream plucked his last few words from her mind. With the rattling report and the wounded blood-curdling cry still ringing in her ears, her last conscious thought as she slumped forward and fell to the ground was, *At least there's no pain, but God, what a way to go.*

There was nothing Tony could do. He had run back into the clearing desperately trying to reach Anna's side.

He'd lain quietly after peppering the poachers and sat, watched, and waited. As the elephants disappeared from the clearing he saw one poacher rise and scamper away, while the other writhed around in pain. He then flicked his eyes over to Anna. He saw her fear and the sheer horror contort her face, but he knew he couldn't go to her. For now, he'd have to bide his time.

Four down, but how many to go. Surely that'd be it?

It wasn't. In horror he saw her turn and another man step from behind the termite mound.

Tony was up and running across the clearing as the man lifted his gun; he was screaming a blood-curdling cry as he fired from the hip. He briefly saw the poacher's AK burst into life as Anna slumped forward before they were both hidden within a light lead-born shroud of swirling brick-red dust. He hurdled the log and ran into the dust as his FN clicked empty. He immediately saw his bullets had plucked the poacher's AK from his hands, but not before they had smashed into him and shattered his forearm.

'Bastard!' Tony screamed. He saw Anna lying at his feet.

Although he was wounded, the scream rallied the man who turned and staggered from the scene.

Tony would have chased him but instead hurled his rifle with another scream after the stumbling figure, before slumping down to his knees beside Anna. It never crossed his mind to use the rifle cradled in her lap.

'Good one Tony,' he cursed as he lifted her lifeless head, 'you should've stayed with her, she never deserved to die. *Damn it!*

From far away out of the blackness a bony finger beckoned. She felt the hard earth underneath as somebody lifted her head, but before she could reach the light the terror of it came rushing in to crowd her mind. Anna's eyes flew open as she instantly came to. The first things she saw were Tony's cool-blue eyes and the naked concern marking his face. In terror, she threw her arms around his neck.

'It's okay, it's okay, he's gone now.' Tony gently placed a hand on the back of her head. 'It's over now, you blacked out.' Yet as he said the words, he couldn't help but scan his eyes around the clearing. 'Well, at least I hope it is.' Thankfully, he saw no movement. It was then that Anna's shock set in as she began to cry. 'Okay, shhh now,' he hushed as he began to gently rock her in his arms.

Over the next five minutes, Anna cried like she had never cried before. Like a fountain, the tears welled-up from deep within, gut-wrenching sobs that wracked her body to a silent streaming torrent of tears. Twice Tony tried to disengage her arms, but she was having none of it. Though she didn't realise it she felt safe in his arms, like with her father when as a little girl he would wake her from a nightmare. Acting on instinct as if her life depended on it, there was no way she was letting go.

Resigned to the fact, Tony rocked and hushed her until finally her tears and trembling subsided. He felt her body go limp as she relaxed within his arms. When she let out a long heavy breath, he knew she was over the worst.

'How are we getting on?' he asked gently. No reply. 'Okay, I suppose we could stay, hadn't planned to do much else this afternoon.' Again no reply.

Anna opened her eyes and blinked into his shoulder. She was pressed up against a huge tear-stained wet patch and it was then she realised how safe she felt. Notwithstanding her father, she had never felt this secure in anyone's arms before.

It must be the shock, she found herself thinking, *he could never measure up to Pop*. She let out another heavy, trembling breath.

'Shhh, that'll do.' Tony hushed, as he tried to disengage her arms again.

'Hush up yourself, and don't do that.' She'd decided he may not be her father, but a little longer within his arms won't hurt. Then after a couple more minutes, she found her voice again. 'You called me a silly bitch.' Tony groaned. 'And that's right,' she accused as she finally lifted her head off his shoulder, 'You slapped me.'

'Yes well ... I ah ...' he mumbled into silence, then thought about Ben. *It's your fault ya little pixie* he half-heartedly cursed his friend, *Leaving me in the lurch. Where the hell are you when you're needed?*

CHAPTER 48

Hwange National Park, Zimbabwe

'PSST ... HEY, psst.'

The position Ben was in could be best described as less than envious. He had really excelled himself this time and even Tony would be hard pressed to believe the mess he'd got himself into.

'Joshua, psst, hey Joshua,' he called quietly from beneath the thornbush he was hiding under, then hurriedly added in a much louder voice, 'No, no don't. Oh shit!'

Joshua, one of the game rangers from Hwange National Park's Main Camp, a tall willowy man, had just descended from the raised game-viewing hide at the Nyamandhlovu Platform. The platform was situated in a shady perch, about six miles south-west of Main Camp and overlooking the Nyamandhlovu Pan, one of the many well-used watering holes dotted about the Kalahari woodlands and thornveld that make up most of the park's trackless wilderness.

He had spent the day on the platform with a small group of tourists who had taken one of the Shamwari Safari's day trips to the pan; they had viewed a multitude of wildlife ambling in to drink throughout the day and it was now nearing sundown. The safari company's Land Rover would be arriving soon to take the group back to Main Camp. The group showed little interest in Joshua as he went to relieve himself on a nearby thornbush.

Joshua dribbled to a stop as his mouth fell open in shock; he had chosen to urinate on the bush Ben was hiding under.

'Put that great shank of meat away before you drown us both,' Ben said, wiping a hand over his now splattered face.

For several seconds Joshua stood dumbfounded, gaping down at the little man. 'What?' he eventually managed to squeak, before clearing his throat. 'Ben, what on earth are you doing under there? You've been missing for days.' He shook himself and zipped up his fly. Then in concern, he asked, 'Are you all right?' Ben didn't answer. He was suspiciously eyeing the group that was beginning to descend from the platform, Joshua looked over his shoulder, following his gaze. 'You're not in some sort of trouble, are you? You haven't ..' he flicked his head at the group, 'you know ... with one of the tourists.' It wouldn't be the first time he'd known Ben had made promises he couldn't keep.

'What?' Ben snorted lightly. 'I only wish, just a bit worse this time. Tell me, are Captain Sithole and his Shona goons still camped at Main Camp.'

Joshua was also a Matabele and held similar views as Ben's towards his Shona countrymen. 'Yes, they've taken over one whole bloody corner of the camping ground,' he said disdainfully. 'As a matter of fact, it was them asking about you that made us realise you were missing.'

'Oh gawd,' Ben groaned.

'The others thought you must have gone north with Tony, but I found your Land Cruiser hidden behind the shop this morning.'

'Oh Christ, you didn't tell anybody? Nobody else knows, do they?'

'No I didn't,' Joshua said indignantly. 'Will you come out from under there? They'll think I'm crazy talking to a bush.'

'Believe me, I'd love to, I've been hiding out here for days waiting to talk to you. It's bloody Sithole and his men. They sort of want to have a wee chat with but I'm not that keen.'

'Shit, you've really landed yourself in it this time. Okay, what can I do?'

'Has anybody heard from Tony for a start?'

'No... well yes. Look, will you come out from under there, they're only tourists. Sithole and his unit headed north this morning.'

Cursing and muttering to himself as he delicately crawled over Joshua's wet patch and out from under the thorns, Ben dusted himself down as he asked, 'What do you mean yes and no, has something happened?'

'He crashed his plane and apparently went bush for several days.'

'Shit, the bastard.' Ben immediately knew it was no accident and that he should have checked the plane more thoroughly.

'Hang on a minute,' Joshua wanted to prevent him from jumping to conclusions. 'The Kenyans thought he'd been killed but he eventually turned up at one of the lodges in Selous, and we also got a message from him a few days ago instructing you to hot foot it up into Tanzania.'

'Thank God, where –?'

'Yeah, come to think of it,' Joshua cut in, 'I was at HQ when the message came through. Sithole was there as well, and he didn't look that pleased. You two are up to something aren't you; it's about that container of ivory, isn't it? Oh ho, you are in the shit.' Joshua seemed to find his friend's plight amusing.

Ben didn't even try to explain, 'Look, I need to get out of here and down to Bulawayo without the army seeing me. Can you help?'

'Course I can,' Joshua said indignantly, 'I'll talk to the Shamwari driver when he arrives,' he flicked his head at the group now milling beneath the platform. 'We should be able to get you to the Safari Lodge with this lot. From there you can catch one of the Ajay Motorway's buses down to Bulawayo.'

They began to walk towards the group; the Land Rover would be arriving soon to pick them up. 'So what the hell happened?'

'Joshua, it's a long story.'

Once Tony had flown out for Nairobi from Bulawayo, Ben had decided to try and talk to the soldier in Captain Sithole's unit that he'd told Tony he felt could help them. However, if Sithole and his men hadn't arrived at Hwange by the time they were supposed to, he would head up to Malawi instead and make a few inquiries about the container up there.

As it turned out, Sithole and his men were setting up camp at the camping grounds when he arrived back at Main Camp. His trouble started the next morning.

'Right, time to talk to our friend,' Ben stated purposefully.

It was a crisp morning and Ben had risen early from his cabin and had been discreetly watching the army tents for the last hour or so. Slowly, the soldiers had risen and set about their morning's duties. He spotted his man walking by himself to the camping ground's ablution block.

He was greeted by a tuneless whistle as he entered the men's toilets; standing in front of the urinal was his man. Ben walked up to stand beside the man as he unzipped his fly and assumed the posture.

'Good morning for it,' he said, staring straight ahead at the wall. The tuneless whistle fell silent on the man's lips and out of the corner of his eye, Ben saw the man turn his head towards him. *God, you're an ugly brute. How heavy was the truck that parked on your face?* he silently asked.

The man was short and squat with a permanent scowl engraved upon his chubby face, and Ben could just make out the three stripes on his camouflaged army fatigues that designated he was a sergeant. The man said nothing as he turned to face the wall once again.

Ben decided on the direct approach. He'd found in the past that when a man had his penis in his hand and was standing in front of a urinal, it was socially acceptable to make small talk with a stranger.

'They say a big haul of ivory was found in a container on the road to Bulawayo yesterday.'

'You mean you and Campbell found it,' came a curt reply.

'Ah the bush telegraph prevails again. Well yeah, an accident really,' he replied. 'Somebody must have lost a bundle.'

'Huh,' the sergeant snorted, 'More than a –' came out before he checked himself. 'Yeah, probably,' he finished instead.

It may have been an innocent enough comment if both men hadn't turned to each other, Ben saw the guilt flare within the sergeant's eyes as he saw realisation flicker within Ben's. Turning back to the wall both men were silent with their own thoughts.

Shit, he knows we're involved, the sergeant thought.

Bloody hell, he is part of it. And Christ, I didn't want to be that direct, Ben thought.

Both men finished, zipped themselves up and walked over to the hand basins, each fully aware of the other's actions. Ben knew he now only had one chance to stop this meeting being reported to Sithole. Like the sergeant, by returning his disconcerted look he'd laid open his hand; the sergeant knew Tony and Ben were onto Sithole.

As if inspecting the light stubble on his chin in the mirror above the basin, Ben brought out a US hundred dollar bill from the breast pocket of his khaki shirt. It was a hell of a price to pay – worth five times the amount on the official exchange rate and ten on the black market – but he was hoping it would appeal to the man's greed. He could be a fountain of information into Sithole's operations if Ben could win him over.

It'll be either Tony who kills me if he accepts or Sithole if he doesn't. Here goes nothing, he thought. He held out the bill. 'I was hoping you could help me, maybe answer a few questions.'

The man gawked at the note as he goosed his head forward in disbelief – he even licked his lips. 'Certainly could.' The sergeant clasped his hand around the bribe and after a brief tug of war, when Ben had difficulty letting it go, the note disappeared into his pocket. 'What would you like to know?' The squat figure leered his most agreeable smile.

Taking a deep breath Ben said, 'Everything on the storage and transfer of the ivory.' He knew he'd asked for too much when the sergeant's smile dropped from his face. 'I'm not interested in names,' he tried to reassure him.

'One hundred dollars isn't enough for that sort of information,' the man said, shaking his head – he'd just remembered how violently opposed his captain was to disloyalty. But Ben noticed he made no effort to return the money, and he had admitted to his involvement.

'I could possibly see my way clear to say ... find another one..'

'Two,' the sergeant immediately countered.

No, no. Christ, Tony'll kill me, he wanted to implore. However, he managed to keep his silent anguish to himself. He appeared to consider the demand, but before he could agree another soldier walked into the toilet and stepped up to the urinal. *Damn!* He leaned forward and whispered, 'Tonight after sunset, under the giraffe acacias, out beside the bar and restaurant here at Main Camp,' Ben then turned and walked from the toilets.

It was a crisp evening and Ben had been under the giraffe acacia that arched over the bar and restaurant since well before sunset. As the afternoon's scorching heat rapidly cooled, only the lyrical sounds of silence accompanied him during his wait; a light murmur from the wind, the rustle of the sand, and the gentle hum of an insect overhead. However, he never heard any of these sounds as his eyes incessantly scanned the surrounding teak forest that gradually merged into Kalahari woodlands of thorn trees, grass and scrub.

The first thing he'd done after leaving the toilet was to hide the Land Cruiser; why he'd done it he didn't rightly know. *Just in case my friend gets cold feet,* he had reasoned at the time.

For the rest of the day, he'd discreetly watched the soldiers. There was about twenty in all and though they stayed around their camp for most of the day, nothing looked out of the ordinary.

Ben sensed the sergeant before he saw or heard him – Tony had called his gift of unerringly picking out hidden figures 'Matabele witchcraft'. As he pressed himself into the shadows, he noticed a blur of movement dart behind a nearby tree.

Moves quickly for a big man. Ben had recognised the sergeant's squat figure.

Eventually, after a few more scurried rushes, the sergeant pressed himself up against Ben's tree. Ben reached out and touched him on the shoulder, 'Boo!' he whispered.

'Oh you bastard of a Matabele!' the sergeant vehemently cursed in fright when he recognised Ben.

Ben cocked an eyebrow at the ferocity of the outburst. It should have been his first clue that things weren't as they seemed. 'You have the information?' he asked as he stepped in front of the man.

'Money first,' was his reply.

Ben held out a one-hundred dollar bill, but just out of the sergeant's reach. 'Where's the ivory stockpiled?' The sergeant lunged for the money, but Ben whisked away. 'Where?' he repeated.

'Damn you!' the sergeant swore as he looked back over of his shoulder. He appeared in a hurry to get the money and only briefly hesitated. 'Warehouse, behind the Boabab Hotel, Thomson's Junction, north of the township of Hwange.' He snatched for the bill again and this time Ben let him grab it. 'Where's the other one? We agreed on two.' He was sweating now. Ben could see a light sheen covering his forehead; again, he should have been suspicious. He produced the second bill.

'How often do the containers come through and where's the ivory from?'

'Monthly and from all over, Botswana and Zimbabwe, it's trucked in relays. Now give it 'ere.'

The sergeant made another lunge, but the answer had been too quick. Ben whisked it away again. 'You Matabele dog.'

It was then Ben knew something was terribly amiss. However, before he could react the sergeant had reached behind his back, drawn a Tokarev pistol and had it pointing at his belly. With his free hand, he was cupping his fingers in an impatient demanding gesture. 'The money, come on, *now!*' Ben was then told the bitter truth; he had completely misjudged the sergeant. 'You don't think I'd sell out for a pittance, my life's worth more than that. Plus, I was ordered to remove you and Campbell, before you even approached me,' he chuckled then, 'You're making it worthwhile. Now hand it over.'

It was then that Ben saw the other darkened figures looming out of the darkness.

'You don't think I'd share the money, do you?' He frowned, 'I told them to wait.'

'What about what you told me?' It was all Ben could think of saying.

'Huh,' he grunted, 'that's something you were never supposed to know. But as you'll be telling nobody, what's the harm? Now the money, come on,' he impatiently flicked his fingers.

Jesus, I've really screwed up this time, Ben thought. The sergeant made an impatient gesture towards the bill, Ben looked over his shoulder. *Oh gawd!* The other soldiers were going to overrun them at any moment. He let out a heavy dejected breath and thrust the money forward, but as the sergeant reach for it he dropped it. In desperation, the sergeant lunged forward. Ben stepped in close and swung a hefty foot which landed with a dull thud to his crotch. The sergeant groaned out a wounded breath as he doubled over, clutching not at the money but now at his injured groin. 'Spent those pennies wisely won't you,' Ben managed to say before he turned and ran.

The sergeant fell to the ground. As the soldiers came alongside, one of them cocked the weapon he was carrying.

'Not in the camp, you fool. Remember the tourists.' Ben heard the sergeant wheeze, 'After him. Don't let the Matabele dog get away.'

Until he'd attracted Joshua's attention at the Nyamandhlovu Platform, Ben had played cat and mouse throughout the park with Captain Sithole and his men. Most of the time he was able to easily evade them, but he did realise how proficient their trackers were, he knew if he hadn't been by himself it would have been a very different story. Throughout the first five days he'd noticed the sergeant with the other soldiers chiding and encouraging them during the hunt, but on the sixth day, he was conspicuous by his absence.

The sergeant's spirits were buoyant; he was a happy man. The reprimand he'd received from Sithole wasn't that bad; docked a month's paid, yet what he'd received from the Matabele more than made up for it. *Oh, and the bastard will pay.*

His genitals still ached at times. However, he began whistling his tuneless whistle as he walked up to the Land cruiser, hidden behind the camp's store.

He placed the green duffel bag he was carrying between his feet once he'd lifted the hood. He was undisturbed and worked happily for the twenty minutes it took him to attach, this time, an electronically timed device to the Toyota's electrical system. As he carefully closed the hood and made sure there was no evidence the vehicle had been tampered with, he turned and walked away, still whistling his tuneless whistle.

CHAPTER 49

Los Angeles

It was dull, cool and quiet in Donovan Enterprises tower-block's basement car park, the only light coming from the fluorescent bulbs attached to the concrete ceiling, while the only sounds emitting were from the occasional *pink* of a car's engine cooling down. The stillness was broken as a gentle chime resounded from above a set of highly-polished stainless steel elevator doors; a small square light briefly showed and then was extinguished as the door glided quietly open. A harsh white light pierced the cavernous car park as Donovan stepped from his private elevator.

He was dressed differently compared to his usual office attire; there was no tailored suit, business shirt and tie. Rather, he was dressed casually in a sports jacket, open-necked button-down shirt, Levi jeans and brown loafers. Once out of the lift he stopped, placed the briefcase down he had at his side and stood just over the threshold. He then began running through a mental checklist.

Right, luggage in the trunk, passport and tickets in my pockets. He patted the lapel of his sports jacket. *And travellers' checks, cash, laptop and blank disks in the briefcase. That does it.* He felt he was now ready to embark on the analysis of his poaching racket in Africa.

A movement at his rear attracted his attention; he turned and stepped back into the lift.

Sonya, with her brunette locks in complete disarray and her white blouse unbuttoned revealing a glimpse of a fancy lace bra, was flattening down the tartan skirt she wore over her shapely hips; she had a satisfied smile upon her face. Donovan unconsciously repositioned his crotch as he stepped in front of her. He raised his hand, cupped it around the mound of one of her impressive breasts and placed his lips over her mouth. After a slow lingering kiss, they broke apart.

'Judd that was wonderful,' Sonya murmured.

'Yes, I would have to agree. Oh, and make sure you tidy up the top of my desk.' With a satisfied grin he stepped back out of the lift.

'Most certainly,' Sonya responded with a dreamy smile. 'I'll look forward to your return.'

The door closed and when the elevator had been sent on its way Donovan dropped his grin. 'Don't count on it.'

He picked up his briefcase, turned to his left and walked to a black stretched Cadillac limousine sitting in its reserved spot beside the lift doors. A chauffeur, dressed in a classic grey chauffeur's uniform with peaked cap and jodhpurs, was respectfully standing beside the passenger's door. Donovan never said a word or acknowledged his presence as the door was opened and he stepped inside.

'Ah, Nikolai. A pleasure to see you,' he greeted the Russian who was already comfortably sitting in the limousine, but the warmth of the greeting never reached his lips.

As Donovan sank into the cushioned leather seat he reached into the inside pocket of his sports coat and retrieved a sealed envelope. 'A small job for you to do,' he handed it to Bogatin, 'before I return.' Bogatin briefly revolved it in his hand then slipping it into the inside breast pocket of the suit he was wearing, he dropped his hand back to his lap and impassively waited for the accompanying orders. 'It's Sonya's notice,' Donovan gave a tired flick of his hand, 'Ensure she's gone before I return.'

As easily as he'd dismissed Sonya, he dropped all thought of her from his mind, reached to his side and pressed the limousine's intercom button. 'LAX,' he ordered curtly then released the button. When the Cadillac had driven out of the car park and pulled onto Hill Street, Donovan turned back to Bogatin.

'Right, a few last minute things before I leave. Firstly, my wife – you or somebody else from security is to keep a close eye on her at all times.' He shook his head sadly. 'I don't want any bullshit from her while I'm away.'

'It is already arranged,' the Russian replied.

'Good, now what about this prick that's been screwing her? Anything?' That still galled him deeply.

'A name, maybe. But from what I've been able to find out I don't think he lives in America.'

'Why?' Donovan cut in the question.

'Once he left the Bel Air he drove straight to LAX and caught a flight to London's Heathrow. He knew his way around the city; our people lost him in the underground system.'

'Could be a coincidence. Why else do you think he is a foreigner?'

'Quite simply, because he carried a British Passport. We can only suspect he is an Englishman.'

'Damn!' Donovan knew it would be harder to dissuade a foreigner from seeing his wife. 'Okay, what about his name?'

Bogatin shook his head, 'No luck, and he used two different ones. One at the Bel Air, the other off his passport for his flight. Nothing on either,' the Russian shrugged.

'False names?' Donovan couldn't believe it. 'Surely the passport –'

Bogatin was already shaking his head. 'Nothing?' he queried incredulously. 'Damn!'

'Would you like the names? I have them right –' Bogatin was already reaching into a suit pocket.

'No, no,' Donovan was shaking a hand in irritation; he didn't want to be worried by such trivia. He turned his head to stare briefly out the window, eventually turning back. 'Sabina, the bitch, it looks as though she's being more devious than usual. Probably not enjoying the forced abstinence,' he snorted with a callous laugh. 'Okay, watch her, but remember no surprises from her while I'm away. And if this boyfriend of hers shows up again, make sure he doesn't get away until you've at least got an address.'

He changed topic or at least thought he did, 'Next, this Richard Black, anything on ...?' Donovan never finished the question. He lightly rubbed a disconcerted hand over his face; he could do without this, Bogatin's resigned expression was enough. Oh, shit!' He slumped back in his seat. 'Don't tell me. I know. Nothing.'

He looked out the window again. He hadn't expected any progress. It had been less than a week since he'd first read the name Richard Black, but he was bitterly disappointed all the same. He would have preferred to leave for Africa on a high, with the mess behind him. He knew there was no profit in worrying, so felt it was best to concentrate on what he could control.

'Just do your best. Right, two more things. Ace Security has installed a trip switch in front of the wall safe in my office. If the contact is broken it'll trigger an alarm in your office. If you're not there it can be switched over to security. Now, security has been given strict instructions – if my wife or anyone is caught in there, they're to detain them until you arrive. Then ... well you know what to do. Next, as a precaution I also had the lock changed for my private elevator.' He reached into a shirt pocket and produced a plastic card and a key, 'and more importantly, I've also had the code on the security panel for entry into the ivory room at the villa changed. This is your new card for the room and key for the elevator.' He handed them over. 'I've made sure there'll be no shipments arriving while I'm away, but if for any reason you require access you'll have to contact me for it.'

Both men knew Donovan would never let anyone in the room without him being present, not with the value of the goods inside. Bogatin made no comment as he accepted the card and the elevator's key.

Throughout the rest of the journey, Donovan gave the remainder of his instructions that he wanted either remedied or actioned. All laundering, shipments of gold out of Russia and ivory out of Africa had been put on hold until his return. Because of certain anomalies he had no control over, he had effectively shut up shop while he was away. He was ready to alight from the limousine outside terminal 4 at LAX when he gave his last set of instructions.

'Now I don't want you to screw around sending messages – you'll probably never get me. If anything turns foul on us, Sabina's not that important. You've got my itinerary, so bring it to me personally. If you do have to come, ring my corporate lawyer. You know the procedure, get the wall safe's combination and grab whatever expenses you'll need plus, of course, all the disks. I don't want them left if either of us is away. But for God's sake, Nikolai,' he threatened with a probing finger, 'make sure it's important.'

He stepped out of the limousine and as Bogatin got out beside him he flicked his head at the chauffeur. 'Give him a hand with the luggage, I'll go ahead and complete the ticketing. He turned and walked into the terminal building; confident everything was now under control.

Neither Donovan nor Bogatin noticed the short casually dressed Mexican discreetly watching them from behind a magazine stand as the ticketing was completed. He waited until Donovan had gone through to the departure lounge and Bogatin had walked back out to the Cadillac before he moved. After making sure the Russian had been driven away, and Donovan's connecting flight to New York was airborne, he then went to the nearest phone booth. Dialling a number from memory, he found the call was answered almost immediately.

Sabina snatched up the phone after the first ring. 'Yes?' she stated, keeping words to a minimum so the anxiety couldn't be heard in her voice.

The phone she answered was an extension of her private line; it was a cordless model and sat on her bed stand beside her bed. As soon as she answered it she was already anxiously pacing across the bedroom's white shag-pile carpet.

'He has left, the plane is now airborne,' was the reply she heard.

She stopped and breathed out a slow silent breath of relief before speaking. She was surprised at how calm she sounded when she eventually responded, 'Thank you. Marie will have the money for you this evening.' Her maid had organised her cousin to make sure Donovan left.

Sabina immediately broke the connection and nearly jumped for joy. 'Yes!' she cried in jubilation as a few excited bounds carried her to the bed. It was a huge four-poster king-size, covered with a brilliant white duvet, and it, like the rest of the bedroom, was decorated with acres of white-upon-white. Because of the size of the bed it easily accommodated the belly flop Sabina executed in the middle of it.

'Yes, yes, yes!' she cried again, as she joyously pumped her fists and kicked her feet. She could hardly believe it. 'He's actually gone!'

It was as if a great weight had been lifted from her shoulders; she felt free, she felt like doing something ... something totally outrageous. Her thoughts immediately settled on Richard Black and she soon found herself beginning to giggle in memory. Well, maybe not that outrageous, not yet, anyway. She rolled on her back and gazed sightlessly up at the white ceiling. 'Right, one more call,' she stated, once her thoughts drifted back down to Earth.

Sitting up, she held the phone in front of her as she dialled an international number, then held the receiver back up to her ear, with her eyes fixed straight ahead. A man with a English accent answered. Johnny. She recognised the voice – that's what Richard had called him.

As always when she rang to leave a message for Richard, her heart was fluttering like a caged bird, threatening to burst from her chest. *Here goes ...* this secret agent stuff got her so excited. 'This is White Gold,' she liked the code name, it had been Richard's idea, 'The Racketeer is airborne.' That code name for Donovan had been her idea.

She broke the connection and waited; if the phone immediately rang twice and stopped she'd know the message had been received.

She applauded as it rang once then twice and fell silent. Four days and he'd be there. Then the shit would really hit the fan. She kicked out her heels and rested her arms back on the down-filled pillows behind her head. 'And for that, I can certainly wait.'

CHAPTER 50

Kenya – Tanzania

'JEEZ, HE MAYBE, you know? Maybe they are alike?' It was the closest Anna had come to making a decision about Tony so far today. Yet again, she was comparing him to her father.

Since the altercation with the poachers Anna had experienced virtually every emotion possible. She had felt overawed by Tony's actions, and also humiliated at her inadequacy compared to the professionalism he'd shown throughout her moments of hell. She felt disgust and loathing for what the poachers were attempting to do, but most often, however, disconcerting they were, her thoughts would soon settle back on Tony and when she had felt safe and secure wrapped within his arms.

However, the worst thing was Tony seemed oblivious to the fact. *The oaf hasn't realised*, Anna thought indignantly.

Once Tony had disentangled her arms from around his neck, he had checked on the poachers that he had knocked unconscious. Bitterly, he realised one had come to and escaped; there was now only one still lying face down, snoring softly into the red earth.

Anna had been terrified all over again when Tony had left her, with an AK trembling in her hands as he ran back to the Land Cruiser to retrieve a rope.

In agony Anna had waited, and after what seemed like an eternity Tony eventually returned with the Land Cruiser, to a howl of indignation.

'You said he wouldn't move,' Anna had danced in behind Tony to peer over his shoulder at the poacher once he had alighted from the vehicle. 'But he did, and I ... I nearly peed my pants.'

'Thank God you didn't,' Tony had mumbled under his breath setting to work with the rope.

Once the poacher was securely bound and dumped in the back of the Toyota, Tony had headed straight back to the park headquarters at Voi.

Anna had hardly seen him for the next twenty-four hours as he and a group of four other park wardens went off in hot pursuit of the poachers.

They had caught all bar one of them, the leader Tony had first clobbered, and after completing the appropriate paperwork Tony had joined Anna back at the Voi Lodge. He'd had a hurried lunch with her before they began the final two hundred odd mile leg of their journey, to Anna's new project and the Ngorongoro Crater.

After arrowing down a dusty brick-red road, with the great white-capped mountain of Kilimanjaro looming above them, they soon crossed over near Taveta into northern Tanzania.

'Why so much of a hurry?' Anna queried as another of the Tanzania's road signs flashed by, it had been illustrated by a leaping buck and read 'Danger – game area'. The last hundred miles they had travelled may have been filled with conversation but it hadn't exactly been driven at a leisurely pace.

'There was a message at Voi HQ; we have to pick up somebody at Sanja Juu – Kilimanjaro's International Airport.'

'Oh.'

Tony didn't notice the disappointed note in her voice, she was starting to warm to him and really enjoy his company. Under his rough exterior was somebody truly dedicated to a cause he believed in. If Anna had analysed her disappointment she probably would have been shocked; she was feeling jealous towards the intrusion.

'Who is it?' she tried to ask casually.

'You'll see,' was the only reply she received.

Anna again saw a side of Tony's personality she never knew existed; affection. It was a gruff manly type she realised as her jealousy stung deeper. However, that was until she was introduced to the little man who Tony had fondly clasped around the shoulder.

'Anna, I'd like you to meet my off-sider Ben Mzamo. Ben, Anna Hagan.'

'Ah, the good doctor I presume.' Ben acknowledged as he swept an appreciative glance over her well-presented features, 'Well, things are looking up.' He ended with a good-humoured grin and Anna liked him instantly.

Once she had released his proffered hand she fell in beside the two of them as they walked through the airport's car park. As they talked she couldn't prevent the smile that creased her lips. They were the most unlikely looking pair she had ever seen, Tony so broad and tall and Ben so slight and short, but she did recognise there was a bond, a type of intimacy even, between them that must have been forged over many years spent together.

Anna remained quiet for most of the remaining hundred or so miles it took them to reach the Ngorongoro Crater. She hardly even noticed as they swept through Arusha, the starting point for most safaris in northern Tanzania and administrative headquarters of the area, she was so transfixed by what Ben was saying.

He was in the back, leaning forward between the two front seats talking to Tony and bringing him up to date with what had been happening in Zimbabwe since his departure. Eventually, Anna could keep silent no longer.

'You mean the army was trying to kill you?' she asked, horrified. In the last few days she had unwittingly become part of a world she had previously never realised existed.

Ben turned and answered as if it was an everyday occurrence. 'Yes Anna. The people we're dealing with don't feel comfortable with the likes of me and Tony.'

He turned back to Tony and completed his report without being interrupted again. When he'd fallen silent, Tony began asking his questions. 'So you believe this warehouse near Thomson's Junction is genuine?'

'Has to be,' Ben answered, 'the sergeant never thought I'd live to pass it on. Yeah, it's genuine.'

'Well, I doubt if he would've had enough guts to tell our friend Captain Sithole that he's let the cat out of the bag – could be useful. We can probably use it.'

'Yeah, if the Captain and his goons don't get to us first. We ...'

A slight gasp and the horrified expression on Anna's face that accompanied it distracted Ben; to her the way they spoke had an unreal quality. It was the candid way, she decided, they discussed death, their possible deaths, which made matters worse.

Tony also noticed Anna's expression. A few days earlier he would've rubbed home the point to emphasise how dangerous his job was. But his attitude had changed towards her. Because of her recent experiences, she knew it was dangerous, and after what she had been through he didn't want to distress her further. So before they could expand their conversation to include Donovan and his meeting with Peter Nkomo, Tony intervened, 'Okay Ben, leave it for now. We'll talk about it later.'

It was Ben's turn for a startled expression to skip across his face, Tony's comment may have appeared casual, but Ben had never heard him speak with so much compassion. He was quiet for a couple of minutes and his amazement changed to intrigue. He decided to question Anna, for he knew

Tony wouldn't be forthcoming.

'So tell me, Anna. Been an interesting assessment, has it?'

'Interesting?' she blurted, 'Bloody hell …' her early horror was forgotten, 'you can say that again ... And he slapped me, did you know?'

'Oh, I see,' Ben said, but he was now more confused than ever.

Tony eventually saved him as he launched into his own version of their brush with danger in Tsavo East before Anna continued with what he knew would be a distorted sequence of events. 'It was just a tap really. You see Ben, what *really* happened was…'

It was dark by the time they had driven up onto the rim of the Ngorongoro Crater, and it was only because of Tony's position that they were let through the Lodoare Gate and into the Ngorongoro Conservation Area after dark.

Anna's base, off the crater floor itself, was to be at the closest of the three lodges to the Crater Village; the Ngorongoro Crater Lodge. It was an old rustic lodge built back in the 1930s and was perched giddily on the edge of the crater's rim, amongst the temperate evergreen mountain forest that sprawled down into the extinct volcano.

The reason why this particular lodge had been chosen was because of the many detached cabins it had dotted around the rural setting of its grounds, one which had been permanently set aside for research purposes for Anna and the WWF.

Once the three of them had had a generous evening meal in the lodge's log-cabin style dining room, and a nightcap in front of the roaring log-fire in the bar, Tony saw Anna to her cabin. He made sure she was settled in and that the gas heating was working before he arranged to meet her the next morning before sunrise. She thanked him coyly and saw him out.

As she closed the door Tony felt she'd been acting rather strangely. However, he shrugged and dismissed the thought.

Probably eager to get started. Huh, scientists eh? he mused. He walked away again, completely misreading her reaction.

CHAPTER 51

Ngorongoro Crater

'GOSH, WASN'T IT cold last night?' Anna said to Tony as she shrugged a down-filled vest over the tan shirt she was wearing. 'You'd never think I'd only just been down in the Antarctic,' she said as she shivered slightly. She couldn't get over how warm it was during the days, but how cold it could get at night.

'Worse in places down south,' Tony answered, 'Come on, I want you to see the crater as the sun rises.'

It was still dark as they walked from Anna's cabin towards Tony's Land Cruiser where they were met by two shadowy figures talking quietly beside the vehicle. One was small, that would be Ben. 'Who's with Ben?' she asked of the taller one, standing probably six inches above him.

'Your assistant. She heard about our arrival and was waiting beside the vehicle this morning.'

'She?'

'Hmm, yes, another woman.' Even in the morning gloom Anna recognised the humorous twinkle in Tony's eye.

'And more power to us, buster,' she rounded on him good-naturedly. 'Ben tells me her name is Jessica.' They soon reached the Land Cruiser.

'Hello, I'm Anna Hagan,' she said as she held out her hand in greeting in front of the tall woman. 'Tony tells me you're Jessica.'

She must have been about six-foot. She was dressed in a light blue patterned sun-frock that agreeably showed off her long limbs and willowy good looks. She had fine features and a radiance that made her black skin glow.

'Yes, doctor,' Jessica answered as she accepted the hand and shyly bobbed her curly black head.

'Anna will do fine.' She liked the girl instantly.

'Yes doctor,' the girl repeated just as shyly.

Anna would have pressed home the point but Tony intervened, 'Yes, well. Big day ahead.' He hustled Anna into the front and Jessica into the back with Ben. 'You can get acquainted later.'

Tony had stopped the vehicle at the top of the steep descent that led down into the crater. It was a rough narrow winding road, but in the half-light before dawn it as well as everything below was invisible from the rim, hidden not only by the gloom but also by a thick billowing mist. However, as the first of the morning's rays drew back the veil they finally revealed the haunting beauty below.

'My lord!' Anna breathed, staggered by what she was seeing.

Stretched out below her was the world's largest unbroken volcanic crater, containing a hidden world of teeming wildlife supported by an abundance of vegetation. There was lush rainforest cloaking its circular rim, while savanna bush and acacia woodlands flourished on its floor two thousand feet below. Lying as it did on the eastern edge of Tanzania's game-rich Serengiti Plains, yet being incomparable in all its self-contained glory, the crater's one hundred square miles was the most densely packed game area in Africa.

They sat in silence, awed by the wild Eden they were viewing. Only when the sun's rays shimmered on the crater's central soda lake, and the distant surrounding mountains had risen into the blue haze above, did they finally venture below.

Halfway down the steep hairpin track the sprawling constellations of black stars dotted about the floor finally became recognisable as wildebeest and zebra, the principal species of the crater. Once on the floor, the tension after the bumpy first-gear ride faded away, and muscles relaxed as they left behind the thick bush on the rim and began a leisurely journey of enchantment through the savanna country on the crater floor. The sun was warm and a smell like freshly cut grass carried through the vehicle's windows on a warm gentle breeze.

They first stopped in the south beside the swampy Lerai Forest, where Tony knew they would find the crater's elephants. The forest was made up of umbrella and yellow-barked acacias and it wasn't long before the herd made their presence known; noisily stripping bark and breaking branches they slowly came into view. Tony couldn't prevent himself from slowly shaking his head in wonder.

'You know, I've probably seen these animals half a dozen times and they always leave me speechless.'

'I see what you mean; they're huge,' Anna answered, 'Look at the size of their tusks.'

Totally unconcerned by the vehicle's presence, probably knowing they lived in a protected haven, four of the largest remaining tuskers in Africa fed within yards of the spellbound group. As they slowly ambled back into the forest their majesty left a deep impression on not just Tony, but all within the Toyota of what the grandfathers of the species must have once been like when their range spread across the full breadth of the African wilds. With a visible shake, Tony roused himself. The trip into the crater was for Anna's benefit and they still had a lot of area to cover and other wildlife to see.

When they came upon the shallow central lake they saw the mixture of volcanic ash and the water had left a white desert rim around its shores. But it wasn't this brilliance that drew their attention; it was the great swathes of vibrant pink rising and falling above the water like mist, formed by the thousands of flamingos that made the lake their home. While watching the flamingos they saw a pair of cheetah cut across the edge of the lake, and further along hippos basking in the early morning sun. But when they eventually left the lake behind, strangely, the relaxed air they'd experienced was also gone.

They saw herds of wildebeests gazing fitfully amongst nervous gazelles and zebra, while even the herds of buffalo wandering by looked decidedly wary, and even two tank-like black rhinos seemed particularly cautious as they fed. But when a group of crested cranes suddenly took flight in a moment of panic for what seemed like no apparent reason, Jessica overcame her shyness; she found she could no longer hold her curiosity.

'Why on earth is everything so nervous?' She'd seen a shifty looking jackal and a few spotted hyenas skulk by, but she was positive it was more than that.

It was Anna who answered, slightly taken aback by the question. 'Jessica, you of all people should know,' she said as she swivelled around in her seat, 'The main reason for our research project of course.' She pointed out the window over Tony's shoulder to a partially shaded rocky out-crop that commanded a good view of the crater floor. 'The crater supports the highest density of large carnivores in Africa and there they are; lions, the major reason for our project.'

'Oh,' was Jessica's only reply.

A pride of lions, in various tawny heaps, lolled about under shady trees or basked on the rocks. They had obviously only just eaten for their bellies appeared full as they were settling down to sleep away the day until it was dusk and time to hunt again.

Until mid-afternoon they explored the crater floor while Anna familiarised herself with the self-contained piece of Africa that would be her home for at least the next couple of years. It was with a growing sense of excitement that she found herself back in her cabin with Jessica at the table beside her. She was beginning to plan how they would start the project.

'Right, first things first. Do you mind if we shorten your name a little? Jessie. How about it, how's Jessie sound?'

'I would like that, doctor, very much.' From the moment they had met there had been an instant rapport; it was clear they would soon be fast friends.

'Okay the next thing, now watch my lips, and repeat after me, "Anna", you will call me "Anna". Doctor makes me sound so old and fuddy-duddyish.' Once Jessie had repeated the name after a series of self- conscious giggles, she continued. 'Good. Now you look awfully young for all your experience. How long have you worked at the crater? Your experience will be invaluable.' Anna sat forward, eagerly awaiting the answer; it would cut months off the initial familiarisation of the crater and its lions.

Jessie swallowed heavily, 'Experience?' It sounded like a word she'd rarely used or heard of before.

'Yes, at the Nairobi office they said I would have an experienced assistant to help me set up.'

Silence.

Anna started to become suspicious. 'Jessie, tell me you do know the area. Don't you?' she pleaded.

'Yes, I am Masai. I was born not far from here, across the border ...' She fell into silence and the pause she made screamed a silent 'but'.

Anna couldn't help herself, she voiced the silent word, 'Yes ... but?'

'But as for experience, I only left university the end of last year.'

'No wonder you didn't know about the lions.' Anna groaned, she sounded mortally wounded as if stabbed in the chest and Jessie was convinced she was about to have some sort of a fit.

'Doctor, I mean Anna, are you all right?'

Eventually, Anna found her voice, 'You mean you've no practical experience in zoology?'

'No, but the man who will be our cook does,' Jessie's attempt to console her, it only made matters worse.

'Cook?' Anna cried incredulously.

'Yes and the guide that will be with us down on the crater floor used to be a hunting guide.'

Anna brought her hands up to cover her face in disbelief, she had been given a research project that surpassed any she had ever worked on before and any she would probably ever be likely to work on again. The crater was like a small island habitat, a naturally isolated oasis that she knew would provide major insights into the long-term consequences of inbreeding and genetic inconsistencies. Yet to correlate and document such information she needed trained people, experienced people to help her, she couldn't do it alone. *A cook, a recent graduate and a bloody hunting guide!*

She finally dragged her hands off her face. 'This'll be interesting,' she muttered. She looked over at Jessie who had an 'it's all my fault' expression on her face, even though she didn't have a clue what had upset Anna. Anna laid a reassuring hand on her wrist, 'Don't worry, Jessie. It's not your fault. We're both going to be busy for the next few months that's all. At least the theory you did at university will help?'

'Theory?' queried Jessie, again it sounded like a word she'd never heard of before.

Anna took a deep breath and then tentatively asked, 'What exactly did you study at university?'

Jessie proudly puffed out her well-developed chest, 'As a schoolteacher, I was the top in my class.'

Anna gaped at her assistant for many moments, but eventually she was unable to contain herself, she threw her head back and began to laugh like she hadn't since… she couldn't remember.

Anna had finally been welcomed to Africa.

CHAPTER 52

'So let's get this straight. Besides finding out about the warehouse, you also succeeded in giving away three hundred dollars. Is that right?' Tony rounded on Ben. They were sitting outside on the Crater Lodge's terrace overlooking the crater; they didn't notice the great cedars, olive and pillar trees overflowing down the rim or even the spectacular view. In front of them may as well have been the Sahara Desert; the scenery was wasted, for the last few minutes they had been engaged in an animated discussion.

It was Ben's turn. 'Huh, well at least I didn't have to total the Cessna to find out how they poach in the Selous Game Reserve,' he huffed as he crossed his arms defensively across his chest and stared out across the crater.

Tony finally realised he'd been too harsh with his earlier comments – neither of them worked well when they were apart. 'Okay Ben, we've both done some good work, even if it has cost us.'

'Huh,' the little man huffed again without turning his head, but Tony's next comment had his full attention. 'I don't know whether you'll be interested, but ..' he began casually, 'I met Peter Nkomo the other night.'

'What!' Ben's head snapped around.

'I thought you would be,' Tony responded with a wry smile. That and the comment disarmed Ben completely and Tony launched into his report. He told him about Peter's house in the Nairobi suburb of Muthaiga, his call to Richard Black in London, the subsequent information sent down in the diplomatic bag, and of course the meeting he had at the Carnivore.

'I can see how frustrated you must've felt, having to have the assessment done,' Ben reasoned.

'No, not really. It gave me a chance to think things through. Plus, I needed you up here as back up.'

'So you'll want me to go up to Nairobi and pick up Donovan's itinerary from the High Commission then? We'll need it if we're to track him down. It'll give you a few more days with –'

'What are you talking about?' Tony cut in as he frowned. 'I've got to go up and pick up the new plane, it should be ready by now.'

'Well, I thought with you and Anna, you two could –'

Tony cut in again, 'What on earth are you going on about?' Then the penny dropped; he was flabbergasted. 'Holy mother ... you didn't think that I ... that we ... good God, man, with her?'

It was Ben's turn to disarm Tony completely, 'But why the hell not?'

It was such a direct question Tony couldn't answer it. 'Well, I ... ah ...' he then found his tongue. 'Christ, can we change the subject; we've a few other pressing matters.'

'Yes, Tony,' Ben replied with a deadpan face, but both men knew what he was thinking. Bit slow off the mark aren't we, Campbell?

'Just leave it out, I'm leaving you here to help her set up her camp on the crater floor until I get back with the itinerary, and that's final. I'm leaving tomorrow.'

'Yes, Tony,' Ben answered again, flatly.

'Look, we don't even get on very well.'

'Yes, Tony.'

'Oh, drop it.' He got up to leave. 'I've got more important things to do.'

But as he walked from the terrace all he heard tailing after him was, 'Yes, Tony.'

As luck would have it, Tony was on the terrace alone with Anna that evening. Bewildered, he looked around. 'Where on earth have Ben and Jessie gone?' They'd only just finished dining with them.

Anna had also only just noticed they were alone, but she didn't bother answering. Instead, she looked out over the darkened cavity of the crater below. For several minutes she gazed down into the darkness before finally she spoke.

'Every zoologist dreams of working in a place like this.' She turned to Tony and he saw her eyes flash with emotion, 'I thought I'd never find a place like this. God. and I thought I had it all when I was stationed down on the Ice. Do you know how much can be learnt from a place like this?'

Tony was intrigued; he'd never heard her speak with so much feeling before. 'No, tell me.' Notwithstanding his misconceptions of scientists he found he was interested and he unconsciously reached for his ivory disk.

'The lions here are totally isolated, right?' She noticed Tony nod, 'So they must be breeding from a shrinking gene pool, and even you have to agree that that can cause inherent defects due to inbreeding.' Tony nodded again. 'But what most people don't realise is, is that it's not just these lions and populations of other mammals like them that have this problem.' Tony was becoming less intrigued; Anna was speaking with so much passion it was slowly turning to fascination. He found her intensity alluring. 'All around the globe the world's wildlife, whether here in Africa, in South America or Asia, is shrinking into fragmented islands – smaller and smaller isolated communities – because of human expansion.' She pointed a questioning finger at Tony. 'And do you realise your elephants are no different?' She didn't wait for an answer. 'They, just as many other mammals, are being squeezed into smaller and smaller areas where they're forced to live, and because of that it's like a population bottleneck where there are becoming fewer and fewer mating partners to go around. It's like ah ...' she looked for an analogy. 'Uhm, I know,' she flicked her fingers, 'Do you play poker?'

'Well, sort of. I know how if that's what you mean.'

'It's like animals have become part of a high-stake game with a crooked dealer. After beginning with a fifty-two card deck the players wind up with, say, five cards that are dealt over and over again.' She frowned thoughtfully. 'Do see what I'm getting at?'

'Sure, of course.' He'd become engrossed. 'But what happens? Are they born deformed or what?'

'Eventually, they may be.' Anna shrugged.

'But surely it can't be as devastating as the likes of, say, poaching?'

'Maybe not on the surface. But if mammals inbreed for long enough, often there's an abnormal sperm increase, infertility rises and the birth rate falls. But the most devastating thing in the long-term is the hidden killer: each animal's immune system is weakened.'

'So what are you saying? How do we protect them?' Without realising it, for the first time Tony was truly interested in a scientific view of wildlife preservation. He had a glimpse into a new and very different world.

'What I'm saying is that it's all very well having protected wildlife parks and reserves, but if these populations are cut off from new bloodlines, an epidemic could wipe them out?'

Tony rocked back in the chair he'd sat down upon as he looked up at Anna. 'So in years to come the work I'm doing could be wasted?'

'Exactly.' She pointed a finger at him to emphasis her point. 'If it's not done properly, that is.'

'Hell, I admit I never realised. You *do* do important work, don't you?' Tony was looking at her in a new light.

'Yes I do,' Anna stated, without a hint of arrogance. 'It may not have as startling results as yours, but I feel it's as important.'

In those few brief moments Tony had seen past the tip of his nose and the importance of his work. However, not only was he seeing into another realm of wildlife preservation he was now seeing another truly dedicated conservationist, someone who helped the world's wildlife using an entirely different approach to his own.

'So what will your information tell you?' He got up and stood beside her.

'Well, it's like anything, really. The more you know about any problem, the better equipped you are to fight it. All that may be needed is new bloodlines, but usually it's not as simple as that. Tell me, if you continually fought the poachers and not the middlemen, would poaching stop?' Anna shrugged into silence, she didn't expect an answer.

Both went silent for several minutes with their private thoughts. Tony had gained a new respect for zoology – and for one zoologist in particular – while Anna realised she'd found an empathetic man who was just as dedicated, if not more so, to wildlife conservation as she was.

'What more can Ben and I do to help you? Have you got everything you need?' Tony finally broke the silence.

Anna couldn't prevent herself from laughing, 'You, sir, must have a warped sense of humour.'

'Ah,' Tony understood immediately, 'been introduced to Africa have we? What are you missing?'

'Missing! It's what I've got I'm worried about.'

'Well, if he can be of any use, you've got the use of Ben for the next few days while he helps you set up your base on the crater floor.'

'Ben?' Anna queried disappointedly, as a brief frown skipped across her face.

'Yes, I'm leaving for Nairobi tomorrow. I can make a few noises on your behalf if you like.'

'Oh,' as she said it, Tony realised Anna was no longer laughing.

She decided to be frank with him, 'I was hoping that, perhaps, you'd be staying a little longer.'

Tony was lost for words, 'I ah, er, well ...' he gave up in the end; he didn't know if it was a professional request or a personal one. *Christ, here goes,* he thought, *either make a complete fool of myself or drive her away.* He cleared his throat then swallowed heavily before speaking, 'I think, I mean I know, I'd love to stay ...' he paused, hoping she'd take it the right way.

'But?' Anna continued for him.

'Yes but,' he hurried on as he stood up and slipped his ivory disk back into his pocket, deciding to come straight to the point and tell her about the Donovan investigation. 'Look, Anna, you remember when you told me about how you knew *of* me from that assassination attempt when I was with Operation Stronghold in Zimbabwe?'

'Yes,' she nodded.

'Well, that plane crash I had just before first meeting you at the airport wasn't an accident. It was another attempt by the poaching racket we're investigating. The same one who that tried to kill me before.'

'Good lord.' Anna, full of concern, had taken a pace closer and placed a hand on his upper arm as she stared seriously up into his eyes. Tony continued, acutely aware of her hand's presence and her gaze.

'You also heard of the trouble Ben had down in Zimbabwe. Well, that's only the half of it. We're currently onto probably the biggest poaching racket in Africa.' He could see disquiet burning in her eyes as she took in his every word. 'And during your first night in Nairobi, I had a run in with one of the men running it, who tried to kill me.' Her hand tightened. 'Now his boss, an American who runs the racket, is flying in or has flown into Africa to view the racket's operation.'

'An American, but who is ...' Tony held up a hand so he could finish.

'Now I have to get back to Nairobi,' he said, 'to pick up an itinerary of this character's trip.'

'But ... good God, how on earth ...' Anna had so many questions tumbling through her mind she had trouble deciding which to ask first. 'Who gave you his itinerary?'

Tony opened his mouth; he was about to tell her Richard's name, then remembered it had been given in good faith. 'It's a long story,' he answered instead, 'Actually, British Intelligence of all people.'

'Hell, no wonder you thought me a pain.' Anna dropped her hand. 'And you've put up with me all this time. God, I feel awful – and I called you arrogant when you were only trying to do your job.'

'Oh, I don't know,' Tony had decided Anna was showing more personal than professional concern, or he hoped to hell she was. 'Maybe I was being overbearing at the time.'

The mood between them was delicately poised but Tony couldn't bring himself to do or say anything more. His feet felt like lead and his tongue felt like rubber in his mouth. *Come on, Campbell. Do something, anything,* he wanted to scream, but before he could say anything Anna spoke and the moment was lost. 'So when will you be back for Ben? You two obviously work well together.'

'In the next day or so.' He went to step back but felt Anna's hand grab his arm again.

'No, I didn't mean ...' like Tony she too had felt the shift in mood, but unlike him she wasn't about to let it slip away.

As if startled, for the next few seconds they stared at each other. Then, as if drawn together by a magnet, they found themselves slowly come together. Tony bent down his head as he wrapped his arms around her body and Anna leant in towards him as she lifted her face. Their lips were brushing against each other's when ...

'Ah, there you two are. We've been looking for ... oops!'

Without immediately breaking their embrace Tony turned his head to see Ben and Jessie walk onto the terrace. Anna let out a slow heavy frustrated breath as she briefly rested her forehead on Tony's chest and they then broke apart.

Both Ben and Jessie were still in the set postures that they'd assumed when they'd realised they plunged into something intimate, Ben still had his mouth open as his eyes darted from Tony back to Anna and back to Tony again.

'Yes, my fine little friend. You certainly have found us.'

'Right.' Ben relaxed his stance while Jessie was trying to stop herself from giggling. 'Oh yes, we just came past reception. Jessie's got a letter for you, Anna.'

'It's from America,' Jessie indicated with a twinkle in her eye.

Anna accepted it excitedly, 'It'll be from Sarah, my old roommate.'

Although none of them moved they left Anna alone to read the letter, they never noticed the slight frown skip across her face as she looked at the back of the letter at the sender's name and address. Tony was talking as she opened it.

'So where the hell have you two been, anyway?' he asked suspiciously.

Jessie flushed as Ben started to speak a bit too hurriedly, 'Oh, a walk, to watch the sunset. We ..' he would have continued but was prevented by a gasp from Anna. Her face had turned deathly white; she had thrown a hand up to her mouth as she stared down at the letter.

'What is it, Anna?' Tony asked, full of concern.

Dumbly she looked up into his face. 'It's from the caretaker of my old apartment block; he got my address from a letter I sent to Sarah, my roommate. Tony, she's been murdered.'

This time there was no hesitation as he took her in his arms. The tears were slow in coming and didn't spill until Ben and Jessie had respectfully left them alone.

It was early morning before Tony saw her to her cabin. She had let him read through the letter and the explanation that the caretaker had given. For the rest of the time Anna had talked about Sarah. Tony mostly sat and listened. It was as if Anna was trying to impress every facet of her friend within her memory. She spoke mostly of their good times and their secret moments shared together, yet as she spoke she realised one friendship may have passed but another was beginning to form.

CHAPTER 53

Nairobi

'Ah, very English but most impressive, Peter, most impressive.'

'I fear I'd describe it as more Colonial than English. It's the servants you see. They're of a very un-English shade, wouldn't you agree?'

Donovan let out a bull laugh; he found Peter's comment extremely amusing. 'Rich coming from you, isn't it?'

He and Peter were standing outside Peter's Tudor mansion, in front of a line of white-jacketed, red-sashed African servants who were lined up outside the front door on the dwelling's pebble driveway – they stood in strict formation like a guard of honour, welcoming Donovan to Kenya.

It was now mid-morning on the day Tony, Ben and Anna had arrived at the Ngorongoro Crater. Donovan had left Los Angeles three days ago. The time it had taken him to get to Nairobi had been taken up with travel and, of course, obligatory company meetings in New York, Paris and London. So far it had been a fruitful trip; all subsidiaries profits were on the rise and new markets had opened up. He hoped as Peter arranged for his luggage to be taken to the guest wing and showed him through to his study that this part of his trip would be as productive.

Once Peter had dismissed the entourage of burly bodyguards, especially organised for Donovan's visit, and was sitting behind his carved oak desk, Donovan didn't wait to be offered a seat but chose the Chesterfield against one wall, extracted his laptop from his briefcase and laid it on the highly polished oak coffee table in front of him.

'Right, you know my itinerary and how tight it is. So let's get down to business. From the top, how are the operations?'

For the next four hours, with only a short break for a light lunch, they discussed most facets of the Africa-wide racket. As they were coming to the end of the discussion, Donovan admitted he was impressed with most aspects of the operation.

'Only two points that concern me here in Africa; firstly this container discovered in Zimbabwe, any chance of salvaging anything from it?' Donovan asked as he began saving the information he had typed into the laptop.

'Afraid not. The press it caused made most officials too jumpy. We've lost the lot.'

'Damn!' Donovan cursed half-heartedly, but he was already resigned to the fact. 'It made our Asian friends rather jumpy. Most of the ivory had already been sold forward and they weren't that keen to have their money outstanding for another month.'

'We won't experience problems with the sale of future consignments will we?' Peter asked, full of concern, conscious of any loss of profit – or more correctly, loss of his profit.

Donovan chuckled lightly. 'Most saw my point of view. The stubborn ones eventually came around with a little persuasion from Nikolai. An amazing asset that man,' he added as if an afterthought. 'Okay, what about the new route? I don't want any further consignments using the old one.'

Peter had already decided on two different routes and had made tentative arrangements for both; all he needed was for Donovan to sanction his decision. 'It will cost slightly more for the next, say, six months, then it can be amended again. But I believe we should split the load. Ship the Zambian ivory on its own through Botswana, bypassing Zimbabwe completely and down to Durban, while we still continue to use the main warehouse and drop-off point in Zimbabwe for both the Zimbabwean and ivory from Botswana.'

'And how do you plan shipping it from the warehouse?'

'An empty, or partially empty, container comes in from Malawi, loads the ivory as before, but goes down through Botswana like the Zambian ivory, instead of the old route.'

Donovan immediately saw the advantages. 'So if it's opened and checked when it first enters Zimbabwe, they'll have to give it a clean bill of health and re-seal it with Zimbabwean seals.'

'Exactly.'

'Okay, what about a Zimbabwean custom's seals and a punch?'

Peter shrugged, 'It won't be a problem.'

Donovan remained briefly silent as he considered Peter's plans. As with most of what Peter did, it had been well thought through. But he wasn't ready to simply give his agreement. 'I'll think about it. I first want to see the warehouse – I presume it's the same one at Thomson's Junction we're talking about?' Peter nodded. 'Good, I'll decide after I've seen it. Right, last but not least, Tony Campbell. I take it he and his assistant have been taken care of?'

Donovan leant back on the Chesterfield, closed his eyes and clasped the bridge of his nose in a gesture of resignation when he noticed the despondent look in Peter's eyes. He eventually let out a heavy breath of long-suffering. 'What the bloody hell happened this time?' Shaking his head he got up and began pacing the room.

Peter delicately cleared his throat before beginning his explanation. 'The plane crashed as planned. He disappeared for several days but apparently must have somehow walked away from it.'

'Shit, bloody marvellous. Christ, he's like the proverbial rubber ball. Then what? How did you find out he'd survived?'

Peter would've rather not told Donovan about their confrontation at the Carnivore, but he knew if he tried to conceal it, it would make matters worse. 'Well, he actually confronted me at a restaurant here in Nairobi.'

'What!' Donovan exploded, 'He knows you?' He stood in front of the desk with his fists balled and resting menacingly on its top.

Peter tried to keep his composure; he wasn't used to being treated like this. 'Initially, he appeared not to, but I fear he knows more than we realised.'

'Bloody hell, he suspects even more than Sithole's involvement?'

'I'm afraid so.' Despite his forced composure Peter couldn't prevent himself from shrinking down in his chair. 'His exact words were, "You're finished, Nkomo, you and Donovan both".'

Donovan's shoulders slumped, 'What? He knows about me?' His head had jutted forward in disbelief.

'It appears so, yes.'

Donovan pushed himself off the desk and walked back to the Chesterfield and slumped down upon it. *Bloody hell, were the Hagan fiasco and Tony Campbell somehow linked?* he had to ask himself. *Surely not.* He turned to Peter, 'Where is he now? Christ, he has to be taken care of.'

Peter lifted his hands with palms uppermost in a gesture of ignorance. 'He seems to have disappeared. For a week now I've had men searching the country for him.'

Donovan was lost for words; all he could do was shake his head in disbelief. 'And his assistant?' he eventually asked.

Peter couldn't help himself; he tried to shift the blame. 'Unfortunately, Captain Sithole has again let us down, he's also missing.'

Donovan ignored the snide remark. He rose from the Chesterfield and stood in front of the desk again, thrusting out a determined finger and speaking softly but with a voice as cold as ice, 'Peter, I don't care how you do it but get rid of them – both.

'It's already being taken care of, here and in the south. They won't get away this time.'

'Yeah, well make bloody sure they don't.' Donovan looked at his watch; it was typical of him not to dwell on something that was presently out of his control. 'Right, we have a plane to catch. We've the operations up north to view before we head into Tanzania.' A thoughtful expression skipped over his face. 'Now this crater that we're due at in the next few days, it's supposed to have some of the biggest tuskers left in Africa in it, is that right?'

Peter was glad for the change in topic. 'Yes, Ngorongoro. You should find it an interesting place,' he replied as both men got up to leave the study.

CHAPTER 54

Ngorongoro Crater

ANNA FELT TERRIBLE and wished Tony hadn't left for Nairobi that morning. *Not that he could've probably made me feel better anyway.*

She had moped around close to tears for the first few hours since dawn, trying to keep her mind off Sarah. As with her father's murder, thoughts of loss and sadness kept roving through her mind. *Why? Who on earth would do such a thing?*

The main difference with Sarah's death was that there should have been more than enough to keep her occupied, but so far she had been unable to bring herself to begin work.

Come on, she wouldn't want to see you moping around like this, she told herself.

Dejectedly, she looked at the boxes of information in the corner of her cabin. She knew what they contained and with a heavy sigh she dragged them to the cabin's table to begin her analysis. Within a few short minutes Sarah's death had been put aside and Anna had been transported into another world.

Anna had achieved her doctorate because of the extensive research she had done into a small near-extinct group of panthers that clung tenuously to survival in Florida. Even though the felines here at Ngorongoro were of a different species, upon arrival she'd felt immediately at home and comfortable with the work that had to be done.

As with her studies on the Florida panthers she knew she was working with a limited feline population, but this time with a huge difference. Every one of the lions living in the crater had its family tree known and documented; five hundred individuals, most now long since dead, spanning five or six generations that had originally descended from just fifteen lions.

This incredible piece of zoological detective work had taken ten years to complete by two earlier researchers. Using earlier research data, countless films, and hundreds of photos from professional and tourist photographers, they had methodically pieced together the origins of and tracked down every lion that had lived on the crater floor for the past quarter of a century. They'd known that transient males would show up from time to time, but because of the strength of the large coalitions of crater-born males, they were easily able to be evicted, driving away what the crater's lions needed most – new genes.

Armed with this background information Anna knew the current population had been subject to close inbreeding and genetic decline. Part of her job was to find out how much of a loss in genetic diversity and reduction in reproduction the crater lions had suffered. However, her main focus would be on the long-term consequences of inbreeding.

Would the lack of genetic variability in the crater lions' immune defence systems render the population more susceptible to an epidemic? Logically, she knew the answer, but without scientific research it would remain a hunch.

Anna's first job was to acquaint herself with every one of the lions living on the crater floor. To begin her work she had to know which were the breeding adults, or where in reality the future population would come from. So placing aside all bar one small box of information, she was ready to begin when a light knock at the door brought her back to the present. It was Jessie.

'We are all ready to go down into the crater.' She was hesitantly standing on the threshold; she'd seen the state Anna had been in earlier that morning.

'Jessie, great. If you'd help me with this stuff, then we can get underway.' Despite her earlier feelings, Anna was surprised by how cheerful she not only sounded but also felt.

Feeling somewhat relieved herself, Jessie eagerly offered assistance. 'As we'll only be down for the one night, just that small rucksack on the bed. I'll carry the box.' Then as an afterthought, she inquired, 'Has Ben got everything else?'

'Ah, if you mean the boxes of stuff that came with you and Tony, and those things with the wires, yes, he took them down with him earlier this morning.'

'Okay Jessie. The first part of your education as a research assistant begins,' she said good-naturedly. 'That stuff and those things with the wires will be referred to from this day on as "research equipment",' she said the words importantly. 'Appear learned, is the first rule to being a scientist.'

Jessie giggled; she was going to like working with Anna.

Outside the lodge Jessie led Anna to the short-wheel-base Land Cruiser Tony had organised as her vehicle while she was at the crater. It was on long-term hire from one of the other nearby lodges; the more modern Ngorongoro Wildlife Lodge.

Standing around the vehicle were two black men dressed in khaki shirts, shorts and rawhide sandals. 'Ah, the knowledgeable cook and the gun-wielding guide,' Anna murmured. 'They certainly look a likely pair.'

With a smile, Jessie introduced the cook, a rather round man with black curling hair, lightly dusted to a silver grey. 'This is Tembo, he understands English, well, some anyway.'

Anna was presented with a beaming smile of white teeth. 'I am honoured, doctor,' he said with a brief bow.

'No please call me – oh, never mind.' Maybe being called doctor was something she would have to put up with. 'Tembo, the elephant,' she said. It was one Swahili word she'd learnt from Tony, and by the reaction she got it was exactly the right thing to say; he excitedly nodded his head in confirmation.

However, Jessie could restrain herself no longer, she leant over and whispered in Anna's ear, 'In Swahili *tembo* also means "beer".'

'Oh, I see,' and her next words won the man over completely. 'Ah, an elephant with a great thirst.'

Managing to suppress the urge to follow Jessie's delightful laugh, Anna turned to the next man. He too was of middle age, tall and slim, but not yet showing the signs of is age through his woolly black cap of hair. He was obviously a shy man as he could only bring himself to briefly look Anna in the eye before dropping his head and beginning to bashfully shuffle his feet.

'This is Joseph,' Jessie said. Like Tembo, Anna liked him instantly.

After the introductions the three Africans stood expectantly looking in Anna's direction, obviously waiting for something to happen. First taking a quick glance over her shoulder, she turned back to Jessie. 'What's everyone waiting for? Shouldn't we get going? Won't Ben be waiting?'

'Yes.' Jessie nodded. It was her only reply. Everyone still watched Anna expectantly.

For a few more disconcerting moments Anna stood bewildered beside the Land Cruiser, then the penny dropped. 'Oh my God!'

'Don't –' Anna partially squawked before clearing her throat, 'Don't any of you drive?' she eventually got out. All three shook their heads, with patent trust still etched across their faces.

'You're the doctor,' Jessie simply stated.

What's that supposed to mean? Anna quailed inside. 'But it's … it's a …

oh God, a bloody four-by-four with the steering wheel on the wrong side.' She took a couple of hesitant paces towards it as if it were some grotesque prehistoric monster, and looked in the window. 'And, oh no. It's a stick shift.' Anna was used to driving only automatics.

After tentatively positioning herself behind the wheel she turned the key, God, it started! *'Come on Anna it's supposed to.* She tried to calm herself. *Right, do what Tony did.* She tried to remember what that was. *The big lever's for the gears and small ones for the four-wheel-drive.* She engaged both, let her foot of the clutch and with a great lurch they were off.

Anna didn't register if the others were aboard; all she could think of was the rocky track that would take them to the crater floor. 'Two thousand feet in two miles,' she remembered Tony saying; she didn't know if she could do it.

No, I'm going to have to wait for Ben, she thought as her courage left her. But she was already passed the Wildlife Lodge and before she knew it, she was committed.

Fifty minutes later the drive of terror was over and they had arrived safely but shaken, at the campsite Tony and Ben had chosen earlier to the left of Lerai Forest. Ashen-faced, Jessie, Tempo and Joseph hurriedly alighted from the vehicle and all stood well back waiting for Anna to turn it off.

Anna sat rigidly behind the wheel; her hands were gripped around it like vultures' claws and she was oblivious to the smoke slowly wafting from all four of the vehicle's brake hubs. Eventually, Ben's voice brought her round. 'I think it's angry.'

'What?' it was all that came to mind as she slowly turned her head and looked out the window.

'When we get angry, we usually fume,' he looked down at the smoking hubs. 'I think you must have made it *very* angry.'

Anna let out a sickly laugh, before blurting out. 'God, Ben it was horrible.'

'Yes, it is steep isn't it? Come on, Tempo's put on a pot of tea.'

CHAPTER 55

THE CAMP WAS set up under the over-hanging branches of an umbrella acacia, on the edge of a grassy plain that swept down to Lake Magadi, the central soda lake. Behind the camp was the rainforest that stretched up the rim, while in the distance on one side was the Lerai Forest, and on the other low grassy hills that rolled out of the crater's rim.

The campsite was made up of a number of differently sized tents. The central and largest was for Anna, Jessie and their research equipment, which easily gave them enough room to compile their data. Next there was a smaller one for Tempo's supplies and cooking equipment where he would also sleep and a pup tent beside it for Joseph, and finally two small open-topped tents; one a simple gravity-fed shower hanging from the tree, while the other, positioned discreetly away and screened by a wall of thorn-bushes, was for ablutions.

Anna and Jessie sat in collapsible camp chairs outside their tent and finishing their tea. Tempo was over in the supply tent fussing over his equipment, while Joseph was already off scouting around the camp.

'Gosh, you've been busy,' Anna stated once she'd finally regained her wits as she looked around the camp.

'Did have a little help.' Ben motioned towards a couple of Masai tribesmen still busying themselves with clearing the outer edges of the campsite. 'Hired them with the Land Rover I got from the Crater village. But I've still got a fair bit of other stuff that has to be put somewhere.'

'Research equipment,' Jessie chimed in importantly, trying to look learned.

'Exactly,' Anna agreed with a light chuckle at the private joke. 'It can all go in behind us.' She indicated to her and Jessie's tent.

'What's it all for?' Ben asked standing beside Jessie in the main tent, a question she would have loved to ask but she didn't want to show her ignorance.

Spread across a trestle table in front of them was Anna's research equipment. She started at one end and worked her way along. Pointing to a box of books she said, 'Scientific journals and backup data.' Next was an open leather case. 'That, you'll probably recognise. Joseph will be using it.' It was an adapted bolt action Anschultz .22, now an effective tranquilising gun. 'Some of the lions will need to be darted once we've identified them all.'

Jessie had lost her reserve. 'But how will we know which lion is which? The other day they all looked the same to me.'

'Simple really. All you need is a good pair of binoculars and ... these. Mugshots, with a difference.' Anna opened the box she had brought down from her cabin. It was filled with lion identification cards compiled over the years by previous researchers. Each had a name or number, several head-on photographs and numerous comments.

Ben looked at the first few before shaking his head. 'Like Jessie said, they all look the same to me.'

Anna was about to comment but Jessie interrupted. 'Hang on a minute.' She carefully studied a number of the photos. Although there were some noticeable differences – ear notches and scars being amongst them – it wasn't those she was looking at. 'The patterns above the whiskers, they're different.'

'Well done, Jessie,' Anna was genuinely surprised and equally impressed. 'We'll make a zoologist out of you yet. That's how researchers accurately tell felines apart. Like a fingerprint they're unique. Some you'll immediately recognise by sight, but when you're unsure, the whisker spots never lie. Using these and the new ones we'll make up is how we'll begin our research.'

'What's this?' Ben had lost interest in the ID cards. It was too technical for him; a lion was a lion as far as he was concerned. He was looking at a box-like apparatus with numerous nobs, wires and pads protruding from it.

'It's one of the pieces of equipment we use after we've darted a male. When we've taken the blood tests we use it. It's an electro-ejaculator.'

Ben had a dumbfounded look etched across on his face; he was still none the wiser. Jessie, blushing slightly, leant down and whispered in his ear.

'What!' he blurted, he was horrified. 'You use it to pull them off? It's a jerk-off machine!' He backed away from it.

'I suppose, to put it bluntly, yes,' Anna answered with a smile; she'd never looked at it like that before. She could see Ben was slightly embarrassed by his outburst, so she continued. 'The blood samples and semen we refrigerate in that portable fridge there,' – it was a dual twelve-volt gas operated model sitting beside the trestle table – 'before being flown out for analysis in the States.'

Ben's horrified expression had returned. This time he was looking at the fridge. Chilled blood and semen. It was too much for him to bear; he shuddered slightly. In his view, refrigeration in the bush had one purpose and one purpose only. He'd seen enough, so sadly shaking his head he turned and walked from the tent. *Waste of good beer space*, he was thinking.

Ben had gone with Joseph to find out what crater animals made their home near the campsite; it was better to be forewarned than sorry he'd told Anna. So Anna with Jessie, who was as it turned out a very bright and fast-learning assistant, were left to make their preparations. They were categorising the ID cards into specific prides and Anna, oblivious to the scrutiny Jessie was giving her, was vacantly staring at a photo of a big black-maned lion. Jessie eventually interrupted her line of thought. 'You like him, don't you?'

'Sorry, what?' Anna queried, shaking her head slightly as she brought her mind back into focus.

'Tony, you like him.'

'How did you know I was thinking about him?' she asked in surprise. Despite the news of Sarah's death he'd kept popping into her mind.

'Oh, just a hunch.'

Anna placed down the card. 'You know, I've never argued with someone so often before. He's sworn at me, challenged me, and even hit me once, but you know I've never before met a man whose has turned out to be so appealing, with a real passion for what he is doing. And to top it off, he's shown me a world, both good and bad, I never knew existed.' She was quiet for a couple of moments before speaking again. 'I used to measure men against my father before he died, and though I haven't quite worked Tony out, I think they may just be alike. Yes, Jessie,' Anna finally was able to admit, 'I do like him.' With a twinkle in her eye and smile on her lips, she fixed her eyes fully on Jessie. 'And you? Don't you think Ben's a little short for you?'

Squirming uncomfortably in her seat made it clear this was definitely one topic that Jessie wasn't ready to talk about. Jumping up from the seat she walked over to one of the camp stretchers and hurriedly changed the subject. 'Ah, I found this with the equipment. Is it yours?'

Anna let her off the hook; that was enough girl-talk for now, anyway. She immediately recognised the rucksack Jessie was holding, it was the one Tony'd had with him during their trip to the crater.

'No, but I know whose it is. It's Tony's; he must've left it with Ben before he left for Nairobi.' She reached out for it. 'Most of those clothes will probably need washing.' She opened the flap to look inside. 'I can get them done with mine when we go back up tomorrow.'

Surprisingly, the clothes looked neatly packed. However, what did attract her attention was a legal-folder sized report sticking down the back of the clothes. It wasn't the report as such, but the partial name she saw on top of it. She pushed a shirt collar out of the way to view it better.

'Jessie continue on with those ID cards will you please,' she said absent-mindedly once she'd seen the name.

Once Jessie had turned back to the cards Anna didn't hesitate in pulling out the report. Dumbly, she stared at the name before rousing herself. 'I'm stepping out for a few minutes. Just continue there.' She didn't wait for an answer as she walked out of the tent.

The thoughts Anna was having about Tony were very different from those she'd had ten minutes previously. She was sitting by herself in the passenger's seat of the hired Toyota Land Cruiser. She had read through the report, which was meaningless to her. It gave background information about a man she'd never heard of before, a Peter Nkomo. However, there were two names that did attract her attention. The first was Donovan's. The report was entitled **EXTRACT: DONOVAN FILE** and the signature on the last page, in clearly legible handwritten script, read, 'Richard Black'.

Life had dealt her another savage blow. Like a sudden change in weather, all feelings she had begun to develop for Tony were blown away. How, she didn't have a clue, but he was somehow involved with Donovan and that South African she'd met – Richard Black – and what she knew about them was they were definitely involved in her father's death. She felt her feelings towards Tony would never be the same.

As she stared sightlessly out the vehicle's windscreen, her melancholy finally slipped away and her resolve hardened as her anger flared. Anna had certain questions to ask Tony. And by God he'd answer them.

CHAPTER 56

Los Angeles

SEVERAL HOURS AFTER Anna had made her way back to her tent after reading the report, half a world away in a different time-zone a woman slightly more attractive than her was caught up in a turmoil of her own.

Sabina wet her lips. *Pucker up girl, here we go.* She steeled herself, then looked at her watch, 7.03 am. Damn! *Already three minutes late.*

She slid her security cards through the card lock on the side door beside the main entrance of Donovan Enterprises' tower block. After a few seconds, once the card's magnetic strip had been read and the information registered, the door opened.

She walked straight up to the young blond guard sitting at a dazzling security console positioned in front of the bank of high-speed elevators. It was constructed of brushed stainless steel and had a low flat top which rose up at a forty-five degree angle to house a battery of lights and security screens.

Thank God he's young, she thought, ignoring the actual console, *And good looking, too.*

He sat up straight and dropped the Playboy he was viewing as soon as he recognised her. He cleared his throat. 'Mrs Donovan.' He floundered for something to say. 'You're up early today.'

Sabina, with her heart pounding like a locomotive, gave him her security card; despite the casualness of her outward appearance she was nervous. However, his comment eased her anxiety and gave her the opening she wanted. Raising a seductive eyebrow, she looked down at the Playboy then at the young man's groin, 'Probably makes two of us.' The man blushed bright scarlet and she hurried on, appearing not to notice, 'My husband has donated the Chinese pavilion from the board-room to be auctioned for charity today. I would like it, please.'

'The one in the middle of the table?' he asked as he leant forward in disbelief. *God, it must be priceless.*

'Yes, is there a problem with that?' Sabina asked as she frowned, trying to look concerned. As she made the comment she moved around to his side of the console, bent from the waist, and made sure he got a good view of her cleavage as she placed her shoulder bag she'd been carrying at her feet.

'Of course not,' he said trying to stay calm. It wasn't his job to question the boss's wife, who also happened to be a board member of the company that paid his wage. *God, some people have more money than ...*

He lost the thought as Sabina rested her buttocks against the console. She had been told to wear something sexy, and that's just what she'd done. She had chosen a red, stylish silk suit with a deeply cut jacket and accompanying miniskirt. As she sat back, she ever so slightly bent her knees which immediately raked up the mini, showing off far more of her shapely unclad legs.

'Will you please get it for me?'

'Ah ...' it was like an anguished cry the guard finally uttered; he'd caught the briefest glimpse of a dark fringe beneath her white lacy knickers.

'Sorry?' she straightened her legs.

'Ah ...' came the cry again as he slowly raised his eyes, they settled on her virtually sheer, frilly-laced cleavage. Finally, he managed to revive his wonder-struck mind. Without lifting his eyes he spoke to her breasts, 'I'm sorry, Mrs Donovan. I can't leave my post.' This was something Sabina already knew. 'But if you'd like to wait, the next shift comes on in about half an hour. I could get it for you then,' he eagerly said. Which was again something she knew.

Acting irritated, she looked at her watch and stood up. He flinched as she began to speak. 'Oh, how frustrating. It has to be on display before the auction rooms open.' She let out a heavy, annoyed breath. 'I'll have to get it myself.'

The guard swallowed heavily, opened his mouth briefly and then snapped it shut. He was caught in a terrible turmoil. Only specific personnel were allowed into the office section of the tower block after hours, unless of course they'd been cleared and he knew Sabina hadn't been. He opened his mouth again to protest but closed it. 'Oh God,' he lamented before hardening his resolve. 'I'm sorry, Mrs Donovan, but I can't allow that.' His eyes briefly flicked to hers before resting once again on her generous chest; he even licked his lips.

Shit! Sabina silently swore. It was harder going than she'd anticipated. *'Right, let's see how hardened your resolve really is.'* Standing in front of him she leant in gently and pressed her thigh against his arm and pouted. 'It's for a worthy cause, and if it's not there before opening it can't be auctioned.' As she spoke, she also laid her hand gently on his shoulder.

To the guard, seated as he was, first the bare skin of her leg and then her touch felt like fire. Like an inferno it seemed to rage through his body until it finally settled to ignite his groin; he felt it flare, inflaming his desire before he swallowed heavily again. *Christ, the boss's wife.* He was positive she may have said one thing, but her actions – *Jesus, they had to be a come on. No, surely not?* As his doubt clawed deeper and slowly took hold, he again opened his mouth to refuse, 'I'm sorry Mrs –'

However, Sabina had already anticipated his refusal. 'You know, I've always found blond men attractive.' She raised her hand and lightly ran her fingers through his hair before turning and picking up the Playboy. It had been laid face down on the centrefold and displayed a stark naked Hispanic girl, with hooded eyes, lounging on a tangle of white satin sheets. She had erect up tilted nipples, her coltish legs were spread, and she was fully exposed. Sabina sucked in her breath before continuing to speak 'And I'm glad you like your women dark.' She turned and looked him in the eyes. 'When was it? Half an hour you said you get off?' She then dropped the magazine.

As his head snapped up and he saw the inviting smile in her dark alluring eyes, his refusal died a swift and hurried death. 'I'll get an elevator for you,' he said, but his silent voice spoke very different words. *Yes, yes. Christ, Sabina Donovan. Yes, I'm in. I'm in!*

However, Sabina's thoughts were very different. *Thank God* was all she thought. Too much rode on her getting past security.

Producing a key from the end of a chain, the guard inserted it into a panel in front of him; he slotted it into a keyboard and twisted. A row of vertical lights turned from red to green. He had isolated and switched on an elevator for her to use. 'The one closest to me. Here, I'll show you.'

As he rose and passed her, Sabina lightly brushed a breast against his upper arm and delicately grazed his groin with the back of her hand. *Just so he doesn't change his mind,'* she reasoned, but despite the anxiety she felt, she was finding the alluring mix of tension and playing the seductress had begun to turn her on.

Only one of the eight elevators had a green light showing above it. The guard pushed its button just before the doors slid noiselessly open. He then leaned inside and pushed floor twenty-five. 'I'll only be able to give you ten minutes.'

'More than enough time. Well, for now at least,' Sabina purred, lightly stroking a finger down his jaw as she brushed past him, moving into the lift.

Stepping back from the door, she saw him blush again, and as they closed he and the longing of his face was snatched from view.

Realising what lay ahead, Sabina was quickly able to forget about the guard, yet relieved all the same she slumped back against the lift and uttered, 'So far so good.' As the office part of the tower block was deserted at this time of the morning, for the next five minutes she knew she would be alone.

When the lift arrived at the twenty-fifth floor – the floor that housed the board-room, company lounge and bar, and the corporate personnel offices – Sabina already had taken off her high heels and slipped on a pair of Adidas trainers she'd produced from her shoulder bag. She dumped the stilettos and shoulder bag in front of the door so it couldn't close and ran to the board-room. With scant regard for the value of the Chinese pavilion, she scooped it off the table and hurried back with it to the lift. Unceremoniously, she dropped the treasure on top of her bag.

'Right, next the stairs.'

Her breathing had started to become laboured by the time she had run down the five flights. She took a deep breath as she stepped into her husband's outer-office. *That's strange*, she thought. Even though it was early she'd half-expected to see Sonya, or at least some evidence of her behind her desk. It was empty and what's more it looked as if her workstation hadn't been used for days. *Maybe she's taken leave while Judd's away?* Sabina didn't dwell on the thought.

Briskly, she walked through the outer office and up to the keypad on the side of the heavy teak doors. *I hope to God he hasn't changed it.* She pressed the numbers – 7,0,5,1. Sabina heard a buzz and numerous clicks. She then tried the doors and they opened.

Tentatively she pushed her way through into Donovan's office; again it had an abandoned air to it. As soon as she'd entered the office she went to the concealed doors of Donovan's private elevator, pushed the nearby button and waited for the panels to withdraw and the lift to present itself. When inside she sent it down to the basement car park.

Once the lift had come to a stop and the doors had opened, she didn't alight, but waited for the three men who stepped from a nearby Oldsmobile limousine to enter, before sending it back to the office; Richard Black had again crossed the Atlantic, only this time he wasn't alone.

'Enjoy your night?' Sabina asked.

'Wonderful, thank you.' Richard replied sarcastically, however, he soon changed his tone. 'I see you took my advice.' He swept an appreciative gaze over her revealing outfit. 'Impressive.'

Despite herself, Sabina blushed.

Late the previous day Richard and his companions had picked up a company limousine waiting for them at the long-stay parking at LAX. The limousine, plus its three passengers had spent a long lonely night in the basement car park.

Although she hadn't been introduced, from the few words he had spoken she recognised the shortest of the three men as Johnny; with his inquisitive probing look he was just as she had imagined. But as for the third man standing opposite Richard, he was another matter altogether.

Like Richard and Johnny, he was casually dressed, rubber-soled shoes, jeans, and a loose fitting shirt, but he had an engaging presence that hung about him like a cloak. He was by far the tallest and when she saw him move it was with an athletic grace. He was in his early forties, had short sandy hair and a creased brow, typical of a man in authority or one who worried a lot, while also carrying a slightly crooked nose from several obvious breaks. However, it was the intensity and colour of his eyes that really held her attention; they were a fierce yellow like those of a predatory cat.

Sabina shuddered lightly; she was pleased he was with them and not a man they would be meeting along the way. As if to confirm the thought he stooped and retrieved a silenced 9 mm Berretta from the carryall he had at his feet. Like her, everyone noticed the movement. Richard said, 'Remember Dave, only if necessary.' The only response he received was an irritated frown.

Richard was also pleased the man was with them because he knew him far better than most. His name was Dave Old and he was an independent agent who had worked with Richard when he chose, which as of late hadn't been for a number of years. Dave now resided in South Africa and frankly could be called one of the best security consultants in the world; his methods may have been novel, but they were extremely effective.

Several weeks prior Richard had received a call from Dave who'd said, 'Blackie, I'm bored. I want a job.' So Richard had immediately included him in on the cross-Atlantic run. He had a hunch a number of Dave Old's resources would be needed before they were ready to head back to London.

Holding the handgun at his leg Dave addressed Sabina directly for the first time. 'The secretary, is she at her desk?'

As she answered Sabina realised the effect the man's presence had had on her. Her heart was pounding and she spoke in a husky breathless voice. 'No it appears she hasn't been there for days.'

Dave frowned lightly. This was unexpected but would make it easier to fulfil their plans. Before he had embarked on the job, he and Richard had been precise with their preparations. Although the job had appeared simple on the surface, he wasn't prepared to move until he knew exactly what he was up against. He'd requested floor plans of the tower block, details of current security and dossiers on all the likely people they could possibly meet along the way, he didn't rely on Richard's vast resources for these, he expected them. As the elevator gently chimed to indicate they'd reached the office, he was as ready as he'd ever be. The doors opened and he stepped out.

Dave did a quick circuit of the office before picking up his carryall and letting any of the others out. He walked over and dumped it on the coffee table in front of the portrait of Donovan's great-grandfather.

Richard turned to Sabina. 'Good work. You'll be expected back in the foyer. You'd better go.' She hesitated. 'Look, only your husband and this Russian, Bogatin, have a key to work the elevator and as for the keypads into the office, it's probably the same.' He glanced sideways at Dave who was intently studying the edges of the portrait. 'Anyway, why do you think I brought him?' he indicated Dave with a nod of his head. 'Go on, we know the guard's routine and I've got a cell phone if I have to contact you. You'll be expected,' he reiterated. Now satisfied, without a word she turned to slip out the door. As she did so, Richard couldn't resist patting her on her shapely behind.

Dave turned to Richard once the door was closed. 'Him? Huh, thanks, pal. And whatever happened to professional ethics?' He didn't wait for an answer; he was once again concentrating on the portrait.

Sabina was breathing heavily by the time she had slipped back on her high heels, and to quell her heaving breath she hugged the Chinese pavilion to her chest. She took a deep breath once the lift had reached the ground floor and stepped out.

'I was about to send a search party,' the guard tried to joke as he handed back Sabina's security card. He'd been trying to think of something witty to say ever since she had left.

'You know us women, had to powder my nose,' she replied in explanation with a seductive lift of an eyebrow. As the guard's colour began to rise she carried on, 'Now, did you say in half an hour you'll have finished your shift?' she queried, leaning forward, making sure he got an eyeful. He quickly nodded, unable to speak or raise his eyes.

Sabina stood upright. 'Oh dear, I've remembered I have a prior appointment.' Without another word she turned on her heels and casually walked away from the tower block.

She looked at her watch as she stepped out of the building. Seven twenty. So early in the morning to burn your bridges. Sabina knew that if Donovan caught her, her life wouldn't be worth living.

Striding to her nearby Porsche she discreetly looked up the road. Yes, the tan Cadillac that had followed her from the villa was still parked on its spot. 'So far so good,' she reasoned. 'Time to dispose of the pavilion and lead them on a merry dance.'

'Right, the guards should check the door every two hours. First check in about, what, an hour and a half,' Richard said looking at his watch. 'Other than that, we should be undisturbed.' He turned to Dave. 'Well?'

Tucking his handgun in the waistband at the small of his back, Dave produced a pair of lightweight pigskin gloves. Slipping them on, he then drew a penlight torch from his pocket and approached the portrait.

After cautiously scanning around the portrait, he grunted. It looked like a simple job. 'One magnetic trip switch, by the looks of it. No other security devices or concealed wires. Just a run-of-the-mill wall safe.' He went back to the carryall and produced two more pairs of gloves. 'Put these on, I don't want to leave any prints.' Neither Richard nor Johnny replied as they did as they were told.

'Right, here goes nothing. You two stand over by the lift, and take your briefcase with you, Johnny, in case we have to do a runner.'

Dave produced several metres of white electrical cable with two small rectangular metal tags, as thin and sharp as razor blades soldered onto either end; he also produced a pair of long needle-nosed pliers. Holding the torch in his mouth he walked back up to the portrait.

Using incredible dexterity for the size of his hands, he held the two tags together and nimbly clamped the pliers over them. Positioning his head to the side of the portrait, he began to glide the pliers and the tags behind the painting towards the magnetic switch. Pushing forward with the pliers he eased the tags in between the magnets. 'So far so good. All I have to do now is open it.'

Leaving the wires dangling down behind the portrait he went back to the carryall. Putting away the pliers he produced a long insulated electrical screwdriver; again its bevel had been honed to a thin razor edge. He walked up to and slipped it between the two tags. 'Here we go.'

He was about to give it a quick flick when somebody tested and shook the handles of the teak doors. Keeping the hand still that held the screwdriver, with a liquid blur of movement from the other Dave had drawn his Berretta. He then stood as if cast in stone, aiming the handgun at the door.

Christ, they're bloody early. If the door opened, he'd be forced to shoot. *Damn!* he anxiously cursed.

However, it wasn't the death his shot would bring that caused his anxiety; it was the prospect of the ruination of such far-reaching well-laid plans. Continuing to hold his aim he prayed, watched and waited. The doors shook again.

After five long minutes, Dave decided the guard had left. He slipped the gun back into the waistband at the small of his back, drew in a breath and twisted the screwdriver. The portrait swung open, revealing the wall safe with the magnet's circuit still connected by the tags and length of electrical cable.

Dave let out a breath. Nothing happened, no alarm, no flashing lights. 'Piece of cake. Well, sort of.' With the back of one glove he wiped his brow. He approached the safe. 'Now the tumbler.' Richard had stepped up to his side. 'Right, now recite the combination.'

'Right 33, left 49, right 23, left 77.'

It only took the once. Dave tried the handle and the safe door swung open. 'All yours, Blackie.'

For now, Dave's job was done; he had the rest of the morning to wait.

CHAPTER 57

'The disks'll be on the top shelf, in the containers, they're apparently unmarked.' Richard spoke to Johnny, 'Grab them and, well, you know what to do.'

The little man, with eyes twinkling, immediately reached in and gathered the containers Richard had indicated. He then headed with his briefcase past the massive ivory columns and up the marble steps, to Donovan's ornate walnut desk. Once Johnny was out of the way, Richard stepped up to the safe. He whistled lightly and spoke over his shoulder to Dave. 'Nothing like keeping a reserve for a rainy day.'

Dave looked past him into the safe. Stacked on the shelves below where the disks were kept were several bundles of a multitude of numerous currencies as well as a number of gold bars. Richard was frowning with interest when Dave saw the gold bars. 'Hell, a small fortune. What a pity we have to appear to leave everything in the safe undisturbed.'

Richard nodded. The last thing he wanted was for Donovan to make a hasty return from Africa before their business in LA was completed. The plan was they would leave everything as they found it and be gone without a trace. Well, that's what Richard had told Dave and Johnny.

As Dave began walking about the office, viewing the ivory collection around the walnut walls, Richard went up to Johnny. Already the little man had made the desk his own. Strewn about it was notepaper, blank disks and a laptop produced from the briefcase.

The plan was to use the laptop, and if necessary Donovan's computer, to copy the disks. It could halve the time necessary in the office if the need arose. But as they had most of the morning before they would risk leaving, giving Sabina a clear division between her early morning visit and her other morning's activities, it was probably unnecessary. Even so, after Johnny had set up the laptop he flicked on Donovan's computer and screen.

'Well?' Richard asked Johnny who was now scrolling through the file menu of the first of the disks he had planned to copy.

'Not a problem. I'll be finished well before we're due to leave. Should be able to copy the lot.'

'Hang on a minute.' Richard stopped his assistant with a hand on his shoulder; he was peering at the laptop's screen, 'That file … no, no, the one above it, the one titled **Hagan**. Yes, that's right,' Johnny had positioned the cursor over it. 'Can you print it out?

'Sure.' Johnny transferred the disk to Donovan's computer and called up the file.

'This'll be interesting,' was all he heard from Richard as he set the laser printer in motion.

As it turned out it was only a small file and the printing took no time at all. One quick read of the printout and the final words 'file closed' had Richard's mind reeling in shock. *Oh shit!* He hadn't expected this at all. *Bugger!* But he had to be sure.

Looking at his watch, he calculated. Three hours ahead in Washington, he should be in his office. After retrieving the cell phone from the briefcase, he dialled for an operator and asked for directory assistance. He was soon put through to the number and man he wanted; his contact with the WWF in Washington. After a few tentative words, he breathed a sigh of relief. *Thank God*, he silently applauded, and then casually asked, 'So where is Anna working now?' This time, after the response he received, he was unable to keep his next comment to himself, 'Christ almighty, Tanzania, at Ngorongoro? Sorry, what?' He'd briefly forgotten about the person on the other end of the line. 'Uhm … oh, Tanzania. It's just I've heard it's a dangerous place. Thanks all the same. Must go.' He hung up before he had to reply again. Christ, dangerous place, that's an understatement.

For nearly a minute Richard paced around Donovan's office, Anna's presence in Africa was entirely unforeseen and not the least bit convenient. *Damn!* Because of his past links to her father, she was a sacrifice he didn't want to make, but for his plans to proceed – he swallowed heavily and grimaced. *Christ, I'll have to let the bastard have her. Mind you, that's only if they meet.* But even before he'd finished the thought he instinctively knew that she and Donovan would. He placed the phone down and with a heavy resigned tread walked away from the desk.

'What the bloody hell are you looking at?' Richard demanded when after half an hour he looked up at the desk. Without answering, Johnny sadly shook his head and concentrated back on his copying. He knew exactly what Richard's phone call to the WWF's office in Washington had been about; it was clear he didn't approve of his boss's lack of action.

Richard eventually threw up his hands. He'd wrestled with his conscience for long enough. Johnny had been the straw that had broken the camel's back. *Christ, I owe him that at least.*

Despite his agents accepting that they operated at their own risk, Richard felt responsible for Mitch Hagan's death. He knew he hadn't given him enough information and he now felt obliged to do something to prevent his daughter's death. He walked back to the cell phone but hesitated. Tony Campbell could help her, but he was reluctant to make the call. He had specific and carefully laid plans for Tony and they definitely didn't include Anna Hagan. He looked again at Johnny, now staring up at him.

'Yeah, yeah, all right, all right. One conscience is bad enough.' They had worked so long together; he knew Johnny could read him like a book. He looked at his watch again as he raised the phone and dialled for an international operator.

Eleven hours ahead in Kenya – 6 pm. An operator eventually came on the line. 'Yes, a Kenyan number, please. I'll also need directory assistance – the World Wildlife Fund's office in Nairobi.'

After what seemed like an eternity while Richard paced up and down in front of the desk, he was eventually connected. 'Hello, yes?' It was a bad line and he had to raise his voice, 'Tony Campbell please?' Not available was the answer. Richard was overcome by a cowardly sneaking sense of relief; maybe his plans could remain intact. 'Well, when is he expected back?' The Australian accented voice on the other end didn't know, so Richard considered ending the call but, *Damn!* his conscience had started to niggle at him once again. He cupped his hand over the receiver. 'What's the number of this blasted phone?' he asked Johnny. After repeating it down the phone, he implored, 'Please, as soon as you can contact him, get him to ring this number. Yes, that's right, it is an American number. Yes, urgent. It's to do with poaching–life and death.'

Richard eventually rang off, placed down the phone and without looking at Johnny, walked away from the desk. *Well, at least I tried, what else can I do?* The only trouble was there was a hell of a lot more he knew, but as of now Anna Hagan was on her own.

Johnny had finished copying the disks, packed up all his gear, except the laptop, turned off Donovan's computer and placed the disks back in the safe. However, he was still in a world of his own, scrolling through the more interesting files he had copied. As he scribbled on scraps of paper, Richard left him to it, he knew he wouldn't be getting any sense from the little man for days. Both he and Dave were lounging on the leather couches in the office's informal discussion area, clearly bored.

Richard looked at his watch, 11.00 am. 'Come on, we may as well get moving.' He rose and walked up to Johnny. 'Pack up the briefcase. We're about to leave.'

After checking Donovan's desk to ensure Johnny had left it the way he'd found it, he walked back down to the safe. While waiting for Dave to make his preparations to close it he carefully repositioned the container of disks and then stood aside.

'Johnny, over beside the lift. Open the door and be ready to leave,' Dave ordered. After closing the safe and twirling the tumbler he turned to Richard. 'Ready?' he asked and received a nod. 'Okay, swing the picture to.' The portrait swung to cover the safe and closed with a gentle click as the magnets met. With Richard pressing against the picture frame, a quick yank on the electrical cable pulled them out and left the circuit intact. Richard was still standing beside the portrait as Dave packed his carryall and walked over to join Johnny at the lift.

'A neat job,' Richard was congratulating himself. 'Just as planned. Now for a few minor alterations.'

Richard could feel the puzzled eyes of Johnny and Dave on him as he walked up the marble steps towards an exquisitely carved ivory lace ball. It wasn't just one lace ball; there were three of different sizes, the smaller ones having been artfully carved inside the larger. Because of the intricately carved patterns and the thousands of man-hours that had gone into it, it was priceless. However, with little regard for its value he scooped it out of its walnut panel recess, dropped it on the ground, and because of its delicacy he was easily able to crush it underfoot. He heard a light gasp of horror from Johnny but ignored it. He left the crumpled pieces where they lay and moved onto another piece.

It was the thirty-five thousand-year-old mammoth ivory stylised figurine. He picked it off its shelf, threw it once in the air, but caught it before it fell. He then dropped it, but this time into his pocket, it would be leaving the office with him.

Quickly scanning around, trying to make a decision, he then moved back down into the informal discussion area. Standing beside the coffee table, from his pocket he retrieved an ivory disk, about the size of an American silver dollar but slightly thicker. He bent down and carefully placed the ivory disk just beneath one of the leather couches.

Satisfied, he stood upright and looked at the bewildered pair of men standing beside the lift. 'Okay, you can put on your overalls and get mine ready.'

First, dumbly, Dave and Johnny turned to stare at one another, before Dave bent down and retrieved three pairs of white overalls from his carryall. As they shrugged them on they saw Richard move to stand in front of the portrait; he appeared to be studying its frame. 'Ready to leave?' he asked over his shoulder. He didn't wait for an answer as he curled his fingers around the frame and yanked the portrait open. All hell broke loose.

'Jesus bloody Christ, what the –' Dave shouted, but the words were plucked from his mouth as an alarm bell rang and a siren began to scream in the distance.

Richard needed little encouragement to hurry as he ran to the lift. He was met by disbelieving stares from both Johnny and Dave. It was Dave who eventually found his tongue, 'What the fuck do you think you're doing?'

'A creative diversion,' he answered, then, 'Well?' he asked as cool as ice, 'What are we waiting for? I think we can leave.' He had a number of press contacts to speak to and a reputable courier company to find. He turned to Johnny. 'To the basement carpark, if you please.'

CHAPTER 58

ANYONE NOTICING BOGATIN's face wouldn't have realised he was thoroughly bored. With partially hooded eyes, he sat impassively behind the wheel of his Corvette as he drove down Hill Street in downtown LA. Since Donovan had left for Africa there wasn't exactly a lot for him to do; organising and checking surveillance on Sabina wasn't exactly inspiring work.

He indicated and pulled the car up to the security check at the entrance to Donovan Enterprise's tower block's basement car-park. The guards knew exactly who he was and that he had security clearance – after all, he was in charge of it. Once he'd stopped, he carefully noted the questions asked and the checks that were made. Too many ex-employees knew the consequences if the precise procedure wasn't followed. As he waited for them to process his pass he noticed three white overall clad men walking along the narrow footpath beside the vehicle ramp, about to leave the car-park. They were walking in single file and he clearly recognised the red embroidered emblem blazed across the left side of their chest: 'Ace Security' it read and as the company had a contract with Donovan Enterprises their presence didn't arouse any suspicion. He absent-mindedly watched the trio, even the carryall the tall leading figure carried or the briefcase the smaller middle man had, didn't unduly attract his attention. However, as he swept his gaze over the third man, like striking a match, something sparked within his memory. Although it was turned away and shadows obscured his face, he looked vaguely familiar and immediately Bogatin's suspicion began to flare.

He lent out the window towards the guard. 'Those three men, the Ace Security ones, have them –' as he began to speak his carphone started to ring. He snatched it up and the words he heard stilled those on his lips.

'What! A break-in, in his office. Shit! When? Damn! Remain where you are.' As he floored the Corvette, shooting down the ramp and leaving the security kiosk in a haze of harsh blue smoke, the three overall clad men – who had slightly quickened their pace – were now the furthest thing from his mind.

As Bogatin rode up in Donovan's private elevator, he dragged a snub-nosed Smith and Wesson .38 from a shoulder holster beneath his suit jacket and checked the load. Using surprising speed for his squat toad-like features, he had alighted from the lift and swept the handgun around Donovan's office before the lift's doors were fully open.

After another twenty seconds and a quick search he knew the office was empty; just the open portrait and broken ivory carving appeared out of place. He ran for the big teak doors. Yanking them open, he was presented with three security guards with guns drawn. 'You and you,' he pointed to the first two guards, 'to the front foyer with me,' then to the third, 'and you guard the door; the office will have to be searched.' Trailed by the two guards, the Russian hurriedly set off through the outer-office to the floor's bank of elevators.

Bogatin soon had a myriad of security guards scouring the tower block and questioning everyone who was leaving the building, trying to identify the intruder. He was at the security console in the building's vestibule and in the midst of the confusion he found out about Sabina's early morning visit. As Donovan had requested, he'd had her tailed since he had left for Africa, and the security manifest at the console pre-empted what he would have found out when he made his twelve o'clock check with her surveillance team. Shaking his head in irritation, he knew he'd be needing another security guard. He looked at the time on the manifest; 7.03 am she'd entered and seventeen minutes she'd been in the building. He then looked at the security guard's nightly report. 'Chinese pavilion?' It didn't make sense. But sure enough after radioing through to the guard on the twenty-fifth floor he knew it was missing from the board-room's table.

'Donovan will have a fit.' He knew it was a prized piece, probably several hundred years old. However, he was still suspicious and would wait keenly for the surveillance report that was due in at noon of her last twenty-four hours' activities. He read the security report again, '"Auction" she said. 'Jesus, he will hit the roof.' Throwing the report back on the security console he decided he would look into it later.

It was twelve o'clock by the time he got back to Donovan's office. So far the search for the intruder or intruders had revealed nothing. He stepped through the teak doors. 'Anything?' he asked one of the two guards he'd organised to search the office.

'Just this.' The guard placed an ivory disk in his hand. Bogatin briefly studied it before placing it in his pocket; he'd examine it more fully later.

'What else?'

'The portrait's been opened, a carving broken and there appears to be a piece from the collection missing.'

Bogatin cursed inwardly. Donovan would explode, and he wasn't thinking about the safe, he knew all too well of his employer's virtual obsession for his collection. He'd have to worry about that later he decided. 'Okay, the safe. Has it been opened?'

'Unless they had the combination, it appears not.' The other guard had joined them and confirmed his colleague's thoughts.

'Right, both of you out. There's not much more that can be done.'

Once they had closed the door Bogatin walked up to the shattered ivory lace ball, it was obvious it had been done on purpose – crushed into a creamy-white heap onto the carpet. He then spotted the vacant shelf where the missing piece had been. *Jesus, in all that is sacred, he will hit the roof. Christ, the mammoth ivory figurine. They couldn't have picked a more valuable piece. It must be worth millions.* He breathed out heavily, 'Oh, shit.' He didn't envy telling Donovan about this one, but he'd have to face it later. The security check on Sabina was due.

He walked to the phone on the coffee table in between the two rolled back elk hide couches. Dialing and bringing it to his ear, he stared vacantly at the portrait of Donovan's grandfather as he waited for the call to be answered.

'Bogatin,' he identified himself. 'What of Mrs Donovan?' he asked. 'What auction?' He grunted, 'And the Chinese pavilion, she has sold it? And she's been there all morning? Right, keep me informed.' He ended the call once he'd been told what he suspected. *Donovan will have kittens,* he thought.

He dialed another number; it was his secretary this time who answered. 'Bogatin,' he identified himself again; he didn't wait for a response. 'Mr Donovan's itinerary and the number in Kenya where he was to stay. Ring me back when you have them ... no, I'm in his office.'

Bogatin anxiously paced around the office while he waited for the call. 'Yes,' he answered as he snatched up the phone after its first and only trill. 'Right,' he scribbled the number down in a notebook, 'And place his itinerary on my desk.' He curtly ended the call, looked at his watch and grimaced as he calculated, 'It'll ... uhm ... be just before midnight ... I think.' And for the second time that day a call was placed from the office to a number in Nairobi.

'Damn!' Bogatin cursed as he cradled the receiver. 'Unavailable.'

He hated having to do it, but Bogatin knew he'd have to make a decision. Donovan's parting words came back to mind: *Now I don't want you to screw around sending messages, you'll probably never get me. If anything turns foul on us, Sabina's not that important. You've got my itinerary, so bring it to me personally.*

But was this important enough? It appeared as though the safe hadn't been opened but Bogatin was more than aware of what it contained, and the fact that somebody had got past the guards, entered the office and stolen the mammoth ivory figurine was an enormous breach of security. *No, until whoever did it and how has been identified,* he reasoned, *the disks can't afford to stay. Damn!'* But still he hesitated; he would've rather spoken to Donovan first. He reached into his pocket and drew out the ivory disk the guard had given him. Looking at it he reasoned he had no choice.

He looked up at the portrait and steeled himself as he made up his mind. *No, he'll want to know and not want me to leave them behind.*

He reached for the phone again and from memory dialled Donovan's corporate lawyer. He identified himself, gave a brief code and waited. After a few minutes he scribbled a series of numbers beneath the Nairobi phone number in his notebook. Before hanging up he repeated them back to the lawyer, 'Right 33, left 49, right 23, left 77. Got it.'

Walking up to the open portrait and safe, he flexed his fingers before setting to work on the tumbler, and for the second time that day Donovan's disks, along with several wads of money, left the safe. However, the difference this time was that they wouldn't be returned. With the containers of disks tucked under his arm and the money stuffed into his outside suit pocket, Bogatin closed the safe and finally left the office.

Two hours later, ten frustrating minutes of which had been spent questioning Sabina Donovan, the Russian was in the air. He was sitting by himself in the business class section of a Continental Airlines flight heading for New York. He was no longer wearing a suit but dressed casually; he wanted to be comfortable for what he knew was a long trip ahead.

So with a briefcase, containing a number of computer disks, now securely wedged between his leg and the plane's internal wall he settled back to wait. With the sequence of connecting flights his secretary had arranged it would be at least twenty-four hours, or thereabouts, before he landed at Tanzania's Kilimanjaro International Airport, and it was there or close by he expected to meet his employer. A prospect he didn't relish.

CHAPTER 59

Nairobi

THIRTY-SIX HOURS AFTER leaving the Ngorongoro Crater Tony eventually arrived in Nairobi. Normally the two hundred and sixty-five miles would take him at most six, maybe seven, hours to drive, but as he passed close by Kenya's Amboseli National Park he felt he was obliged to stop at the park's headquarters and speak with the head warden there.

Tony had spent a day and a half in the park, and during that time he had learnt that the rangers had been experiencing a recent uplift in poaching. However, it wasn't until the early afternoon of the day following his arrival that he realised why. Without explanation he muttered one word, 'Donovan,' as he ran from the headquarters to his Land Cruiser. Instinctively, he knew the American was now in Kenya and that his personal presence had triggered a resurgence in poaching, not only in the park but probably throughout the rest of the country as well. The sooner he got hold of Donovan's itinerary, the sooner he and Ben could put concrete plans in place to have him and his racket closed down.

As he headed for the Kenyan capital he was appalled at himself, for most of the past day and a half his thoughts had been distracted, he had let his personal life impinge on his professional one; for that period Anna Hagan had hardly left his mind.

'Hell of a woman, looks, spirit, and real desire for wildlife preservation. Christ, I've been blind.'

Even though Nairobi was only a hundred and forty miles from the Amboseli Park, it still took Tony just over four hours to reach the capital. The hundred miles of the A104 were excellent but the fiercely corrugated dirt roads to get to it nearly shook his fillings out.

He arrived at Nairobi just on dust as the British High Commission was closing. Luckily, for a week now they had been expecting his visit and he had little trouble picking up the second instalment of information Richard had sent for him.

He was horrified by the time he'd had a chance to read it, and with a vague sense of disquiet he entered the WWF's office on Harambee Avenue. However, as he did so he didn't notice the two Kikuyu tribesmen sitting in a Toyota pickup on the opposite side of the road.

When he walked in through the smoked glass door Craig Maitland was tidying up his desk ready to leave for the day.

'Tony, where the hell have you been?' Craig twanged in his Australian accent.

'Good to see you too, Craig,' Tony responded sarcastically.

'Christ, I've been trying to reach you for a day and a half.'

'Ah, remember that assessment I was forced to have.' He didn't wait for an answer. 'That's where I've been.'

'But you left Ngorongoro yesterday morning.'

'Yeah, I've been at Amboseli. I have actually still got a job to do.' He then asked suspiciously, 'What's all this about anyway?'

'Amboseli, of course,' Craig chastised himself as he realised that's where Tony would have been before carrying on, 'Oh, some joker from the States rang up in a flap wanting to speak to you.'

'An American?' Tony asked, bewildered. He hardly knew anyone in the States.

'No, sounded South African. Left a number for you to call, said it was about poaching and ... he was a bit dramatic, mentioned the words "life and death".'

'Richard Black.' Tony knew straight away. 'Where's the number?' he demanded urgently. It was Craig's turn to have a bewildered look on his face. 'Come on, he wasn't joking,' Tony was already snapping his fingers impatiently.

Tony snatched up the phone without asking and dialled the number as soon as he was given it. Although it was early morning in the States, the voice that answered sounded surprisingly wide awake. Tony recognised the English accent immediately. 'Johnny, Tony Campbell. I presume it's Richard that wants a word with me?'

'You presumed right. Hang on, I'll get him.'

Tony had a long minute's wait before Richard came on the line. He didn't sound nearly as fresh as Johnny or as willing to speak to him as he could have. 'Tony, yeah, Richard. Hell, we've been waiting for over a day now for you to call.'

'Yeah, yeah,' he answered impatiently, 'It must be important.' His earlier disquiet had turned to anxiety.

'Okay, sorry. Even though this is an open line there's no other way to tell you what I have to ... it's Donovan. We've just cleaned out his files, had them for a day and a half now, some bloody interesting reading. Now I'll need you to try and keep him there while we attempt to put together a case. Or – well, you know what I mean. But while you're doing it, there's a personal favour I'd like to ask.'

Tony didn't like the sound of this. He didn't want to run off on some errand, and certainly not after he'd read through Donovan's itinerary.

'Donovan had one of my people here in the States killed, an FBI agent that doubled for me; he'd been looking into his money laundering. Now somehow, don't ask me how, but his daughter's got wrapped up in it after he was killed. Donovan thinks he's already taken care of her as well, but to cut a long story short he missed his mark. She's now in Africa and it looks as though they may run into each other. I know it's taking you off track, but can you help?'

Tony fell silent. Richard heard his heavy long-suffered breath but didn't interject. It'd have to be his choice to help – if he wouldn't, so be it.

Tony sat heavily on the corner of Craig's desk. He didn't like the sound of this one bit, especially if it meant missing a crack at Donovan. 'Oh, Jesus, Richard. Why now of all times?' Richard didn't respond, 'Okay what's her name and where is she?'

'The FBI agent's name was Hagan ...'

Shit! Tony stood bolt upright, 'And his daughter's name is Anna.' *Jesus bloody Christ!* And Donovan was due at the crater that day he remembered from his itinerary. 'Shit, you could've told me.'

On the other end of the phone Richard was first bewildered then intrigued, he hadn't expected such a reaction. 'Well, that's what I was trying to do. I take it you know her, then?'

'Know her?' Tony stated incredulously, 'I've just spent the last week with her, that's all. Yes I know her. Christ, it was me who dropped her at the Ngorongoro Crater.'

From Tony's response Richard realised what he thought was a negative was a positive. Either way, whether Tony could help Anna or not wouldn't matter. Just the fact they knew each other, and well as it seemed, added a whole new dimension to his plans. What a stroke of luck. As he spoke he ensured he kept the excitement from his voice. 'Tony, I don't want to tell you what to do, but ...'

'You're going to, anyway. Look, Richard, you don't have to I'm on my way ... if I'm not too late already.' Tony was about to hang up when Richard stopped him.

'There's something else you should know. The man who killed her father, a real nasty piece of work, will have joined Donovan by now. His name is Bogatin, ex-Russian mafia, and, Tony, if he's there he'll bear watching.'

'Thanks for the tip.' Tony had hardly heard the words; he was already preparing himself to get back to Ngorongoro as quickly as possible. He hung up without even saying goodbye.

'What the hell was all that about?' Craig demanded.

Tony had forgotten his presence. 'Oh, what? It's a long story,' he said. 'Look, has a new plane been organised for me? Like the man said, it's life and death.'

'Shit, Tony, what the hell are you wrapped up in?' Craig asked.

'Poaching, as always, bloody poaching. But this time like I said about a week ago, I'm onto the biggest investigation I've yet encountered.' Again he ended without explanation. 'Have I got a plane or not?'

Craig shook his head in irritation; Tony was forever keeping information to himself, so bloody infuriating. He huffed disconcertedly. 'Yes I've got you another bloody plane, a Cessna 310. It's at Wilson Airport waiting to be picked up. But I'm warning you, Tony,' he threatened with a rigid finger, 'it's only on loan.'

'A 310, things are looking up. Good, I'll be in touch then.'

Tony turned to leave but was met by the burly figure of one of the two men who had watched him enter the office. He was about Tony's size but his whole bearing spoke trouble. He was clearly not a man to be taken lightly. From instinct, Tony immediately realised that he and his companion behind him were Peter Nkomo's men. Where normally he wouldn't initiate contact, he threw caution to the winds; his phone call to Richard had changed his view of Donovan, Peter Nkomo and, more importantly, anyone who was going to stand in his way from getting to Anna as quickly as possible.

He walked up to the man as they entered the office and spoke in Swahili, pretending not to notice the machete hanging at the man's side, *'Jambo ... karibu ndani ta fadhali.'* (Hello ... please come in.)

The man was taken aback by the friendliness of their intended victim. However, he soon lost the sentiment when he felt Tony's fist driven up under his diaphragm. He doubled over; the air was forcefully expelled from his lungs as the machete clattered to the ground. Tony then pole-axed him with a double-handed chop to the base of his neck. The man had nowhere to go except topple forward to the ground.

'What the hell do you think you are doing?' Craig screamed.

Tony answered as he kicked the machete along the floor and under Craig's desk to his feet. 'Welcoming them, of course. As you can see, they've probably just come for a friendly chat.'

He turned to meet the second man, and stopped in his tracks; if the first man was big the second man was huge. Tony gaped at him; he was a man-moving mountain. Like the first had obviously intended, he stepped over his colleague and advanced on Tony with a machete dangling at his side.

'Definitely a friendly chat wouldn't you say, Craig.' Tony spoke over his shoulder as he stepped in towards the man, swung his foot and snapped a kick, which landed with a meaty thud in his groin. The man never flinched, never even changed the expression of menace on his face. He continued to advance, now raising the machete above his head.

As if hacking through jungle, the man swung and heaved the blade at Tony's rapidly departing figure. Dancing and sidestepping a hurried retreat, Tony soon found himself behind the desk.

'Christ, do something,' Craig wailed. This was part of Tony's work he definitely wanted no part of.

'Grab the phone, call the police,' Tony implored as he bent over and groped for the other man's machete he'd seen at his feet. *Thunk.* The man understood English and cleaved his machete into the phone, demolishing it. 'Shit, circle around to the door. We're going to have to make a run for it.'

Like an executioner advancing on a sacrificial lamb, the machete-wielding thug was now circling the desk. 'Go.' Tony had grabbed the other machete and with a great heave, upended the desk towards their assailant before turning and following Craig as he ran.

The nimble Australian was out of the door first and running for the street. Tony was hot on his heels but as he skipped over the prone figure at the door he found his ankle had been clasped as if caught in a steel vice.

'Shit, here we go!'

Managing to keep on his feet, Tony raised his machete like a sword and fended off a downwards hacking stroke from the second man, who by now had hurled the desk out of the way and was taking the advantage his colleague had given him by grabbing Tony's ankle.

With a great chink of striking metal Tony managed to meet and fend off the blow, but he knew held as he was, he'd have little hope of fending off many more. He saw the next great slice come chopping down and managed to dodge to the right; he avoided it as it slashed into the doorjamb just above his head.

'Christ, too close for comfort.'

Like a badly struck axe, the machete was embedded heavily in the door-surround. Taking advantage of the brief reprieve, Tony hacked downwards and cleaved through the man's wrist which held his ankle. An agonising groan and great gush of ruby-red blood saw him free, but before turning to run he raised his arm and with all his might threw an overhand stroke at the man still trying to free his machete from the door.

The weapon left Tony's hand, tumbled once in the air before striking with a meaty welt, impaling itself in the assailant's chest. As Tony turned to run all he heard was a dull groan from the man clutching his severed wrist and the breathless anguish of the man skewered through the chest. He never looked back as he caught up with Craig, standing flabbergasted just beyond the door. Grabbing him by the arm he dragged him out onto the street.

'They were trying to kill you,' the Australian said dumbly, shaken by the experience.

'I think you mean us. They wouldn't have stopped at me.'

'Jesus, Tony, what the hell have you got yourself into?' They had just reached and hurriedly climbed aboard Tony's Land Cruiser.

Tony grunted in response as he reached for the ignition. 'Poaching, as before, always bloody poaching.'

He gunned the big petrol engine and headed for Wilson Airport before Craig could protest. He had a plane to catch, and as of now the mess in the WWF's Nairobi office was Craig's to tidy up.

CHAPTER 60

Ngorongoro Crater

LAX, JFK, Heathrow, Jomo Kenyatta and finally Kilimanjaro international airport. Although Bogatin had spent twenty hours either in the air or waiting to board the next plane, because of the time zones he had travelled it was still only eight in the evening on the same day that he had left Los Angeles. Bone-weary and walking with the mechanical steps of a zombie, he entered the large lounge and dining area of the modern Ngorongoro Wildlife Lodge. After asking to speak to Mr Donovan, and being accosted himself by several bodyguards, he eventually found his employer and Peter Nkomo sitting on the lodge's veranda, perched high above the crater rim.

Wearily, with a dumb expression etched upon his face, he went to stand in front of Donovan.

As if seeing an apparition from the dead, Donovan stood bolt upright. Realising the Russian's state, he offered him a seat before beginning to ask the first of his many questions. He had noticed the briefcase clutched protectively at Bogatin's side. It was a simple question. 'Well? I take it there have been problems?'

'We have had a break-in. Into your office.'

'Christ, not the safe. What about the disks?' Donovan was clearly distressed.

Bogatin indicated the briefcase; Donovan breathed a sigh of relief. 'Okay, what happened?' he asked as he tentatively sat back into his seat.

The Russian briefly glanced at Peter before swallowing heavily; he wasn't looking forward to this. 'I was called to your office several minutes after eleven this morning, Los Angeles time. The portrait's trip switch had been triggered and the portrait had been opened.'

'Shit, the safe. It hadn't been opened?' Donovan asked pensively.

'It appears not, no.'

'So nothing was missing or out of place when you retrieved the disks?'

'Not that I could see,' the Russian indicated with a tired shrug.

'I think the safe was of secondary concern and may have even been found only by chance. It seems the break-in had another purpose.'

Donovan frowned briefly. 'Another purpose?' he queried initially not comprehending, then uttered, 'Oh shit! Not my collection?' The safe, for now, was the furthest thing from his mind.

Bogatin frown gravely, this was the moment he had been dreading of all. 'I am sorry but, yes.'

'What, how many? They didn't take the lot?'

Bogatin cleared his throat. 'Ah, only the two.'

'Gone, stolen, what?'

'One gone, the other destroyed and left.'

'What?' Donovan's anger had finally driven through to the surface; he didn't know which was worse. His lips turned into a twisted scowl; he spoke his next words quietly but they were full of menace. 'Which ones? What happened?'

Bogatin hesitated only briefly, deciding it was better to get it over and done with in a single breath. 'The lace ball, destroyed – crushed underfoot – and the mammoth ivory figurine, stolen.'

Bogatin initially felt better for saying it – he'd been stewing on the prospect since the break-in. However, the feeling soon left him when he saw his employer's reaction. He again swallowed heavily and flicked a disconcerted glance towards Peter who was transfixed by what he was seeing. Both men were used to seeing Donovan composed, controlled and deliberate; they were witnessing a side of him they'd never seen before.

Donovan's whole body had gone rigid, jaw clenched, his massive shoulders bunched and fists balled into steely hammers. His eyes had glazed and flashed in an ignited murderous sheen; his veins were beginning to stand out rigidly down his neck, while his colour had risen to a consuming violent red and he was shaking. His obsession for his collection had overshadowed all reason, and what's more, the lace ball and figurine had been his most prized possessions.

It was nearly a minute before Donovan could gain some semblance of control and speak again. But even then his words clearly spoke of the fury that still blazed within. 'How? And' – he raised an incriminating finger – 'you'd better tell me you know who did it.'

Shamefaced and feeling utterly exhausted Bogatin was unable to answer. He apologetically raised his hands and simply stated, 'I am sorry, Mr Donovan.'

'So there's no indication of how they entered?' With his jaw still clenched

Donovan bitterly shook his head. 'So much for your bloody security measures. Come on, man. You must have some idea.' He was clutching at straws, searching, grasping at anything that could ease the distress of his reeling mind.

'Well, I was in the carpark when I was called, and ..' something about the carpark and what he'd seen tugged at his lethargic mind. He tried to retrieve it but, not wanting to further provoke his employer's wrath, hurried on, 'I entered the office by way of your private elevator while security answered the call from the other direction. Neither of us encountered anybody that shouldn't have been in the tower block.'

'I take it you had enough sense to search the building?' Donovan had become condescending now.

'Yes, but nobody was found.'

'Shit!' Donovan's anger had risen again. 'The office, anything there?'

With a sneaking sense of relief Bogatin remembered he did have something, after all. He reached into his pocket and withdrew the ivory disk. Although he felt it was pitifully inadequate to start any kind of investigation, at least it was something and may stem Donovan's anger to some degree. He handed it over and it appeared to have the desired effect; Donovan finally had something to focus on.

Rolling and studying the disk in his hand Donovan found his reason returning. 'Okay, so the intruder dropped it?' Bogatin nodded. 'Right, it's a start.'

Peter had propped forward and was trying to get a closer look at the disk. Donovan frowned, still highly annoyed. 'What is it, Peter?' He was in no mood for idle curiosity.

'The ivory disk – no, surely not?' he said in disbelief. 'Yet I think I've seen it, or one like it before. May I, please?' he asked, apprehensively holding out his hand. He was still conscious of Donovan's earlier display of rage.

Once he'd received it Peter only studied it briefly before whistling lightly. 'Well, I'll be. I know who this belongs to, but,' he repeated his earlier uncertainty, 'surely not?'

Donovan was in no mood for Peter's apparent doubt. 'Come on, man. Whose is it?' he snapped.

Peter quickly leant forward holding out the disk. 'I find it hard to believe but,' he indicated one side of it, 'this carving is unmistakable.' It stood out proud of the disk and was a skilful reproduction of a huge bull elephant in miniature. Peter turned it over. 'The inscription puts it beyond doubt.' The engraved words simply read, 'Tony, All the best. Regards Stronghold.'

'Well?' Donovan snapped again, clearly irritated. Peter still hadn't answered his question.

'Stronghold is the rhino protection operation down in Zimbabwe's Zambezi Valley. And the Tony, well, that's Tony Campbell.'

'What? Campbell?' Donovan said incredulously. 'Christ, that bastard.' In irritation he shook his head. Like a fox terrier on a bull, Tony Campbell seemed to be forever snapping at his heels. 'Jesus, again he rears his ugly head. Are you sure it's his?'

'I've seen him with it once, inspected it even, and I also read when he left the rhino operation it had been specially carved and presented to him as a parting gift. It has to be his, but how on earth did it get into your office? That's what I'd like to know.'

'Campbell,' Donovan whispered, he now had something – or in this case, somebody – to focus his anger on. He looked Peter full in the eye. 'But he does know me. What was his comment to you in that restaurant? "Nkomo you're finished, you and Donovan both." And when I arrived you said he'd disappeared, for over a week now. The bastard!' Donovan rose and walked to the edge of the veranda, he looked briefly out across the crater's darkened void before turning back to Peter. 'And he still hasn't turned up. You've heard nothing, I take it?' Peter shook his head. 'It has to be him. Somehow he knows far more than we ever imagined and is taking advantage of it. Christ, he's going to pay.' He walked back to stand in front of Peter and clenching his fist he implored, 'I want him and want him alive. Jesus, like I haven't wanted anything before.' He then turned to Bogatin. 'I'm not at all happy with why you've come, but you did the right thing, and I'm now more than pleased you're here. Once we have Campbell we need to find out what he knows, how he acquired it and where the hell my figurine is.' Donovan's mouth twisted into a malicious leer. 'I take it you'll oblige me with your, ah, skills, shall we say?'

'With pleasure.' Although he was suffering miserably from his trip Bogatin could almost taste the revenge. He'd taken Donovan's anger and the break-in personally and would look forward to avenging his damaged honour. So as per Richard Black's specific, carefully laid plans – courtesy of the forged ivory disk he'd had made – Tony Campbell was now the focus of attention.

Donovan breathed a mollifying breath. Until Campbell had been located, there wasn't much he could do. He turned back to Peter. 'I feel it's time to eat. So could you speak with the maitre d' and organise our table?'

It was a dismissal and both men knew it. As Peter went in search of the maitre d' he accepted Donovan wanted to talk to Bogatin alone.

When Peter had walked from the veranda Donovan sat down again, leant forward and suspiciously squinted; his sixth sense told him there was more. 'Now, Nikolai. What of my wife?'

Bogatin grimaced; he'd seen and experienced enough of Donovan's anger for one day. He steeled himself. 'There have been problems with her, also.' He saw Donovan resentfully shake his head as he carried on. 'Earlier that morning she entered the tower block –'

'Oh, Christ. She wasn't involved?' Donovan cut in.

'It appears not. As you requested she has been under surveillance. Her last twenty-hour's movements were known.'

'Well, what was she up to, then?'

'She left with the Chinese pavilion from the board-room.'

'What! But why?'

'I'm sorry Mr Donovan; she had it auctioned for charity. It went for a pittance.' As Bogatin had expected, Donovan hit the roof.

'The little bitch. I'll kill her.' For several seconds Donovan couldn't speak. Sabina's act plus the break-in were too much for him to bear. He eventually found his tongue. 'Millions, that, the lace ball and the figurine. Christ, they're worth millions. Gone, lost. Jesus, I'll kill the bitch.' If it weren't for Tony Campbell, the vengeance he wanted to inflict and the information he needed, he would've cut short his trip. 'Shit, she'll pay.'

It took him minutes this time to gain control, and be able to place the thought of Sabina and her actions aside. There would be plenty of time for her on his return to Los Angeles, he reasoned. *No, it has to be Campbell I concentrate on.* For it appeared he had not only harmed him personally but professionally as well.

As the maitre d' arrived to have them seated through in the restaurant with Peter, Donovan appeared to be back in control. However, like a sleeping volcano, fury still smouldered bitterly within him, but at least now he had a target at which he could vent that pent-up rage. And as had been planned half a world away Donovan's attention was focused firmly in Africa and away from certain activities far closer to home.

Once they were seated and had begun their entrée, Donovan looked over at Bogatin's normally impassive face. It was then he intuitively knew there was something more. 'Surely not? what else?' he queried, dejectedly.

For the last ten minutes the Russian had been sitting as if in a stupor; jetlag had finally caught up with him. He had been chewing mechanically and barely taking in his surroundings. However, for the last five of those ten minutes he'd been staring at a figure sitting on her own at a corner table in the restaurant. 'I am sorry Mr Donovan,' he drawled in his heavily accented English, 'but I believe I have just seen a ghost.'

Neither Ben nor Jessie had taken much notice of the change in Anna. She had become aloof, but they put it down to a delayed reaction due to her friend's death. She had asked Ben to drive her and Jessie out of the crater just after lunch, saying she couldn't face the prospect of trying to drive the Land Cruiser up the rocky track herself, so they had left it at the camp with Joseph and Tempo for safe keeping. Her reason, or more correctly her excuse, for wanting to leave so early was that she had a lot more research data to process. In reality, Anna wanted to be left alone.

That evening when Jessie and Ben invited her to dine with them she asked for a rain check and instead went off on her own to have a quiet meal at the nearby Wildlife Lodge. For several hours she had sat by herself near the bar's log fire until moving through to the restaurant to eat. As she was nearing the end of her meal, she noticed the maitre d' seat two men who were obviously about to dine with a third already seated. There also appeared to be a number of other men discreetly accompanying them at nearby tables. She hadn't really taken much notice; the tall black man and the squat one with the Slavic features had meant nothing to her. Although the third man had his back to her, for a few fleeting seconds she was sure he looked vaguely familiar. However, she'd gave up wrestling with her memory before the thought had really began to form; instead, her mind was once again filled with Tony and his assumed betrayal.

By the time the three men had finished their entrées, Anna was ready to return to her cabin back at the Crater Lodge. After paying for the meal, as she passed by the three men, she looked down at the face of the man whose back had been to her. Her heart missed a beat as her breath constricted in her throat. Those walnut-brown eyes that met hers were the most evil and malevolent she had ever seen.

She hurried past their table and out of the restaurant, but by the time the cool night air had struck her she already doubted who she'd seen. In Africa? Surely not. It was the same face that had stared blankly back up at her from the newspaper articles she'd studied a lifetime ago at the Los Angeles' public library. However, as she shivered briefly and hugged her vest closer around her chest, what she had no way of realising was her thoughts were similar to those uttered by the man she'd just seen.

'Here in Africa? The Hagan woman? But who the hell did you... back at ... Surely not?'

But by this time Bogatin had lost the dull edge that had blunted the keenness of his mind; he had watched Anna pass by beneath his hooded eyes. 'I'm sorry, Mr Donovan, but this time I am certain.'

'But who ...?' he repeated. Because of all he'd heard that night, he'd lost his normal rationality.

By using his Midas touch Donovan had never experienced a business project going south on him and now he refused to recognise, or perhaps didn't see, that a string of seemingly unrelated events could herald a catastrophic collapse for his ivory racket. He balled up his napkin and placed it on the table beside his plate.

'This time, Nikolai, do the job and do it properly.' It may not be Campbell but at least he was beginning to strike back. Bogatin never said a word as he rose and followed Anna into the cool night air. Once he had left the restaurant, Donovan turned to Peter.

'Once you have finished your main, I would appreciate it if you'd follow to make sure. Take some of your guards if you think it's necessary.'

Not waiting for or even considering Peter would respond, with an effort, Donovan placed his napkin back on his lap. He cursed inwardly at what he viewed as another inconvenience, and what's more he'd lost his appetite.

CHAPTER 61

THE RURAL ASPECT of Anna's log cabin outside was in stake contrast to the warmth and comfort inside. However, its warmth never permeated further than the depth of her skin. She had bathed and taken up station in front of the gas fire, and as she had slept fitfully the previous night, she felt tonight was going to be no different. Again she reached for the report she had taken from Tony's rucksack, and again she experienced the same betrayal, but this time tempered with her earlier disquiet, for the report had mentioned the name of the very man Anna was sure she had just seen.

Eventually, however, unable to find a plausible solution for them both, she tossed the report on the table and decided to turn in for the night. Yet unlike the previous night, once her head hit the pillow she was fast asleep, a sleep that was broken by a creak of her cabin door. As she lay with her eyes closed, quietly half-listening to the peaceful noises of the African night, it wasn't until a rough hand clamped down over her mouth that she realised she wasn't alone.

CHAPTER 62

Nairobi – Ngorongoro

'CRAIG, I'M NOT interested. If the police want to arrest me because I left the scene of a crime, so be it.' The two of them were still in his Land Cruiser and had just parked beside the Cessna 310 that was to be Tony's new plane. Tony ignored the Australian as he swivelled around in his seat looking for his rucksack.

'Jesus, mate. There's blood all over the office; you hacked off one joker's hand and impaled the other. What the hell am I going to tell the police? I found them like that?'

When Tony remembered he hadn't had the rucksack at Amboseli and must have left it with Ben, he retrieved his webbing belt and FN and turned back to Craig.

'They probably won't even be there when you get back. The police are probably the last people they'll want to talk to.' He jabbed an accusing finger at the Aussie. 'Plus, the police are only going to want to talk to me if they know I was there. Look, Anna Hagan and Ben are in trouble and they need my help. You can either help or hinder, the choice is yours,' Tony let the statement hang.

Craig threw up his hands in resignation.

Tony continued, 'Right, either take the Toyota to the long-stay carpark and get a taxi back or sort it out tomorrow. Oh and by the way, a warning, I wouldn't go back to the office till tomorrow.' It was his parting comment as he stepped down onto the airport's tarmac; his mind was now focused on other things.

Craig drove off when Tony was halfway through his pre-flight check. However, if he had known of the Australian's intentions they would have left him an unhappy man.

Tony had never flown a twin-engine plane before, but that was the least of his worries. In just over an hour and a half's time he would be over the crater and as yet he didn't have a clue where, or whether, he'd be able to land.

Although it was a twin-engine, soon after take-off Tony found the 310 wasn't as fast as the single-engine 210 he'd previously had and its service ceiling was about ten thousand feet lower, but for all its failings it was a hell of a lot more responsive and easier to fly. Ninety minutes after takeoff he flew over the crater's rim and found himself above its darkened hollow below.

Damn. Where to land?

He thought about the strip at the nearby Lake Manyara National Park HQ but even that was twenty miles away, and considering he had no transport it would be another couple of hours before he could hope to get to the Crater Lodge itself. Resigning himself to that he thought, *Christ, it'll have to do.*

Tony was about to turn on the new destination when he remembered Ben should have finished setting up Anna's campsite down on the crater floor by now. *I wonder?* he thought, as he considered landing in the crater itself.

He could just make out the glint of Lake Magadi in the south, so using the shiny silver surface as a reference he headed towards it. He lost as much height as he dared, and when he was directly over it, he flicked on the landing lights. The lake in front of him lit up in stark contrast to the rest of the blackness all around. He grunted; he'd misjudged his height and had a good fifty feet between him and the water's surface. Gently losing more elevation, he pointed the Cessna's nose to where he judged the campsite should be.

He was too far to the left he realised as he spotted the domed foliage of the umbrella acacia tree – and yes, he'd seen a vehicle. With a growing sense of elation he thought, *Maybe they decided to spend another night down there, after all.*

The camp, its tents and the stationary Land Cruiser were snatched from view as he roared overhead. The next thing Tony realised was that his heart was in his mouth as he gasped out loud in shock; the crater's rim and the rainforest were racing up to meet him. Reacting instinctively, he yanked back on the control wheel, throttled forward for full power, and prayed. *Christ, I'll never make it.*

Remarkably, like an acrobatic kite, the plane attempted the near vertical climb. Forced down in his seat by the g-force, he could hear the engines indignant howl and feel the whole body of the plane beginning to shudder in protest beneath his seat, but as he felt the scrape of foliage on the fuselage underneath, he breathed a heavy sigh of relief. *Jesus, you might not be as fast, but thank God you've got more grunt.'* It was only the Cessna's twin engines and extra power that allowed him to climb so steeply and out of trouble.

Shaking slightly, with his nerves partially shot, once he had levelled out Tony decided he'd make one more pass before attempting to land. Although it was dark, illuminated by the landing lights the plain in between the lake and camp had looked smooth enough. He reasoned there should be enough room to land.

Lowering the undercarriage, Tony gingerly brought the Cessna down, but the closer he got to ground the worse it got; with no peripheral vision he had fly in by touch. Reducing speed as much as he dared, he followed a set of tyre tracks that led from the camp to the lake. He felt the wheels touch and smoothly run towards the acacia tree. When he judged he'd run over a smooth and long enough area to land, he increased power, climbed and banked back the way he'd come.

This time he lined up to land. 'Two planes in as many weeks, it won't look good,' he said aloud as he felt the wheels touch again. He put on full flaps, throttled back and slammed on the brakes. To his amazement the plane came up far shorter than he would have expected. 'Well, I'll be.' He risked running forward and pulled up just short of the camp. However, as he closed it down and stepped from the plane, with his FN clutched at his side, he knew neither Ben nor Anna were at the camp.

The two Africans standing bleary-eyed and staring dumbly towards him, around a freshly revived fire must be Anna's cook and scout. Walking up to them he asked in Swahili, 'The Matabele and the doctor, where are they?'

The two men gaped at him in aghast disbelief. Never before had they heard of a plane landing in the crater, let alone at night, and the sight of Tony materialising out of the darkness hadn't helped, especially with a rifle clutched at his side.

'Well?' Tony demanded, 'they are friends.'

Tembo answered saying, 'Earlier this afternoon, they left and went back to the Crater Lodge. They will be back tomorrow.'

Tony pointed at the Toyota. 'The truck, does it work?'

Tembo nodded, 'The doctor, she does not drive well. They left it. The Matabele took them back.'

In different circumstances Tony would have laughed out loud. Instead, he was already running towards the Land Cruiser.

Tony cut the normal time it takes to get out of the crater by half and in a great cloud of dust he braked to a halt in front of the Crater Lodge. He went first to Ben's cabin; the door was unlocked so he walked right in and flicked on the light. Bleary-eyed and blinking owlishly, two black woolly heads followed by their naked torsos popped up from beneath the blankets. He had disturbed Ben and Jessie at a most inopportune time.

Ignoring Jessie's presence, Tony demanded, 'Anna, where is she?'

'Tony, what? Anna? Ah, we haven't seen her since ... I think she'll be in her cabin.'

Tony thrust the barrel of his FN at Jessie. 'There'll be enough time for that later. Get dressed. We've got problems, big problems.'

Ben was already climbing out of bed; he'd recognised the concerned voice and had seen the FN. 'What's happening?' He was already reaching for his khaki shorts.

'Donovan's at the crater and believes he has a score to settle with Anna.'

'Jesus Christ, Donovan, here?'

'Yeah, the man himself. Now I don't know where he's staying. But find out and quickly. It'll be either here or the Wildlife Lodge. See if he's got any bodyguards and if so, find out how many. We may be able to hit him here. If not, we'll have to make a run for it to safer ground.'

'Bodyguards?'

'Yeah, they'll be Nkomo's goons. I've run into a couple already this evening. When you've found out, meet me at Anna's cabin.' Tony was out of the door before Ben could respond.

Ben turned to Jessie as he slipped on a shirt, 'Get dressed and find the vehicle Tony arrived in. It'll be the only one warm, probably out front. Wait for us there.' Slipping on his veldskoens, he was already following Tony out the door.

Since arriving in Africa Anna had taken to sleeping in one of her father's old T-shirts, one of his few possessions she had taken to Africa with her. It was a deep blue and nearly hung down to her knees.

Bogatin was disappointed when he stripped off her bed covers and found that she wasn't naked underneath. Savagely, he rolled her onto her stomach, rammed a knee between her shoulder blades, and to prevent her from screaming shoved her head into her pillow. As he wrenched her hands behind her back and began to tie them, he spoke for the first time. 'Your roommate, she was good, she struggled a lot. I hope you are the same.'

Anna's wild struggling stopped as the horror of it struck home, he had mistaken Sarah for her, it was then she screamed into the pillow. He was going to rape her too. *And, oh God, my eyes.* Her struggles increased as she fought for her life.

'Yes, like that. I'll enjoy that.' Once her hands were tied, Bogatin grabbed her by her raven locks and yanked backwards; the scream Anna was about to voice was violently plucked from her throat. With his teeth and free hand Bogatin grabbed the sheet and ripped off a strip. Gagging her he let her head drop back to the pillow. Anna twisted her head and through terrified eyes looked up at the Russian's callous face.

'Now let's see what we have here?' Bogatin raked up Anna's T-shirt to expose a pair of tanned, smooth, shapely buttocks – she wore no knickers underneath. Anna renewed her struggling.

Even with his immense strength Bogatin was having trouble holding Anna's thrashing form. But his next comment sapped all her strength. Like a rag doll, she went limp and lifeless. 'You mustn't take after your father. When I killed him he never struggled.'

Anna's world caved in and she let out an anguished sob. It *was* Donovan she had seen, and this barbarian was obviously doing his bidding. He had killed the two people in the world she had loved most, her father and Sarah. She'd also thought she'd found a friend with Tony, but like with the others a wicked twist of fate had plucked him away. What was the point in going on? She accepted that the humiliation she would soon be feeling would be followed by her death.

As she closed her eyes Anna's world turned upside down. There was a crash behind her and then the pain she felt wasn't as she had expected. Her ears rang and though her eyes were closed there was a painful flash beneath her lids. Then a heavy thump told her life, after all, hadn't dealt such a savage blow.

CHAPTER 63

THE RINGING IN her ears, Anna knew had come from the single crack of a rifle; the crash, from the door smashed against its hinges; while the flash that still hurt her eyes, from the stark muzzle shot magnified in the darkened cabin; and the thump, she recognised was from the man collapsing behind her.

'Bogatin!' she heard somebody hiss.

Instinctively, Tony had known something was wrong. For one, the door wasn't properly closed and as he tentatively pushed it open he heard an agonised sob. As he flung the door against its hinges even in the moon's pale light the sight he saw told him what he'd dreaded most of all; the tied up figure, the naked buttocks, and like a character from a sordid movie, a man bent over about to be caught in the act.

Tony remembered Richard's warning and instinctively realised who it was, he brought his rifle to bear, tapped the trigger and as he saw him fall, in loathing he hissed out his name, 'Bogatin!'

Anna heard her name but didn't have a clue who was saying it. She felt a hand lower her T-shirt and another gentle one on her head.

'Anna?' asked a concerned voice, 'Are you all right?'

She felt the gag being removed and the rope untied from around her wrists.

'God, the bastard!'

It was then she recognised Tony's voice, but she was puzzled by the anguish it contained; she recognised it as genuine.

Anna rolled over and stared dumbly up at the distress she could clearly see marking his face. 'You,' she began. Then, like a discarded shawl, her earlier confusion fell away. 'You!' Her anger at his assumed involvement rose to rear its ugly head again. 'Get away from me you bastard! You're involved with him.' Anna jumped off the bed and cringed away.

'What? For God's sake.' Tony was even more distressed and now as equally confused by her outburst. 'With him?' Baffled, Tony looked at the prone figure at his feet. 'No, Anna. Don't be absurd. Come on, what's wrong?' He reached out a hand.

'Get away!' Anna wasn't listening; she sidled up against the bed.

But like a contagious disease her anger had triggered Tony's.

His whole bearing changed; he balled his fists and menacingly hunched his shoulders. Being associated with poachers for Tony was like waving a red rag to a bull, but coming from the woman who had stolen his heart made it ten times worse. Fixing a pair of cold-blue eyes on hers through the dulled night-time light, while pointing an accusing finger at Bogatin, his mouth contorted out of shape. 'I've dedicated my life to save what his type destroys.' In disgust and fury he shook his head. 'I also risked my life to get back to you and you, you accuse me of being involved with the likes of him?' with disdain he spat out the final word. 'He and his master are everything I abhor in the world. Surely with the time we've spent together you should've read me better than that?'

His vehement disgust lanced the malignant anger of her mind, but she still was suspicious. 'But the report,' she pointed to it, just recognisable on the table, 'The one from your rucksack. It mentions Donovan and Richard Black. The men who had my father killed.'

'Richard? Richard Black?' Tony queried incredulously, 'Involved with your father's death?' Even to Anna it was obvious he found the notion absurd. He was starting to lose his anger. 'The only way he was involved with your father's death was that your father worked for him. Richard Black is part of British Intelligence, and your father was running an investigation for him – into Donovan.' Tony shook his head in disbelief. 'I was speaking to him not more than two hours ago. It was him who told me, implored me, to come back here. Not that I needed much encouragement, but he'd somehow found out there was a chance you two would meet.'

'Oh God, I'm sorry.' She'd jumped to conclusions, the wrong conclusions. 'I thought ... because of the report ... I put two and two together and – God, I'm sorry.' She felt foolish. 'I should never have doubted you.' It was then she looked into Tony's cool-blue eyes; he *was* like her father. Stepping over the Russian's lifeless body she hugged him.

Although it felt like the most natural thing in the world, Tony only allowed the embrace to last for a few brief seconds.

With distaste, Anna looked down at Bogatin. She twisted away from him but continued clutching Tony's arm. Never before in her life had she ever wanted anything dead and she felt guilty at her sense of relief. 'Is he ... did you kill him? He killed Pop and Sarah, he told me, before ...' She couldn't finish.

Looking down at the pool of blackish blood around the Russian's head Tony realised it must have been a headshot. He hadn't aimed as he barged through the door but had fired from the hip. 'I think that is something we can safely assume.' He changed the subject. 'Okay Anna, whether you realise it or not, the man Ben and I have been tracking, who if I assume correctly has already tried at least twice to kill us both, is this guy Donovan.'

'Good God, the American you told me about two days ago that runs the poaching racket.' She was stunned. For months now hers and Tony's lives had been intertwined by the actions of that corrupt and loathsome man. *All this time, if only ...* she silently lamented.

'Yes. He's one of the kingpins in the illicit worldwide ivory trade, and now he's here at the Crater.'

'I know. I've seen him, at the Wildlife Lodge. Tonight I had a meal there. He was with a tall black man and –'

'Peter Nkomo,' Tony broke in.

'The man in the report,' Anna said. 'But there were a lot of other men with them. Big men. At the time I wondered who they were.'

'Shit! Bodyguards.' Tony knew now wasn't the time or the place to go after Donovan. 'Anna, we're going to have to do like we did with the poachers in Tsavo, but this time you have to do exactly as I say, okay?' He said with both hands on her shoulders. She quickly nodded; she'd learnt once and it was enough. 'Get dressed quickly and pack, but only what you need. Keep the light off and wait for me here.'

'Oh God!' Anna had yet to let go, she knew Tony was going to leave her like he'd done with the poachers.

'Anna, I have to.'

'Well kiss me then.'

'With pleasure.'

It was fleeting but still hungry, deep and sensual, and probably the one kiss they would always cherish. Tony was gone the moment their lips had parted.

'Shit, they're everywhere,' Ben said.

He had found Donovan was staying at the Wildlife Lodge, and during his brief reconnaissance he'd counted half a dozen of what had to be bodyguards. That was bad enough, but when he realised three of them were heading towards the Crater Lodge he knew the worst.

Against such odds and without a gun Ben felt entirely naked. All he'd been able to find as a weapon was a short gnarly *knob-kerrie* one of the lodge's servants must have left behind his cabin.

Having to run part way through the forest to get past the bodyguards, he soon arrived at the Land Cruiser Tony must have used parked in front of the Crater Lodge. Puzzled, realising it looked remarkably like the one hired for Anna, he nearly ran headlong into two struggling figures beside it. Ben's blood boiled; one he recognised as Jessie, the other a tall well-built black man.

Without ceremony, Ben stepped in and heaved the *knob-kerrie*, it collected the man with a dull thud at the base of his skull, Ben cursed, he'd misjudged, it hadn't knocked him out. The man released Jessie and spun around to meet him. *Christ, he knows me.* Ben saw recognition spark within his eyes.

'You Matabele dog,' the man uttered.

Not waiting to be introduced, this time as he saw a dull flash of metal, Ben swung the stick with considerably more force and smashed it into the man's temple. He and the pistol he had drawn fell to the ground. Dropping the *kerrie* and scooping up the handgun – he noticed it was a South African 9mm Z-88 – Ben grabbed Jessie by the hand and ran for Anna's cabin.

'He wanted to know whose vehicle it was. I didn't tell him,' Jessie said defiantly as they ran, 'I also think he was a Zulu. He spoke like you but different.'

'Good girl,' Ben congratulated, but her words puzzled him. *A Zulu, in Tanzania?* Running down one of the paths to Anna's cabin, Ben and Tony nearly started an altercation of their own.

'Christ, you little bastard, I nearly plugged you,' Tony berated, when he recognised his friend.

'Speak for yourself,' was Ben's answer. He held up the pistol. 'Relieved it from a friend, he'd found the Cruiser you used.'

'Bugger!' Tony softly swore. He briefly pondered, before looking at Jessie. 'Anna should be waiting in her cabin. Go to her and bring her to the vehicle.' She was up and running before she had to be told again. Tony turned back to Ben. 'Well? I take it Donovan's guarded?'

'They're everywhere and some on the way, we haven't a hope of getting anywhere near him.'

'Damn!' He pointed to the pistol, 'How many rounds?'

'Just the one clip, and you?'

'Shit! The same, the rest are in my webbing belt, in the Cruiser.' He would've preferred to confront and attack, but it only took Tony a few seconds to realise the only course open to them. 'Come on, we'll have to make a run for it.' Both men were up and running for the Land Cruiser.

Anna hadn't bothered changing out of her T-shirt. She hurriedly pulled on a pair of knickers and baggy shorts and for footwear she chose a pair of trainers with no socks, but as she pulled on her down-filled vest she nearly died a hundred deaths. Whirling around with her hand thrown up to her chest in fright, she saw a dark figure slip through the cabin door.

'Anna?' called a whispered voice.

'Oh God, is that you Jessie?'

The two women met with a fearful embrace beside Anna's bed, it was then Jessie choked a horrified gasp as she saw Bogatin's lifeless figure. 'Is he ..?'

'Tony shot him ... he was about to ..' again she couldn't finish. 'Where is he Jessie? Where's Tony?' Anna had already forgotten the Russian.

Shaking herself, with an effort Jessie soon found her wits. 'He sent me; we're to meet him and Ben out the front. Anna, I'm scared.'

Realising Jessie must have had troubles of her own, she knew she'd have to take command. Anna grabbed her by the shoulders, 'Come on, the last thing Ben and Tony needs are a couple of snivelling women. You help me and I'll help you, okay?' She saw Jessie steel herself. 'Good.' However, she wished she felt as brave as she sounded. 'My rucksack's at the foot of my bed, and I'll grab Tony's. Everything else can stay.'

'Jesus, I'll be!' Tony had rolled the figure Ben had pole-axed onto his back. 'Do you know who this is?' He never waited for an answer. 'It's Peter Nkomo.'

Ben never hesitated; he pushed Tony out of the way, lowered the pistol and placed it on Peter's forehead. He would have pulled the trigger if Tony hadn't stopped him. 'What did you do that for? the bastard deserves it.'

Tony had to drag Ben down beside him as they crouched behind the Land Cruiser. 'Think, man. It's Donovan we need. Without Nkomo he could leave the country and go to ground.'

'Okay, what then?'

'We leave him, head for safer territory and hope Donovan will follow.' Of course, a man half a world away had already made sure he would. 'The way I see it, with all we know, and Anna still alive, there'll be too many loose ends. He'll want them tidied up.'

'I don't like it. What if he doesn't?'

'Well, we haven't got much choice, but let's see if we can help make up his mind. Wake the bastard up.'

'With pleasure.'

Ben first searched Peter, and after finding two more clips of ammunition for the pistol, he then propped him up against the front wheel of the Land Cruiser. He was about to set work on him when the two scurrying figures of Anna and Jessie materialised out of the night gloom.

'Get in,' Tony ordered, 'we're leaving soon, plus you'll probably won't want to see this.'

Ben's first lash with the pistol broke Peter's nose. Shaking his head with blood streaming over his lips, Ben proceeded to slap him across the face. 'Wakey, wakey,' he called through gritted teeth. When Peter's eyes had focused, Ben rammed the gun into his forehead. 'I have somebody here who wants to talk to you.'

Despite the pain and tears in his eyes, Peter recognised Tony immediately. 'You!' he said defiantly.

'That's right, very perceptive. I have a message I'd like you to pass on to Donovan.'

'Go to hell.'

Tony looked at Ben. 'He seems to be lacking a few manners.' Ben never hesitated; he ground the pistol into Peter's broken nose.

When Tony was sure he had Peter's attention, he spoke again. 'Now be sure and tell Donovan he not only missed his mark with me again but also for the second time with the Hagan woman. If he wants us, this time he's going to have to come down to Zimbabwe, but he better make sure of it because otherwise ... I've got enough information to blow him away.'

Anna's urgent voice interrupted him. 'Up the road, we've got company.'

'Shit,' it was Ben who spoke; he'd taken a quick look over the vehicle's bonnet. 'They're the three I avoided earlier.'

'Damn!' Tony looked down at Peter, 'Tonight you live, but next time I'm going to kill you.'

As Tony turned away Peter realised he meant it. The next thing he knew the Matabele had pistol-whipped him again. As he faded from consciousness he swore a silent pledge. Even if Donovan was unwilling, he knew using Sithole and his men he'd track them down if it was the last thing he ever did.

'Well, where to now?' Ben asked over his shoulder as he shafted the three bodyguards with Tony's FN as they flew past them in the Toyota.

'Familiar territory,' was all Tony answered as he concentrated on his driving.

For the next twenty minutes if Anna thought her trip down into the crater was terrifying Tony's ride was ten times worse, and it was only when they had reached her camp that they realised the reason for the trip.

'Good God, you were serious about Zimbabwe,' Ben uttered when he saw the twin-engined Cessna.

'Look, Ben, we fought a war in the bush down there. If we're going to fight another, I'd rather it's in a country we know.'

'But what about Sithole? Donovan won't hesitate to use him and his goons.' Tony noticed Ben's gaze had shifted to the two women who had now alighted from the vehicle. 'We could've handled ourselves, but with them it's not going to be the same.'

'Look, we'll have to worry about them when we're in the air. Now grab everything we can use. We've got a long flight ahead of us.'

CHAPTER 64

Donovan was horrified, aghast in total disbelief. What he'd viewed as an inconvenience was definitely now a major problem. His normal reason had left him as he now ranted in an all-consuming rage. The condition and thoughts of those around him preyed little upon his mind. Frankly, in that moment Donovan had lost control. The show of anger he'd exhibited early in the evening was like a stillborn child compared to the fury and wrath he now displayed.

He was in his hotel suite at the Ngorongoro Wildlife Lodge, brawling at the top of his voice as he stormed around the sitting room. He never registered the tasteful decor – stylised to an African theme – or the elegant furniture, which consisted of a comfortable patterned suite and solid wooden dining table. Instead, his outrage was directed at the two sorry looking figures that stood beyond the patterned suite in front of a picture window that displayed the darkened panorama of the Ngorongoro Crater below. He was angrily striding through the screed of papers that he'd hurled off the table, as his embittered words brutally lashed at their intended victims.

Striding from the centre of the room he passed the three-seater settee and violently smacked the report he'd been carrying down on a coffee table, in front of the two downcast men.

'And what the bloody hell do you call this?'

The first of the two things that Anna and Jessie had left behind had reared their ugly head. It in itself may not come back to haunt them, but by its very presence it would ensure something far more dangerous would.

Donovan, with hands on his hips, flashed his raging walnut-brown eyes from one man to the other. For the first time in many minutes his vehement outpouring had stopped and it was clear he wanted a response. 'Well come on,' he blazed, 'don't just stand there!'

It was the second of the two things that Anna and Jessie had left behind that answered. 'I'm sorry, Mr Donovan,' Bogatin answered in heavily accented English, 'but I found it in the Hagan woman's cabin just before I left.'

Tony had missed his mark. He had indeed shot the Russian as he'd intended, however, the wound had been far from fatal. The bullet had nicked him just above the temple and the force of it had knocked him out, but other than losing a pint or so of blood and leaving a gouge through his scalp, it had left him far from dead. He now had a thick white bandage wrapped around his skull and an incessant pounding within his brain, but these he felt were of little consequence compared to the rage his employer had heaped upon him.

'But for God's sake, what was it doing there?' Donovan switched his scowl to the second man. 'Well? Come on, man. After all, it's written about you.'

Peter couldn't answer. What the hell could he say? He'd only had a chance to briefly glance at it. *And it should be me that's worried,*' he thought bitterly. *Christ, it was like a damn biography!*

Compared to Bogatin's, Peter's injuries looked horrific. He had a lump the size of an egg on one temple, his nose was crooked and flattened further across his face, and he had a badly swollen eye and a stitched up gash from the other temple running down into his cheek. To say Ben had done a good job on him was an understatement. However, in one regard his injuries and Bogatin's were the same. With a similar relentless beat, their heads hurt like hell.

When Peter didn't answer Donovan huffed out a heavy exasperated breath. 'Oh, Christ. Take a seat.' He walked past them up to the window and stared out at the blackened African night. 'Christ, the Hagan woman with another reference to Richard Black, and with my name blazed across the report's front cover. Shit. And what the hell is "EXTRACT: DONOVAN FILE", supposed to mean?'

He nearly lost his cool again, it obviously meant there was more, and by the explicit contents of the report probably a hell of a lot more. Using an extreme force of will, he managed to quieten his reeling mind. *Richard Black, Anna Hagan and that bastard Campbell are all involved together. How is what we've got to find out.* He knew exactly how it would have to be done.

After several more minutes of contemplation, he let out another long-suffering sigh and felt that he was now gaining some semblance of order. He turned and in a meticulously deliberate voice first spoke to the Russian. As he did he registered a release of tension. Peter and Bogatin were relieved as they realised he was now back in control.

'So you have no idea who shot at you?' Bogatin shook his head; he thought it best to hold his tongue.

Donovan looked at Peter's disfigured face. 'But you feel it was Tony Campbell?'

'I believe so, yes.'

'Okay from the top again. You found the vehicle and this African girl, then Campbell's Matabele knocked you out,' he briefly shook his head in disbelief. 'Then what happened?'

In as dignified manner as he could muster, Peter began his less than glowing explanation. 'I was roused by Campbell and the Matabele,' he brought up a hand and gingerly touched his nose, 'Campbell then said he had a message for you.'

'Which was?'

'He said to say you'd missed your mark with him and the Hagan woman again.'

'So they do know each other?'

'When I came too she was in the vehicle and there was familiarity in her voice as she spoke. Yes, they know each other.'

'Oh, Christ. Damn it!' Donovan uttered bitterly but without his earlier venom. 'What else did Campbell say?'

'If you wanted them, you'd have to go down to Zimbabwe.'

Donovan frowned. *How on earth did Campbell know I was here at the crater, or in Africa for that matter?* he had to ask himself. However, he voiced a different thought. 'But would he say that? Would he give away his whereabouts?'

'It's his style, yes. He would use that sort of bravado.'

'Okay, and?' Donovan knew there was more.

'I can still remember his exact words. They were, "but he better make sure of it because otherwise, I've got enough information to blow him away".'

Donovan rocked back on his heels. *Jesus, maybe he had got into the wall safe*, he reflected in horror. Not that he would choose to mention it, but the file on Peter sounded awfully familiar. He quickly ran through his mind the sequence of events that had preceded Tony's words. Firstly the FBI agent and his vague allegations. He'd been taken care of. Secondly his daughter, her investigation, the discovery of her father's fax and diary and the first mention of Richard Black. He bitterly shook his head. Then, bloody Campbell's break-in and the new report on Peter. He pondered briefly. Somehow they were linked. They had to be working together.

He reached into his pocket and drew out the ivory disk Bogatin had given him earlier in the evening. Staring down at it he reasoned there was only one course of action open if they were to prevent themselves from being exposed and their ivory racket destroyed.

His greed for money, lust for ivory and arrogance prevented him from even considering a return to Los Angeles. He turned to Peter.

'Contact Captain Sithole and tell him he should expect guests. But if he catches up with them before we arrive, tell him to make sure he takes them all alive.'

'With pleasure,' Peter said with utmost conviction. He had a score to settle.

Donovan spoke then to both men. 'We need Campbell and this Hagan woman; it's imperative we find out who this Richard Black is and what exactly his true involvement is. If we don't,' he warned, 'not only the ivory trade, but all of us could very well be sunk. Now get some sleep. Tomorrow we leave for Zimbabwe.'

CHAPTER 65

Tanzania – Zimbabwe

ANNA, JESSIE, TONY and Ben had been in the air for about six and a half hours since making their hurried departure from Ngorongoro. It was just on dawn and shafts of golden-yellow light were lancing out from beneath the distant eastern horizon.

Tony, with help from Ben, had told the women of the true extent of Donovan's ivory racket and their involvement with it. He had brought them right up to date with what he'd learnt several hours before from Richard Black. His plan was to drop Anna and Jessie off with friends in Botswana at Maun before venturing back into Zimbabwe to go after Donovan.

'But what will you do when you get back into Zimbabwe?' Anna asked, slightly perplexed. She had leant forward between the front seats to speak to Tony and Ben. She hadn't come to terms with the direct way Tony chose to remedy his problems. 'You won't ... well, you know ..'

'Anna, put it this way,' it was Ben who answered, 'we'll do what's necessary to close down his ivory racket.'

She shivered. Closing down Donovan's poaching racket hinged on so many things and she knew it wasn't something that could be walked away from if they happened to go wrong. She changed the subject. 'Will we actually have enough fuel to get to Botswana?' She'd noticed the fuel gauges; one was sitting on empty and the other looked decidedly close.

'Ah, not quite,' Tony replied. They were already flying at the extreme edge of the Cessna's range, 'We'll have to refuel at Hwange Airport, and even then we'll be running on fumes.'

The prospect of parting company with Tony left Anna feeling slightly hollow inside, but his comment about the lack of fuel strangely didn't seem to worry her at all. One thing she had learnt to do was to trust him. With all she'd experienced in the short time she had known him, her life depended on her doing just that. With a wry smile Anna realised when they were in Tony's world if he said jump, she'd immediately ask, 'How high?'

To take his mind off their lack of fuel Tony changed the subject. 'Okay,

I want an inventory of everything we've got.' He turned first to Ben. 'What did we pick up from Anna's camp?'

'Not much I'm afraid. Some biltong and ah ... Anna's dart gun.'

'Dart gun?' Tony queried in disbelief. 'What the hell for?'

'Well it, ah, seemed like a good thing to do at the time. At least it's a weapon of sorts.'

'Yeah of a sort,' Tony replied sarcastically. 'The sort you leave behind. What else?'

'Only what I'm sitting in.'

Tony directed his next question to Anna, 'What about you?'

'Yours and my rucksacks. Other than that, nothing.'

'Good, I thought it'd been left behind. The first aid kit in it may be needed.'

'Now you, Jessie?'

'Same as Ben I'm afraid, only what I've got on.' It was a bright yellow patterned sun-frock she'd worn to dinner with Ben the previous night.'

'Okay –' Tony was about to itemise what they had, what he and Ben could use, and what they'd have to try and get once the women had been dropped off at Maun, but Ben interrupted him.

'Hwange's airport up ahead.'

Tony heaved out a quiet sigh of relief; the second fuel gauge was now touching empty. 'Right, we'll fly over once while I radio through our request to land – just to make sure there are no nasties lurking.'

Tony pushed forward the control wheel and lost elevation. While they did the low-level pass, and as he identified himself and asked to land, the airport looked and sounded deserted; there wasn't a soul to be seen and no response came from his request.

'I don't like it.' Ben looked anxiously down at the small airport's deserted runway and buildings. 'I know it's early and the first flight in from Kariba isn't due for another couple of hours, but surely there'd be somebody about.'

'Yeah, I know what you mean.' Tony was as equally suspicious; he glanced again at the fuel gauges. 'But we're going to have to risk it.'

As Tony banked to the right and lined up the runway, without stopping his landing procedure he gave his orders. 'I'll land and run in as close as I can to the pumps. Ben you take the FN and scout around. Anna, while I'm refuelling, you cover me with the pistol, I'll show you how.'

With a feather-light touch, the wheels kissed the runway. He reduced power, pulled on full flaps and gently eased on the brakes, but before he knew what was happening Ben was yelling at his side.

'Christ, full power! Quickly, take off, take off. It's a bloody trap!'

From the corner of his eye Tony also picked up what had attracted Ben's attention. In the early morning sunlight there was a glint of glass reflected from beside the control-tower, and he knew it could have come from only one thing: a sniper's telescopic sights. In the next few brief seconds, using his soldiers' eye, he picked up three more cunningly positioned marksmen.

'Damn!' Tony berated himself. 'Bloody Sithole, he's been tipped off. Bugger! I flew right into it.'

Tony pushed in the flaps while he throttled forward for full power. Making his intentions clear as the Cessna's twin engines bellowed, he saw perhaps a dozen soldiers run from their hiding places amongst the airport's buildings. 'Here we go,' he said in a conversational tone, 'hold onto your hats. I don't think they want us to leave.'

And sure enough, soon after he saw the muzzle flashes from the soldiers' weapons, the Cessna began to shudder as a hail of bullets hit home.

Despite Anna and Jessie's screams, the shower of shattered glass and jarring impact of white-hot lead, Tony managed to keep his cool. As soon as the wheels left the ground, he kicked one rudder pedal and eased the control wheel over to follow the turn. The Cessna banked away from the storm of bullets and the airport's buildings.

'Is everyone all right?' Tony asked anxiously once he felt the bullets stop smacking home, and when the Cessna had levelled out onto a truer line.

He breathed a sigh of relief – most bullets had been shot too high and behind the plane – only a few minor cuts and bruises he was told. He'd expected better from Captain Sithole's men.

'Now what?' Ben shouted over the bustling wind beginning to howl through the shattered windows.

'Shit I don't know, it's amazing we're still flying. Damn!' He cursed himself again as he shot a look at the fuel gauges. 'Wherever we go it can't be far. If she doesn't fall apart, we'll be going down soon, anyway.'

'Oh God,' Anna moaned. Ever since she'd met Tony her life had been turned upside-down.

'Hey, what about the airstrip at Hwange's Main Camp?' Ben piped up, ignoring the women. 'It's only six miles away.'

'Good thinking.' He should have thought of it himself. 'But that's if we can make the strip.' Then as if to emphasise his point, without warning, one engine cut out. 'Oh, Christ! If we make it, then what?'

'I hid the Land Cruiser behind the shop. It hadn't been found before I flew up to meet you so it could still be there.'

'Let's hope so. I can see the strip.' Tony lined up to land. 'Oh, shit!' The second engine coughed once and died. 'Being on loan and all, Craig'll be pleased.'

Luckily, the Cessna had enough airspeed for Tony to glide it in for a comfortable, if not conventional, landing.

'Right, Ben, out. See if you can fetch the Cruiser. If not, one of the park's Land Rovers, we'll have to explain later, Sithole and his goons won't be far away. Here, you'd better take this.' He handed over the pistol.

Ben had already alighted and was running from the now stationary plane when Tony turned to Anna and Jessie. 'Grab everything. Jessie, you take one of the rucksacks from Anna and both of you follow me.' He grabbed his FN and webbing belt. They were close behind him when he jumped to the ground, running with him for the edge of the strip.

'Thank God,' Tony breathed. He could hear the distinctive throaty whine of the Land Cruiser's big petrol engine. At least with Ben's rifle and all their other equipment aboard, they now had a chance of surviving, or at least being able to put up a decent fight.

When Ben skidded the vehicle to a halt beside them and had alighted, Tony was giving orders again. He turned to the women saying, 'In the back.' Then he grabbed Ben's arm and walked with him out of earshot, 'Okay, what do you reckon?'

'Shit I don't know, Christ, it's not going to take Sithole long to realise we've landed. We can't go south, we'd have to go past the airport, and by the time we reach the park's main gate he'll have already blocked the road up to Victoria Falls.'

Tony silently pondered for a few seconds and made up his mind. 'Right, we still have to get Anna and Jessie to safety.' He flicked his head in the direction of the park. 'Then if we want a crack at Donovan, we'll have to come back for him.'

'In the park?' Ben stated incredulously, he was looking passed Tony's shoulder at Jessie and Anna anxiously staring back at them. 'But Sithole and ... shit Tony on our own, sure, we could hide from him. But not them? I've seen how good his trackers are; they'd find them for sure.'

'I didn't mean the park exactly; I meant we're going out there.' Tony raised an arm and pointed due west.'

'You're joking!' Ben stated, perplexed. 'You can't, not with them!'

But Tony wasn't listening; he had turned and was already striding back to the Land Cruiser.

Taking his seat behind the wheel he said over his shoulder to Anna and Jessie, 'Ready for the trip of your life?' These perhaps weren't the most appropriate words he could've used. Once Ben was seated in the passenger's seat, he ignored his faux pas and the little man's disconcerted look. Gunning the big petrol engine they left the bullet-ridden plane and Hwange's Main Camp behind.

CHAPTER 66

'YES, CAPTAIN. I must admit I'm impressed. It appears to be a well-run operation.'

Donovan, Bogatin, Peter and Captain Sithole were standing in the middle of the warehouse at Thomson's Junction. It was a small corrugated iron clad warehouse about twice as large as an average sized three-bedroom suburban house. It had one cavernous room, a concrete floor and a small cubical office tucked just inside its high-stud entrance way. The four men were standing amongst the many rows of elephant tusks, perhaps four to five hundred in all, that stretched from one end of the building to the other. It was evident by their number it had been another excellent month. Sithole's men, not just for the benefit of Donovan, had weighed, stamped and laid out the tusks according to their size and quality.

However, Donovan was showing an unaccustomed lack of interest in the ivory. Usually, even with it in its raw state, he would take advantage of his annual African pilgrimage and spend hours inspecting virtually every available tusk. Flicking a disinterested hand he commented, 'Okay I'm satisfied. As Peter outlined earlier, we will reroute the ivory.' He then changed the subject. 'But as of right now we have a far more pressing problem.' He directed his next question to Sithole, 'What about Tony Campbell and his fugitives?'

Only half an hour earlier, Donovan, Bogatin and Peter, having left Peter's bodyguards in Tanzania, had arrived from Bulawayo. Before leaving Ngorongoro, Peter had organised the near-new safari Land Rover he'd had imported from South Africa for Donovan's Zimbabwean visit to be driven down from Harare to Bulawayo Airport for their use. They knew about Tony's early morning escape but Donovan had decided to attend to business first.

Despite his bearing – dressed in freshly starched and laundered camouflaged army fatigues – and the confident air Sithole exuded, he never felt confidence within. Every time he met Donovan he stood in awe of the man; he fancied he could even feel the power he radiated. However, this time, especially after Peter's earlier warning, he felt Donovan's presence was almost overpowering; it was clear the man's anger was simmering, like a bubbling cauldron, just below the surface. Sithole cleared his throat as he prepared to give what he knew Donovan would find an unsatisfactory answer.

'Just after dawn they attempted to land at Hwange National Park Airport, they, ah, obviously anticipated my men were waiting. The plane was fired on but they still managed to get away.'

Donovan was frowning with concern when he cut in, 'I said I wanted them alive.'

'Yes, I'm sorry. My men get over-enthusiastic at times.'

'Well, make sure it doesn't happen again,' Donovan warned with a rigid finger. 'I take it, with the lack of bodies you have, they got away?'

'Yes, and it appears uninjured. The plane was found several miles away within the park.' Sithole paused, this was the part he wished he didn't have to convey.

'Come on, get on with it, man,' Donovan snapped, he was in no mood for procrastination.

'As yet we have been unable to locate them.' All Donovan did was shake his head in annoyance. Sithole hurried on, 'But they can only be in the park. Roadblocks had been set up before they had a chance to leave.'

'Oh, Christ. I don't care how long it takes to bloody well find them, especially Campbell and the white woman.'

'Also, the Matabele and the Masai woman,' Peter cut in, touching the gash on his cheek, 'I want them captured – alive.'

Sithole had never heard Donovan, and more especially Peter, so insistent about a request. It was a tall order. To achieve what was asked meant he would probably lose a number of his men. Therein lay the major problem; they had been handpicked because of the callous disregard with which they went about their duties, and only by using an iron hand could he keep them in check. As he glanced sideways at Bogatin's silent menacing figure, he hoped that this time would be no different. Otherwise, the consequences could get a trifle messy. He decided to change the topic. Flicking his fingers he called to his sergeant who hovered nearby.

'Today's edition of the *Bulawayo Chronicle*.' When he had it in his hand he spoke again, 'Mr Donovan, not that it is any concern of mine, but it intrigues me. Why donate to the wildlife protection organisation that is causing us the most problems?' Donovan remained silent, it was clear by his blank expression he didn't have a clue what Sithole was talking about. The Captain opened the paper up to page three and handed it over. 'I read about it in today's edition, I've circled the article.'

As he read the article only Donovan's eyes proclaimed the fury that seethed within; it was the final straw. 'This time Campbell has gone way too far.' He thrust the paper at Peter and walked off down to the far end of the warehouse on his own. He had to control himself; an outburst would be justified but not in front of Sithole's men. The quiet rage he carried built with his every embittered step, for like with his passion for ivory he was consumed but consumed this time with an uncontrollable compulsion that wouldn't allow him to rest until he had caught, interrogated and destroyed that bastard Tony Campbell. The last assault of Richard Black's planned psychological war had hit home and found its mark.

Intrigued, Peter only briefly watched Donovan walk away before looking down at the article. He sucked in a horrified breath then looked up at Sithole. He spoke in Shona so Bogatin couldn't understand. 'My advice to you is to find Campbell as soon as possible, the longer he remains at large the greater jeopardy both our positions are in.'

'But why?' Sithole, using the same language, asked in dismay.

'Because, my friend, he didn't donate the figurine at all. It appears Campbell stole it.'

The Reuters article was a glowing report about a stylised mammoth ivory figurine, reputed to be at least thirty-five thousand years old that had been anonymously donated to the World Wildlife Fund in Washington to be sold on for wildlife preservation. Although the figurine had originally been bought for an undisclosed sum by private auction in Czechoslovakia many years before, it was reported to be worth in excess of a million dollars, and apparently had sold to an American of an unknown identity. The article hinted Donovan had been that buyer.

'Surely with insurance he'll get it back?' Sithole reasoned.

Peter shrugged, truthfully it really didn't concern him. 'Anything more on the unidentified stranger that met Campbell up at Victoria Falls?'

'Ah yes, photographs from immigration. I have them in my Land Rover.' But before he could send for them he was prevented by a soldier who ran up to salute and stand to attention in front of him. 'Yes, what is it, Corporal?' he asked as he returned the salute.

'Their vehicle has been found, and it appears all four are now on foot heading west. One appears to be slightly injured.'

'Excellent, excellent.' Sithole excitedly rubbed his hands together. 'Which one is injured?'

'It appears to be Campbell; it can be seen in his tracks.'

'Good, even better. They are in the park?'

'Yes, Captain. The vehicle was found near Mitswin Pan.'

Sithole frowned. 'Are you sure?' he asked, mystified. Mitswin Pan lay in the southwest of the park, a good thirty-five miles from Main Camp as the crow flies and at least ten miles off any of the park's serviced tracks.

'Yes, Captain, positive. Only by chance did one of the trackers pick up the tyre prints where it left the track. Its position has just been radioed through.'

Even though it seemed Campbell was injured Sithole's excitement had switched to anxiety as he turned to Peter. 'The pan is in the Kalahari sandveld and not more than twenty miles from the Botswana border.'

'Good God, you mean ..?'

'That's right,' Sithole answered for him. 'Campbell's running for the border. The mad bastard's going to take them across the Kalahari Desert on foot.'

Peter turned to Bogatin. 'You'd better get Mr Donovan.' When the Russian had gone he turned back to Sithole. 'Can he make it?' he asked full of concern.

'It will depend on his injuries and the white woman, but with his skills and the Matabele's, more than likely, yes.'

'You've found them?' Donovan had walked up to Sithole's side.

'We found their vehicle in the south-west of the park and they are on foot, heading west for the border.'

'Into the desert?' Donovan asked in disbelief. Even he realised how daunting a prospect that was.

'It appears so, yes. But Campbell may be injured.'

'Damn!' Donovan swore bitterly, 'All the more reason to track the bastard.' He'd wanted to be in on the chase but the images of the Kalahari that popped into his mind put paid to that idea. 'So, now what?'

'But by now they could already be well into foreign territory.' Sithole shrugged with resignation.

It was a lame excuse and Donovan knew it. 'So? You poach in the area all the time.' No way was he going to let Tony get away.

'Yes, but further north in the Chobe woodlands and the forest reserves.' As Sithole would have to accompany his men to make sure the fugitives were taken alive, he was looking for every excuse to avoid venturing into the Kalahari wilderness.

Donovan was rapidly losing his temper. 'Don't give me that crap. If Campbell gets away and with what he obviously knows, in Zimbabwe, you'll be in it up to here.' He raised a hand level with his throat. It seemed to have the desired effect, Sithole could clearly see the wider ramifications – Zimbabwe's military justice was brutally effective against its renegade officers.

Sithole showed a remarkable change of face. 'Of course, I will lead my men in personally.'

'You will also take Nikolai with you.' Donovan might not have wanted to venture into the desert wilderness himself but he didn't have any qualms about sending in others, and with Bogatin accompanying the captain he knew the job would be properly done.

After questioning the corporal who reported that the vehicle had been found, as well as after a few cryptic radio conversations, Sithole quickly planned the operation. All four men were now standing around the long-wheel-based Land Rover Peter had driven up from Bulawayo Airport.

'Because of the nature of the operation, and as it will be run in foreign territory, radio messages must be kept to a minimum.' He placed a long-distant portable set on the Land Rover's front seat. 'I will contact you when we have them.' He then got two of his men to hold up a large-scale map of western Zimbabwe and eastern Botswana on the side of the vehicle. He first explained where Tony's Land Cruiser had been found.

'But why on earth did they leave it?' Donovan asked. It seemed absurd.

'They would've had no choice. One of my men organised a surprise,' he ended without explanation and Donovan didn't pursue the matter as the Captain carried on. 'Now, I believe they have two options. One, head for or catch a lift on the Francistown/Kasane road into the small township of Nata about seventy-five miles south from where they'll cross the border, or two, head up for Kasane by catching a lift on the road or by way of the tourist routes within the Chobe National Park. Nata is twenty-five odd miles closer, but knowing Campbell he'll pick the least obvious, or neither.'

'How can they be stopped?'

He began indicating on the map. 'We'll have to drive them away from Nata. A small unit of men will be deployed further into the south-west to cut them off, while with my main body of men Nikolai and I will drive them deeper into the Kalahari or towards the north-east of Chobe, away from the main tourist routes. If they get that far, at this time of the year we shouldn't have too many problems with tourists because of the heat.'

Donovan was impressed with Sithole's planning so far. 'Okay. What about Peter and me?'

'Well I think you should circle around and enter Botswana at Kazungula near Kasane, and stay at the Chobe Game Lodge. It's just inside the park, overlooking the Chobe River and well within radio range. Once you're there and when we have them, which may take several days, I can radio ahead and organise a rendezvous deeper within the park.' He looked at his watch, now anxious to get underway. 'I'll have my men on their spoor before dark, but unless there is a decent moon the hunt won't resume until tomorrow, first light. If you hurry you'll get to the border well before it closes, and be at the Chobe Game Lodge before dark. I will have one of my best men accompany you.'

Within ten minutes Donovan, with Peter driving, was heading north. They were accompanied by a squat army sergeant now dressed in civvies who was sitting contentedly in the back. Like Donovan he too hadn't relished the prospect of venturing into the Kalahari's heat. In fact, he was so gladdened by his timely reprieve he had to prevent himself from whistling his tuneless whistle.

In turn, Bogatin with Sithole, and his unit of twenty hardened soldiers were heading away from the warehouse and travelling south.

Other than their necessary equipment and supplies, the only other thing they were accompanied by were the photographs Sithole had forgotten to pass on to Donovan.

CHAPTER 67

The Kalahari

'GOD, I'M CURSED,' Tony had uttered in disbelief. Never before had he had so many plans stifled and things go wrong while trying to break a poaching ring. 'So much for tracking down Donovan.' The shoe was definitely on the other foot.

As he had originally intended, Tony's main aim was to get Anna and Jessie safely to Maun before venturing after Donovan. The revised plan was to run for the nearby Botswana border, pick up the tar-sealed road that bordered Hwange and head south to Nata. From Nata it would then be into the westbound dust and across the hundred and eighty miles of Kalahari sands to Maun. Well, that's what he'd planned.

Once thirty odd miles had been travelled since Main Camp, Tony had slowed the Toyota and with Ben's help, eased it off the track. They had spent ten careful minutes sweeping away all sign of their exit from the road, and satisfied their work would pass casual inspection, they headed due south. Off the beaten track, as they had ventured further and further into the Kalahari's sandveld, it was far slower and harder going. It was another fifty minutes before they stopped beside the Mitswin Pan.

'Right, this'll be our last stop before Nata,' Tony said as he pulled up just beyond the pan. He turned to Jessie and Anna. 'There should be three water bottles somewhere in the back and one in my rucksack. Take them down to the pan and fill them up.' He noticed Anna grimace slightly as she looked out at the shallow muddy water. 'Out here, Anna, any water is precious. Wait till you get out of the Cruiser and face into the west, then you'll realise why – you take what you can get.'

Anna's expression didn't change until she did as she was told. It was her first taste of the Kalahari. Even though it was only mid-morning, it was like opening a sauna door when the desert's wafting heat briefly licked her face. Clutching Tony's rucksack at her side she'd definitely lost her squeamish expression as she followed Jessie down to the water's edge.

Tony and Ben left the girls and walked in the opposite direction, back along the sandy tracks the Toyota had made. 'What the hell have you got that for?' Tony rounded on Ben; he had Anna's leather case that housed the dart gun.

'Just wanted to see if there was anything in it we could use.'

'Come on, we've got better things to do.'

As Tony rested his FN against a thornbush and slung his webbing belt above it – out in the bush he made sure he was never without it – he noticed the pistol was tucked into Ben's waistband, but he'd left his FN back in the Land Cruiser.

Ben rested the leather case beside Tony's FN, and looking back the way they had come, said, 'Even if we drive nonstop, it still won't be till tomorrow morning before we even get a chance at Donovan.'

'Yeah,' Tony began to answer, but before he could say more there was a violent concussion, as simultaneously a savage shock wave rammed into their backs.

'Christ! What's that?' Tony snatched up his FN as both men dived for cover.

The sight they were presented with was one of blistering, twisted metal and angry orange flames; Sithole's sergeant's explosive device had just destroyed the Land Cruiser and everything in it.

'Christ, the girls!'

Dancing around the blazing wreck Tony was the first to find them. They were half sprawled at the water's edge and with shocked expressions, were staring back at the demolished vehicle. 'Thank God.' They'd both been crouching at the time of detonation and the blast had driven over their heads; they were dazed but uninjured. 'God, I'm cursed. So much for tracking down Donovan.'

Anna had relaxed the grip she'd taken hold of Tony's arm but still held on, it was several minutes after the explosion and she and the others were all staring numbly at the charred and blackened Toyota – she was certainly experiencing a different world since she had arrived in Africa. 'Now what?' she asked Tony. It was a question the others had dreaded to ask.

'Huh, we walk.' The question had roused him. He knew if they were to evade the chase that was sure to come he'd need his wits about him. And they'd soon have to get going. 'Right, what have we got?'

'Your rucksack and FN, four water bottles and the pistol. Oh, and the dart gun.'

Despite the circumstances Tony snorted with laughter, 'Of course, how could I forget the dart gun? Well done, Ben.' Looking briefly at the two women he knelt and emptied his rucksack. 'Anna, you'll have to change your T-shirt and Jessie you're going to have to lose the sun frock. Those colours will be seen for miles.' He handed Anna a tan shirt and Jessie a pair of khaki shorts and matching shirt. Leaving the rest of his clothes out, he only replaced the first aid kit, three of the water bottles and two lightweight thermal blankets back in the rucksack.

Anna was surprised with herself; she felt no regret at the prospect of losing her father's T-shirt if it meant surviving. So be it. Pop would understand. She didn't need a material object to remember her father by.

After a quick look around she realised not only was there little cover to change but also now wasn't the time for modesty. What's more, as she scooped off the T-shirt and bared her naked breasts, she discovered as Tony's eyes roved over her body she found it strangely appealing. Yes, she had certainly ventured into a new world, in more ways than one.

As she began buttoning up the shirt she looked over at Jessie, her fingers stilled as her mouth dropped open – she thought she'd done well with her forwardness. Once Jessie had stepped out of the yellow sun frock it was abundantly plain for all to see she'd been naked beneath, and as is accepted by most African tribes she showed no shyness about her nudity – to her it was natural. To her maybe, but not to Anna. When she saw Tony and Ben frankly observing Jessie's naked and rather comely figure, her sense of modesty was fired.

'Now that's enough of that!' With her shirt only partially buttoned up, she grabbed Tony and Ben by the shoulders and yanked their bodies around. 'Give the girl some privacy.'

'Yes well ..' Tony mumbled, before adding with a wicked grin. 'I must say, however, I do find this view rather more appealing.'

'What?' Anna frowned, slightly puzzled as she looked out at the Kalahari's scattered bush and sandveld, before looking up into his grinning face. His eyes were firmly fixed down onto her exposed cleavage and a dark-brown up-tilted nipple. 'Tony Campbell!' she exaggerated primly, as she clutched the shirt closed with one hand and jabbed him in the ribs with her other elbow; her modesty had returned. 'That'll be the last look you get, mister.'

'Ah, I rather hope not.'

'You wish.'

With eyes twinkling and light smiles tracing their faces, they stood for several seconds staring at each other. Although they weren't even touching it was the most intimate moment they had shared together. But before the moment could grow and take tangible form, Ben cleared his throat. At least he was still aware of the gravity of the situation.

'Jessie has changed. I think we're ready to go.'

Tony broke away from Anna's enticing gaze, his mind clicking back into focus. 'Right.' He turned to Ben 'There's a thin leather thong in my bag, get it.' He sat down and proceeded to take off one of his veldskoens. When Ben was back, he ordered, 'Okay, you know what to do.' The little man never hesitated and as he crouched in front of Tony who proceeded to tell the girls what was in store for them. Seeing the two pairs of big serious eyes he knew he had their complete attention.

'We're going to hot foot it for the border. It's probably fifteen, twenty miles away, with the Kasane/Nata road being as far from the border as that again. Once at the road we'll have to try and hitch a lift, but if we can't soon after arriving, we won't be hanging around. At most, we've probably only got half a day's head start. And no disrespect,' he looked from Anna to Jessie, 'but Sithole's unit will travel a hell of a lot faster than us.'

Anna could feel her stomach beginning to churn. She knew that once they were on the move it would be better, but she was searching for something, anything, to keep her mind off the gruesome consequences of being caught. 'What are you doing,' she asked, as she looked down at Ben. He was tying the thong tightly around Tony's big and second toes. 'Won't it hurt?'

'Slightly,' he shrugged, 'but that's the point. A trick we used in the war. A good tracker will immediately know if a man he's tracking is injured. He can tell by his prints. This thong won't hinder me much but it will be enough to show in my prints.'

'But why?'

'A good tracker not only has to be able to read signs,' he began to explain, 'but also out-think his prey. I want them to think I'm injured, it may make them sloppy. It's just a ruse, one of many they'll have to contend with along the way. They may be chasing us, but I don't intend for us to run as prey.'

'What happens if we can't get a lift at the road?' Jessie hesitantly asked.

Christ, we may not even make the bloody road, Tony bitterly thought. Jessie, he figured would be fine because of her upbringing, it would be Anna who would slow them down. Without voicing his doubts he tried to quell her fears, 'Plan B, of course. But we'll worry about that if and when the time comes.' He stood up, humped his rucksack on his back, made sure the pistol Ben had given him was firmly tucked into his waistband, and with Anna's dart gun clasped at his side, turned to Ben. 'Okay, burn the clothes, etc.. You've got the FN, so ... I suppose I'll see ya around.'

CHAPTER 68

ANNA COULDN'T BELIEVE it, she'd been working on automatic pilot for ... *God, for how long?* She didn't have a clue. All she knew was that they'd thankfully stopped again. It was dark, cooler, and Tony had allowed her and Jessie to slump down on their backs.

Anna hadn't even been able to ask why Ben had left them; once they were up and moving there was little chance. It was wiser to conserve her energy, concentrate on moving her legs and on what Tony was directing them to do.

Once on the move, the first thing that struck her was the heat. With the baking torch of the fierce Kalahari sun steadily growing higher, it felt as though they were walking into an open furnace. The next thing she realised when she'd actually managed to ask Tony, 'How long before we reach the desert?' and after he'd grunted his reply, 'This is it,' was that the Kalahari wasn't a desert in the true sense of the word. Sure, it was a brown-grey sand they were travelling over, but unlike the Namib or the Sahara there were no naked rolling sand dunes. Instead, the land may have been without any major features, but it was covered with vegetation; scattered grasses, bush, scrub and tree savanna, dotted with the occasional low rocky outcrops.

She had thought the first hour and a half was bad enough. Tony had set out at a cracking pace, and without breaking stride or slackening the tempo, he had directed and shown them where and how to tread. But the next hour leading up to the terrible heat of noon was murder; Tony had forced them to break into a jog, a pace he didn't slacken until it was too hot to move – the burning noon hour.

Feeling exhausted Anna slumped thankfully down beside Jessie under the twisted limbs of an acacia thorn. At least in the shade, and with the cooling evaporation of her sweat-drenched clothes, the surrounding heat was bearable. Tony had briefly inspected and massaged her aching feet and then given them all salt tablets and allowed them to drink. With a whimper she had raised the water bottle to her lips and, with something approaching ecstasy, had drunk – the water from the pan may have been muddy and tainted with animal urine but in that moment it had tasted like nectar. After only a couple of swallows she handed back the water bottle; she'd learnt to conserve each mouthful. The first time she had been allowed to drink, her thirst had taken on a mind of its own. Tony had had to snatch the water bottle away or she would've squandered the lot.

Since setting out her breath had rasped through her throat like sandpaper, while her saliva had turned white and sticky within her mouth, but worst of all it had been the thought of water that plagued her the most. When she'd first asked to drink the only reply Tony had given was, 'Never drink on the first thirst. Otherwise, it'll never slacken.' And sure enough soon after he had snatched the water bottle away it had abated ... for a while.

While they lay in the shade waiting out the fierce midday heat Anna found it was too hot to sleep, but at least the pounding headache she'd had until then had gone. However, all too quickly Tony had them up and either anti-tracking or into their jog again, stopping for only a few brief minutes, the occasional salt tablet and drink every hour.

They had moved like that until well after the last flash of day and when the stark blue of the Kalahari heavens had taken on its blackened night-time shade. Until, finally, Tony had allowed her and Jessie to stop and slump down in the sand on their backs.

If Anna was wrought with disbelief, Tony was doubly so. He couldn't believe her stamina and how quickly she'd picked up and – more importantly – done what she'd been told. He had thought she would be their Achilles' heel; instead, she had performed far in excess of what he'd imagined.

For the first hour and a half Tony had shown the women the basic art of anti-tracking. When Anna had picked it up and appeared to still move freely, he tried a jog and ran them up into the fiery noon hour. He judged it finely; he noticed the few minutes leading up to the stop both girls had begun to tire, the first signs of real fatigue setting in. But the thing that had really impressed him was the discipline she'd shown when he'd given her the water bottle – he'd only had to tell her once.

All throughout the afternoon and evening he'd watched her run, and it was only in the last half-hour that her legs had begun to wobble with fatigue. Also, during the last few times they'd tried to anti-track, he'd seen that both women had left clearly visible signs.

After a quick scout around, now knowing exactly where they were, he walked over and knelt at Anna's head. He lifted it and lay it back down in his lap. As he began to massage her temples, he spoke, 'You, my girl, are extraordinary. It's as if you've got native African blood running through your veins.'

'Hmm,' she murmured before adding, 'not quite African, but similar. And after today, I suppose, thank God I've got it.'

Tony was silent for many moments, he didn't understand. 'What do you mean?'

Anna tilted her head back and looked up into his darkened face. 'What do ya mean, what do you mean?' Surely I told you?' Then she dropped her gaze. 'Yeah, I suppose not. It's just that with what we've been through it feels as though I've known you an eternity.' She lapsed back into a weary silence.

'Come on, get on with it, girl. Spit it out.' Tony was intrigued. 'Oh, I'm part North American Indian: Mohave. The desert's in my blood. The tribe actually still lives along the Colorado River that divides California and Arizona.'

'Good lord, no wonder. I never thought to ask where you got your olive complexion.' It now made sense. 'No, you didn't tell me. Frankly, I was staggered at how you performed today; you even did better than Jessie.'

Anna could feel a surge of energy pulse through her veins. That alone seemed to do more than a full night's rest could've ever done. 'Yeah, and you better watch it, buster, we're an extremely warlike breed – a bloodthirsty lot.'

'Tell me about it,' Tony snorted. 'You think I don't already know?' Some of their past altercations were still fresh in his mind.

Anna would have responded, she was feeling a hell of a lot better but Tony's hands had stilled on her temples. His body had stiffened; she knew his bearing signalled danger.

'Not a word. Pass it on to Jessie.' And before she knew it, he was gone.

As the two women crouched fearfully, it seemed like Tony was away for an eternity. The first thick darkness that preceded the red afterglow of the Kalahari sunset had now abated; the moon had risen and was bathing the scene in a pale-grey gloom, and with the rising of the moon the heat had left. Anna was shivering slightly and it was because of the desert's night-time chill. However, it was Jessie who fearfully gasped and clutched her when two shadowy figures miraculously appeared; intuitively Anna had known it was Tony. She turned from him and greeted the second man. 'Ben you rascal. Where have you been?'

'Just watching our backs.'

Tony could never say what had attracted his attention before leaving Anna's side. However, he was thankful all the same when he recognised Ben's tiny barred owl call. He tucked the pistol away as he returned the call. When Ben reached his side he didn't waste time with pleasantries.

'Well?'

'I don't know. They hadn't turned up before I left.' Ben took a swig of his water bottle. 'I burnt the clothes and everything else we'd left behind, before sweeping clear most of the site.'

'Could you follow the sign we left, easily?'

'I swept the worst of it. During the night and even with this moon they'll have difficulty, but in daylight, well ... no, they'll follow it. I've seen them. Sithole's trackers are good.'

'Damn!' However, it was as Tony expected.

'But hell, I must say I'm surprised, it's Jessie's prints that show up the most.'

'Yeah, we've got a woman with hidden talents, come on we better get back to them.'

'Now what?' Anna asked once she was at Tony's side.

'Time to try and catch a lift.'

He turned without further comment and within twenty yards they all stepped from the Kalahari's scattered bush onto the first sign of civilisation Anna had seen since leaving the Mitswin Pan. They were standing at the white verge of an endlessly stretching tar-sealed road.

'You mean we were that close?' Anna said in disbelief, 'I never heard any traffic.'

'Yeah, and don't expect to see any either. Not at this time of year.'

Tony didn't risk waiting beside the road. Instead, he used its sealed surface to throw off Sithole's trackers. He knew Nata was about seventy-five miles south, but rather than heading in that direction he headed north – he had decided they would try for Kasane.

After a nervous twenty minutes on the road with still no sign of traffic he decided to head further into the Kalahari and forge up into the Chobe National Park. Although he didn't hold out much hope of success, they'd try to pick up one of the tourist routes and catch a ride either down to Muan or up to Kasane.

As they carefully stepped from the road – all prospect of going after Donovan now gone – he considered Anna's growing aptitude for travel in the sandveld. *Maybe, just maybe, we've got a fighting chance, after all.*

Tony, with Ben bringing up the rear, pushed the women hard for the next half-hour further into the desert. Finally, with Anna and Jessie nearing exhaustion, they stopped for the remainder of the night at a low rocky outcrop, partially screened by a smattering of stunned acacia thorns.

Ben, with one of the thermal blankets, had discreetly taken Jessie away and left Tony and Anna on their own. They were in a small sandy-floored basin surrounded by a wall of rocks.

After taking off the leather thong from around his toes, despite the trek Tony found he couldn't sleep. He was sitting with his back up against a rock staring out into the darkness. Anna was stretched out under the other thermal blanket on the basin's floor. She had her head in his lap and he thought she was asleep.

'What are you thinking about?' Her quiet voice roused him.

He snorted softly, 'Another time, another war.'

'Did you used to fight like this?'

'That's how Ben and I learnt. Jesus, it's probably the only thing we're good at.'

'I doubt it.'

Tony wasn't listening. 'Do you know you ran over the equivalent of a full marathon today?'

'And I swore the first one I did would be my last.' She changed the subject; she didn't want to think about the predicament they were in. 'What else were you thinking about?'

Tony didn't hesitate, 'You,' and Anna could hear the tremor of passion in his voice.

'I believe earlier today you had a wish?'

'A hope, actually,' he corrected her as he lifted her head and slid down beside her.

After throwing off the blanket, now lying on her back looking up at Tony through flaming passionate eyes, Anna reached up and tangled her fingers into the hair at the nape of his neck. She'd found a man she could truly respect, yet with the dreadful looming prospect of losing him before they'd had a chance to really be together.

'Tony, I want to forget about tomorrow. Help me, please. I want tonight to be one I can cherish.' She drew his head down so she could reach his lips.

Although Tony could feel a hungering for her welling up from within, he knew that because of her tiredness he'd have to be unhurried and gentle. As their lips touched he realised his hunger had been replaced by a deep and eager craving. Long, slow and probing they kissed; he could sense her need but chose to draw out their pleasure. He broke away and kissed her graceful neck and heard her sigh a contented moan.

As she threw back her head to allow him to kiss down her throat, he began to undo the buttons on her shirt. Finally throwing it open he was greeted, illuminated under the light of the silvery moon, by her two proud neatly formed breasts, topped by pert fiercely erect darkened nipples. It was he this time who breathed out softly in yearning as he slowly lowered his head.

The tiredness Anna felt seemed to intensify the aching pleasure she began to feel. The slow and gentle kiss sparked a smouldering glow, then his lips on her throat fanned the ardent flames, and as she felt her shirt thrown open she hollowed her back and raised her chest. 'Yes, like that,' she breathed. His tongue twirling around her nipple had ignited a furnace within.

As he nibbled and caressed each nipple, Anna could feel his hand smooth down her flat stomach; its hardened, calloused touch intensified her weary pleasure. He eventually reached the belt and waistband of her shorts. To help him she sucked in her belly and lifted her buttocks. He skilfully flicked open the belt, popped the buttons of the fly, and in one gentle movement pulled off her shorts and knickers. His next tender stroke had her sighing again, tilting her hips and parting her legs with need.

Tony was now fully aroused, his lust blazing fiercely within his groin. He heard her sigh as he lightly ran his fingers through her silky smooth raven V of pubic hair, to finally rest them over her sex. He parted the supple folds of skin and felt her moistness, as well as sensing her incredible yearning. While he lowered his lips to her breasts again, his fingers lingered at her groin, soothing, massaging, probing – this time he heard her moan.

'Tony, please now. But I want your skin against mine.' He pulled off his shorts and shirt. 'Quickly, please.' She had seen his full and hardened arousal, which intensified her own firing lust. He came over her; she tilted her hips further to meet him and as she felt him enter she opened her mouth to shudder a breathless stifled moan. Her weariness fell away as she rode with him the gentle waves of pleasure. With each slow luxurious stroke, she felt him strong and vibrant, equalling her own yearning thirst of passion. Wave upon sensual wave they rode together.

Tony felt invincible, powerful beyond belief, controlled by an absorbing force he and Anna had helped create, which had now taken on a life of its own. He voyaged through a sea of rolling passion, meeting and eventually surpassing each consuming wave, to finally float and drift with Anna through a tranquil expanse of glowing sensual warmth.

Floating, drifting and peaceful, in that special moment Anna's world was now complete. She looked up into Tony's smiling eyes and when they finally found their focus, she reached up and kissed him on the lips. She sunk back down with a contented sigh, knowing never before had she experienced such absorbing pleasure. With twinkling eyes and a tired but happy lopsided grin she found she had to declare, 'I can say with certainty, there is definitely something else you're good at.'

CHAPTER 69

UNLIKE TONY AND his small band of fugitives, Sithole and Bogatin were traveling in comparative luxury. Once at the Mitswin Pan, Sithole immediately sent a Land Rover and a stick of four men south to sweep the sandveld from Nata north. Also, as a precautionary measure he'd already done the same up north; a unit of four men was working down from Kasane. With two Land Rovers, his two best trackers and the remainder of his men he set off into the Kalahari. He used similar methods to those Tony and Ben would have used when running down poachers spoor, the V formation; one tracker at the point with three others fanned out either side in case of ambush.

Although Sithole hadn't fought against Tony during Zimbabwe's war of independence, he'd heard of his reputation and didn't put it past him to do the unexpected. So not only did he change his running men every hour, but also ensured he, Bogatin and the resting men were well back from the hunt. He'd emphasised, 'If contact is made, radio back and detain or follow from a distance.' His men knew what to expect if his orders weren't followed.

Using these techniques he had made the border by nightfall. There had been an hour and a half's wait before the moon had risen, and then by using some heavy-handed diplomacy, tempered by a certain degree of frustrated patience, his trackers had finally followed the spoor through to the Nata/ Kasane road by dawn.

It was a cloudless morning; the air was fresh — contrary to the fire the day would bring — and it wasn't fully light when Sithole stopped his Land Rover just beyond the road. With Bogatin at his side he walked up to the tracker squatting down beside its tar-sealed surface.

'Well?'

The tracker, a small wiry man, made a loud hoick in his throat and spat with disdain on the ground by the tracks. 'They have made far more ground than expected. With his injury Campbell, as well as the white woman, have moved well. They arrived here, perhaps, an hour or two after dark.'

'Damn!' Sithole smacked the swagger stick he carried against his leg. 'Any sign of them being picked up?'

The tracker shrugged, slightly perturbed. 'I can't tell.' Even he knew he wasn't that good.

Sithole turned to the Russian. 'It appears they may have got away.'

Bogatin stared at him from beneath hooded eyes. In the fifteen-odd hours they had been together they had exchanged less than a dozen words, and the Russian chose not to add to the meagre tally; his bearing spoke louder than anything he could've said.

'But of course my men will check.' Sithole stated contemptuously. He had grown an intense dislike for the Russian and his silent manner.

He first ordered both his tracking teams to sweep north and south along the opposite side of the road, before radioing through to his two other units to check at both Nata and Kasane. Within half an hour the first radio message came through from Nata – it was negative. There had been little traffic, and what there was had been through that morning and stopped at the settlement's garage; there had been no hitchhikers picked up. It was another long thirty minutes before the next message came through. This was from Kasane and also negative. All Sithole heard was there had been only southbound traffic. Then, an excited voice called for a radio break. It was his tracking team sweeping north along the road.

'Spoor found, three miles north. Well concealed, but heading north-west.' Ben's night-vision had missed the briefest smudge on the road's whitened verge allowing Sithole's team to pick up their trail.

Although he didn't want to, Tony roused Anna well before dawn and was heartened by how fresh she looked once she was up and dressed.

'Same as yesterday I suppose?' she asked. Surprisingly, the prospect didn't seem that daunting. Their lovemaking and the few hours of sleep had further galvanised her resolve.

'I'm afraid so.'

'God,' she exaggerated a groan, 'and I haven't had a chance to carbo-load.'

It was then Tony realised she'd been holding out on him. From his experience only serious athletes knew about and used the term freely. 'Okay, hot-shot. We'll see how far you can run today.'

As he went to awaken Ben and Jessie he found his spirits had risen again.

After reapplying the leather thong, using the same procedure as the day before, Tony, Anna and Jessie had gone forward on their own and left Ben to cover their rear. Every hour they rested and every second hour they anti-tracked for about twenty minutes. It was after noon and the sun was standing high above in the far blue heavens, while the temperature had soared to the extreme, causing the harsh desert earth to send wafting heat hazes up into the sky. Tony was looking for a suitable place to rest out the hottest midday hour. He had spotted a tall acacia thorn shimmering in the distance. However, before he could veer off towards it he stopped abruptly. Anna ran headlong into his back.

'What? What is it?' she thrust aside the numbness that had taken over her mind.

'Shhh,' Tony silenced her with a raised hand. In the ensuing silence he felt more than heard what had attracted his attention; a vibrating concussion carried on the air. Tony's spirits slumped. 'Damn, gunfire!'

He turned and slumped to the ground. As he untied the leather thong he said, 'There'll be no midday stop.' He looked up at the sun. Probably five hours to dark. It was their only chance. 'Right, do as I do, step where I step.' He got up. 'We've got a hard afternoon ahead.'

For the next hour they anti-tracked. It was nowhere near perfect and he hoped to God that Ben had survived his altercation and could cover up any mistakes. After an hour of stepping from one clump of grass to the next, crawling under low slung thorn-bushes and twisting, turning and crisscrossing over their hidden line of spoor, he put Anna at the point and Jessie in the middle, while he brought up the rear. He pointed to the heat distorted horizon, 'Run,' he ordered, 'I'll tell you when to stop.'

It was just on dusk. For three and a half-hours Tony had had the women running with only intermittent stops. Half an hour earlier he'd noticed Jessie's legs flop and splay to the sides with fatigue and now Anna's were doing the same. He saw a small outcrop of rock amongst the scrub up ahead and out to the right. 'Anna, to the rocks, you're stopping for the night.'

Tony found a niche to conceal the women. 'Drink, salt tablets, then try and rest. I'll be back when I can.' He took off his rucksack and gave it and the dart-gun to Anna. 'It's not much, but if you have to, use it. You know how?'

With solemn eyes she curtly nodded before stepping forward and briefly hugging herself to his chest. She was trying to think of something to say, but before she could, Tony broke the embrace, grabbed a water bottle and was running back the way they'd come.

By himself Tony was able to stretch out his legs; he'd been chaffing at the bit running behind the women. Although they had done far better than he had ever imagined they could, it was still only just over half the speed he was used to when running on any kind of spoor; sixty, seventy miles a day had been common during the war. But notwithstanding the exertion that had been expended, and the distances the women had travelled, their biggest problem was their meagre supply of water and the desperate need they had for food; without either they were doomed.

With all his senses focused he had been running for about an hour when he found himself diving to the side. A minute later, after recognising Ben's call of the barred owl, he was reunited with his friend.

'I take it that was Sithole?'

'No, the bastard was nowhere to be seen. Just his goons.'

'Okay, what happened?'

'They found where we'd left the road at about seven thirty and where we'd slept by nine. For the next three hours I watched his trackers work. There were two of them, an hour on, an hour off.' He shook his head in disgust and took a swig from his water bottle. 'Every sign you left that I covered they soon unravelled.'

'What about the gunfire? Did they spot you?'

Ben took on a wounded look. 'Don't be silly. At the rate they were going, three more hours and it would've been over. I waited until the tracking crews were swapping. The leather thong had obviously done its trick. Christ, they were bloody careless, they never even put out a guard – I shafted both trackers.'

'Yeah, and?' Tony urgently asked.

'Killed one outright and shot the other through the guts, then I ran for it. I found where you'd anti-tracked, covered what I could and waited. It must have taken a couple of hours for a new tracker to be brought up; he's not as good and was still trying to unravel the sign when I left.'

'Where will they be now?' Tony was trying to form a plan.

Ben shrugged. 'Still trying to unravel the spoor or just this side of it.'

'Right, this is what we're going to do.'

'The bastard!' Sithole's full rage was directed at Tony; he had just arrived and parked his Land Rover at the scene where Ben had shot his trackers. He was standing, fuming beside the dead one still lying shot where he lay. He desperately needed something to vent his anger, so lashing out he kicked the prone figure and gained a measure of satisfaction as his boot staved in the dead man's ribs. But it still wasn't enough to abate his growing fury.

'Oh, Christ, bury him!' he bawled at his cowering men, 'And do something with him.' He pointed an irritated finger at the wounded man slumped beneath a nearby tree and then angrily strode back to his vehicle. He knew once he'd radioed his other units it would be at least a couple of hours before he'd have another tracker on the spoor, and what's more, he instinctively knew it wouldn't be the last he'd be hearing of Tony before the night was through.

'Huh, so much for that, my grandmother could have unravelled it,' the new tracker stated emphatically to himself. It was well after dust, the moon was up and he'd found Anna, Jessie and Tony's out-going spoor heading into the northwest.

In reality, he hadn't unravelled the confusion of hidden signs and prints at all; he'd been totally bamboozled and only by chance had blundered onto their outgoing tracks. He gave a curt order and got his four out-runners to form up in their running V – to conserve his men Sithole had cut-back the numbers directly involved in the hunt.

Within a minute the tracker was running with his head down along the well-defined line of spoor. He had just noticed something was different about Tony's prints and was thinking of inspecting them closer. Those thoughts and most else left his head as a carefully aimed shot crashed out. He died with half his skull blown away.

Simultaneously, from the opposite flank a raking volley of automatic fire riddled the remaining men. All four fell to the ground; two returned fire, the others lay unmoving. They hadn't run into an ambush, they had run past one and were being fired on from behind.

From their muzzle flashes Tony marked the position of the two remaining men. His ploy had worked. As he shot the tracker, Ben's continuous rattling volley had drawn the remaining soldiers' fire. Working with the surprise he still commanded, Tony was up and running, charging their position. Twenty yards, fifteen, ten, and then holding the pistol double-handed, stretched out in front of him, with only five yards remaining he opened up. The first man died not realising what had happened; the second as he turned with a bullet between the eyes.

Within seconds of the charge Ben was at his side. 'Grab a rifle. What sort is it?'

'Another FN.'

'Good,' he dropped the pistol on the ground. 'Right, their water bottles, whatever rations they're carrying and fill up your webbing belt,' Tony had already knelt and was yanking a belt off one of the dead soldiers. 'Then we'd better gap it. Company'll be due any minute.'

Sure enough for a few brief seconds as they ran to the northwest, they began receiving heavy fire. But as they ran, crouched over, jinking and swerving from side to side, as quickly as it had started it stopped. What puzzled Tony was he was sure the firing had ceased after a curtly bellowed order. He didn't let the thought worry him; he had their next ambush to plan.

CHAPTER 70

TWICE MORE, UNDER the protective cloak of darkness, Tony and Ben set and sprung an ambush, both times with slight success; one down and one injured. After each altercation Tony couldn't believe the luck they'd had, escaping without a scratch. However, shortly after they had broken the second time the awful truth came crashing home.

'Christ, they want us alive!' Without further thought of setting another ambush, like men possessed, he and Ben headed for a distant outcrop of rocks.

Sithole had never felt so frustrated, he'd anticipated Tony and Ben's line of retreat and almost exactly pinpointed the positions of their ambushes; he knew they were heading northwest, into the Chobe National Park. Being on foreign soil he couldn't afford a prolonged and drawn out chase or to have his men make anymore-costly mistakes. Throwing caution to the wind he brought up all his men, bar one small stick, and put them to the spoor. Knowing the woman weren't with them, he reasoned it would only be a matter of time before they were reunited and be forced to either break and run or dig in and make a stand. With his superior numbers, he felt confident he would have them within the next twelve hours.

'It will be soon now; they will be with the women before first-light.' It was Bogatin who spoke. He was staring sightlessly through the Land Rover's windscreen out into the morning's strengthening light and they were his first words for many hours. 'I can feel it. We will have them soon.'

Sithole immediately realised he'd mistaken the Russian's silent demeanour for a lack of interest in the hunt. As he swivelled in his seat to face him he saw for the first time his eyes were alive, sparkling with a murderous sheen. In that moment Sithole recognised he was a man who had hunted often, the same prey as that now being chased. Despite the abhorrence he felt for the man, he could feel his empathy growing.

'Yes, it will be soon.'

As if realising for the first time he wasn't alone, Bogatin slowly rotated his head and looked Sithole full in the eyes. The murderous sheen was gone to be replaced with open contempt – his look spoke louder than any words.

The Captain had heard Russians were racist and he knew beyond the shadow of a doubt he was sitting in front of one of the biggest of them all. If it weren't for Donovan's protection he knew at that moment if he'd been able he could have killed him outright and left the bastard to rot in the desert.

Thrusting aside his bitterness, he reached over the back of his seat and retrieved a brown manila envelope, thrusting it at the Russian. With casual disregard he said, 'Your employer will be interested in these.' Once Bogatin had flicked on the cabin's courtesy light and pulled out the envelope's contents his interest quickened and he recognised a startled expression skip across the man's usually impassive face.

'Good God! This man, are you sure he's the one who met Campbell at Victoria Falls?' Like a stack of dominoes a whole sequence of events tumbled into place.

'Positive.'

'God, he's the one I saw in the car park with the other two, just after the break in. Donovan must be told,' Bogatin voiced out-loud, but to himself. He was looking at a photo of Richard Black, and he knew it was the fourth time he'd popped up in as many different places, one; dining with Sabina at Malibu, two; at the Bel Air, three; as was identified here in Zimbabwe, and four; he now clearly remembered seeing his side-on profile walking out of the tower block's carpark at the time he was alerted to the break in. Still holding the photo he turned back to Sithole and commanded, 'This Campbell, describe him.'

Sithole's intrigue made him disregard the pretentious manner of the Russian's request. 'I'll do one better.' He reached over and retrieved another manila folder. 'Here's his file.'

Extracting the contents, Bogatin was presented with another photograph of a man he knew he'd never seen before: it was a head and shoulders view of Tony. 'Damn, he wasn't at the break-in at all. It has been this other bastard all along. He must have set it up,' he picked up Richard's photo. 'Sabina, the little bitch.'

Sithole's intrigue had turned to fascination, he couldn't contain himself, 'Who's been set up?' He craned his neck and looked at Richard's photograph. 'What break in? And who the hell is Sabina?'

Bogatin ignored the questions and instead demanded, 'I must speak to Mr Donovan, now. It's imperative.'

The curt rebuff was like a harsh slap across the face, 'Impossible,' Sithole, just as abruptly discarded the request. But before Bogatin could argue the radio squawked. As they were on foreign soil there was no call sign and the message was brief.

We have them, pinned down. Our line of spoor will lead directly to them. The message was repeated once before the radio fell silent.

'You can wait and tell him personally. The radio is not to be used, especially not now.'

Even if Bogatin tried to respond Sithole wasn't listening, he'd reach for the Land Rover's ignition and turned it on; this part of the hunt he definitely wanted to be involved in.

Tony and Ben reached the girls in the darkness just before dawn. They hadn't moved from the niche and it was clear neither, despite the previous day's exertions, had slept little if at all; it wasn't a gladdening sight.

Both women's relief was evident but with fearful eyes locked on Tony's face, Anna said, 'Throughout the night we heard gunshots ... we thought ...' She didn't finish.

'Come on, only dogs worry and they get shot,' Tony tried to lighten the mood. 'Now finish your water we've ah ... acquired some more. Plus I've got a couple of presents for you both.' He produced four high-energy chocolate bars and his words and the gifts had the desired effect. Tony witnessed a pathetic sight as both girls hesitantly reached out their hands.

'Food,' they uttered in harmony.

'Yes, and I'd eat them now before the sun comes up. As you can see, they've already melted several times.' While they were distracted he hurried on; it was best to get them moving before they realised the full extent of the trouble they were in. 'Right, you can eat those on the run.'

However, before they had run half a mile they ran into the small stick Sithole hadn't included in with his main body of men. The Captain had sent it to circle in front of them to intercept their anticipated line of flight; the soldiers had set up a skirmish line and cut off their escape. Several minutes later they found themselves scrambling back into their rocky outcrop.

'God damn it, they're everywhere!'

Because of the lie of the rocks Tony and Ben had to split up; it was too exposed at the top to try to hold their position from there. Tony was around one side with the women cowering at his feet, while Ben was around the other side defending it himself. They were now surrounded, but the worst part of all was the scrub was thicker than usual leading up to the outcrop; it helped hide the surrounding Shona.

As it was now fully light and several hours after dawn, from his slightly elevated position, Tony could see out in the distance. Well out of rifle range and on another slight rise, was an army Land Rover with a man dressed in camouflaged fatigues standing on its roof. He knew it was Sithole, and with the occasional glint of sunlight reflecting off glass he realised bitterly that the bastard was directing his troops with a pair of binoculars pressed to his eyes. Every few minutes the figure reached down and spoke into a radio at his feet.

What had puzzled him when he'd first spotted the Land Rover was that there were two men on the roof, but as he was dressed in a tan safari suit, he knew the second man wasn't one of Sithole's soldiers. The man was gone now so he didn't let the thought concern him further.

There was a lapse in the incessant rifle fire that had peppered the rocks above Tony's head; Sithole was obviously repositioning his troops. Tony looked down into Anna's frightened eyes.

Although terrified, when she spoke, she sounded remarkably calm. 'We're going to die aren't we?'

'Of old age and together if I've got anything to do with it,' Tony responded, yet without conviction. Although the soldiers below were shooting to miss, if they couldn't hold out until dark they'd be overrun for sure and he didn't know which was worse – dying now or waiting for an uncertain fate.

'But seriously, it can't be long now. Twice already they've nearly succeeded.'

Yes, Tony thought to himself, waiting for nightfall was like a distant dream. Anna was right. He'd only just managed to fend off the two previous concerted attacks. Many more like those and it would be a different story. However, this time as he held her gaze he spoke with conviction, 'All I know is, for some reason, they want us alive. And because of it, we'll always have a chance.'

He would have reached down and laid a reassuring hand on her face, but he heard Ben's urgent call, it was his belly whistle snort of a reed buck. Tony knew he wouldn't have called if it wasn't critical, it told him Ben needed help, and quickly

'*Bugger!*' He wished to Christ that he hadn't dropped the pistol. He picked up the dart-gun at his feet, it was pathetically inadequate but it was all he could leave with the girls. 'It's loaded and ready to fire. Shoot at anything that moves and then scream blue bloody murder.'

This time Anna's voice quaked with fear, '*No Tony, don't leave!*'

'I have to,' he said, and before she could plead again he was gone.

'What is it?' Tony had dived in at Ben's feet.

'They must be all out here in front. There can't be any over your side. Two groups, either side and one in the middle.' He pointed.

'Shit, they're going to try and storm us. How much ammo?'

'Plenty, but the bitch keeps jamming.' Ben was using the semiautomatic they had retrieved after their first ambush. 'What about you?'

'No I'll need ... oh, shit, here we go!'

All at once, all three groups of Sithole's men came charging from their different positions. Tony and Ben were up and firing and both sets of troops faltered under their incessant hail of bullets. One more blast and his would be forced to make a hasty retreat. He pressed the trigger and, *Oh, Christ*, the FN clicked empty. Frantically reaching for another clip, he risked a look at Ben.

Ben's group, with one killed and another hobbling, were already turning back. He switched his aim to the central group, fired one round and heard his rifle clunk – it had jammed. Madly trying to re-cock the weapon he soon realised his actions were hopeless; the middle group was storming up the rocks. Reversing the rifle, he stood and began heaving it like a club. His first swing collected a soldier in the temple, the second the side of another one's ribs then thankfully he heard Tony's FN open up.

Ramming home the magazine, Tony didn't have to aim. Looming up just in front of him was a Shona poised ready to pounce. The first bullet caught him in his stomach, and the second in the middle of his chest. He stood and shot one handed to the right, wounding another Shona in the leg while using his other arm to fend off a rifle butt aimed at his head. The blow glanced off his forearm and he would've easily over-powered the man, before turning to shaft those soldiers Ben was just managing to keep at bay. He knew they had a chance if they could stifle this attack. With the few fit soldiers left, they could easily hold out until dark. However, as soon as the thought began to form it was snatched from his mind and with it went all his reason. From behind him he heard a woman's terrified scream. He dropped his guard and turned. 'Anna!' he bellowed in anguish before collecting a meaty whack to his head and falling unconscious to the ground.

'What was that? It wasn't a soldier?' Anna queried fearfully. She was sure she'd seen somebody dart out to the side, yet she knew it wasn't a camouflaged strip she'd seen.

'Maybe it was Tony or Ben,' came Jessie's equally fearful reply.

Anna knew that with the rifle fire behind, it couldn't possibly be them. With her finger curled around the dart-gun's trigger she scanned the bush in front of her as she tucked the rifle's butt up under her arm. She hoped to God she didn't have to use it. Even with all she'd been through she still didn't know if she could shoot at another human being. As she swept her gaze to the left, a blur of movement caught her eye. Swinging the rifle to cover that flank she saw a rock land on the sandy soil and tumble away.

'Anna, look out!' Jessie gasped.

The rock had been a ruse.

She swung back to the right and screamed in terror. 'Ahh!' Thrusting the dart-gun forward, she breathed in trepidation, 'No, you're supposed to be dead.'

Bogatin had to concede, 'This time the black monkey has got it right.' As he threw the rock he knew the women were alone, so maybe after all he would have his way with the raven-haired bitch. As he touched the furrowed scab on his head, he callously thought, *Yes, you'll truly pay.*

As the rock landed and began to tumble, he moved and darted towards the women. He displayed far more speed and stealth than his squat form suggested he was capable of. He was nearly up and on top of the girls before they knew he was coming; however, he hadn't anticipated the speed the Hagan woman showed. As she screamed and brought the rifle to bear, he stopped to stand stock-still on the edge of their rocky niche. He then heard her fearfully exclaim, 'No, you're supposed to be dead.'

As both girls cowered back up against the rocks, moving only his eyes, he first studied the rifle. Looking at its magazine he realised immediately it was only a .22. Then looking at the size and reconstruction of the over-sized barrel, he saw it had been modified. Why and what for he didn't know or really care, but instinct told him the rifle was more harmless than it seemed. Yet when he looked into Anna huge round fearful eyes, it was then he laughed and deliberately stepped down into their niche.

Initially, Anna couldn't respond; it was like the poachers in Tsavo East all over again. *No, I can't shoot another human being.* She was petrified, scared stiff as a board. This time she intuitively knew Tony wouldn't be coming to help; Bogatin would have his sordid way. He stepped forward a pace.

'You couldn't hurt a fly. Like your father and roommate before you ..' menacingly Bogatin took another pace, 'you're mine.'

His words made something snap deep within and Anna's fear dissolved to be replaced with a cold and all-consuming loathing. She raised the rifle and as her finger pressed against the trigger she could see the Russian had read her change in mood. 'You bastard!' She pulled the trigger.

There was a crack, followed by an almighty welt as Bogatin was forced to stumble backwards. The dart had flown straight and true, embedding itself in the middle of his sternum. Dumbly, he gaped down at the flighted projectile sticking out of his chest as he felt a cold liquid sensation beneath his skin, and then ... nothing, nothing happened. Reaching up he plucked out the dart and tossing it away he began to chuckle. 'This time you are truly mine.'

CHAPTER 71

BOGATIN'S ONLY MEMORY after plucking the dart from his chest was walking forward to stand over the two cowering women, then his vision blurred, his head began to spin, and he collapsed. The dose of tranquilising drug, M99 that he had taken in his chest was potent enough to stun a five hundred-pound lion so it left him virtually comatose on the ground.

He drifted in and out of consciousness, on the brink of suffering complete paralysis. He remembered soldiers roughly grabbing the two women and wanted to tell them to leave the white woman for him, but he couldn't move a muscle let alone speak. However, during the periods when he was able to assimilate his thoughts, above all else he experienced was wave upon agonising wave of pain within his chest and back that the massive dosage of M99 had caused.

His muscles gripped, spasming with a mind of their own. Then briefly came sheer and utter relief as each spasm subsided, only to be replaced by the clenching talons yet again. With each rasping breath his mind lurched as the harrowing torture took hold once again. The only reality at that time was all-consuming pain.

Pain had become his master as weakness filled his mind, for he could gain no respite from the devil that now lurked within. Nothing helped; nothing quenched the clutching, seizing pain.

He felt wave upon fluid wave of agony washing over his body, its evil waters lapping, bathing, drenching him in the absorbing pangs of pain, while playing games with his reeling, lurching mind. Then finally it passed, leaving again the throbbing ache of relief, yet to soon be replaced with the dread, the knowledge it would soon return.

But this time as the fingers of the living monster began to whisper down his spine, he had no time to think, no time to act, for as it began to roar its silent jealous rage, he gratefully felt the enveloping darkness taking hold instead. He finally experienced peace as he tumbled down into a darkened, smothering pit of gloom.

Bogatin never knew how long he rode the pain or wallowed in his world of darkness, yet there was one particularly lucid period when he was rolled upon his back by that black monkey and his men. He could even recall the words that Sithole had said, but in his lethargic drug-induced state, though they seemed important, he couldn't comprehend their meaning.

'We will leave the racist white bastard; he's already as good as dead. I'll tell Donovan that Campbell killed him during the fighting.'

Then Bogatin had been left alone.

As he opened his eyes he realised, although he still couldn't move a muscle the pain had gone and he could think coherently; his mind now clear. The next thing he knew he could hear a melee of fluttering and a great disruption of air. Swivelling his eyes, in horror he saw a line of vultures settling on the rocky crest above him. He wanted to shout at them to leave but couldn't form or voice the words. In terror he saw them looking, not into, but down at his eyes.

In that brief moment the scores of people he'd brutally killed flashed through his mind. They were laughing as they stared out at him through gaping empty sockets, while extended in their hands were their eyes he'd sadistically hooked out and squashed.

Finally, his vision cleared as one huge white-backed vulture fluttered down from its perch. It was probably a coincidence, but as Bogatin's mind lurched in terror he reasoned the bird was an instrument of revenge as it hopped over and began to peck out his eyes.

CHAPTER 72

Chobe National Park, Botswana

PETER COULDN'T BELIEVE the change in Donovan. It had seemed like an eternity since he'd last acted and spoken in his usual deliberate manner. Ever since Bogatin had arrived in Tanzania. *But now, thank God, he's back to normal.*

Peter was driving the safari Land Rover, with Donovan in the passenger's seat opposite, while Sithole's sergeant was in the back. It was nearing midday, and after an hour's traveling they had left the beautifully decorated Moorish-style Chobe Game Lodge far behind. First, by traveling along well-defined tracks beside the Chobe River, then, by weaving through thick savanna-type woodlands still near the water's edge, they found they were still within the National Park but now well away from any of its regular tourist's haunts.

Donovan lightly rubbed his hands together. 'How much longer?' he asked excitedly. The reason they'd left the lodge was because the sergeant had received a coded message from Captain Sithole. It had briefly stated that Tony and his small band of fugitives had been captured, and it had given the coordinates for a rendezvous.

Peter briefly consulted a map on the seat beside him. 'Shouldn't be long now.' He was weaving up a gentle incline through an open forest of mopane trees, 'Just over the rise.'

'So he has them at last. I was beginning to wonder.' Peter would have agreed, they had reached the top of the rise and the edge of the trees, but was prevented from speaking as Donovan breathed, 'Good God!' in complete and utter wonder.

They came to a stop on the verge of an open plain; it seemed to stretch forever into the west. It was fringed on one side by riverine vegetation that lined the Chobe River and on the other, by green and brown shaded woodlands that swept to the south. Both men were now gawking out across the plain at an astonishing array of wildlife like neither had seen before. But what really captured their attention was the hundreds of peacefully feeding elephants that littered the golden grassy plain.

Like his great-grandfather before him, virtually on the same spot, Donovan's wonder turned to jubilation; he had never seen so many elephants congregated in one place. As he turned to Peter his words may have been similar to the ones spoken all those years ago. They avidly portrayed the misconception that over a century of slaughter had caused.

'Look at all those elephants; we could go on poaching ivory forever.'

Peter nodded in agreement. 'Yes, as our forefathers must have experienced, with herds like these, there will always be elephants for the taking.'

Donovan nodded in agreement before he stilled all movement. 'Did you bring the rifle?' he urgently asked. It was clear he was excited. While in Africa, if a decent trophy appeared he wasn't above doing a spot of poaching himself.

'Yes. It's concealed beneath the back seat as you asked,' Peter stated as he tried to see what had attracted Donovan's attention.

'Good. And the park rangers?'

'It's been taken care of. I have a man who works for the Department of Wildlife and National Parks. We won't be disturbed.' It was then that he saw what had triggered Donovan's excitement.

From the trees two elephant bulls had emerged from the forest to their left. One had big enough tusks but the second, he carried a set unlike any Peter had ever seen in the wilds. The tusks weren't nearly as big as those taken nearby over a hundred years before, but by today's standards the bull that carried them was obviously one of the continent's last living treasures.

With callous disregard to the heritage he was about to try and destroy, Donovan ordered, 'Get the rifle, I'll take them both. We'll leave the sergeant here; he can bring up the Land Rover when it's done.'

Believing they were protected within the sanctuary offered by the park, it was comparatively easy for Peter to lead Donovan up to within fifty yards of the two peacefully feeding bulls. As he brought up the rifle, a Weatherby .460 Safari, and peered into its telescopic sights he didn't bother to conceal his position. Unlike his great-grandfather he wasn't a hunter or marksman; he killed for neither passion nor need. His motive was solely to quench his lust for ivory. He pulled the trigger.

'Damn!' He'd only wounded the beast with an ineffective shot and it staggered backwards to stare down at him in total disbelief.

Another shot crashed out, then another. Each found their mark but as they were fired blindly they never killed the bull. But by this time it knew Donovan was its aggressor and was wheeling away, back to the protection offered by the forest.

Another shot barked out to reverberate across the open plain. The elephant flinched and hunched his back but not before it was swallowed by the trees.

'Damn!' Donovan bitterly cursed again as the bull disappeared. He switched his aim and snapped off a shot at the other rapidly retreating bull hot on the heels of its companion. The shot crashed out. It had been a reflex shot and a total fluke; the bullet rammed into and severed the elephant's spine.

By the time Donovan had walked the fifty yards to the spot where both elephants had been, the wounded bull in a pathetic show of courage had dragged itself around and, with its back legs splayed awkwardly to the side, it was trying to rise and charge. As it trumpeted in vehement anger and violently bucked its head, Donovan showed no remorse or pity. The only reason he was so quick in dispatching the beast was so it couldn't damage its tusks.

Peter was at his side when the elephant finally collapsed lifeless to the ground. 'Pity about the other one.' He tried to gloss over the macabre display he'd witnessed.

Donovan shrugged disinterestedly, not considering the wounds and pain he had inflicted. 'This one'll do.' He changed the subject. 'Signal the sergeant. While we wait, he can cut out the ivory. Sithole and his friends can't be too far away.'

CHAPTER 73

TONY REGAINED CONSCIOUSNESS as he was being bundled into the back of one of Sithole's Land Rovers. He landed unceremoniously beside Ben on the hard metal floor – the two soldiers who had thrown him in took up station on the padded bench-seats either side to guard them. It was then that it came crashing back to mind. *Oh Jesus, the firefight, the Shonas charging up the rocks and ... nothing. Christ, I took a sucker-punch.* Then suddenly he remembered Anna's scream. He looked over at his friend – what he saw wasn't a pretty sight.

Like Tony's, Ben's feet were tied as well as his hands behind his back. He was lying on his side, his eyes were closed and Tony could see he'd taken a terrible beating. One eyebrow was cut and the eye was badly swollen; his nose looked broken and he had a huge fat lip. All Tony could feel was the lump on his head and where somebody had obviously kicked him in the ribs. He'd gotten off lightly compared to his friend.

'Ssst,' he hissed. Ben's good eye popped open. 'The girls?' he whispered.

Ben lightly nodded and whispered back, 'They're fine, Sithole's Land Rover.'

'Hey!' barked a soldier, 'No talking.' Ben received a rifle butt in the stomach for his trouble.

As Tony watched his friend wheezing, struggling to regain his breath, he thought it best to wait out in silence wherever they were going. At least he knew Anna was safe, so he closed his eyes and waited. He estimated it was about three hours before they stopped.

'Ah, Captain, so you eventually caught them. Well done.'

Sithole's two remaining Land Rovers (he'd already sent the others back to Zimbabwe) had just pulled up beside the elephant Donovan had shot. Donovan and Peter had come over to greet them, leaving the sergeant to finish hacking out the elephant's tusks.

'Eventually, yes,' Sithole addressed Donovan, alighting from the vehicle, 'but at a cost. Because they were needed alive I lost ten of my men, good men, five also wounded.'

Donovan shrugged dispassionately, 'A small price to prevent us from being exposed.'

However, Sithole wasn't finished. 'The Russian, he is also dead.' Donovan lost his nonchalance; Nikolai had been an integral part of his business, his anger immediately flared.

'Oh, Christ!' He could've done without that. Yet his anger wasn't for the Russian's death, it was for the inconvenience of finding a comparable replacement. Good men like Bogatin were hard to find. 'Right, where the bloody hell are they?'

As Tony and Ben were dragged out of the Land Rover and dumped on the ground, Tony quickly scanned his surroundings. He knew approximately where there were; he recognised the vegetation and after the waterless Kalahari he could easily smell the nearby river. Yes, it'd have to be the Chobe. Next thing he heard was voices behind him. One had an American accent.

'Untie their feet and make them stand.'

'But ..'

'Just do it,' Donovan commanded.

Once he could stand Tony turned around and he quickly took in the rest of the scene; safari Land Rover, dead elephant and somebody hacking out its tusks. At the sight of the elephant he could feel his blood beginning to boil. His gaze then swept to the men standing in front of him. Although he'd never seen him before, he instinctively recognised the broad-shouldered white man with the shock of black wavy hair and the malicious walnut-brown eyes. His eyes locked on his as he hissed, 'Donovan, you bastard!'

Donovan stepped in and struck him a savage blow across the face. 'That's for the break-in, and this is for the Russian.' With his other hand he connected with another resounding blow.

Tony didn't have a clue what he was talking about but that was the least of his worries. Shaking his head, he staggered backwards and received an almighty thump from a rifle butt a soldier behind had thrown into his back; he ended up collapsing to his knees.

'Get that bastard out of it,' Donovan rounded on Sithole. 'In fact, all of them, except the sergeant can be sent away. I want as few witnesses as possible.'

'But ..'

'Christ, just do it!

As Sithole was sending away his soldiers, but telling them to stay within radio range, Tony regained his feet. His face and back were throbbing and he could feel one eye beginning to swell. He was standing beside Ben and in front of him were Donovan and Peter while the sergeant had just dragged over and dumped the elephant's green ivory tusks beside them. Nobody had said a word since Donovan had barked at Sithole to get rid of his men.

Tony turned to Peter. 'I must say your looks have improved.'

Peter scowled which tugged at the quickly healing cut running down his cheek; the expression pulled his whole face out of line. 'More than yours and your Matabele scum will have by the time we've finished.'

'Shut up, Peter!' Donovan snapped, and then he called over to Sithole returning from the departing Land Rover. 'Get the women.' He turned back to Tony. 'Now we'll see how much of a smart arse you'll choose to be.'

Although they were petrified with their hands tied behind their backs, Tony was heartened to see both women moved freely and looked unscathed. But before he could attempt to caution Anna to try to remain aloof, when Sithole led her up to stand beside him what resolve she had been able to muster fell away. Being allowed to lean against him, with terrified eyes she looked up at him and tearfully sobbed, 'Oh Tony, what are they going to do?'

'Just be strong. I won't let them hurt you.' Although he was unable to embrace her, through his words he tried to give her strength.

'Oh how noble,' Donovan chuckled with a humourless laugh. 'At least now, Campbell, I know where your weakness lies.' His face and voice hardened. 'Now take her away from him.'

As Anna was dragged away by Sithole, she wailed in terror, 'Tony, no!'

'You bastard,' Tony voiced as he took a menacing pace towards Donovan, but the sergeant quickly moved in and rammed a rifle butt up into his solar plexus.

As Tony bent over spluttering, Donovan grabbed Anna by her raven locks and twisted, making her cry out in pain. 'Do something like that again, Campbell, or try any clever answers to my questions, and she'll be the one who gets it.' He viciously twisted harder and made her cry out again. 'Get my point?'

'You're dead, Donovan,' Tony declared as he raised his head and regained his upright stance.

'I think not. It is you and your friends that will have that honour if you don't answer me properly. Now, who helped you organise the break-in?' He saw the briefest frown of ignorance skip across Tony's face before the expression was quickly masked.

'Go to hell,' was the only answer Donovan received.

'Good acting, but you left a trail a blind man could follow. Missing this are we?' From his pocket Donovan produced the ivory disk Bogatin had given him.

Looking at the disk, Tony was bewildered and he didn't try to hide his expression.

'You cost me millions, now who helped you?' Menacingly, he grabbed hold of Anna's hair again.

'Listen, arsehole. I don't know where you got that from but I've still got mine in my pocket. And as for a break-in, I don't have a clue what you're on about.'

'Search him,' Donovan ordered, and sure enough Sithole brought to him Tony's disk. Comparing them Donovan could see they were alike but slightly different, he began to feel uneasy. 'Bullshit!' he barked to hide his growing disquiet; the last thing he wanted was to display any uncertainty. 'We know it was you who broke in.' He placed the disks in his pocket.

Sithole couldn't contain himself any longer. 'Ah, although I don't understand Mr Donovan, I believe there is something you should know. The Russian must have discovered something before he died.' Without waiting to be asked, he turned to the sergeant, 'Get the two manila envelopes on the back seat of my Land Rover.' When he had them he handed to Donovan the one he'd received from Zimbabwe immigration. 'I showed these to him. They are of the man that met Campbell and his Matabele up at Victoria Falls.'

Extracting one of the photographs Donovan immediately became just as startled as Bogatin had been. He recognised the face as the same one belonging to the man photographed leaving the restaurant with Sabina at Malibu. 'Damn,' he breathed. He remembered feeling uneasy about the dates, times and his description. He looked up at Sithole and demanded, 'What did Bogatin say?'

'He asked if I was positive, then mumbled something about a break in. I presume he was referring to the same one.'

'Come on, man.' Donovan's disquiet had returned. 'What *exactly* did he say?'

'I can't be certain but I think his words were, "he was the one I saw in the car-park with the other two, just after the break-in".'

'And ..?' Donovan couldn't believe his ears.

'He looked at a photograph from Campbell's file and said he hadn't been there and that it was him' – he pointed at the photo Donavan was holding – 'all along. He indicated it had been a setup.'

Donovan wasn't the only one who Richard Black had set up. If it hadn't been for the fact that Anna was involved Tony would have been impressed by the devious way it had been done. *Jesus, the bastard*, he thought bitterly. *He could've told me.* Thrusting aside his resentment, he chuckled a humourless laugh, 'Having a few problems are we? Thing's not as they seem?'

'Who is he?' Donovan thrust out the photo of Richard towards Tony.

'Go to hell.'

However, as Tony spat out the words Donovan saw recognition flare within Anna's eyes. She knew the face. 'So, you little bitch. You know him as well.'

'Anna, don't!' Tony implored. Although he was bitter about being set up and having Anna and the others involved, there must have been a damn good reason why Richard wanted Donovan's attention focused in Africa. Maybe, indirectly, there was a chance of stopping his racket after all. 'He's going to kill us, anyway!'

'That's exactly right, but only if you don't tell me what I want. Now who is he and what does he do?' He grabbed her hair again and twisted.

'I don't know – ahh!' Tony's words had galvanised her; if he said don't, she wouldn't.

Donovan tried twisting harder. 'Who is he?' he demanded again through clenched teeth, but all he succeeded in doing was making her cry out louder and triggering Tony back into action.

As the sergeant clubbed Tony, Peter chipped in, 'Let's see how close these two are.'

He grabbed Jessie by the hair, and found with his other hand he had to thump Ben to the ground, preventing him from trying to defend her.

His brutality breached Anna's newfound resolve; she couldn't let her silence bring pain down upon her friend.

Before Peter could do anything to Jessie, Anna spoke. 'Okay, leave her,' she pleaded. The relief that showed in Jessie's eyes was pathetic. 'His name is Richard Black and Tony said he was with British Intelligence.'

'Richard Black?' Donovan breathed in shock, his anxiety had now turned to patent alarm, 'And British Intelligence?'

Sithole cut in again, 'There is also something else the Russian said, it may be important. Right at the end I clearly remember him saying, "Sabina, the little bitch".'

'Oh my God!' The awful truth came crashing home, 'Right from the start it's been my bloody wife!' The magnitude of her deceit stunned his horrified mind.

It was Tony's laughter that eventually lanced his stupor. 'Huh, now it makes sense. All that information and those files. Good God, betrayed by your own wife.'

In complete and utter dismay Donovan dumbly stared at Tony's laughing face. It had indeed been an elaborate set up while he'd been focused in Africa, *What the hell's been happening back at home?* He began shaking his head incredulously. 'Christ, I've been blind. Sabina *has* gained access to the files.'

CHAPTER 74

Los Angeles

ON THE OTHER side of the world and twelve hours prior to Donovan's realisation, there was a different sequence of events taking place.

It was clear to everyone who saw Sabina as she stepped out of the elevator at the tower block's twenty-fifth floor, that she was dressed for business. She wore a battleship-grey business suit with the same colour briefcase clutched at her side. Her hair was pulled back and piled high on top of her head, highlighting her dark Mediterranean features.

As she pushed her way through the double doors into the boardroom, she fancied she could feel the nervous energy crackling about the room. Initially ignoring the directors and guests who sat around the highly polished walnut table, she strode to its head. It wasn't until she had placed her briefcase on the corner of the table, snapped its clips and sat down that she looked about those present. The agitated stares that met her stony glare did nothing to quieten the anxiety she felt inside. She was about to take the biggest gamble of her life.

The directors' faces that met her – most she had known perhaps not well, but for years. There were twelve of them, all experts in their fields; accounting, legal, investments, and, of course, freight-forwarding and importing-exporting. However, besides sharing that similarity they also all had another similar trait; the reason Donovan had arranged their appointments to the board. They were either weak men he could easily manipulate or vulnerable men who were not beyond reproach.

Sabina cleared her throat, preparing herself to speak. With these men alone she would never have a hope of pulling off what she was about to attempt, not without the presence of the other four men seated either side of her at the head. 'I would like to thank you all for attending this extraordinary meeting I have had to call at such short notice. But due to the gravity of the events that have recently come to light, I can assure you it was a necessity.'

The main reason Sabina had only given each man an hour to attend the meeting was that she didn't want the remotest possibility of any of those present being able to contact her husband; it was now six in the evening in Los Angeles while in the early hours of the morning in Africa.

Sabina noticed a number of the directors stir uncomfortably, but before any of them were able to question her actions she was speaking again, 'You will be curious at the identity of, and reason for, our guests.' She indicated the men and it was clear that three of the four, by their dress and indifferent demeanour, were government men; short back and sides, stony-faced and wearing grey three-piece suits. However, the fourth, well, he clearly had an aura of his own.

'Yes, Sabina, it had crossed our minds,' one of the directors drawled sarcastically. He was a southerner; a weasel of a man named Carl Jackson and the one Sabina was worried about the most; Donovan's right hand man and creative accountant.

Looking directly at him and fixing him with her most concerned look, she asserted, 'I wouldn't get too distressed, Carl. You will learn sooner than most. It's you they will want to question first.' She could see disquiet grow in his face so she chose to keep him in suspense and finished without explanation. *The bastard can sweat,* she decided. His sarcasm had further hardened her resolve. She turned back to the rest of the directors and, while watching their faces, she introduced the men.

'On my far right is Mr Ooms from the Inland Revenue Service, beside him Mr McCarthy from the FBI,' she could already hear quiet murmurs of concern drift around the table. She ignored them and carried on. 'On my far left is Mr O'Connor from the CIA and beside him,' she chose not to introduce him by name, 'an overseas guest from British Intelligence.' She paused while the IDs of the three American's were handed around – it was obvious to those present they were authentic. She waited until the uneasiness their presence caused had sunk home, before continuing, 'It is enough to say that the reason for their visit is of the utmost concern for all of you as directors of Donovan Enterprises.'

Now fully into her stride Sabina open and reached into her briefcase and extracted a sheath of photocopied documents. 'It pains me to inform you gentleman, but ..' she began handing out the documents. 'this is a photocopy of a warrant for my husband's arrest.' When she heard the gasps and murmurs of astonishment, only by using an extreme force of will was she able to keep an expression of triumph off her face, but she couldn't help adding, 'It also distresses me to tell you it is likely more will follow.' She noticed Carl squirm the most. As she sat back down, she indicated a hand to her left. 'I will invite our British guest to briefly explain.'

Richard couldn't believe the skill with which Sabina had artfully managed to rock each of the directors. So far everything was running according to plan. 'Thank you, Mrs Donovan,' he stated without a spark of familiarity twinkling in his eyes. 'Gentlemen, I will make this short. You will all be thoroughly briefed when questioned by myself and, ah, my colleague.' He swept a slow sombre stare around the room. 'Several months prior my organisation was alerted to the fact that Mr Donovan and a number of his companies, Donovan Enterprises being one of them, have been heavily involved with a money laundering and smuggling operation of huge international proportions. From the information since gathered, it has become evident the United Kingdom is being used as an illegal entrepôt for vast sums of laundered funds. And as you can appreciate, my government has taken a less than favourable view of your Chairman's and your company's activities – hence the joint venture with your country's government organisations. So far Mrs Donovan has been most helpful. I hope each of you will be equally so.

'Now, due to the enormity of the situation and its ramification to a company of Donovan Enterprises' size and international reputation, we have chosen to undertake this investigation in-house and behind closed doors. We have also consented to Mrs Donovan's request that you may have a brief meeting, say, five minutes, before we begin our interviews.' Richard stood, as did the other guests, adding before walking from the room, 'I trust you will use the time wisely. We have a long night ahead of us.'

The gathering was stunned into silence as the men left. Carl Jackson who broke their bewilderment as he spoke to the lawyer who was head of the company's legal department. 'Christ, can they do this?'

'With all three of them, the IRS, CIA and FBI, they can do anything they damn well please. Plus, from experience, they hate being shown up by foreign organisations. They'll use all their clout on this one.'

'But can't we force them into court and wait for Judd to …'

Carl never finished as the other directors tried to talk all at once. They could clearly see the complications Donovan's alleged illicit activities could cause for them personally. One thing they had learnt about him was that he certainly wasn't above being involved with dubious activities, and secondly, if it meant saving his own hide he wouldn't hesitate to implicate any or all of them. If the allegations were correct, he was the last person they wanted back in America.

Sabina stood up and forcefully slapped a heavy folder she had extracted from her briefcase on the tabletop; its resounding smack silenced them all.

'For God's sake shut up!' She saw Carl was about to respond, so pointing an accusing finger at him, she got in first, 'You shut your mouth. If Judd or any of the company's subsidiaries are involved in illicit activities you have to be involved. Nobody here is going to sink themselves to help save your hide.'

He might have tried to defend himself, but most of the other directors immediately realised how true Sabina's words were.

'Yeah, shut up Carl. We'll not take a fall for you or Judd for that matter.' A number of them came to her support. She knew they were clutching at straws and running scared – just the way she needed them.

'From my experience with those men, when they interviewed me this afternoon, when they say we only have five minutes that's all we've got. We're lucky they consented to that,' she added. 'So let's make use of it.'

She opened the folder and began handing out the sheets of paper she had slapped on the table; she placed a single sheet in front of each man. At the top it simply read in bold type: AGENDA, and underneath were listed two items: 1. Removal of Judd Donovan from his office as Chairman of the Board. And: 2. Appointment of new Chairman.

She looked around the room, making sure each man was fully aware of what she was proposing. 'Whether each of you realises it or not, the company's articles of association state, I quote,' she extracted a copy of the articles from her briefcase, "In the event of any board members being criminally indicated, the board is vested with the power to temporarily terminate the said director's appointment and position on the board. Furthermore, in the event of his conviction the termination is automatically deemed permanent."

With a heavy sigh she deliberately placed the articles down on the table. 'It saddens me, gentlemen, to do this to my husband, but I feel it is wise for us to distance ourselves from Judd and his actions. That is of course until the whole untidy affair is sorted out.' As she looked from face to face, in most she could see their patent relief. She had offered them a scapegoat and if expressions were anything to go by, it appeared most would willingly accept it.

Sabina was positive she would gain the two-thirds majority she needed to pull off her husband's termination.

Deliberately looking at her watch, she stated, 'We have little time, gentlemen.' She cleared her throat as she could feel the tension around the table rise. 'Item one; I nominate the termination of Judd Donovan as Chairman of the Board. I call for a seconder,' she held her breath as she realised she was teetering on the edge of cementing in place the biggest ruse she'd ever been involved in, in her life. Unbelievably, half the board seconded the motion, and the subsequent vote was passed. One down, one to go.

'Item number two; appointment of new Chairman of the Board.' She deliberately looked around the room, seeing most shrink ever so slightly into their seats; it was clear with the potential ramifications nobody wanted the job. She wondered if now, her reason for sitting at the head of the table – in her husband's old chair – was obvious. 'I call for the nominations for the new Chairman of the Board.'

Several minutes later Sabina walked into the guest office – small, tastefully furnished but functional – that had been set aside for her whenever she had business to attend to in the company's tower block. She quietly closed the door and rested her back up against it.

'Ah, the new Chairman of the Board I take it,' a voice greeted her. It was Richard Black, casually lounging in one of the office's chairs.

'Madam Chair *Person* to you, thank you very much,' she responded with a haughty flick of her head, before turning back and giving him the wickedest of smiles. She began to laugh. 'It happened as you said it would. They took it hook, line and sinker.' She skipped across the room as Richard rose, and wrapped her arms around his neck. Kicking her heels in the air she made him support her weight as she laughed deliciously into his ear.

'Well, I suppose congratulations are in order.'

She dropped back to the ground, still laughing, 'But it was so easy. I just said what you told me to say.'

'Plus added a bit of personal flair. Remember, I was there for part of it. But come on, there's still a long night and probably a couple more days to go,' he reminded her.

'Christ, don't I know it.' Sabina brought herself back down to earth. 'Right, now what?' As usual, things concerning Richard Black weren't as they seemed.

'Okay, Johnny has still been unable to uncover anything substantial from the disks. Even with what we've got, your husband has covered his tracks extremely well.'

'So how much time have we got? How long will the others play along?'

'The IRS will be in it for the long haul. Although it's only circumstantial evidence I supplied, because of the creative tax returns the company has been filing in recent years, they've been looking for any excuse to go through your husband's personal affairs as well as the company's. So, no trouble there.'

'And the FBI and the CIA?'

'Well, the FBI was the hardest; they were pretty reluctant to act. I had to call in a few favours. They'll only hang on until the end of the directors' questioning. If nothing-substantial surfaces, well ...' he shrugged, 'who knows? But the CIA, now they're content to sit on the fence. Because of the nature of the company's business, if anything does turn up you can bet they'll be after their pound of flesh.' Richard shook his head. 'I'll warn you now, if with your new clout as Chairman to get into the company's books we are able to nail your husband, there'll be a downside. The CIA will call in the favour and you can guarantee it'll be with interest.'

'It's "Chairperson" and I can live with that. Well, let's hope we come up with something.' She changed the subject. 'What about Dave Old? How's he getting on?'

'I spoke to him just before the board meeting. He's about ready to move. And I take it the guards at the villa are still refusing to leave without notice from either your husband or Bogatin?'

'Fraid so.'

Richard breathed out heavily in regret. 'So be it.' If he'd surmised correctly it would be the culmination and possibly the most important part of his plans. 'Okay, you've spoken to Dave and he's told you what to do. Just be back here as soon as possible after the job is done – I may need your womanly charms.' He bent down and briefly kissed her lips. 'Right, we've both got work to do.'

CHAPTER 75

DAVE HAD BEEN watching the villa for several days now. From his surveillance he had learnt the guards' shifts, their numbers and – most importantly – their routines. He looked at his watch; it was just after dark and the night-time shift had been on for an hour now, just easing into their routines. There were four in all and he knew exactly where each of them were to be found.

Dave was crouching amongst shrubbery just inside the villa's wrought-iron security gate. For the briefest second his position was illuminated as a set of car's headlights skipped over the shrubs. The outline of the Porsche 944 was clearly recognisable as it stopped in front of the gates. 'Ah, Sabina. Right on cue.'

Sabina's heart pounded like mad as she sat in her Porsche waiting for the gates to open. *I should be used to this by now,* she reasoned, *what, with all I've been through.* She had long since come down from her adrenaline high experienced during the board meeting and was now suffering from withdrawal. *God, at least the shaking's stopped.* She steeled herself as the gates began to open. *Well, here we go again.*

Once she was able to drive through the automatic gates she would normally flaunt security procedure and floor the Porsche, sweeping past the guard and on up to the villa. But tonight she would be following the procedure according to the letter of the law.

Easing her foot off the clutch, she coasted forward and stopped beside the security kiosk. Lowering her window, she was met by a uniformed guard; he walked up to the window and shone his flashlight full in her eyes. Bolstering her courage Sabina took a deep breath and turned to the light.

'Get that bloody thing out of my face.' Her words were spoken with such venom the guard took half a pace back. He hadn't expected the cutting rebuke let alone her stopping at all. As he stumbled back Sabina had twisted her head out of the window, choosing to give him no respite from the lash of her tongue. However, 'Next time, you moron –' was all she got out.

Dressed in a matte black, one-piece boiler suit, with the same colour rubber-soled boots on his feet, Dave came out of the shrubs noiselessly like a blacken liquid blur. Sabina gasped as he clamped an arm around the guard's throat. However, it wasn't Dave's presence that had frightened her – that was planned and expected – it was his face; smeared with camouflage cream, it looked hideous.

With his free hand Dave first drew the guard's gun and tossed it into the shrubbery. Next, he reached for his walkie-talkie. Bringing it around and up to the guard's mouth he said, 'Call her in.'

His message was brief. 'This is the gate. An arrival, Mrs Donovan. Out'. 'Good man.'

Although he was young, fit and a big man, Dave held him easily. He marched him backwards to the kiosk, released his arm from around his throat and as he turned him slightly, pole-axed him with a punch to the side of his jaw. Once the guard had slumped unconscious, Dave drew a roll of two-inch wide duct tape from a concealed pocket on his leg. He bound his hands behind his back, feet around his ankles and then firmly stuck a strip over his mouth before unceremoniously dumping him out of sight in the kiosk.

As Dave walked back to the car Sabina's jaw hinged open in amazement at the speed and obvious professionalism he had used to dispatch the guard.

'Close it. We've still got work to do. Now the one at the front. You know what to do.' Dave turned and merged back into the shrubs.

Licking her lips and swallowing, she snapped closed her mouth. Slightly stunned, she let out the clutch and drove up the redbrick driveway. By the time she reached the villa's porte-cochere, her mind was firmly back on the job.

As soon as she had left Richard at the tower block and managed to lose her normally ever-present tail, Sabina had driven to the Beverly Wilshire Hotel, on Wilshire Boulevard, at the foot of Rodeo Drive in Beverly Hills. She had gone straight up to the room she'd previously booked and spent an hour changing and artfully applying her makeup. As she pulled the Porsche up underneath the porte-cochere and stepped out she was a very different woman from the suit wearing, business-type executive she had portrayed several hours earlier. Wearing her hair down, white high heels, skin-tight blue jeans and a simple white see-through blouse with a lace patterned bra underneath, she looked alluring beyond belief. And sure enough, her next victim was standing right where he was supposed to be.

Unlike the guard at the gate, this one was wearing a dark three-piece suit; Donovan may have preferred men on the ground as opposed to fancy high-tech electronic surveillance, but he didn't want uniformed guards walking around the villa detracting from its beauty. As if noticing him for the first time, standing beside one of the porte-cochere's pillars, Sabina looked directly at him, slightly cocked her head to the side and subtly pushed out her hips. Her makeup, clothes and stance brought the moment to a climax as the guard's breath constricted in his throat.

'Jenson, isn't it?' Sabina purred. She had to admit this was the type of secret agent stuff she liked.

The man cleared his throat. 'Ah, yes, ma'am, it is.' Like the guard at the gate he too was tall and fit looking, but older, obviously more experienced.

'I've always admired you, you know.' Sabina began to seductively walk towards him.

'You –'his voice caught; clearing it he tried again, 'You have?'

'Of course.' She was now standing in front of him. 'But I've never had the courage to approach you. Are you married?' As she asked the question she saw his eyes drop to her chest; the ride up with the window down and the excitement from the gate had hardened her nipples and their rigid darkened outlines were clearly visible through her bra and blouse.

He was getting bolder now and Sabina felt the first twinge of doubt as he raised his eyes and lightly smiled and answered, 'No, ma'am. It's the job, you see.'

Sabina must have driven up from the gate too quickly. She would have to give Dave more time to arrive. Thrusting aside her misgivings and slightly elevating her chest, she reached out and ran her index finger down the lapel of his jacket.

'Well then, as my husband …' she began, but again gasped with fright. Although it was twenty yards from the edge of the porte-cochere to the garden, she hadn't seen Dave stealthfully move behind the guard. Like an apparition his arm and face materialised and reared up behind him. Sabina threw a hand up to her chest and took a step back as Dave went to work.

First the gun from the shoulder holster, then the walkie-talkie from the clip on his belt, and as he'd done with the guard before, he brought it up to the man's lips and ordered, 'Do it. Call her in.'

However, this one had far more spirit. He stepped half a pace forward and tried to drive an elbow back into Dave's solar-plexus. Dave was already a step ahead. Thrusting his hips around, the elbow missed and he twisted his arm-lock down onto the man's windpipe, cutting off his air. 'Bad move, pal.' Dave then spoke to Sabina, 'Grab the radio and hold it to his mouth. Press the send button on the side when I say.'

Reaching to a holster strapped to the side of his leg Dave clasped his free hand around the butt of a black shaded, silenced pistol; it was a Desert Eagle .50 Action Express. Bringing it around and holding it to the man's head, he hissed, 'Now call her in.'

'Up yours,' was his only reply.

Without hesitating, Dave lowered the weapon and pushed into his groin. Deliberately cocking it, he uttered, 'A fate worse than death, wouldn't you say? Now call her in.' But still the guard hesitated. It was Sabina's words that changed his mind.

She tutted and sadly shook her head. 'It would be such a pity, and the last one I saw him do that to left so much blood.'

'Okay, okay.' He didn't need further persuasion and Sabina didn't wait to be told to press the send button.

'Now bloody well call me in.'

'Yeah confirming. She's arrived, parked her car beneath the porte-cochere. Over and out.'

As soon as Sabina had flicked off the button, Dave did the same as at the gate. When the guard was unconscious, he slotted the Desert Eagle back into its holster and dragged the limp figure to the front door. He waited for Sabina to open it and quickly bundled the man inside onto the Cipolin marble floor.

'Right, here's another roll of duct tape. Do the same as with the one down at the gate then turn off the alarms and unlock the French doors from the study out to the veranda, but remember, don't open them,' he warned. 'After that, it'll be time to strut your stuff.' Dave was about to slip back into the night but stopped. 'Good work out there. Well-timed words.' He chuckled lightly, 'But I thought we agreed I was supposed to be the intimidating one.'

Sabina would've responded but he had already gone out the door.

The next guard was easy enough; there were no radio messages that had to be given or other precautions to take. Dave found him in the cobbled courtyard between the villa's garage and its back entrance that led into the kitchen. He walked boldly out of the gloom with the Desert Eagle extended.

'Hi, you don't know me,' he stated to the astonished man, 'And you know, we'll probably never be close. In fact, this is the closest we'll ever get.'

Using lightening speed, he lashed out with his other hand and caught the man on the point of his jaw; he went down like a ton of bricks and Dave trussed him up where he lay. As he let himself in through the kitchen door with the key Sabina had given him earlier, he prepared himself for the fourth and final man.

After Sabina had done as Dave requested she ran up the sweeping Cipolin marble staircase to her bedroom on the second floor. Once in her bedroom, before flicking on any lights, she drew a set of lace curtains over a pair of French doors that led onto a small balcony beyond. However, curtains over a window to her left remained open. Her bedroom was on the opposite side of the villa to the front door and marble-floored vestibule; it was at the end of one wing and lay at right angles to the pergola-shaded veranda outside her husband's study.

Peering out through a crack in the curtains, Sabina could clearly see down through the pergola to the darkened red-bricked veranda below. 'Come on where are you?' she anxiously whispered, wanting to get on with their plans. She knew the last guard should've been patrolling down there somewhere. After peering out for a minute she caught a faint glow, flicked out from beneath the eaves of the overhanging roof below. *Oh, the bastard.* He'd been leaning near the study door out of sight, 'He's been smoking. That's a dereliction of duty.' With a light snort of laughter she soon realised her concern was misplaced. 'Yeah, right. As if with what you're about to do you care.'

The guard was approximately where Dave had said he wanted him, so she flicked on a tall standard lamp that would clearly silhouette her behind the curtains and – proceeding to do as he had earlier described – she began to strut her stuff.

The man was thoroughly bored and with Bogatin away, he knew he didn't need to keep up his guard. That bastard was forever on the prowl. Although he was the most experienced and longest-serving guard at the villa, the Russian's unwavering views towards security meant there would never be more than a professional rapport between them.

Just after he flicked his cigarette away a light was switched on above him. 'Ah, the bitch is home.' In the past Sabina hadn't exactly endeared herself to the villa's security staff.

Looking up at the French doors his thoughts quickly changed. He could clearly see Sabina outlined behind the sheer net curtains and – *God!* – she was undressing.

Without making it too seductive and obvious, Sabina began peeling off her clothes. First, she kicked off her shoes and then wriggled out of her

411

jeans. Moving to stand side on, she slowly undid the buttons of her blouse. Dropping it behind her she then hooked her hands behind her back and unclasped her lacy bra. Once she had dropped that to the ground she feigned a leisurely stretch, giving a clear outline of her pert neatly formed breasts. When she'd gauged the stretch had been going on for long enough, she dropped forward from the hips. Allowing her breasts to swing free and unsuspended, she scooped off her knickers. Hooking them on the end of her foot, she kicked them away.

Deciding to push her charade that bit further, she turned to face the French doors and parted her legs. Exaggerating her next gesture, she bent forward slightly and ran her fingers from her knee up the inside of her thigh, then throwing her head back and lingered her hand ever so briefly over her groin, she thought, *First the entrée; now the main course.* She turned and stepped out of the light towards the window at her left.

The guard couldn't believe his luck. There she was, undressing, right before his eyes, *But damn ... those curtains.* He licked his lips and repositioned his quickly swelling groin. *Christ,* her side on view had been something else. *But now ... oh man, oh man.* Her hand was running up the inside of her thigh, and, *Oh, God,* it was lingering at the top of her legs. The display was all the more erotic because of the enticing mystery offered by her silhouette. *Christ, if only ...* but before he could fully vocalise his wish, Sabina moved and her image was snatched away.

Like a thirsty man having his first glass of water whisked away from just beyond his lips, he was left reeling at his loss. *Bloody hell, she's going to the open window.*

Having to dance forward and out to the side of the veranda to see through the pergola and up over the overhanging eave of the roof, he clearly saw Sabina standing in the middle of the uncovered window. *Holy mother,* she was totally naked. Her arms were thrown to the sides clasping the drapes, her breast with no evidence of a bikini line stood out free and proud, her tapered waist flared generously down to her hips, and, *Oh, gawd!* – he was able to glimpse the top of her darkened pubic V.

However, that was the last image he remembered as he fell unconscious to the ground. In his rapture he had never heard the study's French doors open or the soundless footfall of stalking feet.

As Dave clubbed him, he applauded Sabina again. It had worked far better than he'd ever imagined it would. Once he'd taped up the guard and dragged him into the study, Sabina had already slipped on a pair of sweatpants and top and joined him beside her husband's mahogany desk.

As she proceeded to tie up the laces of her running shoes, Dave spoke. 'The new set of guards we organised will be here by dawn and..' he chose to congratulate her, 'well done, it went like clockwork.' He paused and sadly shook his head. 'But you could've waited a bit longer at the window.'

'But you just said it went like we planned. I mean ... didn't it?' she asked concerned, now full of doubt.

Although she'd dealt with him often over the few days since the break-in, she still felt uncomfortable in his presence – it was as if he hadn't accepted her. However, when she saw the wicked glint in his laughing yellow eyes, she knew it was a joke.

'Yeah, but you still could've stayed.'

'Oh, you wish.'

'Probably.' His smile then reached his face. 'No seriously, Sabina, well done. I can see why Richard's put so much faith in you.'

'Thank you. I think I needed to hear that.' She wasn't yet used to being given praise by a male and her thoughts were immediately drawn back to Donovan. 'I wonder what he's doing?' she queried, dejectedly.

Dave immediately knew who she was talking about. 'Not too much, we can only hope.' Her melancholy was starting to affect him. What with all he'd found out about the man and what he was doing to the continent of his chosen home, it was no wonder. With an effort he roused himself. 'Come on, you'll probably be needed back at the tower block and I've certainly got more than enough to do here. Let's hope it's not going to be in vain.'

CHAPTER 76

Chobe National Park

GOD IT'S BEEN *Sabina and that Richard Black all along!*

Donovan had underestimated Sabina. Still slightly dazed by the enormity of his realisation, he turned to Peter and implored, 'You have to get me to an airport as quickly as possible.'

Although he didn't understand all of what had transpired, Peter knew it was vitally important to get Donovan on his way back to Los Angeles. One thing he did know was that the continuation of his income could very well depend on it so he made a quick calculation. 'The closest commercial one is at Victoria Falls. We will have to go back across the border.' He looked at his watch. 'But there is still plenty of time. There is a direct flight for Harare that flies out at 5:30.'

'Whatever. Just make sure I'm on it.'

'And what about them?' Peter asked with contempt as he motioned towards Tony, Anna, Ben and Jessie, still standing with their hands tied behind their backs.

Donovan slowly turned to gaze dumbly at each of them as if he'd never seen them before. He lightly shook his head, realising they had only been a ruse. *Why hadn't I seen it?* he berated himself. It was then his anger began to burn. He had to assume it was this Richard Black who master-minded the plot; the bastard had played on his emotions and nearly won. *Christ, the smashed lace ball and stolen figurine were evidence enough, and – Jesus – he'd planted the ivory disk.*

Retrieving the two near-identical disks from his pocket and looking at them again he felt his anger change form and smoulder. Unlike the emotional outrage he had experienced since finding out about the break-in, it had become a cold, calculated loathing.

'So you say we have plenty of time to catch the flight.' It was a statement not a question, so Donovan didn't wait for an answer. 'They are of no value to us.' He looked at Sithole. 'The women can be given to your men then killed, but because of the trouble he has caused I want to see Campbell die.'

With a stifled cry, Anna managed to break the grip Donovan still held her by. As she did so, Peter thrust Jessie towards Ben. Looking at him, he asked, 'And the Matabele?'

Donovan shrugged; he would seek his retribution on Campbell. 'He's yours, but like Campbell he must be killed before we leave.'

'With pleasure, but I also want his woman.' Peter didn't wait for a response but turned to Sithole, 'Your pistol. I'll cover them while you call up your men.'

Tony's mind was reeling. He knew what would happen if Sithole's soldiers got hold of Anna, he'd seen it happen too often during the war; guerrillas attacking and brutally raping anyone from nuns to farmer's wives and their children. As Sithole handed over the weapon and warned Peter not to let them move, Tony whispered to Anna to get in behind him. He didn't have a clue what he'd do, but he would rather have Anna killed out of hand than after Sithole's men had satisfied their carnal lust. He prepared himself to attack, the sergeant would be first. However, before he could move, Ben had turned to face the sergeant. As Sithole had turned away he began to speak in Shona.

'The information you sold to me about the warehouse at Thomson's Junction was most enlightening, thank you.' Sithole stopped dead in his tracks and the sergeant swallowed heavily as Ben pushed on. 'It's a pity we were unable to act on that and the other information we got as well. But no doubt you'll be able to sell it to somebody else.' For Donovan's benefit he switched to English. 'Oh, and by the way, thanks for the tip-off about the container and letting me go.'

By this time Sithole had turned around. He had noticed despite docking the sergeant's pay for missing the Matabele at Main Camp he had appeared more flush than normal, and while he'd never been able to prove it, he'd suspected Peter had had an informant working within his ranks. Although no words were spoken, the sergeant could clearly see anger flare within his Captain's eyes.

'It's a lie,' the sergeant asserted indignantly. He desperately looked from Sithole, to Peter, to Donovan who by now had turned to watch him. 'The Matabele, he lies!'

Tony saw his chance. In that fleeting moment they were all distracted. He didn't yell; he never made a sound as he stepped towards the flustered sergeant. As he swung his foot he glimpsed from the corner of his eye that Ben was following his lead. When his foot crushed the sergeant's testicles against his pelvis, all hell broke loose.

Like Tony, Ben had moved without a sound – he was just thankful it was the sergeant of Sithole's men who had remained behind. He bent forward and ran, ramming his head into Peter's unsuspecting stomach. As he heard the air being forcefully expelled from Peter's lungs, he gave the big Zulu no respite as he drove him off his feet. Once they were on the ground, unable to use his hands Ben hounded Peter with his forehead, knees and feet.

As the sergeant lurched forward Tony drove up a knee to smash it into his lowered face. He didn't wait for or watch the man as his rifle fall to the ground. Briefly scanning the scene, heartened by what he saw, he turned on Donovan.

Anna was initially dumbfounded by the explosive action Tony had triggered but when she heard, then saw Jessie, she too flew into action.

As Ben moved, Jessie screamed to bolster her courage and choke down her terror. She threw herself at Sithole. As they flew to the ground, her courage was further galvanised. She felt her bindings loosen and realised Anna had also thrown herself at the captain, helping pin him to the ground. Using her knees, Anna was working on Sithole's lower body, while with gnashing teeth Jessie aimed for his face as she desperately tried to free her hands.

Donovan was appalled at the melee that unfolded around him. However, as he saw Tony turn towards him it changed to outrage. 'Come on you bastard!' He balled his fists and bunched his massive shoulders, preparing to either defend or attack. He never had to make the choice; Tony had already pivoted on his toes and lashed out with his other foot. Donovan twisted to the side and drove down forcefully with his arm; his forearm deflected the kick, so it landed harmlessly on his thigh. Now it was Donovan's turn to attack.

With Tony's arms still tied behind him, the storm of punches Donovan threw easily forced him to retreat. So, with the element of surprise now gone and unable to adequately protect himself, Tony was forced to roll his head with each punch or take them on his chin. He had little chance of defending let alone overcoming the attack. He saw Donovan step in close, about to drive up an upper cut to his chin, so rearing back his head he smashed his forehead into the American's face. Donovan roared but the blow never stifled his attack.

The next punch collected Tony squarely on the chin and his knees buckled; he stumbled and fell backwards to the ground. Stunned, he looked up at Donovan preparing himself for his final assault. He then glanced to the side and saw the sergeant clutching towards his rifle as he was beginning to rise. The situation was hopeless, and then with a great scream of outrage, Sithole threw off the women. Tony didn't even bother to look how Ben was faring. They had tried but they had failed, beaten by the odds.

He looked up at Donovan then gasped out loud in shock. *Oh my God! Christ*, we're all going to die. He roused himself as he began to cower.

Initially, he'd been bewildered especially by the first of the savage blows that struck his body. He'd even stumbled and nearly fallen. But with the ensuing entourage of each crashing, brutal thump, he soon experienced the pain – pain like he'd never felt before. Turning to run, he was hampered in his flight but soon found despite his terrible agony, he was able to make the trees. Once amongst their gloom he turned back towards his aggressor.

Still confused, the elephant eventually looked past his attacker out at the open grassy plain. He'd only ever known this place as a sanctuary, being protected in it since his birth. But when he saw his friend pole-axed to the ground by another crashing shot, his confusion changed to anger, and merging with the aching pain he felt, he soon became enraged beyond belief. Nothing like this had ever happened in his lifetime, and he was going to make sure nothing would again. He bucked his head and cracked his massive ears. In that moment he was transformed from the hunted to the hunter. He then raised his trunk through his massive tusks and tested for the scent he knew would be wafting on the air. He soon identified the acid-sweet stench of man but in particular the man who had shot at him and mortally wounded his friend.

The bull elephant found his raging anger gnawing deeply at him within his body. However, he chose to use the agony like a tonic. He'd bide his time but when he judged it was right he'd strike. As Donovan walked up to and dispatched his friend, he began to stalk his prey.

'Oh my God!' Tony breathed in horror, he was looking past Donovan's shoulder and the sight that presented itself made him cower.

'Good try, Campbell, but this time you're going to die.' Donovan snatched up the rifle from beside the rising sergeant and slowly began to bring it to bear. 'Time to meet your maker.'

As he levelled the semiautomatic a menacing shadow fell upon him from behind. The next moment the rifle was violently swatted from his hands. It was his turn to quake in fear. The ground shuddered as a high-pitched riotous noise pierced his ears; from behind him came a gut-wrenching maddened scream of anger.

Paralysed, Donovan turned his upper body. He saw two great shafts of ivory, the huge tapered head and the massive grey wrinkled body. Instinctively, he knew – he'd never forget such tusks. This was the bull he'd shot at and wounded earlier that had escaped into the trees.

In mounting terror Donovan watched the great beast crack its enormous ears, rear its head and then raise its twisting trunk. He knew what was about to come and, as his scream of horror mingled with the elephant's trumpeting rage, once again the trunk came swatting down. It collected him on the shoulder, pulverising the joint, and as he was driven to the ground his hip dislocated as his knee popped its joint. The bull left him there and turned upon the sergeant.

Still pushing himself backwards with his heels, Tony couldn't believe his eyes. Donovan was as good as dead and now the sergeant had been impaled with a tusk through the chest. Driving his head down into the ground, the elephant worried the bloodied figure further onto its tusk. When the beast was satisfied the man was dead, he flicked his head and tossed the broken body aside.

As the bull screamed his wrath again, Tony felt a pair of grasping hands on his shoulders dragging him up off the ground. Quickly looking around, he could see Jessie had somehow freed her hands and was helping him to his feet. Both she and Anna had run from Sithole when the elephant had begun its attack. He swept his gaze to Ben. He and Peter were still half sprawled, tangled together on the ground, staring up in aghast disbelief at the angry bull. Tony yelled, 'Quickly, Ben. Roll away!'

The bull had turned to advance on them. Tony's words roused the little man and with three quick flicks he rolled away from beneath the elephant's feet.

As Jessie helped drag Ben towards the others, the bull was already again absorbed in its gruesome work. They heard Peter scream, but the piercing cry was abruptly extinguished as the elephant stomped with its full weight down onto the centre of his chest. Like a piece of rotten fruit his rib cage burst; the crush of bones and splattering of blood signalled his sure and hideous death.

With his foot still on Peter, the elephant swivelled, further mangling his ruined flesh, and reached for Sithole who by now was backing away. He evaded the elephant's first attempt, but as he turned to run, one great swipe of its trunk felled him to the ground. His neck, back and both his legs were broken but still the beast worked on. Grabbing him around the waist he brutally shook his shattered body then when satisfied, with casual disregard, tossed him up over his head. The elephant never looked around as Sithole tumbled to eventually land in a crumpled heap twenty-five yards away. It then turned towards Tony and his cowering group.

Tony watched the great bull stand stock-still for several seconds, listening as if trying to make a decision. It was then that Donovan moaned. Without hesitation, the elephant turned and strode towards him. He was trying to sit up as the bull reached out its trunk and sniffed. Again, it screamed a trumpeting cry of fury; it knew the smell; this was the one who had killed his friend and caused him so much pain.

Pushing Donovan back, it placed a foot onto his chest. However, he never crushed him, just used it to hold him in place. Donovan screams grew shriller as each limb, one by one, was savagely plucked from his body. They weren't extinguished until his head was twisted and plucked from his neck. Like a cannon-ball it bumped and rolled away.

The elephant left the limbs and severed head where they lay. It turned and faced the foursome now rooted to the spot. He bucked his head; his work was done and it was time to leave. But as he turned, preparing to walk to the woodlands to find a peaceful place to die, he flicked his trunk through Donovan's tattered clothes and bloodied flesh. It may have been a coincidence but the gesture tossed up a small creamy disk which landed in the dust at Tony's feet.

Looking down at it, Anna could see it was Tony's ivory disk. 'Good God, I know they're intelligent but surely not ...' she stated in disbelief. 'He couldn't know what you do!' Stunned, they all looked up to see the limping elephant disappearing into the trees.

Tony looked numbly at Sithole and Peter's broken bodies, then at Donovan's mutilated heap of flesh. 'One way of dismantling his ivory racket, I suppose.' Strangely, nobody laughed. 'God, how fitting. Huh – bush justice.' He looked back towards where the elephant had disappeared, then at Ben. 'But at least now, we've got a chance of saving the elephants.'

Or so he thought.

CHAPTER 77

Los Angeles

IT HAD TAKEN Dave a full twenty-four hours to clear the villa of all security systems, install new ones and properly brief the new security guards who would guard the dwelling. As it was now secure, it had become the centre of Richard's operations.

Dave had to admit he was happy with the way his side of the operations had gone. However, it was fair to say Johnny wasn't blessed by the same type of sentiment. Dave found him sitting hunched over his laptop, staring owlishly at the screen, behind the highly polished mahogany desk in Donovan's study.

'Still no luck?' Dave walked in behind him to stare over his shoulder.

The little man dejectedly dropped his hands from the keyboard into his lap; he leant back in the high-backed chair and let out a long-suffered breath. 'Not a bean. I've gone over them for what seems like the hundredth time, I just can't link up the circumstantial stuff.' He sadly shook his head. 'You've got to hand it to the prick. He's covered his back.'

'Well maybe Richard's been getting on better, but last time I spoke to him he was having the same amount of luck. Have you heard from him?'

Johnny would have responded, but Richard himself walked into the study and stopped in front of the desk. By the smug expression on his face it was clear he had news.

'Well?' Dave demanded.

Never one to play theatrics, Richard came straight out with it. 'I've been speaking to Tony Campbell. Donovan's dead. Happened sometime yesterday.'

'You're joking?' Johnny responded, astounded. Then rousing himself, looked down at the computer screen. 'You mean ... God the hours ... all of them wasted.'

'No, not at all. There's plenty we can use.'

Dave cut in. 'How did it happen?'

Richard snorted in amazement. 'He was killed by an elephant. Can you believe it?'

'I can.' Sabina's voice carried to the men from where she'd been listening at the door. She'd been upstairs when she'd heard Richard arrive. She walked the few paces to stand in front of him. 'Quite appropriate, wouldn't you say?'

Seeing there was no regret or sympathy in her eyes, Richard aired his views as honestly. 'I couldn't agree more.'

Taking a seat in one of the chairs in front of the desk, Sabina heaved a sigh of relief, 'Just as well, too. I must admit I was beginning to get worried. From what little we've uncovered from the company books so far, it would've been weeks before a prosecution could've been laid.' She shuddered slightly at the thought of Donovan being back in LA. She then looked up at Richard. 'God, I might've been forced to work for you.'

'I could think of a lot worse.' Richard grinned, looking into her smiling eyes.

'Yeah, yeah, all right.' Dave broke in. 'Knock it off.' Any endearments could wait until they were alone. He had a few questions he wanted answered. 'What else did Tony Campbell say?'

As Richard dragged his eyes from Sabina's, he grimaced. 'Now there's a man that's not too happy with me. He even called me the "c" word – several times.'

'I'm not surprised,' Johnny snorted. 'And Anna Hagan?'

'Apparently, she's fine.'

'Yeah, I know it was a set up to keep Donovan in Africa and get the Russian down there,' Dave cut in, 'but what was it with her?'

'Oh, she just happened to add a bit of spice, kept both Tony and Donovan on their toes.'

'And if he'd actually been able to kill them both?' Sabina asked pensively. She had only just heard the full extent of Richard's plans.

'Ah, but he didn't.'

'Okay, so we can all sleep well at night. But at least we've achieved our objective. The racket is destroyed and the elephants have been given a much-needed reprieve.'

The comment brought a heavy sigh from Richard, his next words were spoken with regret, 'I'm afraid not. I wasn't able to get the full picture, but it appears from what Tony said there had been some type of fracas at the Wildlife Fund's office in Nairobi. I think it's an excuse, but its Board of Trustees pulled most of Tony's funding and cut his anti-poaching scheme right back.'

'No, how could they?' Sabina voiced in astonishment, 'He's helped destroy the world's biggest ivory racket!'

Richard shrugged his shoulders. 'Like us, he hasn't been able to prove it.' He snorted humourlessly, 'And even if he could've, it probably would've given them all the more excuse.'

'So we're back to square one. The elephants haven't been given a reprieve after all,' Dave stated bitterly.

'Precisely. Without adequate resources Tony can't capitalise on what's been gained.' Richard dejectedly shook his head. 'It's inevitable; somebody is bound to fill the void.'

'But isn't there something we can do? It seems such a waste.' Sabina mirrored Richard's disquiet. 'I could get Donovan Enterprises to set up a trust fund or something.'

As soon as she'd said it she knew it wasn't an option. Even from her brief perusal of the company's books so far she knew it may have been a huge multi-national concern, but because of Donovan's greed for power it had become asset-rich yet cash-poor; all its revenue went into running its massive global operations.

'So what's Tony going to do, then?' Johnny asked.

'As of right now, he said he'd quit. Mentioned something about spending time helping out someone in Tanzania. But knowing the type of person he is he won't let it rest for long, he'll struggle on. And Christ, that's exactly what he'll be forced to do if he isn't financed by an alternative source. It'll take millions.'

'Yes, but what price can be placed on an elephant's life?' Sabina asked. 'I'd say it'd be money well spent.'

Richard could see Sabina was beginning to take the hopelessness of the elephants' future plight and the consequences of her husband's past actions to heart. He turned to Dave and changed the topic; he wanted to know about the last phase of his plans.

'The ivory room – have you been able to get in?' His comment had the desired effect. Sabina's disquiet fell away; she'd always wanted to but never been able to see inside the room.

'Haven't had a show. Once I tried to change the codes, the security system computer shut itself down. Whoever installed it, programmed in a fail-safe. It's shut up tight as a drum.'

'And?' Richard knew he wouldn't have let it rest there.

'Well the room's encased in steel, so I'm left with no other option. I'll have to go in through the weakest point, the door.'

Like the study's door further along the hallway, the ivory room's door had appeared to be made of solid redwood. However, Dave had peeled back a thin wooden veneer to reveal a fire-insulated, vault-like door beneath. After drilling numerous exploratory holes, he'd found it was solid-steel and flat-silled, locked in place by three horizontal hardened-steel bolts that were operated by a locking mechanism encased behind the computerised security panel beside it.

Dave had just emptied a carryall of assorted tools and equipment, and carefully laid them out on a small table underneath the security panel. 'Do you mind?' he asked as he turned and looked at Richard, Sabina and Johnny, all trying to peer over his shoulder to see what he was doing. 'A bit of room if you please.'

As they stepped back Sabina watched on in fascination as Dave went about his work. First, he placed an adhesive foot-wide band of Velcro hooks on the wall around the door, before carefully measuring, then marking with a pneumatic metal-punch, four separate points around where each of the locking bolts were slotted into the door. Next, he picked up a cordless drill with a diamond-tipped bit in its chuck; with the points now accurately marked he proceeded to drill each one of them out.

Once the incessant whine of the drill fell silent, he had four horizontal holes around each of the locking bolts. Next, the explosive. It looked like a white pliable putty he had unwrapped from amongst a thick wax-lined paper.

Dave carefully packed each drill-hole with cyclonite before gliding a needle-length detonator into each plug; he carefully measured the length of the wire that hung from each which he then attached to a small black box. Once the wires were connected, flicking on a switch he set a small red light on top of the box flashing. Then it was time for the compression pad.

Dave produced from a plastic bag what looked like a canvas pouch with a small CO_2 gas cylinder attached. He pulled a pin from the neck of the cylinder and with a great whoosh of gas the pouch quickly inflated to the size and thickness of a single-bed mattress. It was then that Sabina realised what the Velcro hooks around the door were for. The reverse side of the compression pad was covered with Velcro mesh; when Dave pressed the pad over the door she saw it was held firmly in place. He then re-packed the carryall, and herding her and the other two men in front of him, he walked them down to the villa's vestibule.

'Right, up against the wall, crouch, and cover your ears.' When they had all done as had been told, Sabina saw Dave position himself beside the entrance to the villa's wing. 'Here goes nothing,' she heard him mumble as she noticed he had what looked like an automatic garage door opener, but smaller, in his hand. He looked at her and winked, then pressed the button.

There was a blast concussion, a dull thud and Dave was striding back towards the ivory room before Sabina had actually realised what had happened. She, Richard and Johnny were back at his side, in front of the door when he uttered, 'Perfect.'

The blackened and now punctured compression pad, with three chunks of twisted metal wrapped within it, had been ripped off the wall and thrown to the opposite side of the hallway while the door itself had three rectangular slots blasted out of it where the locking bolts and chunks of metal would have been.

Dave stepped up to the door, clasped the handle and yanked it open. Richard was at his side as the door swung open. 'All yours Blackie.' Dave stepped back, allowing Richard and Sabina to step inside.

'Oh my God!' Richard breathed in awe as they both stepped into the ivory room. 'I suspected, but I never truly believed that's what he'd actually done.'

He turned to look at Sabina. Her mouth was gaping open, her head was craned forward, while her eyes bulged wide in shock. Dumbly, dragging her eyes away from the treasure before them, she gawked at Richard, unable to find a word to say.

'There must be millions and millions of dollars' worth,' said Richard. 'God, will you look at the stuff!'

Sabina was finally able to rouse herself, 'I'm looking,' she said turning back, slowly shaking her head in wonder.

In front of them, stacked in open pallets from floor to ceiling, was row upon neatly packed row of gleaming yellow bars of gold.

'It always puzzled me what your husband did with the stuff. That'll be the laundered gold out of Russia.' He turned back to Sabina. 'What are you going to do with it all?' he asked in bewilderment. 'Christ, there's enough here to indefinitely finance a small army.'

It was then that Sabina's eyes began to twinkle, and her lips creased as she smiled. 'You know, Richard, I think that's exactly what I'll do. Huh, how appropriate – White Gold.'

Tony Campbell was back in business.

AUTHOR'S NOTE

I HOPE THE reader will forgive me for any liberties I have taken with the construction of this story.

In particular I refer to the exposé of the Indonesian Ambassador to Tanzania, Joesoef Hussein, and his involvement with ivory poaching. The discovery of his involvement was in fact at the beginning of 1989, and not years later as indicated in this text.

Also, I would like to apologise to the owner of Tat Hing Trading in Hong Kong. The company and owner's name were subtly changed, but he would recognise the comparison. His assassination was fictitious and included for the narration of the story only. Whether or not he is still involved in international ivory poaching and smuggling is unknown to the author.

I hope these discrepancies have not impeded your enjoyment of this novel. However, I would like to add as near as my research was able to ascertain the places, ivory prices and weights, the number of elephants killed and the manner of their slaughter are all based on fact. The illegal trade of ivory *is* a real problem, but thankfully one that is being seriously addressed by the EIA, WWF, The Quigley Wildlife Foundation, and many other dedicated organisations around the world.

OTHER WORKS BY AUTHOR

AFRICAN SERIES:

Book 1 – **The Last Rhino**

Book 2 – *White Gold*

Book 3 – **African Lion**

Series Prequel - **Scars of the Leopard**

WEBSITE

Get personalised book information and up-to-date news about the author and his works:

DavidMarkQuigley.com

EMAIL

Be the first know about the author's new releases, awesome giveaways and news by signing up for his VIP mailing list:

books@davidmarkquigley.com

REVIEWS

Did you enjoy this book? If so, I would love to hear about it. Honest reviews help readers find the right book for their needs.

To leave a review, please head to the Book's page on Amazon, scroll to the bottom of the page under "More about the author" and select "Write a customer review".

I hope you enjoy reading this book as much as I did writing it; it has been a pleasure having you as one of my readers. Thank you

Did you know that a portion of your proceeds is seamlessly donated to wildlife causes around the world?

To find out more, please turn to the next page.

To donate: davidmarkquigley.com/wildlife-foundation

Save the Rhino International estimates that almost 10,000 rhinos have been lost to poaching in the last decade. Similarly, the International Union for the Conservation of Nature (IUCN) reports that, as of 2021, Africa's elephants are now considered critically endangered.

"Wildlife needs all the help that it can get. That's what resonates with me the most and why I chose to start this Foundation." – David Mark Quigley

The **Quigley Wildlife Foundation** is a registered 501(c)3 non-profit organisation in Florida that donates to wildlife causes around the world.

The foundation is comprised of five Directors, each with diverse international backgrounds and wide net reach to various organizations and charities around the world.

DAVID MARK QUIGLEY
Author of the Africa series. Born in New Zealand, traveled and lived extensively around the world.

Rhonda J Brenner
Born and bred Floridian. Incidentally, the author's wife.

Robert Luke Noble
Originally hailing from Michigan, now a resident of Naples, Florida.

Terry Dorval
Born in Haiti, now a resident of Naples, Florida.

Doris Sloan Moon
Born and bred Floridian.

With your purchase of any of my books you are seamlessly donating to a worthy cause, as a portion of all proceeds for my books goes to Wildlife Preservation. You can also donate here: **davidmarkquigley.com/wildlife-foundation**

If you would like more information about the foundation, I would love to hear from you:

David Mark Quigley
dmq@davidmarkquigley.com

Printed in Great Britain
by Amazon

81780580R00244